CATHERINE
of LYONESSE

RICK ROBINSON

CORGI

For Paula

CATHERINE OF LYONESSE

A CORGI BOOK 9 780 55257 133 3

Published in Great Britain by Corgi Books,
an imprint of Random House Children's Publishers UK
A Random House Group Company

This edition published 2014

1 3 5 7 9 10 8 6 4 2

Copyright © Rick Robinson, 2014

FSC® C016897

Typeset in 11/15pt New Baskerville

RANDOM HOUSE CHILDREN'S PUBLISHERS UK
61–63 Uxbridge Road, London W5 5SA

www.**randomhousechildrens**.co.uk
www.**totallyrandombooks**.co.uk
www.**randomhouse**.co.uk

Addresses for companies within The Random House Group Limited
can be found at: www.randomhouse.co.uk/offices.htm

THE RANDOM HOUSE GROUP Limited Reg. No. 954009

A CIP catalogue record for this book is available from the British Library.

Printed and bound in Great Britain by CPI Group (UK) Ltd, Croydon, CR0 4YY

Being the History

Of the several Adventures of

CATHERINE

PRINCESS LYON,

Grand Daughter of KING EDMUND the Fourth

Of the House of Guienne,

Who by unhappy Mischance was Raised

In the Court of la Trémouille,

Seat of the King of AQUITAINE.

Containing an Account of the many Trials

Which this same Princess

Did Undergo in seeking to Return to her own Country

And Assert Her most Rightful Claims,

And of the many Deeds

Glorious and Shameful, on Occasion Foolish,

Which did thereby Ensue,

As Related by the most True and Authentick Sources.

THE HOUSE OF GUIENNE

Harold Hardwin
(made Duke of Guienne by Pépin the Great)

⋮

John I (John of Guienne) = Kynthred Eddling (Cynethryth Aetheling)
|
Henry I
|
Edmund I
|
Charles
|
Edmund II
|
Edmund III
|
Henry II   James I
|
James II
|
John II   Katherine of Kelliwick =
| Louis VII of Aquitaine
|

(Names in Boldface indicate individuals alive at the start of chapter one.)

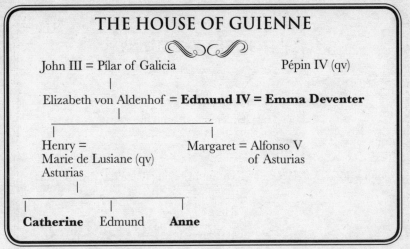

THE HOUSE OF GUIENNE

John III = Pílar of Galicia   Pépin IV (qv)

Elizabeth von Aldenhof = **Edmund IV = Emma Deventer**

Henry =   Margaret = Alfonso V
Marie de Lusiane (qv)   of Asturias
Asturias

Catherine   Edmund   **Anne**

THE HOUSES OF HERISTAL AND LUSIANE

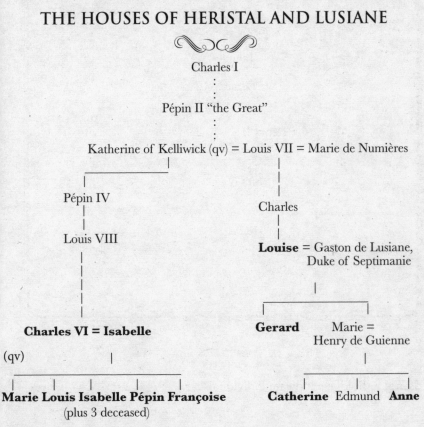

Charles I
⋮
Pépin II "the Great"
⋮
Katherine of Kelliwick (qv) = Louis VII = Marie de Numières

Pépin IV   Charles

Louis VIII   **Louise** = Gaston de Lusiane,
                                            Duke of Septimanie

Charles VI = Isabelle   **Gerard**   Marie =
                                               Henry de Guienne

(qv)

Marie Louis Isabelle Pépin Françoise   **Catherine** Edmund **Anne**
(plus 3 deceased)

Kelliwick Castle, Year of the Crown of Lyonesse 1025
Catherine slipped away from the pavilion where her mother sat amid her attendant ladies, listening to musicians. Not even her Ladyship, Catherine's governess, sharp-eyed as her hawks, saw her climb over the railing-cloths and drop silently onto the soft black earth. She stole among fragrant rose bushes, freezing anxiously when a bee took interest in her, then reached the wall between the gardens of Kelliwick Castle and the stableyard. She climbed into the lower branches of a young oak tree. Here, Catherine had discovered, she could look over the wall into the stableyard, yet still hear the musicians – and have ample warning if her absence were noted.

She loved the stableyard: fine horses tended by leather-clad ostlers; the clink of tack; the pungency of ripe straw and horseflesh. At times the bustle reached a sudden pitch of excitement as riders in red and green livery rode in at the gallop, or leaped into the saddle and spurred out through the stable gate, carrying the commands of her grandfather – King Edmund IV – to every corner of his island realm of Lyonesse.

All at once a party of horsemen burst through the gate, grim faced, snapping out orders in voices harsh and bitter. Among the horses was her father's splendid hunter, its trappings bearing the Royal Arms and marks of the heir apparent. Yet her father was not riding tall in his saddle; his hunter was led by another, and stretched over the saddle was a limp form, booted feet visible below the cloth that covered it.

Catherine stared at the concealed body, at first not comprehending, then refusing to believe. 'Father?' she called out, as though any could hear her above the uproar. Commands rang out with unbearable clarity: to send word at once to his Majesty and the Privy Council – to Princess Mary – to the chaplains. '*Father!*' cried Catherine again, tears filling her eyes as she clung sobbing to the tree trunk.

'Kateryn! We must be off, child!' said her Ladyship.

'Y–yes, your Ladyship,' stammered Catherine. She sat on the truckle bed, arms wrapped around herself in her thin linen shift. The candle guttered low, but through the cottage's horn window shone the harsh flicker of torches. Through the window too came low, urgent voices.

'I must tend to Nan,' cried her Ladyship. 'Here – dress yourself! Quickly! We've no time to waste!' The governess tossed Catherine a bundle of clothes and turned to deal with Catherine's little sister Anne, who started squalling. Catherine struggled into her kirtle and riding-gown, lacing them up herself. She could almost have thought the last three days an adventure, and wished they were.

They were not. Never again would she see her father; and now her mother had led them from the castle to this country cottage, travelling in haste towards the coast to cross the Narrow Sea to the Aquitaine, and none would tell her why.

From outside came hoof beats, a sharp challenge and reply, then a rider leaped down from the saddle. 'What word from Kelliwick?' asked a voice just outside the window.

'The Duke of Norrey has demanded that all ports be closed,' said the newcomer, 'and my lady Princess Mary and the children fetched back to Court. By God's grace the Privy Council yet balks, but Norrey has sent out his own riders—'

'Lud's blood!' cried the other. 'Haste, then, or we are lost!'

'What of the Lord High Admiral?'

'In his cups,' came the reply. 'Yet drunk or sober, Black Jack de Havilland will not dance to his Grace of Norrey's measure – once at sea we shall be safe.' A moment later came pounding on the door. 'Lady Lindley! We must ride!'

'Anon!' answered her Ladyship. She threw Catherine's cloak around her, bodily picked up Anne and threw open the door. 'Come, Kateryn!'

Catherine hesitated. It was all so strange, strange and terrifying. Yet she was old enough at seven to understand that she was now heiress to the throne. 'Why?' she demanded. 'Grandfather is still King, is he not?'

'Princess Kateryn!' snapped her Ladyship. 'There is no time! Come!'

Catherine followed her governess out of the cottage. Most of their escort was already mounted; a handful stood by, flaring torches in hand. Her lady mother was waiting too, and for a moment embraced her, but Catherine could scarcely bear to look at her mother's face. The sorrow and fear she saw were too great.

Then she was lifted high into a saddle, seated pillion behind young Lord Rathbone, who had been one of her father's gentleman attendants. The last riders mounted and tossed their torches into the mud, plunging the scene into a darkness broken only by a half-moon above scudding clouds. 'Onward!' ordered the lead rider. 'To Rosemouth haven, and God speed us all!'

Antoine de Chirac rode through the château gate not long past midday: mud spattered, soaked to the skin, cursing under his breath the day he forsook honest scholarship for preferment in the royal service. The twenty miles from the Palais de la Trémouille to

Clermont sur Brassy were a hard morning's ride at the best of times for a man no longer young, and more accustomed to books than horses. A late-summer storm did not ease his journey. Servants ran to tend to him and his escort of half a dozen Gardes de Maison, and Antoine was ushered into the gatehouse. Only when he threw back the hood of his sodden cloak did the steward recognize him as the confidential secretary to the King of Aquitaine.

'Monsieur de Chirac!' he exclaimed, and bowed.

Antoine wasted no words. 'Is his Majesty here?'

The steward frowned a moment before nodding. Affairs of state were not supposed to intrude upon Clermont sur Brassy, but it was a rule Antoine did not break lightly. The steward ordered a servant to bring hot mulled wine – and dispatched another to inform the châtelaine of Antoine's arrival. Twenty minutes later Antoine, properly clad in his lawyer's purple gown, gold chain of office around his shoulders, followed the steward along a covered gallery to the Great Hall.

The walls were hung with tapestries of hunting scenes, between pillars carved with paired, intertwined letter 'Cs' A fire roared in the great fireplace. Near it a winding stair led up, its entry flanked by two guards. Their silver and blue livery bore the same device of linked 'C's – for Charles VI of Aquitaine and Corisande d'Abregon, maîtresse-en-titre, acknowledged paramour of the King.

The guards snapped to attention and Antoine adjusted his doublet as the lady herself came down the stairs, a woman of some thirty years, her loose white chamber gown matched by white ribbons in the jet-black ringlets of her hair. Only the rich samite of her gown betrayed her true rank, as it also betrayed her elegant figure. The gown's cut was perfectly respectable; its wearer made it enticing. He bowed. 'Mademoiselle!' he declared.

Corisande d'Abregon answered with a deep curtsey. 'Monsieur.' She was not tall, though her carriage and proud Hesperidian features gave her the presence of height. She offered her hand, he kissed it and looked up to her warm smile. '*Mon ami!*' she exclaimed. 'My house is always yours!' She paused, her smile fading to a sober expression. 'Yet you would come only for a matter of concern.'

Antoine nodded. 'Concern, yes, Mademoiselle,' he replied. 'Not, I am pleased to say, alarm.' As Mlle d'Abregon studied him, dark eyes almost violet, he continued, 'His Majesty's cousin Marie has landed at la Fleur, along with her daughters.'

'Marie?' asked Mlle d'Abregon. 'Marie, who is wife to Prince Henri de Lyonesse? She has come back to l'Aquitaine? Why?' She looked more sharply at Antoine. Her frown and arched eyebrows asked, *A scandal?* Abruptly she shook her head, and answered her own unspoken question. 'But no. You say she brought her children.'

'She is a widow, Mademoiselle,' Antoine explained.

Corisande d'Abregon stood silent for a long moment. Finally she nodded. 'You did well to come.' She made a little curtsey and gestured towards the stairs.

They led up to a chamber with large arched windows, open to the air but sheltered from the rain. The chimney from the hall below kept the chamber warm, but the hiss of rain was loud and the stormy air bracing. Beside the chimney hung hunters' horns and weapons; a tapestry covered the opposite wall. In front of it sat Charles VI, King of Aquitaine, clad like a country gentleman in a hunting lodge. Well knit and russet bearded, he looked younger than his forty-five years. Credit went to his frequent hunting and other vigorous pursuits, though in cynical moments Antoine wished the King would give equal exercise to his mind.

Antoine bowed low. 'Sire!' The King motioned for him to rise and gestured towards a stool by the chair. A lute rested against it; Antoine handed the lute to Mlle d'Abregon and sat down.

'You know the law of this house, de Chirac,' said the King. 'I am not "Sire" here, simply Monsieur d'Heristal.' He frowned and shook his head slightly. 'But as you have burst in on me and my lovely Corisande this way, I fear a "Sire" matter.'

Mlle d'Abregon disposed herself gracefully at the King's feet as Antoine repeated what he had already told her. 'Prince Henri – Harry, as they say in Lyonesse – was killed in a hunting accident, nine days past. Princess Marie took her daughters in all haste to Rosemouth, there embarking in the first ship she could hire to cross to l'Aquitaine. She reached la Fleur the day before yesterday on the afternoon tide. She is there now, in the Porte St-Michel.'

'Old King Edmond's only son? Dead?' mused the King, as a serving maid brought in a tray of bread, cheese and wine. He looked up and frowned. 'A hunting accident, you say?' His tone registered doubt.

'Such was the report,' said Antoine. 'Knowing the state of Lyonesse, worse cannot be ruled out. We may assume that Princess Marie fled for fear of her daughters' freedom, if not their lives. Whether needfully or not, I cannot say. I have ordered enquiries, to determine the truth as best we may.'

The King nodded. 'Very good! Yet what now of Lyonesse? *Pardieu!*' he exclaimed. 'It is without an heir!'

Antoine washed down a bite of cheese with wine. 'The Lyonessan succession becomes interesting, Sire – Monsieur,' he said. 'You may recall that Prince Henri's own little son, the one they called Ned, died of a fever last year. So unless old King Edmond should father another son – which his age and condition render unlikely – the House of Guienne will become extinct in the direct male line.' Antoine sipped thoughtfully at his wine. 'Yet Lyonesse has no law forbidding the crown to a woman, as l'Aquitaine does. Therefore, the two properly next in line are Prince Henri's daughters, Catherine and Anne. Who are now with their mother at la Fleur.'

'Ah,' said the King, frowning thoughtfully.

'I advise, Monsieur,' said Antoine, 'that Marie and her children be brought to Court at once. Their present quarters in the Porte St-Michel are scarcely fit for royal ladies.'

The old seaside castle of la Fleur, which would have been a more suitable residence, had been demolished to be rebuilt in the new manner as an artillery fortress. The quality of accommodations was not Antoine's concern. La Fleur was too close to Lyonesse, and too many of its garrison were mercenaries who might be amenable to a bribe. Some fortunate star had delivered an inestimable prize into the King's hands. It would be folly beyond measure to risk its being snatched away again – or destroyed.

'Yes,' said the King. 'You are right, of course: Marie and her children must come to Court. How quickly can it be done?'

'I ordered coaches and escort made ready, Monsieur. They can leave at dawn tomorrow, and with hard driving reach la Fleur in three days.'

'So be it,' ordered the King. Antoine began to rise, and the King motioned him to sit again. 'I will send a rider – no need for you to wear yourself out and muddy yourself again, de Chirac. With my Corisande's consent you may abide the night here as our guest.'

'I would be honoured, Monsieur,' agreed Mlle d'Abregon.

Little risk, thought Antoine, that the King's mistress would refuse an invitation suggested by the King – but her pleasure sounded genuine. He thanked her warmly and turned back to the King. 'A lady of the Court should accompany the officer who formally receives Princess Marie and her children into your hospitality and escorts them back to la Trémouille.'

'So?' asked the King. 'My charming cousins, the Princesses of the Blood, live richly on my subsidies, and have no other use. One of them can go.' He smiled wickedly. 'Send Christine de Marsenne – country air and a swift journey will do her constitution wonders.'

'Your Majesty is very brave,' said Antoine with a wry smile. 'A Princess of the Blood make ready for a journey overnight, and endure a coach driven in haste?' He imagined the expression on the plump face of Christine de Marsenne as she received the royal command. 'Your heartless cruelty will be the talk of the Court for months.'

The King laughed. 'Perhaps it should be, de Chirac!' He shook his head in dismay. '*Sacré Dieu.* Whoever I command will make delays, while poor Marie and her little royal heiresses languish in—'

Mlle d'Abregon had sat quietly at the King's feet,

running her fingers over the body of her lute, the picture of a lady quietly tending her own thoughts as King and minister spoke of matters above her, but now she abruptly set aside her instrument. 'By your leave,' she said, 'there is no need to trouble a Princess of the Blood, nor delay the journey. If it please Monsieur, I will go myself.'

CHAPTER ONE

Encounters at Dawn

Seven years later, the Court of Aquitaine at Aix-le-Siège

Dawn was only just breaking when Catherine de Guienne, Princess Lyon and heiress of Lyonesse, set out from her chambers in the palace of la Trémouille. Followed by her two young ladies in waiting, she slipped from her bedchamber through her Presence Chamber. A couple of her serving women were awake, if barely so, and stumbled to their feet to make their curtseys. Others still slumbered. Catherine let them sleep.

The two Gardes de Maison flanking the outer door grounded their halberds smartly, a sound to wake the dead. They did not ask where a Princess of the Blood was going at this hour. Probably they could guess. Late spring at the royal court of Aquitaine was a time for affairs of all sorts, including affairs of honour, and the Baron de Moine, a famed swordsman, had offended the Comte d'Alembert – the count being so foolish as to demand satisfaction. Catherine had decided that, having turned fourteen, she was now old enough to witness their encounter.

Madame Corisande, she suspected, might disagree, but she need not know – and she certainly would not attend the duel. It would be less than appropriate: having been replaced in the King's bed by Margot de la Fontenelle, Corisande was married now to King Charles's chief minister, Antoine de Chirac, and duels were supposed to be forbidden by royal edict. When *she* was Queen of Lyonesse, thought Catherine, she would see that her edicts were obeyed, or not go through the show of issuing them.

She and her ladies ghosted through empty halls and galleries lit by oil-lamps, went down a stair, then through archways and courtyards to the great Montfaucon garden. The courtyards and gardens too were lit by torches in brackets, though dawn had brightened enough that they were no longer needed.

'Turn right at the next corner, if it please Mademoiselle,' said a voice behind Catherine: her lady-in-waiting, Madeleine du Lac de Montpellier. Her father was an officer of the royal stables and she got on easily with the palace servants, so possibly knew the layout of la Trémouille better than King Charles himself did.

Their way led through further courtyards and gardens, then down to the lower gardens and orchards along the riverbank. Mist rose up from the river below, fighting the encroachment of day, and the outer gardens were not torch-lit. It was cold, and Catherine drew her cloak tighter, but the mist gave the excursion a proper tone of adventure.

They reached a stone parapet. 'Now we shall have to go down a ladder, I fear,' said Madeleine. As fears go, she sounded rather enthusiastic about this one.

Catherine's other lady-in-waiting, Comtesse Solange de Charleville, was less so. 'A ladder? How is this necessary? If the men wish to conduct affairs of honour, as they say, they could show some courtesy to ladies!' Catherine's ladies did not always get on; a year or two older than her, they were bright and sharp-witted, which made their company pleasing, and entirely too pretty, which did not.

'If we go by the promenade it is twice as far, and we would have to pass a guard post,' said Madeleine. 'We would be all right, but the guard-captain might make trouble for Mademoiselle. The delicate eyes of a Princess of the Blood should not see the edicts being violated! Anyway,' she added, 'if the men were Christians, as they say they are, they wouldn't be fighting duels.'

'The devil with the Gardes de Maison!' said Catherine. 'But we need to make haste! Anyway, if we were Christians, as *we* say, we wouldn't be going to watch, would we? So hush, both of you!' She looked down over the parapet. In the shadows she could not tell how far it was to the ground below – surely further than she wanted to fall. 'Can you handle the basket, Madeleine?'

'I'll do fine!' Madeleine swung easily over the balustrade, grabbed the basket she'd filled to break their fast, and made her way down.

'God preserve me,' said Solange, and crossed herself. Then she kilted up her skirts, threw a sack filled with blankets over her shoulder and went down the ladder without the least difficulty. Catherine was left with no choice in honour but to go down herself. What young Gallic ladies could do, a princess of Lyonesse could certainly do. The ladder swayed alarmingly as she felt her way down from rung to rung, but she too made it safely to the ground.

The sun was just rising as Catherine's little party reached the meadow by the riverbank where the combat was to take place. The two parties to the combat, the duellists and their seconds, each awaited under a tree at opposite ends of the open space. Along the upslope side of the meadow were a dozen or more clumps of courtiers who had also risen at this early hour to witness the affair.

Catherine and her ladies settled themselves near the midpoint: she was no partisan of either combatant. Some of those seated nearby looked back and recognized a Princess of the Blood and a small stir ran through the gathering. Abruptly Catherine grasped something that she had considered only in principle, never supposing that it would truly come to pass: she was the highest-ranking witness to the combat.

One member of each party detached themselves and walked to the midpoint – not the combatants, but their chief seconds. There they spoke briefly with a third man wearing a herald's tabard, plain white without heraldic charge. He pointed towards where Catherine and her ladies sat on the blankets Solange had brought.

God's teeth! thought Catherine in her native tongue. It was far too late to slink away, not to mention dishonourable. King Charles's daughters were all comfortably – and sensibly – in bed. So apparently was the King of Aquitaine's younger son Pépin. His brother Louis, the Dauphin, was not at court. *He* would carry this duty off with style and dignity. Catherine stifled an inner sigh. She had no choice now but to go through with it.

The three men came her way, and Catherine got to her feet. Her ladies rose beside her, and promptly knelt. The men came up to her and knelt as well, until she motioned them to rise. The herald inclined his head. 'Altesse,' he said.

It was the Gallic for 'Highness', not a literal reference to Catherine's ungainly height. For once, indeed, that was an advantage: she was as tall as they were.

'The Comte d'Alembert,' said the herald, 'has taken offence at certain words spoken by the Baron de Moine, and demands satisfaction of first blood for the same.'

'Can they not settle their difference peacefully?' asked Catherine, and looked back and forth at the two seconds. The words were mere formula, part of the

17

occasion, as she knew from hearing many accounts of such encounters, but she spoke them with meaning. She was heiress to a throne – the throne of Lyonesse. One day it would be her duty to keep peace among her people. 'Let the gentlemen mend their quarrel without bloodshed,' she said, 'and keep the royal edict as well.'

That was not part of the formula. The herald took it in his stride, merely inclining his head once more. De Moine's second looked sharply at Catherine. 'That is not possible, Altesse!' he said. D'Alembert's second hesitated a moment, then barely shook his head.

'I have done what I can,' said Catherine – again, the formula. Perhaps she could do more, but what? Her forebears had once ruled half this kingdom as well as their own, but those days were long gone. It was not her place to enforce the King of Aquitaine's edicts, even if she could. 'Satisfaction has been asked of first blood,' she said. 'Take care the affray goes no further!'

Heralds and seconds knelt again and withdrew. Catherine gathered her skirts and settled on the blanket. Madeleine produced a jug from her basket and handed it to Catherine – mulled wine, still warm. Catherine took a drink, and the jug made the round of the three of them. A fresh-baked pastry followed.

'Bravely done, Mademoiselle!' said Solange. 'De Moine will not be pleased – nor will your uncle in whose service he is.'

'De Moine doesn't care,' said Madeleine, 'so long as

he gets his fight. As for your uncle,' she added, 'begging pardon, Mademoiselle, but he is never pleased.'

'Then he must learn to live with displeasure!' said Catherine. By now the sun had risen behind the Palais de la Trémouille, silhouetting its cupolas and chimneys against a bright blue sky. The river mist was starting to burn off as the two combatants advanced to the mid-point of the meadow, where the herald now awaited them. Drawn blades gleamed in the morning light.

The duellists were oddly matched, like players in a comedy: d'Alembert on the right, lean and wiry; de Moine on the left, taller but portly. If Catherine had only appearances to go by she would have thought that d'Alembert had the advantage – but de Moine was a renowned swordsman.

For long, long moments very little happened. The two men took a step towards each other, still two blades' lengths apart, rocking on their feet, testing the ground, getting a feel for their balance. Their sword-tips described slow circles; the daggers in their left hands held back, ready to parry a thrust – or seize an opportunity.

'Good for d'Alembert!' said Madeleine. 'Don't be hasty—'

It was de Moine who leaped forward, suddenly; then d'Alembert came at him. The encounter was too swift for Catherine to follow, but she heard the clatter of steel. She had watched Gardes de Maison practise with sword and dagger, but this was different. This was in earnest.

Now d'Alembert rushed his opponent. 'Foolish!' cried Madeleine, and indeed a moment later he was giving ground, flailing to cover his retreat. De Moine let him back up. 'Why should de Moine hurry?' said Madeleine. 'He can take his time!' She continued describing the combat; it might have been utter nonsense, but Catherine sensed that her lady-in-waiting knew what she was about – Madeleine du Lac was the finest dancer among the young women of the Court, and certainly knew her footwork. 'D'Alembert needs to make him work harder!' Madeleine continued. 'He's strong, but fat as he is he can't keep running for ever! Yes!' she cried as the count used a parry to force de Moine back a step, then circled the other way. 'Keep moving! Use your feet!'

The Comte d'Alembert was much too far away to hear Madeleine's advice, and it went unheeded. He advanced again, seemed to force de Moine back – then the baron thrust to full extension, and his opponent jerked as he made contact. D'Alembert stumbled, gained footing for a moment; then, dropping sword and dagger, he crumpled in a heap.

De Moine stepped back from his victim. The herald approached and knelt beside the fallen d'Alembert, joined by a physician with his bag. Presently the herald stood up and came towards Catherine. Again she rose, again he knelt. 'The matter is settled, Altesse.'

'What of the count?' asked Catherine. 'Does – does he live?'

'The thrust pierced a lung,' said the herald. 'He lives, for now, but his case must be uncertain.'

'Let him be tended to,' said Catherine dutifully, though it was already being done. 'This matter is closed.' For the Comte d'Alembert, she thought, the closure might be final.

With the combat ended, spectators began to drift away. A handful detached themselves from a large group at de Moine's end of the field, and came towards Catherine's little party. She took a few deep breaths as a man and woman drew up before her and made their bow and curtsey, precisely.

The man was Gérard de Lusiane, Duc de Septimanie, her mother's brother. The woman at his side was the dowager duchess, his mother Louise – Catherine's grandmother.

'Why did you not come to our side of the field, Altesse?' the duke now asked coldly. Gerard never seemed to quite grasp that Catherine was not a part of his family's estates.

'I was not an adherent of one combatant or the other,' said Catherine. Only now did she fully realize that this was not quite the truth. She knew almost nothing about the unfortunate d'Alembert; she knew a little more about the Baron de Moine – and what she knew, she did not like. He had goaded d'Alembert to this fight – and made a deep thrust to win it, when a scratch would have sufficed. 'I came here to see a matter of honour concluded,' she added, and let slip a little more of the truth. 'But I did not do enough. It might have been settled without bloodshed. And without violating the King of Aquitaine's edicts.'

Her uncle made only a grumbling sound in reply. Her grandmother looked Catherine up and down. 'You have acquired the same bad customs from across the sea as your mother.'

Across the sea was Lyonesse. 'Yes, Grandmère Lusiane.' Catherine looked her in the eye. 'I keep the customs of my house and country.'

'*We* are your house!' said her grandmother. 'The Guiennes are nearly at an end, girl. Old Edmond de Lyonesse is in his dotage. When he dies, all that remain will be you and your sister Anne. Without us you are heiress to nothing. One day soon you shall find that you have need of us. You would do well to remember that.' She curtseyed again, icily, and she and her son withdrew, followed by their retinue.

Catherine was left alone with her ladies-in-waiting. 'Well!' said Solange de Charleville. She had said nothing during the duel. Adventures, at least those pursued out of doors, were not to her taste as they were to Madeleine's. 'I know nothing of your land of Lyonesse and – begging pardon, Mademoiselle – I am not sure I wish to learn. But I am sure the dowager duchess knows little more than I do.'

For her own part, Catherine was left fuming. She was aware that that it could not be easy for a young maid to claim a throne, however rightfully hers. How she could do so from across the sea – from here in the Aquitaine, traditional enemy of Lyonesse – she had, as yet, not the faintest notion. And Grandmère de Lusiane probably did know a little more of Lyonesse than Solange did: her daughter – Catherine's mother – had after all married into the royal House of Guienne. But one thing Catherine knew full well: the house of Lusiane had no power or sway in Lyonesse.

Solange and Madeleine gathered up their things for the hike back up from the river. The mist had burned off; the air was still cold, but the morning sun was warm. A movement of bright colour caught Catherine's eye and she looked east along the river. A party of horsemen was approaching, along the path that Catherine and her ladies had avoided on account of the guard-post. The riders were not Gardes de Maison – and the rich, indeed royal, trappings of the leader marked him as of very high rank indeed.

For an excited moment Catherine wondered if the Dauphin had returned to Court from his service with the royal armies. Alas, it was not the Dauphin, only his brother Pépin. He dismounted and walked up to Catherine. He was two years older than she was, and – having hit his growth the previous summer – a shade taller. Her ladies behind her made their curtseys.

Catherine dipped sufficiently to acknowledge her royal host's son.

'What brings you out on this bright early morning, *cousine* Catherine?' said Pépin. 'I heard rumours of a duel! But surely you would have nothing to do with such a thing.'

'You missed it, cousin Pépin,' said Catherine. 'You should have got up earlier.' At sixteen, Pépin was sufficiently handsome, but Catherine wondered how long his looks would last – she could smell wine on his breath even at this early hour. King Charles had hoped to marry her to him, but the Church had raised objections. Thus were God's wisdom and mercy made manifest.

It occurred to Catherine that the same Church laws also forbade her marriage to Pépin's older brother Louis, the Dauphin. That was less fortunate. The Dauphin might in principle be the son of an enemy, but in Catherine's considered judgement he had all the noble qualities the ancients attributed to their pagan gods. Perhaps it was best that he was so rarely at Court.

'So you confess there was a duel!' said Pépin. 'And you came to watch – hoping to catch someone's eye, perhaps? You won't. I should call out my father's guards to arrest you.'

First her Lusiane relations, thought Catherine; now Pépin! 'Summon them, if you wish,' she said. King Charles doted on his younger son, but was not a fool –

the Gardes de Maison would not take orders from Pépin.

'You don't like me, do you, *chère cousine?*'

'Do you care?' asked Catherine. She picked up her skirts and gestured to her ladies with a turn of her head.

'You will not have to put up with me for a while,' said Pépin. 'But when I come back you may like me even less.'

Is that possible? wondered Catherine. She said nothing, and turned to go.

'I am on my way to Richebourg,' continued Pépin.

In spite of herself, Catherine turned back.

'We are going to take it back,' said Pépin. Your grandfather's goddams have held it long enough!' *Les Goddams* was the name Aquitanians used for her people, for in the days when armies of Lyonesse had campaigned yearly in this kingdom its people had learned only two words in Saxon: 'God damn.'

Catherine *la goddamette*, she thought, and proudly so! It was on her tongue to make a brave reply, but she held back. Prince Pépin cared nothing for policy or strategy – only for the chance to offend her, and win glory in battle for himself.

'Well!' he said. 'So you have nothing to say, *chère cousine?* Catherine de Guienne reduced to silence! A rare treat.'

'You would do better to let deeds speak for you, Pépin,' she said. Long ago a Saxon thane of Lyonesse had crossed the sea, and for his valour in the Holy Land been made Duke of Guienne. The fortress city of Richebourg – Richborough, as it was known in the honest Saxon tongue – was all that now remained of the lands on the mainland granted him for his deeds in the War of the Cross. Catherine remembered her father calling it the landside bastion of Lyonesse. *Evesham's Chronicle* – favourite of all her books – confirmed that the fortress city had withstood many an assault. It had nothing to fear from Pépin! His father's armies were another matter, though – Charles VI of Aquitaine kept thirty thousand men under arms, and a mighty train of modern bronze artillery.

Pépin sauntered back to his party. He mounted up, and the lot of them rode away at the canter, headed towards the river road.

'God damn you, Pippin!' muttered Catherine.

Before it took place, the combat between the Baron de Moine and the Comte d'Alembert had been the talk of the Court of la Trémouille for weeks. Considerable sums of money had been wagered on the outcome. The betting odds had favoured the baron, though not by as much as pure logic might have dictated: many had placed their bets wishfully, on an outcome they hoped for rather than expected.

Once it had taken place the duel was swiftly forgotten – displaced by the much greater news that royal armies were converging on Richebourg to eradicate the last fastness held by the island kingdom across the Narrow Sea. Some who had wagered on de Moine scarcely troubled to collect their modest winnings. Many who had optimistically or carelessly bet on d'Alembert scarcely had occasion to rue their losses, or to regret the winnings they might have gained had d'Alembert defied the odds to win his fight.

Among those who had bet on the Baron de Moine was Solange, and she did not forget the outcome. Hastening from Princess Catherine's quarters as soon as she decently could, she collected her winnings before the duel was relegated to oblivion, as it surely would be. Returning with them in hand, she went into the little chamber she shared with Madeleine, and consigned the coins to her strongbox. She could scarcely avoid being noticed by her fellow lady-in-waiting, and confessed as to where the money had come from.

Madeleine could be very simple about such things. 'You should be ashamed of yourself!' she said.

Solange was indignant. 'My eight douzaines and six sous are not ashamed of themselves – nearly half a livre!' Which was not really very much at all, she thought. She was the daughter of a count, but still as poor as a church mouse. She picked up her sewing basket and sat down.

'A livre and a half – that would be more fitting,' said Madeleine. 'Thirty pieces of silver!'

'I wish it were a livre and a half!' said Solange.

'Anyway, you are the one who told me that de Moine was sure to win.'

'Of course he was sure to win. He is an excellent swordsman!' In her enthusiasm for technique Madeleine forgot all about her lofty principles 'His stance and balance are impeccable: feet, shoulders and wrist, all in perfect rhythm!' Setting down the clothes she was folding into a chest, Madeleine demonstrated a graceful lunge. Then, with equal grace, she shrugged. 'D'Alembert was entirely outclassed, and is lucky to be alive.'

'If *you* can admire, I can wager!' said Solange. 'But I am certainly *not* his adherent,' she added. 'He is a retainer of the Lusianes after all. On top of believing they own Mademoiselle,' she said, meaning Princess Catherine, 'they robbed my family of most of our lands.' Which, thought Solange, was why she was as poor as a church mouse. All that remained of the once-vast Charleville estates was the mouldering castle she had grown up in, a couple of villages with their fields, and some vineyards.

'You never told me this!' said Madeleine.

'You never asked,' said Solange. She loved her family but did not speak of it at Court: why proclaim her provincial origins? 'Anyway, the Lusianes are the least of our problems now. Even the least of Mademoiselle's problems. Corisande has made a great mistake, which is not like her at all.'

'Madame Corisande has only ever made one mistake,' said Madeleine. 'Choosing *you* for Mademoiselle's service. So what is this new mistake?' asked Madeleine. 'In plain words, if you will, and especially not in Latin.'

'*Quæ non certiorem Dominillam Catharinam—*' began Solange, then relented. 'She did not warn Mademoiselle about the attack on Richebourg, leaving her to find out from Pépin. Not the best way for her to learn anything, especially not that!'

'Does it even make a difference?'

Solange shook her head. 'Don't be simple, Madeleine! Certainly it makes a difference, if you're a princess of Lyonesse.'

'I mean, does it make a difference who tells her?' Madeleine had gone back to folding clothes; now she patted down the last kirtle, closed the trunk and sat on the lid. 'Of course Pépin was no gentleman about it! He wouldn't be. But it is her grandfather's fortress we are taking. If I were in Mademoiselle's place, should an angel tell me, I would still look for my revenge!'

Solange decided that she would not wish to take a fortress from Madeleine. But taking one from Mademoiselle might be worse. Princess Catherine had said almost nothing on the way back to her chambers and once there she had dismissed her ladies from attending upon her. Solange had peeked in to see her seated under a window, reading her book of the history of Lyonesse, written in the Saxon language.

A stir from the gallery beyond the Presence Chamber culminated in a sharp double bang of grounded halberds. Solange sprang to her feet, took up her skirts and hastened into the chamber, ready to kneel in case the King himself had come to proclaim the impending fall of Richebourg. I am not remotely presentable! she thought. Madeleine hastened in after her. Even in an ordinary day gown the other girl was eminently presentable, all blonde hair and golden glow. You are quite detestable, thought Solange.

It was not King Charles who entered, but a woman who might have passed for a queen: Madame Corisande de Chirac. She swept into the Presence Chamber, and Solange made her a deeper curtsey than the wife of a royal minister, even the Ministre d'État, strictly merited – certainly a deeper curtsey than a former royal mistress strictly merited. Corisande had given Solange a place at Court. Even more than that, for all her doubtful origin and dubious past she was the cynosure of a great lady, as Solange aspired to be.

'I came as quickly as I could,' said Madame Corisande. 'Is the Princess not here?'

'She has heard the news, Madame,' said Solange. 'Prince Pépin told her, right after the combat between de Moine and d'Alembert.'

'Pépin?' said Corisande. 'Oh!' Although the older woman would say no words about the King's son, her tone, thought Solange, was sufficiently eloquent.

A rustle from the other end of the Presence Chamber announced yet another entry, from the inner chambers. This time Solange knelt, as did Madeleine and Madame Corisande, respectful in the presence of a Princess of the Blood.

Catherine pushed her way through the hangings, holding the massive book Solange had seen her reading earlier. 'Yes, Madame Corisande,' she said. 'Pépin did me the service of informing me that King Charles is sending his armies to besiege Richebourg. Or as we goddams call it, Richborough.' Only then, with an impatient gesture, did she bid the three ladies to rise.

Corisande had not been sure which possibility she had dreaded more: telling Princess Catherine of the campaign herself, or finding that she already knew of it. Of course the Princess had already heard – no one knew better than Corisande how swiftly news spread at Court. She was thus spared telling Catherine of what must surely seem a betrayal. What was, in fact, an act of war against her homeland.

'Well, Madame!' said Catherine. 'I did not know what to say to my cousin Pépin, and I do not even know what to say to you.' Her green eyes contemplated Corisande steadily. 'I suppose we are enemies now.'

She looked older than her fourteen years, thought Corisande – not yet filled out, but plainly on the verge of young womanhood. Almost no one at Court, usually so aware of such things, seemed to have noticed. Any more than anyone at Court, even her usually wise and subtle husband, seemed to have considered this awkward consequence of the Richebourg campaign. Wearing a simple chamber gown, the red hair she was so needlessly self-conscious of pulled back but uncovered, Catherine de Guienne already looked the part of the queen she would become in the not far distant future.

Corisande wanted to hug her, but one does not, unbidden, so much as touch a Princess of the Blood, let alone hug her. 'You are not my enemy, Trinette!' She held out one hand, hoping to draw the girl towards her with the use of her pet name for her, as one would draw a skittish cat.

And she came, her pace as cautious as a skittish cat's, as stately as a bishop in Easter procession. She paused, just beyond reach. 'I do not think you are my enemy, Madame!' she said. 'Yet I am the loyal subject of my grandfather, King Edmund the Fourth.' She clutched the book under her arm. 'Oh, Madame – I do not know what to think!' With that she slid into Corisande's arms, softly weeping.

CHAPTER TWO

Resurgam

'Trinette!' Madame Corisande's voice came from just outside the bedchamber door. 'I must go soon! You need not put yourself through this!'

'I am almost ready, Madame,' answered Catherine. 'I will come!' Standing before her great-glass, she examined herself. She was ready, but now that it came to the point she was in no hurry to go. This was not simply being trotted out before some ambassador as the marriage prize of Christendom, to be inspected like a horse. Today was much worse.

Richborough had fallen – three weeks had now passed since the church bells rang out across the Aquitaine's royal city of Aix-le-Siège. Today the army was to return in triumphant parade. Catherine would put off facing it as long as she could, yet face it she would. The world – and above all her grandfather's people, one day to be hers – must know her for who and what she was.

She examined her gown and herself, with as critical and objective an eye as possible. The black velvet gown had come out well, considering the rushed circumstances under which she and her ladies-in-waiting had put it together. The train was pinned up to display the ecru skirt of her kirtle, and the black worked cuffs of her chemise showed under the gown's wide belled false sleeves. The gown's square neckline was wider than Catherine had anticipated, nearly off her shoulders; it would have been quite daring if she had more with which to dare. She intended to be daring, but not in that way, so she'd fitted a partlet modestly above the décolletage, as befitted an occasion of mourning.

In strict fairness, Solange and Madeleine had done most of the work, hovering over the seamstresses through the cutting and stitchery, and embroidering with their own hands the fine black work of the chemise. Yet Catherine had herself chosen the fabric and sketched out the pattern; examining the result, she was not ill pleased. The gown was very simple, almost severe; still graceful. Her only adornments were sprigs of rosemary pinned to the curved billiment of her headdress, and a necklace bearing as pendant the Royal Arms of Lyonesse. It had been a gift from her father to her mother, long ago. Now it was hers: a reminder to the world – today, of all days – that she was not merely a Princess of the Blood, but heiress of Lyonesse. She made a swift half-turn, and the skirts of gown and kirtle swirled around her legs.

'*Trinette!*'

'Yes, Madame.' Catherine turned the other way, and

tried to see how she looked in profile. The buckram stiffening of her bodice provided a welcome hint of a bosom. Not much, but better than nothing at all. All this gown really lacked, she concluded glumly, was a prettier wearer.

As a child in her grandfather's court, Catherine had supposed herself as fair as any other little girl. Even learning at age five that she was 'half frog' had not troubled her. Then she had crossed the sea to the Aquitaine and the Court of la Trémouille. The brilliant court was bejewelled with beautiful women of every age and station – and Catherine had discovered quickly that she was not one of them. Taller by a head than other girls her age, she'd been ungainly and awkward, all elbows and knees, with a face full of freckles and a mass of carroty hair. *La Grande Rouquine,* they called her, the Tall Redhead, and asked her if it was true that her people ate their meat raw. Stung, she had asked them if they sat on lily pads and caught flies with their tongues, which failed to amuse them.

At fourteen, the freckles had mercifully faded from her face, save for a few that clung tenaciously to her nose – the rest had migrated down to her shoulders, where Madame Corisande insisted that they were attractive. Her hair was carroty as ever, more the colour of a bronze great-gun, but she could pull it back and pin it under her headdress where it wasn't too conspicuous. Tall and scrawny she remained. Her eyes were her one genuinely good feature. Green, flecked with amber, they were large and pretty in her angular face. No one would ever mistake her for a beauty. Yet with some luck her eventual husband might see her as not merely the marriage prize of Christendom, but a lady whose bedchamber he could enter willingly if perhaps not eagerly.

The door flew open and Madame Corisande swept in with a rustle of skirts. 'Princess Catherine, what are you—?' The words died when she saw Catherine, or more precisely her black gown of mourning. '*Pardieu!*'

Catherine tried to make a graceful pirouette to show off her handiwork, but ended in a less than graceful stumble. 'Does Madame think it becoming?' she asked, hoping for an answer she did not expect.

'Becoming?' Madame Corisande shook her head. 'I know this is not a happy occasion for you, dear Trinette,' she said. 'No one requires you to attend!'

'I require myself to attend,' Catherine said. 'You will forgive me? I know it is much to the honour of Monsieur your husband.'

Madame Corisande smiled sweetly up at her. 'There is nothing to forgive, dear Trinette,' she said. 'My husband has done his duty to his Majesty. You must do your duty to your grandfather – though his Majesty will be displeased!'

Good! thought Catherine. If only she had ten thousand longbow men and ten thousand pikemen, and – these days – a train of artillery, he would be even more displeased. Alas, she was merely a young maid, and had none of those things.

Madame Corisande was studying the pendant on her necklace, trying to puzzle out the word chased in gold under the oval display of arms. From the day Catherine had first seen her she had known without question that Corisande was the most beautiful woman in the world. Evidence confirmed this: chevaliers walked into pillars and tripped on stairs when she went past. Corisande was intelligent too. But she was scarcely lettered, and knew not a word of Latin.

'*Resurgam*, Madame,' explained Catherine. 'It is the motto of Lyonesse: "I shall rise again".'

All at once the bottles of perfume rattled on the dressing table and a great dull boom resounded. Then another, and another. 'The cannons!' cried Madame Corisande. 'See how we are late! If you would come we must hurry!' She hastened from the room, not looking back to see if Catherine followed.

Catherine snatched up a crucifix on a silk cord and tied it around her waist, then picked up her skirts and ran after Madame Corisande.

Her ladies-in-waiting were in her Presence Chamber along with her little sister Anne, standing beneath hangings that bore the Celtic cross of St Pelagius and Catherine's own badges of the White Hart and Linnet. Solange and Madeleine were her only attendants of rank, but for all their excellent personal qualities neither was of great family – proof of what King Charles really thought of the marriage prize of Christendom.

Catherine had charged her ladies with her sister's care out of necessity: Anne had her own household within the palace, but her attendants could not be relied on to do anything properly – certainly not on an occasion like this. There had been little time to deal with Anne. Her gown was a plain little sack made of leftover fabric from Catherine's, but Anne needed nothing more – she was just ten, but the most careless observer could see at once that Anne had got all the beauty meant for both sisters together. She was of proper height for her age, graceful, with curly golden hair instead of Catherine's carroty mop.

Catherine took Anne by the hand, and the five of them hastened along a gallery lit by morning sun streaming through high windows. They went nearly at a run, footfalls resounding sharply from the carved wood-panelled walls. The guns had ceased firing, and in the distance came the quick tattoo of drums, the blare of trumpets and the cheers of the populace: the returning victors marching up the rue Ste-Valérie towards the palace. At the entrance to the reviewing pavilion Catherine held back with Anne, letting Corisande and her ladies go ahead. Catherine's earlier hesitancy was gone. She was fully committed to the purpose she had come for – but neither Corisande nor her own ladies must seem implicated in what she intended to do. Anne was too young to be blamed; in any case it was her duty as a princess of Lyonesse, as surely as it was Catherine's.

The pavilion was crowded with ladies of the Court, a dazzle of colours and a glitter of jewels. Her Majesty the Queen was nowhere to be seen. This was no great surprise, since Mademoiselle de la Fontenelle was very much to be seen. So low-cut and tight-laced was her bodice, thought Catherine, that she was more to be seen than befitted a State occasion. Margot and her giggling coterie had taken over the centre of the stands. Their handkerchiefs fluttered like pennons on chevaliers' lances; their every movement a mad tinkling of tiny bells in their uncovered hair. 'Ah!' she exclaimed to her friends, gesturing towards Corisande. 'The song of yesteryear!'

Corisande betrayed no sign of noticing la Fontenelle's existence. Catherine knew she ought to do the same, but an answer came to her and she gave it. 'Yes,' she retorted from the threshold of the pavilion, 'a song held fond in memory when this season's ditty is long forgot.'

Margot drew a sudden sharp breath – the more audible for the bells in her hair and more visible for her remarkable décolletage. She turned and glared at Catherine. '*La Grande Rouquine* has a tongue as sharp as her face!' Only then did she seem to fully register the meaning of Catherine's presence and her black gown of mourning. Her bells fell silent.

Catherine stepped out into the pavilion, and two hundred ladies of the Court of la Trémouille also fell silent. Drums rolled and trumpets blared as the procession came into view, passing through the gates from the rue Ste-Valérie into the palace grounds, but within the pavilion, there was now only a rustle of gowns. With Anne in hand, Catherine passed slowly among the ladies of the Aquitaine, feeling all eyes on her and wishing now that she could disappear. Or at least that she were beautiful. She could then have made a properly grand entrance.

She led Anne to the far left of the reviewing stand, the most widely visible place. Now came the task of explaining to her sister what they must do – and getting her to do it. For all of Catherine's efforts, Anne now knew only a few words in the honest Saxon tongue. 'Listen to me, Nan!' Catherine said, then shifted at once to Gallic: 'Attend closely, and do precisely as I say. As King Charles rides past, you must make only a little curtsey, as I do, as though he were but any gentleman.'

Anne looked up at her doubtfully. 'But we always kneel to the King!'

'Not today, Nan!'

'But he is King!' protested Anne.

'We kneel because we are his guests,' said Catherine. *Prisoners* or *hostages* might be more accurate; but saying so would only upset Anne. 'He is not King of Lyonesse!' Nor did she believe was he even the rightful king of

40

Aquitaine, since Catherine's grandfather, King Edmund, bore the title 'King of Lyonesse, Aquitaine, and the Islands of the Sea' – a just claim proven by *Evesham's Chronicle*. Catherine's tutors denounced it as a pack of lies and caned her for repeating it, clearest demonstration of its truth. There was no time however to explain everything to little Anne, who only squirmed when Catherine read to her from *Evesham*. 'You must do exactly as I say,' she said. 'Curtsey to King Charles – and then kneel when I tell you to.'

'Yes, Catherine,' said Anne, a bit doubtfully.

Charles VI of Aquitaine rode at the head of his army, as was his right – though it struck Catherine that he had spent the brief campaign here at Court swiving Mlle de la Fontenelle, doing no more himself to conquer Richborough than Catherine had done to save it. All the same he looked magnificent in his cloth-of-gold doublet and argent robe thrown open at the shoulders, covered with embroidered fleurs-de-lis to match the trappings of his charger. He bore upright the great ancient broadsword borne by Pépin the Great to the deliverance of Sion – almost as noble a blade as Caliburn, wielded of old by Arthur, that lay for ever unrusted in the pool of Camboglanna.

Yet for all King Charles's splendour, it seemed to Catherine that her father had looked even more kingly when he rode home from the hunt in a mud-spattered jerkin. He had never lived to wear a crown, and the memory came unbidden of that terrible day: her mother's shrieks and lamentations, and their hasty departure. Soon afterwards her mother had retired to a convent, and later died there of her grief. Catherine's Lyonessan servants had been dismissed – even her Ladyship, her governess – and she and little Anne had been left utterly alone in this foreign court.

Catherine blinked a tear from her eye and concentrated on the matter at hand. As King Charles rode past and the throng cheered thunderously, Anne naturally forgot her instructions and began to kneel out of habit. Catherine pulled her back up, and with a firm hand on her arm made Anne curtsey as she did. The gesture did not go unnoticed. Catherine saw several sharp glances, and heard with pleasure a disapproving buzz from ladies near at hand. And I am not done! she thought.

Two dozen paces behind the King rode Louis le Dauphin, the nineteen-year-old heir of Aquitaine. The day was cool, more like April than June, but seeing the Dauphin made Catherine distinctly warm under her chemise. Louis was seldom at Court – M. de Chirac said that the proper education of a Dauphin was not at la Trémouille but among the frontier fortresses – and Catherine found this regrettable. During his last visit, just before her fourteenth birthday, Louis had surprised her in a garden. He'd put his arms around her, greeting her in what he claimed was the fashion of her own people – a kiss, full on the lips – and called her *Catherine la belle.* The effrontery! Today the Dauphin looked splendid in breastplate and morion, bearing in one hand his upraised sword and in the other a golden chain with a broken fetter – for Richborough, the Landside Bastion of Lyonesse, had also been called the Fetter of the Aquitaine.

At the Dauphin's right hand, only half a length back – a most signal honour – rode M. de Chirac in his lawyer's gown, bearing a scroll as symbol of his part in the conquest. Catherine leaned forward, at some risk of tumbling head over heels from the reviewing stand, to see Madame Corisande. She was certainly at no risk of Corisande's noticing; her attention was entirely on her husband. Their happiness pleased Catherine – not least because Corisande was no longer King Charles's whore. Catherine held little against whores in general – after all, St Mary Magdalene had been one – but she did object to kings' whores, since she would one day be a queen.

Then came the drums, the trumpets and the colours: first the proud banner of the King, then the Dauphin's, and those of all the captains whose companies had taken part in the successful campaign. Catherine's heart began to pound, for now came the moment for which she had made all these careful preparations. Behind the banners of Aquitaine, held high and met by cheers, came others dragged through the mire – torn, dusty, dishonoured, greeted by hoots of derision. These banners were charged with the Cross of St Pelagius and the Royal Arms of Lyonesse, which Catherine could yet remember flying so proudly over Kelliwick Castle when she was a young child. The flags with the Royal Arms had holes in the second and third quarters; the fleur-de-lis of the Aquitaine carefully cut out so as not to share the dishonour of the rest. The proud lions rampant guardant, gold on red, were torn and stained, spattered with dung.

'Now!' said Catherine in a sharp whisper. She knelt, and Anne knelt beside her. So it was that in the most visible corner of the reviewing stand, in full view of the ladies of the Court, the approaching companies and the populace, two figures clad in black velvet knelt low and bowed their heads to the fallen standards of Lyonesse.

'*Resurgam!*' said Catherine to herself.

Louis le Dauphin sat in his Robing Chamber as servants unstrapped his breastplate, undid the points of his doublet and set out his travelling clothes. His riding party awaited in the courtyard and Louis was eager for the road. On the opposite wall hung a tapestry of Pépin the Great unhorsing the Caliph al Nasr, and in front of the tapestry stood his father's Ministre d'État, Antoine de Chirac. Louis had ordered a stool brought for him, but de Chirac insisted on standing in his presence.

'You'll not stay for the feast and ball?' the minister asked.

'To see my mother insulted again by the presence of la Fontenelle?' Louis shook his head. 'I think not!' He peeled off his shirt and handed it to a servant. 'Pierre,' he told his body servant, 'fetch me bucket and sponge.' Pierre bowed, and ordered another servant to bring them in.

Louis turned back to the Ministre d'État. 'I don't know what has got into my father! He used to be a man of excellent taste – Madame your wife being a case in point.' Louis paused, aware that he was more than bold. Yet truth was truth, and Antoine de Chirac was a man of the world. 'I mean no insult, precisely the contrary, when I say that she was a dish truly fit for a king. Would be still, my friend, had you not made a respectable married woman of her. My father might at least have chosen a worthier replacement. Yet since I speak boldly I must ask . . . how fares my brother?'

Louis gave M. de Chirac a conspiratorial wink, for Corisande's son – *le petit Charlot* – had never been acknowledged by the King although there was no doubt about his parenthood.

'Splendidly,' answered de Chirac. He held his hand waist high. 'He's this tall now.'

'If my father does not proclaim the boy,' said Louis, 'then I shall, when my time comes.' Bucket and sponge were set down. Louis rose, rolled off his hose and stood by the window sponging himself down. Grey clouds were sliding in from the west. The sooner on the road, the better. 'Best I get back to Richebourg,' he said. 'The Comte de Plassey has matters well in hand, but since the pretence is that I command, I ought to be seen there.'

'You *do* command,' said de Chirac. 'De Plassey sent me a private report that you joined in the entrenchment with your own hands. Soldiers notice such things, Monseigneur.' Louis reddened slightly. Praise from the Comte de Plassey, nominally his second in command and in fact his tutor in the art of war, was not won lightly.

'He also spoke of Pépin,' de Chirac continued. Louis' full and acknowledged brother had not returned with the triumphal army, but lay wounded in the Abbaye St Hilaire, just outside the walls of fallen Richebourg. 'De Plassey's report was not as full as it might have been. Perhaps you can tell me more,' he added quietly.

Louis shrugged. 'Pépin was ... Pépin. Bold, rather than wise.'

De Chirac looked steadily at him, waiting for more.

'What shall I tell you? He disobeyed orders!' Louis called for Pierre. 'Where is my towel?' he snapped. 'Do you expect me to dress when I am dripping wet?' Pierre handed him the towel and withdrew. Louis dried himself fiercely. 'Pépin has never forgiven me for being the elder, de Chirac. Half a dozen good men were lost in rescuing him.' Louis forced himself to calm down. Anger would change nothing. He shrugged. 'It might have been worse, I suppose. Had the goddams been quicker, they'd have made a sally.'

De Chirac did not press Louis further. 'Speaking of goddams,' he said instead, 'their princesses made a great stir in the reviewing pavilion this morning.'

'I thought I saw them!' said Louis. 'Dressed as in mourning. I dared not look more closely.'

De Chirac provided further details. 'The little one, Anne, must be judged innocent, young as she is. It was Princess Catherine's doing, of course – and your father is not pleased.'

Louis laughed, happy to speak of a different subject than the brother who hated him. 'Well! The girl has more spirit than all her grandfather's councillors and captains put together. And she to be their queen one day.' He frowned. 'Why was she on the reviewing stand in the first place?' he asked. Louis liked Princess Catherine, had liked her (not that she knew) from the time she came to la Trémouille, when he had been twelve. He'd found himself touched by the lonely, awkward child who was heiress of the traditional enemy. On his last visit he had also made an intriguing discovery: the gangly girl was becoming a lissom demoiselle. Since their garden encounter he could not get her out of his mind. Now this! he thought. 'Surely my father didn't command it.'

De Chirac shook his head. 'No, Monseigneur. Princess Catherine chose to be present, to signal her protest to the world.'

'A spirited demoiselle!' repeated Louis. He would like to see her again – but on this of all days, doubted that she would care to see him. 'Do you know, I've taken up the study of canon law?'

De Chirac looked sharply at Louis.

'I enquired into the impediment of consanguinity, and dispensations therefrom,' said Louis as he pulled on his riding clothes. 'Discreetly, of course! It would not please my father, since he thought to waste Catherine on Pépin.' He paused. 'We lost three hundred men before Richebourg, de Chirac. De Plassey reckoned it cheap at the price, is that not so?'

'Yes,' answered de Chirac. 'We were very fortunate.'

'Indeed we were,' agreed Louis. He thought of a warm afternoon in spring, and a tall, shy demoiselle in a garden. After a moment's initial shock she had kissed him back with trembling eagerness. 'If the canon lawyers could but set aside that nonsense about cousin marriages,' he said, 'I could make a most pleasing conquest of the whole Kingdom of Lyonesse . . . without a drop of blood shed in anger.'

'The Dauphin has gone away again.'

Corisande smiled at her young friend. 'He must tend to his duties, my child.'

'The education of a prince, Madame?' Catherine made a pout. 'Does he not know enough already? He took Richborough, which was my grandfather's, and his forefathers' before him, for four hundred years! What more has he to learn?'

Her words were as defiant as her gesture on the reviewing pavilion, but her tone struck Corisande as distinctly wistful. 'There are other reasons, dear Trinette,' she said. She had her own duty here: the education of a princess. Her noble husband knew infinitely more about kingdoms; she knew something about kings. 'It does not much please his Majesty to see his son.'

'Why not?'

'When the King sees him,' Corisande explained, 'and the young man he has become, it reminds him that Charles the Sixth shall not rule nor live for ever. One day when the courtiers kneel and say "Sire", they will address Louis the Ninth.' Princesse Catherine bit her lip and had nothing to say. Corisande did. 'This morning, Trinette, you showed your distress at the fall of Richebourg, and set the whole Court talking. So how do you speak of the Dauphin, who led the assault?'

Catherine blushed, suddenly and prettily. 'Madame, I—Louis – the Dauphin – has been a very good friend to me, and not so many have been.' The girl went on, more firmly. 'I should like to be his friend while I can. One day I shall be Queen of Lyonesse, and take Richborough back. *Then* he and I shall be enemies.'

Catherine looked solemnly down as she spoke, but there was something in her eyes. A gallant demoiselle! thought Corisande. Fourteen was not a child, especially at Court, and there was more than one form of gallantry. 'Trinette!' she said sharply. 'Just how good a friend has the Dauphin been to you? When and how?' Princess Catherine blushed again. Corisande had not thought that shy, bookish Catherine de Guienne would engage in dalliance, not yet . . . 'What have you and he—'

Cornered, the girl confessed their springtime encounter.

The Dauphin, Corisande thought, was showing himself a man in many ways. One more reason he was better away from Court! He had discovered what so many blind eyes still missed: the ugly duckling was becoming a swan – moreover, a swan eager to fall in love. Corisande knew exactly where such a discovery could lead. She threw open the window. Unseasonably cool air blew in, sharp against her face, rustling the folds of her gown. Music played from the Montfaucon garden, where the Court was gathering for the victory feast.

'Madame,' asked Catherine suddenly, 'why does Mademoiselle de la Fontenelle hate me? I know she pressed his Majesty to assail Richborough. She does not know Lyonesse from Sicania, but she knew that Richborough was to be mine. I'll take it back, one day, but more brave men must die.'

Corisande sighed. What a tangle the world was! Princess Catherine was right, at least in part; perhaps it was best to admit it. 'Margot hates you for being my friend,' she said. 'Moreover, a maîtresse-en-titre must always fear a younger and more beautiful—' She need only be younger, she thought with a moment's bitter flash. Ah, but Margot! We shall see how you look when *you* are thirty-seven!'

Princess Catherine merely shook her head. 'Hah! If King Charles wants a beautiful mistress, my honour is safe! Margot would better hate my ladies-in-waiting. Then I would not have to!'

The Princess surely did not hate her ladies, thought Corisande; but perhaps she was jealous of them. This half-child did not yet see what was obvious only to Corisande herself – and the Dauphin. Catherine was not exactly a pretty girl, and never would be; her features were too strong. But beautiful was another matter. She would face the world better armed for knowing what it might see in her – if that irritated Margot to boot, Corisande would not be sorry. She clapped her hands, and Catherine's young ladies appeared. The Princess was wrong about herself, but right about them. They were contrasting jewels: dark and alluring, golden and lively. 'Go down to the garden,' Corisande told them. 'Pick flowers, and make a garland for Princess Catherine's head.' Then she bade Catherine stand up. 'Come, Trinette.' She led her into the wardrobe. 'Let us have a look at you. Off with your headdress and coif.'

'Madame?'

'Off with them, I say.'

Princess Catherine removed her arched headdress and coif. Her hair was drawn severely back, twisted up and held with pins.

'Now take those foolish pins from your hair!'

Catherine hesitated. 'But Madame—'

'You saw your grandfather's pennants brought low,' Corisande said, 'and let the world know what you thought of it. Now you must fly your own pennant proudly.' She did not await compliance, removing the pins herself. The bronze-red mass tumbled across Catherine's shoulders and down her back to her waist. A hundred things might be done, thought Corisande, to create a new mode at Court and put an end to Margot's infernal little bells – but right now she only had time to run a brush through the girl's hair a few times. 'Henceforth,' she said, 'I sentence you to a hundred strokes of the brush, every day without fail.'

Next she considered Catherine's gown. The girl had sound instincts: the black velvet gown, hastily made for a grave occasion, would draw chevaliers' eyes to its wearer. For that project, however, the modesty-piece had no place. Corisande undid the lacings of Catherine's bodice, slipped the partlet from her shoulders and stepped back to examine the situation. 'This will not do – not for a lady of fashion. Unfasten your kirtle.' Catherine hesitated. 'Quick, quick, *chérie*!' ordered Corisande, then helped her with the lacings. 'Off with everything: we must find you another chemise.' More lacings had to be undone; she helped the girl step out of gown and kirtle and remove her chemise.

Catherine stood shyly by, stark naked, while

Corisande rummaged through her chest of chemises. She found one, the finest work of seamstresses of Ravenna: sheer as air, with delicate green embroidery at the neckline. 'This will do!' Catherine put it on, then Corisande helped her back into her kirtle and made Catherine breathe out and stand straight as she laced it up. Back on went the overgown. A chain of white gold, from Hayastan and very richly worked, completed the project. Fastened above Catherine's hips, it set off perfectly her tall, slender figure. Here is a woman, thought Corisande, who will be more beautiful at forty than at twenty. Have a care, Margot!

Solange and Madeleine reappeared, Solange with garland in hand. Corisande stifled laughter at their expressions. Who, now, would be jealous of whom? She pinned the garland on Catherine's head, examined her and let one thick strand of hair fall forward over her breast. '*Voilà!*' She led Catherine to the great-glass.

Catherine gasped and turned quite red. 'Oh – Madame! How can I . . . Mademoiselle Margot will—'

'Margot will rue the day,' Corisande said firmly, 'that she ever thought it amusing to call you *la Grande Rouquine*. Henceforth you will find that title used with due respect.'

When Louis VIII, father of King Charles, had decreed a magnificent palace in the new style to house his Court, he had chosen as site the old castle of la Trémouille that guarded the approaches to the royal seat of Aix-le-Siège from north and west. Upon the castle's foundations had risen the palace that was the wonder of Christendom for its grand façade, multitude of windows, broad sweeping stairs – and beautiful women.

Today, the afternoon was unseasonably grey and chilly, but Antoine saw scarcely a cloak on any woman. Ladies of the Court would sooner freeze than conceal a well-turned shoulder or shapely bosom. Jugglers and tumblers performed for the amusement of the company; orange-girls circulated among the courtiers, selling their wares and possibly themselves. Musicians played a quick, high-stepping air, suitable for a galliard; younger courtiers warmed themselves with leaps and turns. Antoine watched with satisfaction. Frivolous it might be: the true measures of good rule were well-fed peasants and prosperous tradesmen, strong fortresses and plentiful soldiers. Yet as the nobles danced, they did not make war on one another or rebellion against the crown. Let them dance to the royal measure, thought Antoine, and be content! His smile turned to a frown at a stir of motion across the garden. Duchesses and counts eased to one side, making way for some greater personage, and Antoine suspected it would be la Fontenelle.

He was wrong. It was two greater personages, the Princesses de Lyonesse, with Catherine's ladies and Corisande in train. A wave of silence followed the little procession through the crowd, then a low murmur of conversation. Chevaliers and ladies stared, then hastily made reverence to a demoiselle of royal rank. Antoine could not blame them for staring. Shy, studious Princess Catherine was subtly and profoundly transformed: proudly erect, hair flowing free, dangerously lovely. Behind her, Corisande glowed with pride at her handiwork.

Princesse Catherine halted directly in front of Antoine. He knelt; she responded with a small, grave curtsey, then bade him rise. 'You have performed a great service to the King of Aquitaine, Monsieur,' she said softly. She did not mention the other half of the balance sheet. She didn't need to.

Antoine had to say something. Mere pleasantries would only make things worse, so he acknowledged her rank while steering the conversation away from Richebourg. 'I have news, Altesse,' he said, 'of a matter that may one day concern you. Hosni Shah, Grand Sophy of Fars, is rumoured to be dead.'

'Of an assassin's dagger?' asked Princess Catherine.

Antoine winced at her quickness in presuming the worst – yet had not her own father's death been suspicious? 'The Grand Sophy is old,' he said. 'His death might be in the course of nature. If the story is true at all – it has been reported before. But if true, it will mean civil war among his sons.'

'And the victor will have his brothers strangled with a bowstring,' said Catherine, 'that no royal blood may be spilled.' She put her arm around Anne, as though assuring her sister that no such usage prevailed in Lyonesse.

'Such is the custom,' Antoine admitted. It was slightly unnerving for this graceful, flower-bedecked demoiselle to speak of assassins and bowstrings.

'Then Christendom may breathe the easier, while brother slaughters brother in Fars.'

'For a time, Altesse. Yet one brother must triumph in the end. He will be young and vigorous, and may seek the glory of his house and the Monite faith in war against Christians. And we Christians are divided. We must one day put aside our differences—'

'Restore Richborough, Monsieur,' answered Catherine sharply, 'and no differences need divide us!' An orange-girl approached, then veered away, either sensing the uncomfortable silence, or judging that one ageing man accompanied by a beautiful woman and demoiselles had no need of other wares she might offer. Catherine's ladies exchanged glances, then Madeleine broke the awkward tableau, asking her mistress's permission to go and pay respects to her parents. Catherine granted it; they curtseyed and stepped back.

'Trinette,' said Corisande suddenly. 'Why do not you and Anne go with your ladies? The Chevalier du Lac will be pleased to hear of his daughter Madeleine's good service.'

Catherine nodded. 'Yes, Madame.' She sounded relieved – perhaps she too found the conversation awkward – but her ladies looked bleakly at one another and Antoine suspected their real intent had been to pay respects to young men. They had no wish to be encumbered by the princesses – still less risk chevaliers' eyes being drawn to Catherine instead of themselves.

Princesses and attendants withdrew, leaving Antoine at last alone with his wife. They watched the demoiselles and child make their way through the crowd. '*Magnifique!*' Antoine exclaimed. 'I presume your handiwork, *chérie*. At least that you took up where God left off. Perhaps it is best that the Dauphin is not here to see her.'

'Indeed!' Corisande laughed, and described the springtime encounter in the garden.

Antoine reflected on the realities of power that rendered impossible what should have been the best match in Christendom. Officially the Gallican Church had ruled it out, on grounds of consanguinity, and happily so since the King had wanted to marry young Catherine to Pépin – possibly the *worst* match in Christendom. Then he put the subject aside, and studied his wife with the objective eye of a statesman. Her black ringlets had the first streaks of grey, and her figure had surrendered the slimness of youth for the splendour of womanhood. He slipped a hand around her waist.

'Monsieur!' She spanked the offending hand, then placed her own over it.

'I should enjoy my gain to the full,' said Antoine wryly, 'since it the kingdom's loss.'

Corisande raised an eyebrow. 'You would have had his Majesty keep me for himself?'

'He did not seek my advice, Madame. But since you ask – indeed I would have!' Antoine shrugged. 'How could I guess what came after?' He had married Corisande as pretence when she was with child: a loyal servant providing a husband to a royal mistress in sudden need of one. Antoine had given her her freedom to come or go as she wished – but she had come to his bed, and he rose the next morning her husband in fact as well as name. 'I shed no tears for my good fortune, *chérie* – but I could have chosen a hundred better to take your place at the King's side.'

'Pouf!' said Corisande. 'I can spend a pleasant day not thinking about Margot at all. It is very easy!'

'You were thinking of her today, Madame – do not try to mislead me! You knew the Dauphin would not be here, and none who *are* here are worthy of Princess Catherine. Your purpose was to show her off, and put Margot in her place, no?'

'Margot was my least of reasons,' replied Corisande. 'Trinette is no longer an awkward child; has not been for some time. I tell her, but she refuses to believe. She might be persuaded when she sees it in chevaliers' eyes.'

'So long as she is not persuaded into their beds!'

Corisande smiled wickedly. 'The one who attempts her will answer to me! Yet I will not always be there. Every beautiful demoiselle is in peril, Monsieur, even more if she does not know it! Yet I confess my guilt; I did it as lesson to Margot as well. She can waste her time insulting me – but today she insulted Trinette!' Corisande gave a sharp little flip of her head, a gesture that could once send men to the galleys.

'Margot did a great deal more than she realizes,' said Antoine. 'She insulted the future Queen of Lyonesse!' The problem that had been gnawing at Antoine made its way to the surface. 'One day Catherine's grandfather will die. She will go back to her own country, and seek to rule – a task I suspect she will find impossible.'

Again Corisande raised an eyebrow. 'Because she is a woman?'

'Because it is Lyonesse! Strong kings have broken themselves trying to govern it. She will need friends to keep her throne, and where can she find them? In kissing her, the Dauphin did her greater service than he thought – she might one day remember that kiss, and seek his alliance.' Antoine continued, 'Along with Pépin and the Duc de Septimanie, Margot has half undone that. Taking Richebourg was not necessary; his Majesty could have been provided with some more useful triumph. Now, if she could, your Trinette would be Edmond *le Conquérant* in the form of a woman, and ride into la Trémouille at the head of thirty thousand archers and pikemen!'

He was referring to King Edmund III of Lyonesse, known in l'Aquitaine as the Conqueror, who had once nearly made good the claims of his house, almost two hundred years past. It was Antoine's duty to see that it did not happen again. Something might be retrieved, however, he thought, even from today. The goddams would be pleased to know that their heiress had knelt to their flags; that she thought herself one of them. He would make sure they found out.

'Monsieur!' said Corisande in a low voice.

Antoine turned and saw Princess Catherine returning, her sister in tow, looking every inch the queen she was to be. 'Ah,' he said quietly. 'Catherine *la Conquérante!*'

Corisande decided that she had been wrong: if only the Dauphin had stayed at Court for tonight it might have given Catherine something better to think about. Time dragged on. 'Where are those girls?' she asked. Catherine's ladies had not returned, lingering perhaps with Madeleine's father and mother – or with others.

Her husband indicated a group of dancers. 'The huntress ventures among wolves!'

Following his gesture she saw Madeleine du Lac – the Court called her *la Chasseuse*: a fine equestrienne, un-erring with the crossbow, she also looked like Diana the Huntress – who was dancing amid a group of young men, leaping as high as a youth herself, golden hair whirling free, skirts flying up to display strong, lithe ankles and calves.

'Who would not wish to be her prey?' said Antoine.

Corisande laughed. 'Monsieur is disgraceful!' She made her way to the dancers. The girl ended her leap with a curtsey, face aglow from her exertions. 'Is this how you attend your mistress, Mademoiselle du Lac?' asked Corisande. Madeleine flushed brighter and begged leave of her companions as Corisande set out to find Solange.

She discovered her at last round a corner, deep in conversation with Armand de Fossier, a courtier of learning and wit, well regarded by Corisande's husband – and nearly twice the girl's sixteen years in age. Their 'conversation' was wordless, eyes closed, their lips pressed tightly together. Neither registered Corisande's presence.

'Mademoiselle de Charleville!'

The two started and drew apart. Solange brushed dark hair from her face and hastily adjusted the bodice of her red and black gown. De Fossier, unflustered, made an elegant bow. 'Madame de Chirac! Mademoiselle and I were discoursing upon one of the ancients, the poet Theomachus. Do you know his work?'

'I can guess!' said Corisande. She turned to Solange. 'Mademoiselle knows, I trust, that Monsieur de Fossier is writing his memoirs of the Court. Discuss enough poetry and you may amuse not only him, but all posterity as well.'

Solange, composure regained, dipped in a graceful

curtsey. 'Yes, Madame,' she said, 'I am well aware of Monsieur Armand's memoirs. I have read them.'

That was an unexpected development, and Corisande wondered how long this liaison had been going on under her nose, but she had no time to reflect further. A fanfare sounded to announce the formal procession into the Salle d'Olympie. All the Court was lined up in order of precedence and Corisande hurried back and took her place beside her husband near the front; for his role in the victory he was honoured with a seat at the High Table.

In all the time she had been King Charles's mistress, Corisande had never sat there; she had always been careful not to overstep the appropriate bounds of her office. Not so her successor. The last of all the Court to arrive was Margot de la Fontenelle. Slowly she advanced the length of the great courtyard, so that all might see her, and none might miss her arrival at the entry to the Salle d'Olympie. As Margot swept past the Duc de Septimanie, his formidable mother curtseyed only slightly and her eyes did not meet Margot's, but she could not hide her satisfaction, Corisande saw, that a Lusiane – for Margot was the duke's third cousin – governed the royal bed.

Margot had demanded, and the King granted her, precedence above all women at Court save the Queen and their daughters – above even his cousins and nieces, Princesses of the Blood. Of these the highest ranking was Catherine de Guienne; thus la Fontenelle's presumption placed them unhappily side by side at every Court function. As Margot came opposite Catherine she stopped short and glared at her before taking her own place. For a moment the bells in her hair fell quiet.

'Our Margot is not pleased,' whispered Corisande to Antoine.

Trumpets sounded and the great bronze doors of the Salle d'Olympie swung open. To the stately beat of a pavane, all filed into the hall and made their way to their places. Scant light fell through the high clerestory windows, but the banquet hall was not dark. Golden lanterns hung from marble columns, and five hundred candles glittered in chandeliers, illuminating tables covered with finest linen, and cups and laving-bowls of gold. From the lofty vaulted ceiling too hung captured pennants of Lyonesse: some old and faded, trophies of victories long past; some new, taken at Richebourg. Another bitter dish at this feast for Princess Catherine! thought Corisande.

Again the fanfare erupted, deafening in the marble-walled confines of the Salle d'Olympie. The highest nobility of l'Aquitaine, and the retainers and hangers-on of the Court of la Trémouille, knelt for the entry of their King. He came in with Queen Isabelle on his arm, advancing in state towards the High Table – and Corisande was intensely embarrassed at the sight of Margot so close to the royal seats.

Corisande did not fool herself. For seventeen long years the Queen had as much reason to detest her as to detest Margot now. Such youthful charms as Isabelle, Queen of Aquitaine, ever possessed had been sacrificed on the altar of the eight children she gave the King, of whom five were living. Men being as they were, especially *royal* men – naturally he would take a paramour. Yet Corisande had aimed to make herself as nearly invisible to the Queen as possible; a woman could sometimes preserve dignity by not seeing what she could do nothing about. Margot left the Queen no room for illusions. Corisande was distracted from further meditation by raised voices at the centre of the table.

'Please, Monsieur! Oh! Please—' cried the Queen, her voice breaking.

'I will listen no more!' answered the King harshly. 'Shall I not be served as I please at my own table?'

'*Majesté*, I pray you, it is not proper that—'

'I determine what is proper at the Court of la Trémouille! Now, Madame, leave off this foolish whining! Else I shall dismiss you, and still be served by Margot.'

Corisande stared bleakly at her husband, who shook his head. The King must have insisted on Margot serving him at table; the Queen was making futile protest. All along the High Table people craned their necks shamelessly to see what was transpiring.

'Monsieur, Monsieur,' wailed the Queen, 'always I have sought . . . I beg you, I go on my knees . . .'

'Peace, Madame! I will hear no more!'

Then it happened. In the midst of her heaving sobs the Queen burst into a nosebleed, speckling the front of her white gown. She tried to stem the flow with a handkerchief – then with a cry of anguish she turned and ran from the hall, leaving in her wake a great hiss of whispered conversation. Her ladies-in-waiting looked uncertainly at one another from their seats at the lower tables, but only her Mistress of the Wardrobe rose from her place and hastened after her mistress.

His Majesty rapped his knife against his cup, his glare sweeping every corner of the Salle d'Olympie, and conversation died quickly. The King took his seat, and with a scraping of hundreds of chairs all the Court took theirs. One figure alone remained standing – slender, flower garlanded, clad in black velvet.

'*Mon Dieu*,' whispered Corisande. She considered making a scene herself to forestall what she feared. Monsieur's hand closed more firmly around hers – to restrain her, perhaps, as much as comfort her. Corisande could do nothing but watch the drama play out.

'You may be seated,' said the King. It was a command.

Princess Catherine did not take her seat. She turned to the King and curtseyed. 'If I may beg the Most Christian King's pardon,' she said, 'I am indisposed. By your kind permission, I might be excused.' Her voice was soft, her words humble – they rang through vast silence like a trumpet blast.

'Excused?' repeated the King, utterly perplexed for a moment. Then his face darkened. 'Princess de Lyonesse, you ask to be excused much this day! Very well, then, we excuse you.' He paused. 'We excuse you altogether! Catherine de Guienne, ungrateful guest, we dismiss you from Court! You shall remove yourself tomorrow to the convent of the Mariate Sisters at Ste-Lucie-en-Avers. There you shall abide at our pleasure, and under instruction of the sisters meditate upon the demeanour – and costume – befitting a demoiselle of royal rank. *Begone!*'

Princess Catherine curtseyed again. She turned sharply, skirts and long red hair swirling around her, and walked away. With tears on her cheeks but head held high and eyes straight ahead, she swept past Corisande and down the whole length of the Salle d'Olympie. Her ladies began to rise; with an imperious gesture she bade them remain. All eyes were on her as she went. Slowly, slowly, the buzz of conversation returned to fill the Great Hall.

'This foolishness is ended,' said the King. 'Let the feast begin!'

Corisande heard her husband's low voice next to her, speaking as to himself. '*La Conquérante,*' he said.

CHAPTER THREE

A Disgrace at la Trémouille

Alone in her bedchamber, Catherine stood before her great-glass in the full plumage of disgrace. In the distance she heard music; the feast must have ended and the dancing begun. Had so much time passed since she was cast into the outer darkness?

She dressed herself down aloud in her privy tongue, taking the part of her governess whom the King of Aquitaine had sent away long ago, but could never dismiss from Catherine's thoughts. 'Lud's blood, Princess Kateryn,' she declared to herself, 'you've done yourself a fine turn now, truly you have. Turned right out of Court, this very day! And for what? For your own wilful pride, by God's truth. How plead you?'

'Why, your Ladyship,' she began contritely – then defended herself boldly and forwardly, as she had watched lawyers do when her father had taken her to trials at King's Bench. 'Not guilty!' she cried. 'If it please your Ladyship, I did but ask leave of the table, *pour l'honneur de sa Majesté la Reine*, and before that made what show I did for my country's good name. What could be the wrong in that, your Ladyship, how so ill it please the King of Aquitaine?'

Tears stung her eyes, for the King of Aquitaine was ill-pleased indeed. Dispatched to a convent! Catherine turned away, breathing deeply to calm herself, then turned back to resume her proceedings against herself. 'Princess Kateryn, silly forward girl, you did all for your own pride, and so you know truly. Confess! Because you are tight-laced, with your hair unbound and flowers wreathed about it, so you look a pretty maid – but still in truth a plain one, be fooled not! Yet so swelled up for pride that you take it on your part to offend a king?'

She lowered her head. 'Guilty, your Ladyship.' What an utter pottage she had made this day of her life! To kneel to her grandfather's fallen flags had been her duty, but then to make a scene of herself – such a scene that the King of Aquitaine ordered her immured in a convent? It could be worse, she knew. He could have sent her to the scaffold. But a convent was bad enough. On the day she had meant to declare herself to the world she was instead cast out of it. In a convent cell she would be forgotten. Men would plot and calculate over the throne of Lyonesse, and their calculations would take no account of Catherine de Guienne.

Yet, she wondered, had it been entirely her own doing? Would she ever have been so emboldened had Madame Corisande not decked her out so? Catherine looked herself over carefully. Setting aside the tear streaks and puffy eyes, the careless observer would not take her for plain at all. Corisande had seen to that! The maid in the glass looked someone else entirely – some bold demoiselle of the Court of la Trémouille. She bit her lip and studied her reflection, her mind racing at the gallop.

With sudden clarity – now that it was too late – she saw how cleverly she was led to ruin. King Charles had humiliated Queen Isabelle before; Catherine had tolerated it as all the women of the Court did, in silence. Why not this time as well? Because Corisande had primped and puffed her up, almost as though she were a rival to Margot. And indeed the King of Aquitaine's eyes had been on her in a way she had not seen before – as though she, Princess Lyon, heiress to Lyonesse, were one more delectable demoiselle of his court.

Had that been Corisande's intent? thought Catherine. To what purpose? The answer was all too clear. Corisande might no longer be King Charles's whore, but – married as she was to his chief minister – she was still his loyal servant. The men of the Aquitaine called Lyonesse their traditional enemy. Why not the women of the Aquitaine as well?

She snatched up her hairbrush and set furiously to work. 'A hundred strokes, indeed, Madame Corisande!' she cried. 'Every day without fail, Madame Corisande!' The absurd circlet of flowers – surely now the only crown she would ever wear – was swiftly reduced to broken bits of petal. Where a couple of blossoms fell by chance intact, Catherine made short work of them with her foot. After a few more ragged slashes, stinging her scalp, she hurled the brush into the great-glass. It shattered, bright shards spinning to fall among the rushes on the floor. Seven years' ill fortune? She had lived seven years here now, in the Court of la Trémouille – had come to think of it as home. In truth it was the lair of her enemies. Such a fool she had been! Now at least she would not have to look at herself.

The door flew open and in swept none other than Madame Corisande, with Catherine's ladies-in-waiting behind her. 'Trinette, my child – I left the ball as soon as I dared—' She stared at Catherine, at the broken great-glass, back at Catherine. '*Pardieu!*' she cried. 'What is the matter, dear child?'

'Nothing is the matter, Madame!' cried Catherine. 'I am disgraced and cast down, but what is that to you? A hundred strokes of the brush, indeed! Why not just one stroke of the axe, or the great-sword as you use in this kingdom? It would have been greater mercy!'

'Dear Trinette!' exclaimed Corisande. 'It is not so dreadful as you think, my child! His Majesty is but vexed, because—' Her hand flew to her mouth, and for some moments she was silent, looking at Catherine as if in deep thought. 'Oh! As wrought up as you were, this was not the day – I fear I have done poorly!'

'No, Madame,' retorted Catherine. 'You have done

very well!' She glared past Corisande at her ladies. 'Leave off gaping, you witless girls! Out! I would speak to Madame alone!' The demoiselles hastily withdrew.

'Princess Catherine!' cried Corisande. 'Dear child – come, let me hold you—' She drew towards Catherine and tried to embrace her.

Catherine shoved her roughly away. 'You play the game so well, Madame – no wonder you ruled so long from King Charles's bed!'

'Trinette!'

'I am not your Trinette! I am Kateryn, daughter of Harry, granddaughter of King Edmund the Fourth of Lyonesse! Or so I was!' Catherine cried. 'Now I am no one! A pretty prize to be decked out and led before the King of Aquitaine! Why, Madame?' she demanded. 'What have I ever done to you, that you should treat me so? Is it simply that you think every woman's desire to be as you are, a lady of fashion? But no – this was high policy! Pépin did not send armies against my grandfather's city! Nor Septimanie, and certainly not Margot! Monsieur your husband – and the Dauphin too! – have brought Richborough low. And now you have brought *me* low as well!'

Corisande looked at her for long moments, splendid as ever, the queen of actresses feigning sorrow. 'Please!' she cried. 'I beg you to listen to me. That is not—'

Catherine cut her off. 'No! I will not listen! What is there more to say? I am cast away as you intended! What reward may you not ask now? Surely it will be granted! Margot can be tossed in the convent cell next to mine, and you can resume your place. Your victory shall be complete! How very clever of you! And not only you, but Monsieur your husband as well! Rather should I say . . . your procurer!'

Even as she said it Catherine knew it for utter nonsense, but she did not care. She had cast down the gauntlet! The chamber fell silent but for the pounding of her own heart. At last Madame Corisande spoke. 'Princess Catherine,' she said, tears glistening in her violet eyes, 'you can say nothing to me that I have not heard before. But I will not hear you speak of Monsieur my husband other than with the honour he deserves. I must beg leave to go.' With the precise curtsey due a Princess of the Blood she withdrew, and Catherine was once more alone in her chamber. For a moment she thought to run after Corisande, throw herself at her feet and beg forgiveness. The moment passed. A royal princess – even one in disgrace – could do no such thing. Whatever Madame Corisande had come to say must remain for ever unsaid.

Catherine got out of her gown herself, ripping the lacings from the bodice rather than submit to being undressed by her ladies. Tearing off Corisande's borrowed chemise, she tossed it onto the pile of crumpled fabric, kicked it all into a corner, then flung herself onto her bed and crawled under the furs and coverlets. There she wept till she was out of tears and had nothing left but to consider her fate. Dismissed to a convent! Her last thought, before she fell into fitful sleep, was that her mother had gone into a convent and died there. No doubt she herself would die in one as well; at least it would end her troubles.

She awoke groggily, to Solange shaking her. 'Mademoiselle, please!' cried the girl. 'There is so much to do—' For the first half-waking seconds Catherine forgot it was not any other morning, and wondered what was so urgent that Solange must drag her out of sleep. Then she remembered everything and came wide awake.

Solange had opened up canopy and chamber; the sky through the window was deep blue, and Catherine winced at the bright morning sun. What right had it to shine on her misery and ruin? Yet why should it care? Someone, no doubt Madeleine, had already had servants remove the evidence of last night's fury. Shards of glass still clung to the frame of the great glass, but the floor was swept clean. Catherine had a flash of irritation at the girl's bustling efficiency. Why should Madeleine be concerned with her apartments, when Catherine would this day be gone from la Trémouille for ever? Let the chamberlain deal with them!

She crawled out of her bed and let Solange help her into a chemise. 'Where is Madeleine, and the rest of the household?'

Solange made an uncharacteristically demure curtsey. 'Madeleine is organizing your things, to take for safekeeping at the old Hôtel de Guienne in the city.' Turning to the dressing table, she gathered up Catherine's ruined gown from last night and put it in her sewing basket. 'By your leave, Mademoiselle, I will do what I can. The chemise is beyond repair, but perhaps the gown can be mended—'

'You can leave off!' snapped Catherine. Solange stole a glance at her, then looked carefully down. Catherine studied her lady-in-waiting, and found it pleasing to be harsh with her. Nothing about Solange de Charleville called for obvious correction. Her hair was pinned back under a workaday black headdress, and her gown was bare of adornment. She had known to dress in keeping with the sombre occasion. Still, even Solange's plainest garb called attention to her – she was far too pretty. 'Do not make a show of yourself, Solange!' Catherine told her. 'It will be your ruin, as it has been mine!'

'Yes, Mademoiselle.'

'And do not speak obediently when you are thinking otherwise.'

'Yes, Ma . . .' began Solange, then trailed off awkwardly.

'Enough! Bring me something fitting to wear. Then have Madeleine and my people await me in the Presence Chamber.'

Solange rummaged through the chests and held up a green riding dress. Catherine doubted that it was suitable to wear to the gate of a convent. But she possessed nothing that was – everything in her wardrobe showed Corisande's influence. Was Corisande laughing at her now, or weeping? Whether the one or the other, it was without consequence. She nodded assent at the riding dress and Solange dressed her in uncomfortable silence, then curtseyed and withdrew.

Catherine sat on her bedside, thinking. To her own fate she was indifferent. Better she had died in childhood of the fever that took instead her little brother Ned! Lyonesse would then have had a prince to inherit the throne instead of a useless princess. Yet her downfall, she now fretted, was also the ruin of her ladies-in-waiting. The rest of her household would easily find other situations. But Solange and Madeleine? Demoiselles of noble blood, their families spent every sou of their dowries to place them here at Court. Now their places had vanished. Catherine detested them for being beautiful, charming and Aquitanian – yet they had served her faithfully and well. It was great injustice that they should be thrown back to their families, daughters without dowries, condemned to poor marriages or none at all.

She went out to her Presence Chamber. The servants of her household were drawn up behind her ladies.

'I shall be brief,' Catherine said. She took a deep breath. 'You know what happened yesterday! My clothing and other things I give to you all, in token of

good service. Solange, Madeleine: see to the distrib-
ution, taking care to be just – and don't keep too much
for yourselves! And . . . I will speak to you both about
your places at Court. I shall do as best I can, though I
know not what.'

A long moment passed – then Solange gathered up
her skirts and knelt. 'Mademoiselle,' she said, 'my place
is by your side. If you must go to Ste-Lucie, then I shall
go with you!' She looked, thought Catherine, exactly
like a very brave woman facing the executioner.

Madeleine glanced down at Solange, gulped visibly,
then also knelt. 'So . . . so too shall I, Mademoiselle.'

Catherine stared at them, astonished. Foolish girls!
she thought. They were no more meant for the cloister
than she was – and no king had commanded them to
one. Catherine had thought herself done with weeping,
or anything else; now her eyes welled up with tears of
gratitude. She curtseyed as to princesses of her own
rank, then ran from the Presence Chamber to kneel
before the crucifix by her bed, giving thanks that
honour had still a place in the world.

Solange, youngest daughter of the Comte de
Charleville, examined Mademoiselle's torn gown by a
window. Madeleine was securing a wagon for the household goods, giving Solange some peace and quiet on a
day with far too little of either. Mademoiselle's dismissal
from Court posed a practical problem, and Solange – a

most practical young woman – had just made an utterly impractical decision.

She and her mother had staked all when she was thirteen, persuading her father – that good, honest, but simple man – to place her at Court. Country marriages befit her sisters, but Solange, like her mother, had aimed for a higher station. While her sisters played country games the family chaplain taught her Latin, and an Enotrian dancing master instructed her in skills a lady at Court must have. Her family was ancient but poor; Solange their last, best hope of retrieving their fortunes after their lands were given over to the Lusianes.

Solange had done well. At the great Court of la Trémouille anyone not extraordinary went unnoticed – unless improved by art. Solange had applied herself to art, with gratifying results. She had caught the eye not of some witless young gallant, but of Armand de Fossier: penniless, of unimportant family, yet destined for high places, favoured by M. de Chirac himself.

Solange was not bustling, orderly Madeleine, who ran Mademoiselle's little household – and would as skilfully manage the great (indeed royal) household that Mademoiselle must one day rule. Yet there was a higher duty: managing not one's servants, but one's mistress. In *that*, she felt she had failed utterly! She studied the black velvet gown in the light. The sleeves were torn, the lacings down the back of the bodice ripped out. Senseless ruin of a fine garment! Her needlework was excellent, and she'd put much care and effort into that gown. It passed her understanding why Mademoiselle had been so foolish. Certainly last night had been a disaster, one she should have foreseen and prevented. Nor had Madame Corisande shown her usual good judgement. The King? Solange would not commit lèse-majesté by thinking of it. As for la Fontenelle – she should be taken to St-Léger and tossed into the gutter where she belonged, but that was nothing new.

Her precious solitude was abruptly shattered by Madeleine, who burst into the room and started shouting. 'Was it not enough to ruin your own life, Solange,' she cried, 'that you must ruin mine, as well? A convent!' She pulled off her couvre-chef and shook her head, blonde hair swirling. 'Now I am lost to life – and I had scarcely begun to live! The executioner's sword would have been greater mercy!'

Solange did not wish to hear it. 'No one made you assent!'

'No one made me? What was I to do?' demanded Madeleine. 'You went down on your knees before Mademoiselle and all the household, saying "Whither thou goest, so shall I!" What was I to do? Say, "No, Mademoiselle; faithful Solange shall follow you anywhere, but I have my own life to live"? I was honour bound, as well you know!'

'Will you listen—'

Instead Madeleine whirled round, strode over to

Catherine's books, and with one sweep knocked the whole row onto the floor. Solange gasped and ran to the precious volumes.

'Books!' cried Madeleine. 'You and Mademoiselle are two of a kind! Fools for books! You think it no loss to be locked in a convent, because you'll be free to read! Well! You should have left books alone, Solange de Charleville, and studied life! Perhaps when you are old and wrinkled they'll let you read! Till then you'll be on your knees! Praying, but most of all scrubbing! That's what they do in convents, you know. Scrub, scrub, scrub! All the day long, all the year ... Can you see us? All in a row, in ugly habits, scrubbing our lives away!'

'Madeleine!' shouted Solange. Was some evil vapour making every demoiselle at Court a fool but her? First Princess Catherine, now Madeleine. 'Don't be so simple!'

Madeleine leaped at her, and Solange went backwards onto the floor. Then Madeleine was on top of her, hands around her neck. Solange could not say a word, could not breathe. She struggled to get up, kicked Madeleine and struck her; for a moment the grip loosened, then she was being choked tighter than ever. Madeleine's riding and dancing had left their mark; she was much stronger than Solange.

'Always you prate of what good friends we are!' cried Madeleine. 'Such loyalty and love in Mademoiselle's service, not like the others at Court! Well! Think it my loyalty and love that I spare you slow death in a convent!' Solange was growing too weak to struggle. What a foolish way to die! Then, wonderfully, she could breathe again. '*Bon Dieu!*' Madeleine sobbed. 'I am lost!'

Solange gasped with relief. She got unsteadily up, pulled Madeleine to her feet and slapped her. 'Madeleine du Lac! Now listen, and don't be foolish! No one is going to waste away in a convent – not you, nor I, nor Mademoiselle least of all!'

'But . . .' stammered Madeleine, 'his Majesty commanded that—'

'So?' answered Solange. 'His Majesty is embarrassed because he made a fool of himself on account of la Fontenelle. And Mademoiselle was also a fool to say as much to his face. Yet if we abandon her now, who are we? What marriage can your father afford to make for you? Do you want to be Madame de Nobody?'

'The Chevalier de Batz-Castelmore favours me!' said Madeleine with artless complacency.

'Enough to marry you without dowry? No, I didn't think so. All our prospects are with Mademoiselle. Future Reine de Lyonesse, in case you have forgotten! So we sigh of boredom for a few months. Do you think Mademoiselle is going to take final vows? No! She is today as she was yesterday and will be tomorrow: *heiress to a throne.* And we, her loyal ladies, shall reap the reward – but only if we stand by her now.'

Madeleine thought on this for a while, and finally

nodded. 'I – I suppose you are right,' she said. 'Oh, Solange! I am so sorry . . . however would I do without you?'

Poorly! thought Solange, but took Madeleine in her arms, and they embraced and kissed one another's cheeks.

Charles VI, King of Aquitaine, glared at his chief minister across his cluttered writing table. He held up a paper. 'Do you know what this is, de Chirac?'

'No, Sire,' Antoine de Chirac said. 'I do not.'

'It is a *lettre de cachet*. To confine the person named in the Tour St Martin at our pleasure.' *At our pleasure*, thought Charles: really, this was often for life. 'All it awaits is my signature. Do you know what name it bears?'

'I would not venture to guess, Sire.'

'Corisande de Chirac,' answered Charles quietly, and watched his minister's reaction. The man's face remained impassive, but his eyes flickered with uncertainty, and fear. Charles was sure of it. It was sometimes useful to emphasize who was the King and who the servant. 'Now tell me, de Chirac, why I should not sign it.'

'Because, Sire—' began de Chirac. He hesitated. 'Because Corisande is merely a foolish woman. As you, Sire, know better than anyone!'

'I know her for the least foolish woman in the kingdom!' retorted Charles. 'The world thinks me a fool, throwing her over for Margot,' he said. 'Just as the world will blame me for yesterday! I know *that* quite well too.'

'No, Sire, that is not—'

'Peace, de Chirac!' Charles scowled at his minister. 'I know what is said! Yes, Margot often makes a fool of herself. Sometimes of me as well. Yet does not Corisande bear the greater blame for last night?'

'Sire?'

'You know perfectly well what I mean! Yesterday she taught Princess Catherine something about herself that she did not know. Now her beauty will be the talk of the Court.' Charles had paid little heed to the princesses of Lyonesse, other than as instruments of policy. Little Anne was a charming and pretty child, and someday she would be a charming and pretty demoiselle, an ornament to his court. But her elder sister Catherine had the charm of an abbess. Were she not a royal heiress, a convent would have seemed just the place for her. Last night, therefore, had been a revelation. Catherine de Guienne, red hair unbound, crowned with flowers, was herself a flower worthy of any prince in Christendom. Charles couldn't take his eyes off her, even as he had ordered the insolent girl out of his Court.

'Margot was displeased,' he said. An understatement: Margot had been furious. 'Whatever the world may think – whatever Margot thinks – I *am* capable of admiring a demoiselle without trying to bed her!' He might imagine it, though. But with a royal heiress it was impossible. And according to the Church, he could not even safely give her and her future throne to Pépin. 'In any case,' he said, 'Margot is convinced your wife did it from spite for her.'

'I am sure,' said de Chirac, 'that it was nothing of the sort. I confess that Madame has no great love for Margot! Yet as your Majesty knows, she has been fond of Princess Catherine since the child came to l'Aquitaine. She had no purpose yesterday other than to show a demoiselle that she is pretty. For which she got cold thanks.'

'Eh?'

'Princess Catherine flew in a rage and spoke cruelly to her.' De Chirac shrugged. 'I do not know why. Whatever Corisande's fault, she has already paid with bitter tears.'

Charles noted that de Chirac was not only exculpating his wife, but reducing Princess Catherine's offence to a mere tantrum. How had he ever thought it a good idea for his then mistress to marry his chief minister? Corisande had always liked the little man, but at the time it had seemed a mere convenience. Who could have guessed that she'd end up not only de Chirac's wife in name, but also his wife in his bed? Thus she remained at Court, beautiful as ever – and a standing offence to his current maîtresse-en-titre. 'Tell your wife, in future, to show greater prudence.' He ceremoniously tore up the *lettre de cachet.* 'She should remove herself from Court, for a time, but I require nothing more. Sometimes I think I should have sent her to the Tour St Martin long ago. Other times I think I should recall her to my bedchamber! Either way the loss would be yours, no?'

De Chirac bowed. 'Indeed, Sire,' he said.

At least the man was honest, thought Charles. To his annoyance, he often thought of the girl whose voice had entranced him when he was still young; the woman whose company had made the world a summer afternoon. The seasons of Margot changed by the day, sometimes the hour. It made her exciting. Yet he sometimes missed those summer afternoons of Corisande.

'There remains Princess Catherine,' he said. 'What use is she? I cannot marry her to Pépin, so to whom *shall* I marry her? The vultures circle, de Chirac – and will circle closer, thanks to your wife's meddling, seeing that she is not only heiress but good-looking. When she keeps her mouth shut. What possible candidate will not end up making trouble for us?'

'Why should she marry anyone, Sire?' asked de Chirac.

Charles laughed. 'What nonsense is that? Lyonesse hasn't much of a king now – but no king at all?'

'Under the law of Lyonesse,' said de Chirac, 'not even her husband will be King, save by her grant of the Crown Matrimonial.'

'So? What is the law without a sword? Is that slip of a

girl going to rule a kingdom? Her tongue may be sharp, but not that sharp!'

'Precisely, Sire,' said de Chirac, and Charles had the sense he'd fallen into a trap. 'Do not underestimate Princess Catherine,' continued his minister. 'She is a demoiselle of much courage. Yet what is her chance of reducing Lyonesse to obedience, much less making them a threat to us? Far more likely she will find herself needing us to protect her from her own unruly subjects.'

King Charles drank from his goblet. De Chirac was annoying, but he could not imagine doing without the man. He drove the coach of State like a master coach-man; without him it was an oxcart. As for princesses, unfortunately they could not be drowned at birth. 'So what does it come to?' he asked. 'You are advising me to do nothing at all about a marriage for her?'

'There is an old tale, Sire,' said de Chirac, 'of a certain Jew who once lived in the Eastern Empire. He was a rabbi and a very wise man. The Emperor, needing a great sum of money, commanded this rabbi to come before him at New Ilium, and demanded of him twenty thousand talents. The rabbi said that all the Jews of the Empire hadn't that much wealth. Whereupon the Emperor ordered him put to death. The rabbi fell on his knees, telling the Emperor that if he would spare him for ten years he would teach the Emperor's dog to talk. The Emperor agreed, and sent the man home with the dog. When the rabbi told his wife she burst into tears, saying,

"You are doomed! How can a dog be made to talk?"'

'Well,' asked Charles, 'how *can* a dog be made to talk?'

His minister smiled faintly. 'The rabbi comforted his wife, Sire, telling her to fear not. "I have ten years," he said. "In that time the dog may die, or the Emperor may die, or I may die. Or – since all is possible with God – the dog may talk." So in this case, Sire. When Edmond de Lyonesse dies, some noble may attempt to usurp Catherine's rightful throne, requiring her to choke back her pride and seek your aid. Or some circumstance arise that we cannot now foresee. Avoid the irreversible – a marriage now for the Princess – and you may avail yourself of whatever fortune brings.'

'Indeed,' said Charles. 'The girl might even learn *not* to talk. Yet I will not rescind my command – to Ste-Lucie she goes, by day's end! Let the Mariate Sisters enjoy her company, until she learns to be seen but not heard.'

'Of course, Sire.' His minister bowed and started to withdraw.

Charles thought of something. 'Wait!'

'Sire?'

'Princess Catherine's ladies-in-waiting. What are their names? Solange de Charleville and, ah, Marianne du Lac? No, Madeleine. I suppose they have lost their places now, eh?'

De Chirac nodded. 'Mademoiselle du Lac's father is a chevalier in the Constable's service, Sire.

Mademoiselle de Charleville, alas, will doubtless have to return to her father's château.'

Charles shook his head. 'That would be a shame, de Chirac,' he said. The girl had a lively figure. 'Find places for them – where they are not lost at the back of the crowd.'

'It shall be done, Sire,' said de Chirac. He bowed again and withdrew.

Charles picked up his goblet and settled back in his seat. Margot would not be pleased, but he was King.

Catherine stood at a window amid the silent emptiness of her bedchamber, looking over the garden below. Madeleine had got hold of a wagon and was carting the last of her things to the Hôtel de Guienne, a place Catherine had only seen from a distance, its grey bulk rearing above the rooftops of the city. As for these chambers, soon nothing would show she ever dwelt here. She would not be missed. Her aunts and cousins, Princesses of the Blood, would happily move up one place in precedence. None of them liked her. Not that Catherine much liked any of them.

Solange was at her elbow, awaiting audience. Catherine turned, and started. The girl had changed from her ordinary day attire into her Court gown: crimson velvet trimmed with black, tight laced and décolleté. Solange's finery was nearly as bold as Margot's, though with an elegant simplicity that made her gallant rather than vulgar. All the same she looked as unlike a maiden on her way to a convent as could be imagined. '*That* is how you mean to present yourself to the Mariate Sisters?' demanded Catherine.

'They will find me much in need of saving from the world,' said Solange, dipping. 'Yet we are all martyrs to la Fontenelle, no? Why not wear today the colour of martyrdom? There will be time enough afterward for my soul.'

'Do not make light of this!' said Catherine sharply. 'This is no Court adventure, Solange, and it is not about Margot! The King of Aquitaine finds me . . . inconvenient.'

'As well he might, Mademoiselle! The Church forbade you to his son, vexing his Majesty no end. Yet you are still the marriage prize of Christendom, even if you do not like to hear it. In the end he must give you to *someone.*'

'I am not Charles of Aquitaine's to give to anyone!' Nor was she the marriage prize of Christendom – Catherine had realized that long ago. Her hand in marriage would convey the crown of Lyonesse? Only if the man in question could also furnish an army. Yet if one had an army, what need of a princess not very pretty and not at all obedient? Abruptly the logic became dreadfully clear. Her sister Anne was not troublesome. She herself was, and therefore need not fear long dreary years in a convent. Usurping a throne would be done boldly –

thus she must, and surely would, be done away with.

Catherine had never thought to fear such things, yet what was her life against the prize of a crown? The Duchessa di Longhi had been younger than Catherine when her uncle had murdered her to seize her state. Lyonesse was a far greater prize. 'God save me,' she whispered in her privy tongue.

'Mademoiselle?' asked Solange. 'Are you all right?'

Catherine gulped down sour bile, and held the windowsill to keep from collapsing in a heap. Death was waiting upon her, and might not wait long. Then, looking over the garden, she conceived a plan of breath-taking audacity. The Palais de la Trémouille was built for stateliness, elegance and pleasure, not confinement. Many ways led out. In minutes she could be away from the palace, lost amid crowds in the quartier Ste-Valérie. And then? She still had her jewels – even one would surely buy her a horse. Ride as swiftly as ever she could to the coast and take passage for Lyonesse. Home!

It took only an instant to form the plan, and another to see it was all but impossible. Catherine knew nothing of purchasing a horse, but she did know the sorts of felons hanged at the public execution ground: cut-purses, ravishers of maids, murderers. If she tried to sell her jewels, she might only get her throat cut. In any case her striking appearance – that curse of her life – would swiftly betray her. Reward would be offered for a tall, thin maid with bright red hair. Someone would be quick to collect it. She could be quietly killed, and who would be the wiser? Then she thought: I *shall* be quietly killed, in any case. So why not try?

'Mademoiselle! What is the matter?'

Catherine turned to Solange. Here was her first obstacle. 'Nothing is the matter. I – I feel lightheaded. I shall walk in the garden before – it is time to depart.'

'Then so shall I,' declared Solange. 'You may ask my counsel if you wish, or say nothing, but I'll not desert you and leave you alone.'

'Are you my guard, Solange? King Charles has guards enough without you!' No sooner did Catherine say it than she cursed her folly. Solange was no fool, and Catherine had all but revealed her plan. Catherine balled her hand into a fist, wondering if she could stretch the girl out unawares. Silence her.

Solange saw it and backed out of reach. 'Mademoiselle – truly I meant no harm! And I am no guard!' she added hotly.

You are a daughter of the Aquitaine! thought Catherine. Yet she had knelt before Catherine and vowed to accompany her to the convent at Ste-Lucie-en-Avers. With a moment's silent prayer, Catherine made a decision: to face her fate like a prince of Lyonesse, trusting in her loyal retainers, as every prince must who battles against great odds.

She unballed her fist and reached out. Gingerly Solange took her hand. 'Listen to me, Solange de

Charleville,' Catherine said. 'And spare your brilliance till you hear me out! You call me the marriage prize of Christendom. Yet so would Anne be, were I cast aside – and Anne is not troublesome as I am. You know that; the whole Court knows it. Did I not say that King Charles finds me inconvenient! I'll not be let out of Ste-Lucie alive.'

'Mademoiselle!'

'I'll not hold you to your vow, nor Madeleine. It was much to your honour both – but if you go with me, do not expect to leave there alive, either.'

Solange's great dark eyes regarded Catherine steadily. 'Mademoiselle,' she said, 'I am at your command. Bid me fly out that window and I shall – though it will ruin a rose bush, and my best gown as well.'

Catherine laughed, then caught herself. 'I mean to fly,' she said, 'but not from a window!' She related her intention to escape. 'I doubt I – we – shall get far, not when King Charles can send a thousand men in pursuit! Yet better that than passively awaiting the dagger or poisoned cup.' She'd sooner face the dagger; at least she could fight back, and look her assassin in the eye. 'We must leave at once!'

'May I speak, Mademoiselle?' Solange did not await permission. 'By your leave, you are a mad fool!'

She was quite right, thought Catherine. As always. It was Solange's most annoying trait. 'I said I would not hold you! I ask only—'

Solange cut her off. 'I too am a mad fool, Princess Catherine! You had not noticed? Yet we should not run off in five directions at once, without thinking! Madeleine shall be back soon. No demoiselle at Court – none in Christendom – is better for this enterprise.' Solange looked down at herself. 'Far better than I! If I fall behind, you and Madeleine must spur onward.' She shrugged, her glance straying suggestively towards her décolletage. 'I shall do what I can to distract the pursuers . . .'

Madeleine du Lac de Montpellier rode back to the palace at the trot, no longer encumbered by the wagon that had carried her worldly possessions, with Solange's and Mademoiselle's, to the Hôtel de Guienne. She'd given the carter and his boy a douzainê to stop on their way back for a roasted fowl and cup of wine. She could have taken her own things to her father's quarters, but would then have endured her parents bewailing her misfortune, and their unspoken fretting over what to do with her now. Much though she hated to admit it, Solange had been right: her family had spent all they could afford, and more, to get her a place as lady-in-waiting. Well, she had still a place, in a convent. *Hélas!* thought Madeleine. I should have strangled Solange when I had the chance!

Riding out through the city gate, she came into the rue Ste-Valérie, with the Palais de la Trémouille rising in splendour beyond it. She urged her mount to a canter for the sheer joy of wind in her face, threading her way amid wagons, market-women and bourgeoisie dressed above their station. Then Madeleine spied a litter bearing the colours of Margot de la Fontenelle. '*A l'avant!*' she cried, and leaning forward she spurred to the gallop. She rode straight at the chair, hoping to panic the bearers and cast la Fontenelle onto the pavement. Only at the last instant did she see that while the livery colours resembled Margot's the badges were not hers. She veered off, glimpsing a terrified dowager who had thought her last moment at hand, and was hurtling directly towards a market-girl with a basket. Madeleine reined in furiously, nearly losing her seat; the market-girl shrieked and threw herself down, apples spilling across the cobbles.

Madeleine sprang down and helped the sobbing girl to her feet. 'Mercy, child, stop bawling!' she commanded. 'I meant you no hurt – I thought I spotted an enemy!' Explanation was wasted on a commoner; the girl merely stared at her. Madeleine fished in her gear for unguent and applied it to the girl's scrapes, then found a few coins. 'For your trouble!' she said, and gave the girl a douzain. She added a few liards. 'And for your apples!' As they were now rightfully hers, Madeleine helped herself to one, wiping it on her skirts before biting into it. She remounted, and rode the rest of the way at a sensible trot.

The chambers of Princess Catherine were empty of furnishings and servants. All that remained were Mademoiselle and Solange – looking at her with most peculiar expressions, and Madeleine guessed at once that there would be no tedious wait for their conveyance to Ste-Lucie. She curtseyed before the Princess. 'I have seen your goods to the Hôtel de Guienne, Mademoiselle, and the bailiff's man signed for the inventory.' His efficiency had not impressed her; in the end he'd signed to be rid of her, without inspection. Had she known, she would have padded the inventory, claiming restitution when the time came. Whenever that might be. She held out the inventory.

Instead of taking it, Solange went past her and bolted the door.

'Madeleine du Lac de Montpellier, I shall be brief,' said Catherine. 'As I am in peril of my life, I have resolved to meet it as befits my rank and lineage. I shall not await King Charles's soldiers, but take to the high-way, trusting in God and my right. I should be honoured by your service – even Solange says that none could serve better – but I will not command you to such peril. Yet you must choose, and quickly!'

'What?' said Madeleine, flustered. Their only peril was of dying of boredom in a convent. This had to be Solange's doing, filling Mademoiselle's head with lurid fantasies when Madeleine was not around to talk sense. She whirled on Solange. 'What have you—' She cut short, and turned back to Princesse Catherine.

The Princess's green eyes regarded Madeleine steadily, but she had a skittish look, breathing quickly, neck and shoulders tensed. Could Catherine be in some real danger? She was heiress to a throne; someone might want her out of the way . . . could it really be? What was more, Solange had admitted that she, Madeleine, might serve better than Solange herself. Which was unthinkable, unless she was truly alarmed herself.

Madeleine was not pleased. All she wanted in life was to be châtelaine of her own lands, riding to the hunt beside her husband, riding home to her children and a cheerful, well-kept household. God, as usual, took no account of her wishes. She dipped to Catherine. 'Beg pardon, Mademoiselle. The whys and wherefores you can tell me later – Solange will think me too simple to understand anyway! Whatever your peril, I shall face it beside you.' *That was that!* she thought. I have been so long among fools that now I'm a fool too!

'Then we must delay no longer,' said Catherine. 'We need to slip out, then find horses somehow. Did you see sign of more guards? I pray the chamberlain didn't think it needful.'

Madeleine shook her head. 'There were the two at your outer door, Mademoiselle, as always. I saw no others.' Leaving these chambers was not a problem, but how to get away from the palace? The usable ways out, Madeleine judged, were all on the far side, gates used by minor officials and servants. Crossing though the gallery was impossible: half the Court would be there, playing the game of seeing and being seen. The kitchens? There were back ways, but Madeleine did not know them, and she did know the kitchen servants – they guarded their empire fiercely; she had never been able to so much as steal an orange, and not from want of trying. Three demoiselles of rank skulking through the kitchens would be exposed at once.

'We must go through the gardens,' she declared. 'We'll have to get through the Montfaucon somehow, but after that we should be all right.' She looked Solange up and down. 'Well! *You* certainly dressed for the occasion – how are we to slip out unseen, you looking like that?'

'How was I to know?' protested Solange.

'Well, if you get run through, at least no one will notice the blood!'

'Silence, both of you!' cried Catherine. 'A hundred girls at Court would do as well for chattering! Solange, you must go at the front. Wrap your cloak around you and you'll seem merely on your way to an assignation. Madeleine and I can follow, and perhaps be taken for your attendants.'

Solange nodded, and so did Madeleine. It was a good plan. No, it wasn't, but Madeleine couldn't think of a better. On any afternoon, twoscore women at Court were on their way to or from their lovers, most scarcely drawing a notice. Yet what man would fail to notice

Solange? She looked splendid in red – the very embodiment of mortal sin. Madeleine looked out of the window over the garden. A gardener was huddled over a bush, trimming it. In another corner were a lady and chevalier Madeleine did not recognize, but they had better to do than examine passers-by. 'Mademoiselle – the garden is nearly empty.'

Catherine nodded, though for just an instant Madeleine saw dread in her eyes. 'Let us go, then,' she said quietly, and crossed herself. It was the first sensible thing Madeleine had seen anyone at Court do these last two days; she too crossed herself as they swept out through the empty Presence Chamber.

At Solange's suggestion they left as always, Princess Catherine in the lead with her ladies following. The two Gardes de Maison beside the outer door merely snapped to attention and grounded their halberds as they always did. In the garden, lady and chevalier took no notice of three demoiselles – Madeleine doubted they'd notice a bronze cannon drawn through on its limber by half a hundred horses. The gardener looked up and his eyes widened for a moment, then he bent back to his clipping. Madeleine liked servants who tended to their duties. On any other day she would have made a point of praising the garden so he could hear it.

The archway to their right led past a fountain. This courtyard was more populated, but no alarm was raised. Solange hastened along at the front, looking very much the furtive lover – thus quite unlike the usual Solange, not one to hide her light under a bushel.

Madeleine thought about horses. If only Princess Catherine had discovered her peril (or Solange invented it) earlier, when her business had taken her to the stables. As her father was an officer there it would have been easy to wheedle the grooms out of three mounts. Now it would be impossible; her father would find out and make a correct guess. The Chevalier de Batz-Castelmore, perhaps, since he had his eye on her? His uncle's hôtel off the rue Ste-Valérie had a stables with half a dozen good mounts. Could she talk him out of three?

Madeleine flushed and swallowed dry. More than talk would be needed. She had placed her life at the service of Princess Catherine; now her honour too would be needed. Could giving him her favour be done in haste? Certainly, if need were great. François de Batz-Castelmore, she thought wryly, was about to become the most fortunate of chevaliers.

Another archway, and now before them the Montfaucon garden – thronged with courtiers on a warm afternoon. Beyond was the palace wing given over to civil officers. Three demoiselles would still be noticed, but fewer would know them by sight. Getting there, though . . . Madeleine wondered now if they should have gone through the gallery, but doubling back round would only increase the risk of discovery. Solange threw back a short, bleak look, then hurried on.

They had not gone a dozen paces before disaster struck. Two ladies came the other way; Madeleine knew both, but neither took notice. Alas, the Marquise d'Aurignac had her son by the hand, a boy of eight or nine. In the nature of boys he observed everything – particularly demoiselles. '*Maman!*' He stopped short, let go his mother's hand, and cut a fine bow. 'Mademoiselle de Charleville!' he cried, his piping voice cutting through a hundred conversations. He looked up, then bowed lower. 'Altesse! And Mademoiselle du Lac!'

At least he noticed me! thought Madeleine. She wanted to hurl the chivalrous lad bodily across the Montfaucon garden. The marquise stared for a moment at Catherine, then swept a magnificent curtsey. 'Princess Catherine,' she declared, then lowered her voice. 'Your actions did her Majesty great honour, Altesse—'

'A t-trifle, Madame,' stammered Catherine, then picked up her skirts and hastened on. Madeleine ghosted a curtsey and hurried after. Perhaps they could still get through the Montfaucon, and then . . . but tall figures in silver and sable converged ahead of them.

Solange haughtily threw back her cloak, and Madeleine had a moment to wish after all that she'd worn her court gown of deep, rich blue instead of a plain riding-dress like her mistress. Half a dozen Gardes de Maison formed a semicircle before the archway, and with a hiss and flash of steel their swords were drawn. An officer stepped forward, the eldest son of the Comte de Thérouanne. He bowed gravely.

'With regret, Altesse, that is not the way.'

To Madeleine's relief Princess Catherine stopped short. She stood facing the officer of the Gardes de Maison, a pace from him and not a hand's-breadth less tall. 'Then I yield myself prisoner, Monsieur.' Her soft voice carried through the bated silence of the Montfaucon garden.

CHAPTER FOUR

A Royal Progress

Catherine thought in the first moment that the Gardes de Maison would set upon her then and there. They did not. The officer stood ill at ease once she yielded, having never before arrested a Princess of the Blood. His men lowered their swords, and she dared turn from her captors to watch the gathering spectacle. Silence gave way almost at once to a buzz of conversation. The throng in the Montfaucon grew by the minute, taking on a festival air. Catherine thought of crowds gathered for an execution, and wondered how long it would take for jugglers and orange-girls to appear.

To her surprise she felt entirely calm. It all seemed unreal – no, not unreal: detached, though she felt she was acutely aware of everything. Pigeons walked bob-headed among the onlookers' feet, and somewhere an agitated lapdog yipped. She had scarcely gone a hundred paces in her escape, and might have done a hundred things better. Yet she had made the attempt! None could expect three demoiselles to win through against all the powers of the King of Aquitaine. Half the

Court had witnessed steel drawn against her – those who had not seen were hearing of it this very moment. All Christendom would hear of it.

The drawn swords Catherine took as an honour. The most famous arrest before at la Trémouille had been of the Comtesse de Beune, who had poisoned her husband when Catherine was eleven. The guards had dragged her bodily out of the Salle d'Olympie, the comtesse shrieking her innocence all the way. Catherine would show more dignity. She was guilty only of being of her house and country, and would not pretend otherwise.

A well-knit young man wearing a short cloak, sword at hip, worked his way to the front: the Chevalier de Batz-Castelmore. 'Mademoiselle du Lac!' he cried. Two guards started towards him to bar his way; with a quick step Solange interposed herself. One reflexively brought up his blade, then lowered it in the face of her glare. De Batz-Castelmore came forward unimpeded.

Catherine expected Madeleine to throw herself at his feet. Instead she merely curtseyed and held out her hand. De Batz-Castelmore bowed and put it to his lips, then drew close and whispered something in her ear. She shook her head vigorously – then looked at him with a sidelong smile. 'Good fortune eluded you this day, Monsieur!' she said cryptically.

A little later Armand de Fossier appeared as well, in his purple lawyer's gown, and took his place next to Solange. Catherine's heart sank back to the harsh world of reality. Madeleine now had her champion by her side, and Solange her advocate. Catherine begrudged neither of them – yet for her there was no one. Time dragged on. At last a stir in the crowd, people drawing aside to make way, and Catherine gave in to wild hope it might be the Dauphin. Of course it was not. It was M. de Chirac, clad like de Fossier in lawyer's robes, but of richer material, his chain of office around his shoulders. Catherine blinked back tears.

With the Ministre d'État's arrival the crowd drew back. The Gardes de Maison put away their swords, mere steel superfluous in the presence of the second eminence of the realm. De Chirac bowed to her, and indicated a nearby door. 'If you would be so good, Altesse.' Catherine closed her eyes for a moment, then looked out over the now-silent throng. This might be the last the world ever saw of her. Taking a deep breath she curtseyed to the assemblage, then followed de Chirac. She tried frantically to signal her ladies to stay, hoping they could melt away into the crowd. Stubbornly they followed her; the guards allowing them through but not their companions.

They were led through a series of chambers like schoolrooms, with rows of writing desks; Catherine supposed the kingdom's business was done here. At last de Chirac paused at a side door, bade her ladies wait, and ushered Catherine into a small closet with hangings of black velvet, a chair and a writing desk. He turned and regarded her, eyes lacking the warmth she had always seen before. Naturally so, thought Catherine. She was no longer a harmless child, and policy had no room for sentiment.

'You are half a child, Altesse,' he said, 'and twice as much a fool.'

He was doubtless right, but Catherine did not care what the minister of the Aquitaine thought of her. 'Do as you will with me,' she said. 'I ask only that you release my ladies, who are blameless, and restore their places at Court.'

'Blameless?' De Chirac raised an eyebrow. 'They seem very much your confederates, trying to skulk out of the palace with you. That could be construed as treason – but his Majesty does not care to see such pretty heads on pikes. Indeed, he has given express command that they be given new places.'

'He has?' Catherine stared at de Chirac with amazement and relief. He nodded, and she bent her head in a silent prayer of thanksgiving. 'Please convey my gratitude to the Most Christian King,' she said – then realized the obvious. King Charles had a known taste for lovely young demoiselles: of course he would not turn Solange and Madeleine out of Court! This was after all the Court of Aquitaine. It only saddened her to think that, brave as they'd shown themselves to be, they should end up like Margot – or for that matter Corisande.

De Chirac saw her expression, or read her mind. 'You

are displeased, Altesse?' He eyed her coolly. 'They are young, and gallant, and should be permitted their illusions for a time.'

I am permitted no illusions, thought Catherine, though I am younger! 'I hope only that they would not – not become—'

'As Madame my wife was? You are of far higher station, Catherine de Guienne, heiress to a throne. Yet a greater prince than you did not cast the first stone, instead raising his hand against it. I hope your ladies never hear – that *you* never hear – such cruel words as you spoke to Corisande, who loves you as a daughter.'

'She betrayed me!' cried Catherine. 'She played her part well, but the purpose was yours! I was a fool, indeed, and understood nothing, but I see the truth now!'

'Truth, Altesse?' De Chirac frowned. 'Let me then ask Pilate's question: "What is truth?"'

'Once I am taken from the Court, removed from the eyes of the world, then – then—' Catherine struggled against faltering courage, and stifled a sob. 'Will it be said that I took suddenly ill?'

'Altesse!'

'Is that not the way of such things, Monsieur? In Fars, brother strangles brother. My sister Anne, good and gentle soul, would never dream of such, but she shall never know. Because she is good and gentle, you think she will serve your purpose – as I would not – one day to rule over Lyonesse in her name.' With a deep breath

Catherine gave her defiance. 'Do what you will with me, Monsieur – yet by Christ's blood it shall not be so! My people cast the armies of the Emperor Theodosian into the sea. So also the Northmen, and likewise shall they deal with you!'

De Chirac smiled when Catherine was done, a sad little smile. 'Ah!' he said, 'I understand you now. You are quite full of fire! God was so kind as to make you a Catherine, and not an Edmund or Henri; else I would not know what to do about you!'

'Makes that a difference?' asked Catherine bitterly. 'Have you not determined to have done with me all the same, though I am but a demoiselle? Do not trouble yourself to lie, Monsieur; I shall not believe you.'

'Then I will trouble myself to speak the truth,' said de Chirac. 'You can believe me or not as you wish. I do not seek to put Anne in your place, as you fear. You remember the language and manners of your country; your sister does not. Your subjects may therefore the more readily accept you, when the time comes. Yet even were you an Edmund or Henri,' he continued, 'you would not find Lyonesse easily governed. No king enthroned at Kellouique ever has. Arthur defeated the Saxons, but was undone by his own. That you are Catherine will not make it easier! Nevertheless, his Majesty's wish is that you be established on your throne and obeyed by your subjects. What touches one monarch touches all.'

Catherine stared at him, not sure what to believe.

'I will tell you something more,' said de Chirac. 'From the beginning of the world, more kings have fallen to enemies within than without – and not a few of those enemies were of their own making. You can hurt my Corisande and reap only tears, but misuse the lords of Lyonesse and you sow the seeds of rebellion.'

'My dealings with Madame Corisande are none of your concern, Monsieur!'

'I have just shown you that they are,' de Chirac replied. 'Besides, she is my wife. You may someday find the wisdom to beg her forgiveness on your knees, but that is beyond my power to command.'

Catherine turned away. A part of her still wanted to run to Corisande and throw herself in her arms, as she so often had. The time for that was over, if it had ever been.

'As you wish, Altesse,' said de Chirac. 'I have given you what counsel I can. There remains the matter of your ladies-in-waiting. Would you be so good as to summon them in?' Catherine did so. 'Mesdemoiselles de Charleville and du Lac,' he told them, 'your service to Princess Catherine is now at an end. By his Majesty's generosity, places have been granted you in the households of Princesses of the Blood, the King's own cousins. You are to present yourselves, respectively, before the Princess du Pré and the Princess de Marsenne.'

A curious quiet filled the chamber. Solange glanced at Madeleine, who nodded almost imperceptibly, then she stepped forward. 'Monsieur,' she said, 'we have given our word to Princess Catherine, to accompany . . .'

'To accompany her in a mad dash to a barbarous country, I believe.' De Chirac smiled. 'I should warn de Fossier and the Chevalier de Batz-Castelmore to beware gallant women! They shall have to learn for themselves. This matter is now closed. Princess Catherine is to spend her time among the Mariate Sisters in contemplation and reflection – not presiding over a household. Go! Your new mistresses await you! The chamberlain will see that your effects are delivered to your new quarters.'

Instead, Solange knelt before Catherine, and Madeleine knelt beside her. 'Command us, Mademoiselle,' said Solange.

Blinking back a tear, Catherine bade them rise and embraced each in turn. 'I release you,' she told them. 'Serve your new mistresses as you have served me, and love one another. I shall remember that there are in this country good and faithful demoiselles.'

Her former ladies-in-waiting curtseyed and withdrew, and were gone.

Catherine turned back to de Chirac. 'If my conveyance is prepared, Monsieur,' she said, 'I am ready.'

Margot de la Fontenelle swept into the receiving chamber of Henri de Vérain, Baron de Moine. She sensed his coolness the instant his servant announced her, but did not let it trouble her. De Moine was slow to rise, but not on account of his bulk – he could move fast enough, thought Margot, when it suited him. His bow was perfunctory. 'I awaited you yesterday afternoon, Mademoiselle,' he said. 'You did not appear.'

'Indeed?' Margot smiled, and made an even more perfunctory curtsey. The Baron de Moine was both her ally and a distant cousin, from another side branch of the great house of Lusiane, but she wasted no time in pretending he was a friend. 'I had other business to attend to,' she told him.

'Am I permitted to guess what other business, *chère cousine*?' asked de Moine. He smiled faintly. 'Presumably not his Majesty's. His only diversion yesterday was an hour with de Chirac. Monsieur, you will be glad to know, not Madame.'

'Do not play with me!' snapped Margot. She took the unoccupied chair, not waiting for de Moine to offer it. He expected the worst of her – most people did – but if her conduct offended it was for good reason. The line between keeping his Majesty intrigued and making him annoyed was a narrow one and Margot knew she risked pushing the King too far. She had risked it the evening before last; things might have turned out badly. Instead she'd gained an unexpected victory – both the Princess and Corisande herself banished from Court. 'I will save you the trouble of consulting your spies,' she said with a laugh. 'I merely indulged in the small pleasure of watching a certain coach leave the palace.'

'Princess Catherine?'

'Of course!' said Margot. 'I would not have missed it for any treasure.'

'Not even for the title deed to Chastaignerie?'

Margot stiffened. De Moine knew how much she coveted the estate of Chastaignerie – and that the King had not given it to her. She raised her chin slightly. 'I shall have it in time, Monsieur. With your help or without.'

'Perhaps.' De Moine frowned. 'I truly hope so, my dear. But let us return to the Princess Catherine. You never miss the chance to insult her in one small way or another. Why do you care?'

'I detest her!' snapped Margot. 'Not for herself, of course – she is without consequence.'

'She is of the senior branch of the House of Lusiane,' said de Moine. 'And heiress to a kingdom.'

'What is that to me?' What, indeed, thought Margot, were kingdoms and provinces? They were pieces on the chessboard in the great game for men. The only pieces women could play were men themselves – and on that board, Margot's piece was the King. 'The girl is la Chirac's tool,' she said. 'And that woman uses her to seek revenge upon me – and power for herself! Is that not reason enough to detest her?' The worst of it was that the King had entrusted his former mistress with informal guardianship over a royal heiress and Lusiane relation. He had never granted comparable authority to Margot herself – not yet.

'Surely,' said de Moine slyly, 'you do not think a Princess of the Blood is a rival for your place? A royal heiress is far too valuable in the marriage market for the King to indulge in dalliance with her.'

'Dalliance? With Princess Catherine?' Margot laughed again – though the joke had lost its savour. That horrid girl had ruled every male eye in the Salle d'Olympie – including his Majesty's – and Catherine had known it too, or she would never have been so bold. Fortunately she had been too bold by half.

'I must tell you, *chère cousine*,' said de Moine, 'that you risk going too far. It was unseemly, humiliating the Queen as you did! Were you not thinking at all?'

'That part was an accident!' cried Margot. 'How was I to know the miserable woman would make a scene, then bleed from the nose and flee the hall? Yet you saw the result!' The entire episode had been a pure stroke of fortune – but there was no need for de Moine to know that. 'La Chirac has lost her darling pet: indeed, I heard that they have quarrelled, and parted on bad terms. What is more, her husband incurred his Majesty's displeasure. Which ought to please *you*, and indeed our cousin the Duc de Septimanie himself.'

Margot knew perfectly well that her powerful relatives had not pushed her forward to catch the King's eye for her own sake. The duke, and his even more formidable mother, wanted influence over the King – and looked for Margot to provide it. She would duly look out for the Lusiane family interests, but first of all for her own. 'I'm sure you know,' she told de Moine, 'that de Chirac had to send his wife away from Court too. So what is your point? I did not come here to endure a lecture!'

'You came for useful advice and instruction,' said de Moine, 'which you are now receiving. Believe me, Mademoiselle, I have your own interests at heart! You have gained much, but it has come too easily, when you are too young. You may have won the place you hold using the neck down, but it can be held only from the neck up. Does the name Diane de Trièxe mean anything to you? I know she was somewhat before your time.'

'Of course I know of her!' Margot did not like the direction of this conversation.

'Consider her fate, Mademoiselle. She won the King's favour because she was beautiful. But she was not clever. And so it happened that after five short years, his Majesty's ears heard a pleasing song, and his eyes beheld a beautiful singer.'

Margot stiffened. The singer had been a young girl of obscure origin, named Corisande.

'The King sent Diane back to her cuckolded husband,' said de Moine, 'who for spite left her nothing when he died. She is still alive, you know. At least she was a couple of years ago . . . living in a garret, eating peasant's bread and broth, clad in the remnants of her old finery.'

'I shall do better than that!' cried Margot.

'You had best!' declared de Moine. 'The Court of la Trémouille does not lack for pretty women, more than two or three of whom would be happy to take your place. The Princess Lyonne is of course not among them – so there was no need, on her account, to cause a scene before his Majesty!'

'It was not on her account, *cher* Henri,' Margot declared firmly. 'I do not expect his Majesty to summon a Princess of the Blood to his bed! Even if she was decked out to look half pretty.' Margot arranged her golden curls carefully over her bare shoulders, her bells tinkling by her ears. 'If you indulged the pleasures of women, Monsieur, instead of only those of the table and the blade, you would understand these things. As you do not, I shall instruct *you*. Of course I have rivals! Why do you think that woman dangled Princess Catherine before his Majesty? The *princesse* was merely bait, to draw him to the hook. To two hooks – those charming demoiselles of hers!'

'Ah,' said de Moine, eyes brightening. 'Mesdemoiselles du Lac and de Charleville!'

Margot nodded. At first she'd paid them no mind, the blonde who was then as flat as a board, the dark one child-plump. Yet every presentable woman was a potential rival, and in the course of three years they had grown to be entirely too presentable. Such girls were dangerous – especially in the hands of Corisande. 'You begin to understand, Monsieur? That woman has been set back! With the Princess dismissed from Court, her ladies too have lost their places. The Chevalier du Lac serves in the royal stables, so regrettably his daughter will not vanish entirely.' Margot shrugged. 'She loves to ride, I believe. Let her confine herself to horses, with no thought of mounting his Majesty! As for la Charleville?' Margot flicked an imaginary speck from her wrist. 'Back she goes, to the provincial dungheap she came from!'

De Moine smiled, showing too many teeth. 'My dear Margot,' he said, 'you are behind the news. My man Vernay informs me that both have been granted new places – with the Princesses de Marsenne and du Pré.'

'What?' cried Margot. 'Impossible!'

De Moine shrugged. 'Fact.'

Margot clenched her fists and shook her head, wishing her bells would drive away de Moine's words. How could his Majesty do this to her? He was playing with her, and she did not like the game. But it was indeed a game, and Margot could play it as well. She would have to think of a suitable move. Had Corisande and Princess Catherine truly quarrelled? If it were true – and de Moine had not denied it – it offered interesting possibilities. Perhaps the Princess could be drawn back to favour the Lusiane family, something her cousin the duke and his mother would greatly appreciate? Still, for now she was dismissed from Court, so there was little point in even thinking of it. Margot concentrated on more immediate gains. 'At the least,' she said finally, more to herself than de Moine, 'those demoiselles are no longer in that woman's company. I shall remain on my guard against them. If they dare to challenge me, they will regret it!'

'Do not look for quarrels, my dear Margot,' said de Moine. 'They are unprofitable. If you carelessly seek out duels, sooner or later you will meet a swifter blade.'

Margot raised her eyebrows. 'You have sought your share of duels, Monsieur! And though you think my quarrels are a mere woman's trifles, where would your favour be with his Majesty, *cher cousin* – indeed, where would the Duc de Septimanie's favour be – if it were not I whom his Majesty summons to his bedchamber?'

It was Catherine's third week in the convent of Ste-Lucie-en-Avers. It might as well have been her third month – or year. No doubt other gaols were far worse. The garden was even pleasant, with the warmth of the sun and mingled smells of herbs. Yet already the days stretched into an endless sameness: a cycle of prayer and labour. Catherine prayed, for the deliverance of herself and her country. She laboured, because there was nothing else to do. She had begun to scratch a tally of days on the wall behind her cot in the novices' dortoir, as was said to be the custom among prisoners.

Her task for now was to scrub the floor of the hall where guests of rank were received. The novice nuns assigned along with her were working their way up from the lower end of the hall – was that some instinct of humility in novices? – but Catherine thought it better service to begin at the head of the hall, applying freshest strength to the place of highest dignity.

Sunlight from the high windows crept slowly across the floor. Kingdoms might rise up, send forth armies to conquer, build mighty castles and splendid palaces, then sink into ruin, in the great gulf of time before the bell would summon them to the chapel for the hour of Sext.

Annoyingly, Catherine found herself missing her ladies. Where were they now? What were they doing, and did they have the least regret at being removed from her service? Probably not, Catherine suspected, the more so since they no longer had to deal with one another. They had not always been in perfect charity. No one at Court would miss her. Certainly not the Dauphin! He had surely kissed a hundred maids at one time or another, and had only kissed her from kindness, because no other would – except for her rank, and her duty to her country, a convent was where she surely belonged. Sighing, Catherine bent back to her work.

A fine summer day, and his subjects lined the royal highway as the King of Aquitaine passed in progress, bound for the liberated city of Richebourg. For merchants and carters, it might be inconvenience, for labourers a holiday, but for all it was a magnificent parade: drums and trumpets, caparisoned horses and splendid coaches, liveried servants and great wagons. It stretched for two leagues along the highway, and took more than as many hours to pass. At the head of all – behind only the silver- and sable-cloaked vanguard of Gardes de Maison – rode the King himself. Simple country people might find the woman riding next to him surprisingly young to be his queen, and surprisingly bold in display, but the more informed knew exactly who Margot de la Fontenelle was, and watched her go by with envy, amusement, or dismay. Few if any noticed, or cared, that the procession was short a foreign royal heiress.

Young men did take note of a demoiselle who rode past at a canter, clad in a blue deeper than the sky, stray golden locks whipping free of her headdress. Madeleine du Lac ignored their glances of admiration: she no more thought of herself as beautiful than a hawk on the wing thinks of air. Her mind was on the household to which she was now assigned, that of Christine de Marsenne, Princess of the Blood – a wretchedly ill-managed household.

She threaded past a gaggle of demoiselles, paying them no heed in her preoccupation. Then one caught her eye: a striking figure in black velvet and crimson, elegant and soignée. Madeleine reined in, pleased in spite of herself to see her former companion. 'Mademoiselle de Charleville!' she cried.

'Mademoiselle du Lac!' With a toss of her head, Solange gestured for Madeleine to join her, and introduced the slightly younger girl riding at her side as Allyriane de Marac. 'How do you fare?' she asked. 'I thought you'd long since fallen behind, with your mistress's household.'

'Then you know how I fare!' answered Madeleine. 'Why do you find me riding up the side of the road, frightening peasants' wives out of their wits?' She shook her head in disgust. The Princess de Marsenne's household had not been assembled, nor its baggage stowed, when trumpet and gun signalled the day's journey. 'I stayed behind with her baggage wagons to keep it all from disappearing. Fine thanks I'll get!' she added. She cursed under her breath. Solange looked more closely at her, and put a hand to Madeleine's left cheek. Madeleine slapped it roughly away. 'I took a fall,' she snapped. 'If you know what's best you'll hold your tongue!'

Solange looked away. 'I said nothing, Mademoiselle du Lac.' Madeleine could have sworn the girl sounded hurt. 'I was merely going to offer service of my things,' she said. 'Some blush on the other cheek, perhaps, so it would show less. But as you have no need of such, I'll waste no more of your time.'

Madeleine took a deep breath. 'Forgive me,

Mademoiselle de Charleville,' she said. 'I did not fall.'
She lowered her voice. 'Madame de Verre – the
Princess's Mistress of the Wardrobe – beat me this morning.' She flushed at the disgrace of having been struck
by so miserable a creature. 'For impertinence. She may
beat me again, for taking too long about seeing that
the Princess de Marsenne is not robbed of everything
she owns.'

Solange said something in a low voice to Allyriane,
then nudged her mount towards the side of the road
and she and Madeleine rode a few yards out from the
Princess du Pré's retinue. 'Tell me what happened,'
Solange asked softly.

'I told the Princess de Marsenne that her servants
are stealing from her!' Madeleine shrugged. 'All
servants are thieves; it is the nature of their station,
surely as monks grow fat. But by God's mercy, let them
attend to their duties first and steal afterwards, and in
decent moderation. Mademoiselle would never put up
with it!'

'The world is filled,' said Solange, 'with things
Princess Catherine would not put up with. Ride a while
with Allyriane and me – but not if your mistress will have
you beaten.'

Madeleine tossed her hair. '*Merde!*' she cried. 'La
Marsenne commands nothing! Madame de Verre rules
her household. Everyone is in terror of her, including
the Princess. She beats us all. For good reasons, bad

reasons, no reason. The servants detest la Verre, and steal twice as much to be avenged.' She laughed. 'If you wish some velvet, tell me and I shall get it for you.' Where theft was the rule, Madeleine disapproved, but it would not stop her claiming her share.

They rode together along the highway's side, skirting hedgerows between long fields of golden grain, and spoke of a hundred things – or rather, Solange did.

Of the weather, which was agreeable.

Of how his Majesty let Margot ride beside him – on progress, in full view of his subjects – which was not.

'Madame Corisande would never have asked such a thing,' said Madeleine.

'Why,' answered Solange, 'do you think Corisande held him for seventeen years? Margot will not last half so long! *Fervor libidinis morit; calor amicitiae vivat*, as Cellius wrote in *De Amore.* The heat of passion fades; the warmth of friendship endures.'

'His Majesty threw over Corisande in the end,' said Madeleine.

'Because he is a man, and therefore a fool about women,' retorted Solange. 'Madeleine, you are so simple!'

'Beware,' cried Madeleine, 'lest I pass on my beatings!' She found herself laughing. 'Yet annoying as you are, Solange de Charleville – I have missed you.'

'Then the household of the Princess de Marsenne must be dreary indeed,' answered Solange. She lowered her voice. 'How unfortunate! The Princess du Pré greatly favours demoiselles with fair hair.'

Madeleine stared at her. She'd heard the stories about la Pré, but never believed them, thought them mere scandal. 'Do you mean—'

'Service in her household is . . . instructive. Tell no one, or I shall poison you!' Solange reached under the fall of her headdress, drew forth a lock of her deep brown hair and twisted it around her finger. 'I am safe enough, dear Madeleine, but you would not be.' She smiled wickedly. 'Yet one never knows. Shall I not present you? You might win high favour!'

'Favour, indeed!' Madeleine snatched the lock of Solange's hair and yanked it, drawing a yelp. Then she glanced past Solange at the younger girl she'd been riding with – honey blonde, comely of features, innocent in manner. She looked sidelong back at Solange. 'You need say nothing, but – what is her name? Allyriane? Is she . . . ?'

'She has not yet been tried. I am teaching her to defend her virtue, if she wishes.'

Madeleine contemplated Solange teaching anyone to protect her virtue, even from a Princess of the Blood. Trumpet blasts rang out ahead, signalling the midday halt. '*Hélas!*' she cried. 'Now I shall be beaten for sure!'

'You will forgive me?' asked Solange, without a hint of sarcasm.

'The beatings are nothing,' said Madeleine. 'Yet see

what I am reduced to? I not only miss you, I miss Mademoiselle! Why did you not keep her from making a spectacle of herself?'

'What was I supposed to do?'

'If you were not preoccupied with being the most brilliant demoiselle in Christendom, you might have thought of something!' Madeleine sighed. 'I wonder how she fares with the Mariate Sisters?'

Solange smiled faintly. 'Wonder rather how they fare with her!' She leaned to embrace Madeleine, and they kissed one another's cheeks. Then Madeleine spurred forward, on up towards her place with the Princess de Marsenne.

CHAPTER FIVE

A Gentleman of the Corso

Sicania, in the Middle Sea, at harbourside
The bagno master showed off his wares with pride.
'Look at them, Signor Capitano,' he exclaimed. 'Not a
thin arm or weak back in the lot!'

William de Havilland watched, not impressed, as the
men were marched past – if march was the word for
the trudge of galley slaves being shown off to a
prospective buyer. He pointed at one with his sword. 'He
won't live a week at sea. Waste your own time if you wish;
don't be wasting mine.' It was a hot, sultry day; the sun
blazed down from a blue white sky. The high-walled
enclosure of the bagno was twice as hot as the waterfront
outside, a place of blazing, shimmering heat and ink-
black shadows. William fingered his pomander. In his
homeland, perfume on a man was a mark of the un-
natural vice; it was necessity for a gentleman in galley
service in the Middle Sea. The Sicanian word *bagno*
literally meant *bath*. It was used sometimes for whore-
houses, sometimes for the prisons where galley slaves
were kept ashore, but here the only whore was the

bagno master, and there was no bathing by anyone.

William indicated a man, a fair-haired Northerner with rage in his eyes. 'I'll take that one.' He picked out a handful of others as they shuffled past: another Northerner or two, a couple of blackamoors, several olive-skinned men native to the Middle Sea, and one man with a wide flat nose and oddly canted eyes who hailed from Wott knew where. He ended up with thirteen prospects, of whom he might actually put ten on the *Golden Lion*'s benches.

'Only those?' asked the bagno master when William was done. 'Surely, Signor—'

'Those, and no others.' William detested the institution of galley slaves as contrary to all reason. No wonder Christian galleys got the worst of it in most encounters with the Monites. William needed men who would row with a will, and rise from their benches to fight when it came to push of pike. He dug in the purse at his belt for the required coins. 'Now,' he told the bagno master. 'Get your scrivener out here, and make out their papers of manumission.'

'Manumission?' The man looked genuinely shocked. 'But Signor – what do you mean?'

'I mean I want 'em freed up!' William lapsed into Saxon as he did when annoyed. He repeated it in blunt, quayside Sicanian, and the bagno master grasped his meaning.

Five minutes later William was standing on the open

waterfront of Palantini outside the fortified gate of the bagno, accompanied by his baker's dozen of newly freed, bewildered former galley slaves. He addressed them in *lingua franca*, the rough seafarers' patois of the Middle Sea. 'You are all now free men.' He reached in his purse again, fished out a handful of dineri, and tossed one to each man: the price of a meal and cup at any waterfront tavern. 'As free men you may go where you list. Or you can sign on with me. I offer you fifteen dineri as bounty: you'll pull your oar, you'll fight – and you'll have the same share of prizes and same right to whore on the beach as any other of my crew.'

The ex-slaves glanced uneasily at him and at one another, muttering among themselves, wondering whether he was madman or trickster. '*Ostrogoto lunatico!*' said one, and William grinned – Lyonessans and other Northerners were often called Ostrogoths here, testimony to a memory undimmed by centuries. With his height, broad shoulders, long blond hair and blue eyes, William was especially often so addressed – not least by one with whom he had a pleasing appointment once done with his business here.

'Enquire after the *Leone d'Oro*,' he told them 'She's tied up just this side of the Arsenal. Red and gold, you can't miss her. Finest *galea di corsari* in the Middle Sea; if you don't believe me, ask anyone. My purser will swear you to the ship's articles and pay you your bounty.'

William turned and walked away, leaving the men

to decide for themselves. From experience, he would get all but two or three. He started up the steep alleys and stairs that wound their way back from the harbour front, making his way towards the Palazzo di Peretti high on the hill. The palazzo lay scarcely two furlongs back from the harbour, a fourth part of a mile, but also a good furlong up – a hot, sweltering climb. The master of the palazzo was one Giovanni di Peretti, an old and fabulously wealthy merchant and sometime paymaster of William's, currently off in the east, trading for carpets and silks. William went round to a servants' entrance. There was no point in standing on pride – his business was not with the camerlengo who handled Giovanni's affairs of commerce, but rather with his beautiful and much neglected young wife Teofania, she of the light brown hair and laughing eyes.

By the time Donna Teofania led William back to the doors of the palazzo the sun was far towards the west, the air was merely warm, and she was feeling very much less neglected. 'You must come back safely, *mi caro Ostrogoto*,' she whispered after their lips parted. 'Every day you are gone I shall go to my chapel, morning, noon and night, and have a Mass said for your safe return.'

William gently eased her arms from around his neck. Stepping back, he knelt and kissed her hand. 'Till I return, Tiffany my fairest!' he said in his own tongue.

He headed down the hill in fine fettle, ready to face

a thousand Monites with sword in hand and Mistress Tiffany's prayers at his back. The alleys were now crowded with people: broad-beamed housewives, shyly smiling maids, and hurtling boys. Smells of cooking filled the air; William discovered that he was ravenously hungry, and found himself daydreaming of a roast of beef on a trencher and a pot of dark, then cursed himself for thinking of them. It only made his hunger pangs the stronger. Worse, the thought of an honest meal grew into the homesickness he usually ignored: cool breezes instead of infernal hot calms; green fields; honest Halverstrand burghers and sturdy ploughmen; the graceful lilting hymns and simple, broadminded piety of the Pelagian Church in place of turgid theological debates and screeching marketplace friars. He couldn't have it, not till his father – Black Jack de Havilland, Lord High Admiral of Lyonesse – was dead. He'd sworn an oath, a fool boy's oath, not to return home while the old devil lived. He was, William thought wryly, like a man who lies abed with a beautiful and accomplished mistress, fantasizing of his wife.

He might never go home at all. All the round world lay at the feet of a man who knew his geometry and could handle a bark. And William had an image: an island under strange stars in the southern sea, with maids black as opals and graceful as willows. He would marry the most gallant and of best wit, fit to bear strong sons and govern as regent when he sailed to the wars.

His forebears had once been Lords of the Isles, his descendants might rule islands yet unknown.

He emerged between rows of houses at the top of a stair above the waterfront – and was jolted from his reverie. A little knot of gentlemen stood on the quay directly under the *Golden Lion*'s short poop deck. They could only mean trouble. In this faithless age, rich in treasures but poor in honour, a gentleman of the *corso* was ever at the mercy of fat, greedy merchants and niggling lawyers. William's conscience was clear. He never took a Christian ship but that he released her on payment of the customary two hundred ducats for the Service of the Cross. If a merchant wished not to pay for honourable protection from the Monites, then let him sail like ships of the Halverstrand Company, with guns charged and boarding pikes at hand. He hastened on.

No guard was posted about his galley. None was needed: without leave from the Podestá, the *Golden Lion* would go nowhere. Palantini harbour was all too snug and secure – half a cable's length separated Castel Santa Chiara above sea cliffs on the north side of the channel, from the Torre de Teoderico on its mole to the south. The Podestá – a man after William's own heart – had armed Santa Chiara with a battery of modern bronze muzzle loaders, and half a dozen cannons royal now commanded the channel, great stubby smashers each hurling a sixty-pound shot.

The chief of the group was dressed in rich sobriety, in

Ravennate fashion – then William was close enough to recognize him. 'Signor Marco Falier!' He bowed. He had embarked as a gentleman-volunteer aboard Falier's galley seven years ago.

Falier bowed in reply. 'Guglielmo de Havilland!' They embraced; as they stepped back, Falier glanced up at the *Golden Lion*'s stern, which was topped by a splendid crystal lantern. 'I see you have prospered!' he said wryly. The Most Serene Republic of Ravenna had no great love for gentlemen of the *corso*.

'I am not poor,' admitted William, 'but the lantern is a gift from a lady. Now I lack only a squadron to follow it. But what brings you to Palantini? Business with the Podestá?'

'Business with you, in fact,' said Falier. 'Not for the waterfront to know. Signor Giustinian – I believe you know the man, Ravenna's ambassador – has offered the use of his house, if you've an hour to spare.'

William nodded. Giustinian's establishment lay a mere hundred paces along the waterfront. The ambassador was not at home; his camerlengo ushered them to a withdrawing room, and wine was brought. For a few minutes William and Falier conversed lightly, then Falier refilled their goblets and began to talk more seriously. 'Lightening merchantmen of two hundred ducats for the Cross is one thing,' he said, 'but I'm told you took a galley of al-Fustat, and sank outright one of Fars. How did that come about?'

'I came aboard her at full stroke,' William explained, demonstrating the encounter with his hands. 'My spur broke up her deck and split her open. If her survivors spoke truth, then ten thousand ducats await some lucky pearl diver.' He shrugged. 'Such is fate.'

'You're no richer,' said Falier, 'but the next Grand Sophy of Fars is the poorer – once his remaining brothers have met their bowstrings and we know who he will be! There is talk of a new Holy League.'

William nodded. Civil war raged in Fars: an opportunity for Christendom, if only it could unite. Ravenna might offer him a captaincy – an offer he would consider. 'Will anything come of it?'

Falier shook his head. 'Talk is cheap, but arms no galleys. I came to speak to you of your homeland.'

The state of his homeland was not a pleasing subject. 'I've never been back,' William said. 'Remember that fool's oath I swore?' Falier nodded. 'So if you want news of Lyonesse, you came to Palantini in vain.' He raised his goblet. 'This wine is excellent; Signor Giustinian is to be complimented. Do you know the three worst fates of a kingdom?'

'No. What are they?'

'The succession of a woman, a child or a foreigner.'

Falier contemplated William over his goblet. 'And Lyonesse faces all three.'

'It faces none of them,' said William. 'Merely a

usurpation – never the best fate, but by no means the worst, depending on the usurper.'

Falier raised an eyebrow. 'Do you plan to offer yourself?' he asked. 'You are of ancient house in your country, and you know how to fight.'

'A girl is to be robbed of her rightful crown, Signor,' William said. 'In the nature of the world, I understand that – perhaps even approve – but I'll not be the robber. The Republic may see little difference between that trade and my present one, but I do.'

'She may be a woman,' said Falier, 'and scarcely more than a child. But Principessa Caterina – your country's heiress – does not seem to wish to be a foreigner. I hear she marked her disapproval of the King of Aquitaine's latest triumph in taking Richborough.' Falier outlined events at the Court of Aquitaine, as reported by Ravenna's excellent intelligence network. 'King Carlo was vexed, and threw her out of his Court. She has now been lodged in a convent.'

'Damned fool maid!' William repeated it in Enotrian for Falier's benefit.

'I thought you liked gallant ladies. You got behind your sword a few times on their account, as I recall.'

William laughed, though the matter was nothing mirthful. 'So I do, and so I have. But there is gallant, and there is leaping from a tower in hope some champion will catch her. She'll only dash her witless brains across the pavement.'

'You are harsh with her,' said Falier.

'Fortune is harsh with her,' replied William. 'Donna Fortuna loves no fools. And being a woman herself she is not lenient towards her mortal sisters.'

The Ravennate senator studied him for a time. 'I confess to being puzzled. You say your princess is to be robbed, and you'll not be the robber – even to win a kingdom. Yet you approve the robbery, and think her a fool to defend her own cause. Your father was right, Guglielmo. You should never have gone to that university in Torcello – learning is contrary to your nature.'

'What has learning to do with it?' asked William, not pleased to have his father brought into this. 'The Duchessa di Longhi was how old? Thirteen? Younger than our princess now is. Her loving uncle took her state from her, and quieted her maidenly protests with a stiletto. The world teaches policy, Signor Marco.'

'So it does,' admitted Falier.

'And so it will,' said William. 'The King of Aquitaine has the Princess, and will do with her as he wishes – it would take thirty thousand men to free her. I have two hundred, leaving me twenty-nine thousand and eight hundred short! A good general of land troops would be needed too. Therefore there will be a usurpation, for better a maiden robbed than our kingdom made a province of Aquitaine!'

'Yet the Senate has taken an interest in your Caterina's case,' Falier said. 'That too might be policy.

We in Ravenna do not wish to see the King of Aquitaine established on both sides of the Narrow Sea.'

The government of the Most Serene Republic of Ravenna, thought William, might not take daggers to young maids, but it was not known for vain sentiment. 'Tell me more.'

'You were a student of Giuseppe Salviani, as I recall, before your – ah – disagreement with the University? So you know that when he is not giving churchmen apoplexy he places his learning at the service of the Republic. He finds the Principessa Caterina's stars to be propitious. You speak of a usurpation,' Falier continued. 'Yet what if the usurper falls short, and there is civil war? That could give Charles of Aquitaine a better foothold than an heiress – especially one who has already shown herself unwilling to be his tool.'

William thought about it. The Princess Lyon was a maid of fourteen or so – he'd been a boy of nine when she was born, two years before his first voyage to the Middle Sea. So lusty was her birth-cry that those outside the birthing chamber took it for a boy's, and bonfires had carried the word the length and breadth of Lyonesse that Prince Harry had a son. There had been much rueful holding of ale-swollen heads – William's father's among them – when the truth was learned. A brother had followed, only to die before his fourth birth-day. Then her father Prince Harry had died, and thus was Lyonesse in wretched case.

The cause might be hopeless for the Princess Lyon, but William could not begrudge her right to fight for it. 'What part is there for me in this?' he asked. 'On my father's death, by the usage of Lyonesse I shall be Lord High Admiral, but he is not yet dead, and he'll not go easily! I could bar the sea to prevent the crossing of the Aquitaine's armies, yet what would make Charles of Aquitaine release our Princess Katrin?'

'We do not know,' said Falier. 'Yet if Donna Fortuna loves no fools, as you say, she gives her favour to the prepared. You have family connections in the Free Estates, I believe?'

William nodded. His mother had been born Petronilla van den Kempen, daughter of one of the greatest merchant princes of the Free Estates, the prosperous Theudish lowlands that stretched northeast of the Aquitaine.

'So, it seems, shall I – at least for a time,' said Marco Falier. 'My father has been appointed as next ambassador to the Court of Aquitaine, an honour he was unable to escape. Before taking up his post he is to make a year's tour of inspection of shipping and shipyards in the Estates. He shall depart with the next convoy of merchant galleys, and the convoy will first call at Rosemouth in Lyonesse along the way. I do not ask you to permanently enter the service of Ravenna, much as I would like to! Yet perhaps the Republic can enlist you as an ally should you be willing to voyage to Rosemouth, to step ashore in your homeland at least. I have proposed you for my father's retinue: a pair of eyes and ears that know something of Lyonesse – and a good deal of war at sea.'

'Do you have flint?' asked Solange. She and Madeleine met daily when they could. The royal progress rode now down a narrow valley, three days from Richebourg. 'Of course you have flint; you have everything useful. I wish to burn a letter.' She held up the offending missive.

'Burn a letter?' Madeleine looked at her quizzically. 'From whom, and why?'

'From Monsieur Armand de Fossier,' said Solange, 'because he tries my patience!'

'How did he get a letter to you, on the road as we are?' asked Madeleine. 'You should be pleased!'

'Well, I'm not! Armand is in the service of Monsieur de Chirac, so he has the use of the royal post,' Solange explained. 'He sent me this bracelet too!' She held out her arm for Madeleine to examine. The gold bracelet was more than de Fossier could afford – Solange knew that perfectly well – but a great lady could not be placated by trinkets.

'That's lovely!' exclaimed Madeleine. 'Monsieur de Fossier sent you that by his Majesty's post, and you're out of sorts with him? Whatever for?' Abruptly she snatched the letter out of Solange's hand and urged her mount forward out of reach.

'Give that back!' demanded Solange.

Madeleine rode fifty paces down the road at a canter. She held the letter up to read, lowering it almost at once. When Solange caught up she handed it back with a toss of her head. 'This is unjust! My one chance to read your secrets, and they are in Latin!'

'Had you heeded your studies,' Solange observed, 'you could read it. I may as well tell you anyway. *Hélas!* Monsieur de Fossier strays. Not only strays, but has the cheek to tell me! See how honour is dead in the world? *O tempora, o mores!*'

'Is that such a bad thing?' asked Madeleine. 'That he told you, I mean! He is begging you to rescue him, no?'

Solange had considered that, but was annoyed anyway. 'Listen to how he excuses himself,' she said. 'I shall render it in Gallic: "My heart belongs only and utterly to you." Mere flattery. What use is his heart without the rest? It gets worse.' She translated another line. '"Madame de Grinaud importunes me." The hussy! "I confess I smile at her, and wish she were you." Well! *That* covers every sin! Next he shall surely lie in her arms, and of course wish they were mine.'

'La Grinaud?' Madeleine raised an eyebrow. 'This I did not know!'

'Tell no one!' ordered Solange. She had not dared tell Allyriane. Everyone in the progress would know inside the hour.

'Who would I possibly tell but you?' retorted Madeleine. 'Did you know that Madame de Grinaud is putting horns on her husband with—'

'You are not amusing me, Madeleine!' Estelle de Grinaud was ten years older than Solange, with two children, a husband who paid her no attention, and a spectacular figure. A pretty head too – quite empty, but Armand was not entertaining his mind. 'How can I defend my rights when we are dragged off to Richebourg? The goddams could have kept it, for the good it has done anyone. We would still be serving Princess Catherine too.' Solange shook her head in disgust. 'Perhaps I shall join her anyway. As all men are faithless, I shall renounce them entirely!'

'When?'

'Hold your tongue, Madeleine. What point asking you to commiserate, when you know nothing of rivals?' With annoyance, Solange thought how this was not simply that Madeleine had not as yet entered into any truly serious affaires, but that she was so beautiful, even just standing still. In motion – just walking, let alone dancing – she was impossibly graceful as well, so Madeleine could not imagine a serious rival if she should set her heart upon a man. 'Now,' said Solange, 'when we get back to Aix-le-Siège I must campaign to win Armand back from her.'

Madeleine shrugged, then gave her slight smile. 'Why

waste time? Take steel to her. Stretch her out and be done with it!'

'You're no help at all!' cried Solange. 'My head may not be so pretty as yours, Mademoiselle de Perfection, but it goes very well with my shoulders, thank you very much!'

'Who spoke of murder?' said Madeleine innocently. 'Call upon her. Demand that she leave her hands off Monsieur de Fossier, else agree to a place and hour. It can all be done properly. I shall be your second, and teach you what you must know.'

'What *are* you talking about?'

Madeleine reached down to a long, narrow pouch strapped to her saddle and threw back the flap, revealing the hilt of a sword. She drew it up, showing a foot of gleaming steel. Solange stared at it. 'My father taught me the rudiments,' Madeleine said. 'The dancing-master has given me lessons as well.' She slid back the blade. 'It's just a sort of dance, after all! He found it amusing, I'm sure.'

Solange was not sure if amusing was the word; no doubt the dancing-master had enjoyed the instruction. 'This is absurd!' she cried. 'Who ever heard of a demoiselle fighting a duel?'

'Who had ever heard of a demoiselle wearing bells in her hair?' said Madeleine. 'If Margot can start a bad new fashion, we can start a useful one. There would be much more honour among ladies if they knew they might be called to account!'

Solange was doubtful. 'Has it made the men more honourable?' she asked, then added, 'Duelling is against the law anyway.'

'So?' asked Madeleine. 'When have the edicts ever been enforced? Besides – once the example is set, I shall be able to slap Margot in front of the entire Court. She will have no choice but to ask satisfaction, and then we shall all be rid of her!'

Solange sighed. She would have to nip this particular folly in the bud. Otherwise one day she might call Madeleine simple, Madeleine would demand satisfaction, and that would be the end of Solange de Charleville!

The high chamber of Richebourg castle was still adorned with the arms and badges of the House of Guienne and the great lords of Lyonesse. The ancient duchies of Ashland, Dunfolk, Prydeland and Tearnac held pride of place; then, marching around the walls, such arms as Avalon, Clarendon, Norrey, Stanbury. Behind the King's seat the morning sun fell bright on a tapestry; here Edmund *le Conquérant* conquered still, his archers' arrows raining down as they had upon the terrible field of Châtelhardie, nearly two centuries past. The Dauphin had ordered all left as it was, a reminder to future governors of the fortress. Antoine de Chirac approved his decision – but for this particular conference it was unfortunate.

The formal meeting of the royal council wound down through minor items and drew to an end. The councillors rose, bowed and withdrew: all save Antoine, whom the King gestured to remain. The rest departed stone-faced, scarcely daring to meet the royal eye, let alone show any expression. They knew what agenda item remained, not to be dealt with by the full council. The whole subject was an embarrassment. Some surely found it amusing – they above all dared not let their amusement show. Antoine would be one of them, had the episode not involved his wife.

When all the other councillors had withdrawn, King Charles held up a letter. 'His Holiness the Gallican Patriarch,' said the King, 'conveys his great regret and sorrow. The Mariate Sisters, it seems, can no longer retain custody of Catherine de Guienne.'

Antoine knew exactly the contents of the letter: he had forwarded it to the King. 'It appears,' he said, 'that the good sisters found the demoiselle unmanageable.'

'Everyone has found her unmanageable,' said the King with half a smile. 'Even Madame de Chirac, no?'

Antoine inclined his head. 'Indeed so, Sire.' He was reminded of it daily. His doublet was imperfectly adjusted, his servants being chosen more for loyalty and discretion than sartorial skill. The state of his attire was trivial – but a reminder of what he did not have this past two months: his wife to warm his bed, tend to him more carefully than any other and provide him with the soundest of advice. Corisande had departed the Court in tears, not only for her temporary exile to Clermont-sur-Brassy, but also for her Trinette.

As for her Trinette, at this moment Antoine did not particularly like the girl. It was liberating, in a sad way, since his duty to his Majesty and l'Aquitaine was to treat the Princess Lyonne simply as an instrument of policy, a jewelled casket holding the crown of Lyonesse. Corisande's tears had made that duty easier.

'You may inform the Patriarch,' said King Charles, that the Gallican Church shall be relieved of its burden. But what then are we to do with her?' he asked. 'Send her back to her own country and be done with her?'

The temptation was strong, thought Antoine. 'Regrettably, Sire,' he said, 'it is not practical. You cannot toss her aside and pretend to have misplaced her. What if you send her back and she calls on you for aid? Or the Duke of Norrey does, in her name? If we do not answer the call, we look weak. If we do, we are marching into the great bog of Lyonesse.'

The King shifted in his seat. 'It will end with that any-way, won't it, de Chirac? What use is this girl? Sooner or later her grandfather will die, and their law says she inherits. So what then? I have to find her a husband, find him an army and still end up in the bog, as you say.' He eyed Antoine. 'Your wife can paint that rose into a sight to behold,' he said, 'but all I see is a million in gold I'll end up paying to be rid of her. And soldiers' widows, de Chirac, soldiers' widows. My gold and God's souls. The girl could at least show some gratitude!'

'Indeed, Sire.' said Antoine. The less said the better.

The King was animated, which meant he was annoyed. 'Her uncle the Duc de Septimanie,' he said, 'has most graciously offered to take charge of her. The Lusianes do have a certain claim to her, you must admit.'

When the Lusianes had exercised their claim on Catherine's mother, thought Antoine, they'd so hounded the lady that she had withdrawn into a convent, there to die. Antoine did not dislike the girl *that* much. And there were matters of policy as well to consider. 'The Duc de Septimanie,' he said, 'is head of a large family, and far too conscious of his royal blood.'

'Eh?' said the King. 'So he is. But thus far he has done nothing to merit losing his head, even if I am sometimes tempted.'

'He lacks the imagination to devise great treasons,' said Antoine. 'Yet to give him – or any great noble of l'Aquitaine – custody over the royal heiress of Lyonesse is to place too great a temptation in his path. Finding a husband for Princess Catherine may be a thankless task, but any suitor Septimanie might favour would certainly not be to your interest. No good can come of a duke meddling with the crown of Lyonesse.' Historical experience showed as much, thought Antoine: long ago a Duke of Guienne had married a Princess of Lyonesse. Three hundred years of headaches had ensued,

Catherine de Guienne being only the latest and by no means the worst.

King Charles nodded faintly. 'Then what are we to do?' he said. 'Must we receive this disobedient girl at Court?'

'Of course not!' answered Antoine. 'Your Majesty alone bestows the privilege of attending upon you.' An idea came to him. 'The demoiselle still holds the title of Duchesse de Guienne, Sire, and the old Hôtel de Guienne stands vacant on the South Bank in our capital. Let her household be installed there. She will be removed from Court itself, but close enough to be watched.' She would also be kept in the hands of the royal administration – Antoine's hands – and away from the grasping fingers of the Lusianes.

The King nodded again, more firmly. 'Lodge her there, then – and keep your wife away from her.'

'I do not believe Madame would find a warm welcome at the Hôtel de Guienne,' said Antoine. Nor would he, for that matter.

For the first time in this meeting, King Charles smiled. 'If no one has charge of the creature, she will have no one to exasperate! She shall have to berate herself, else hold her tongue. That would be a miracle! See that it is done, de Chirac. And let me go a season without hearing from or about her!' With a crook of his finger he dismissed his chief minister.

Antoine rose, bowed low and withdrew. The

conference had gone as well as it could, under the circumstances. But the girl was now his problem to deal with. He had offered the Hôtel de Guienne as policy, leaving aside the practicalities of lodging a troublesome princess there. Now, returning to his quarters, he had to confront them. Ladies-in-waiting would have to be found. Perhaps the two she'd had would consent to return to her service, saving him the trouble of finding fresh victims for an honour without profit. The greater complication would be finding officers to govern her household. Antoine had men competent for the task, but they already had the greater one of governing the kingdom of Aquitaine. He could not spare them to keep a demoiselle in order.

He settled on an expedient option – one that the King, in his irritation, had aptly suggested: as Catherine de Guienne was so prideful, let her govern and supervise herself! In all likelihood she would bring herself down in scandal, rendered unworthy to the world for marriage and to her would-be future subjects for their throne. Young demoiselles as a race were not renowned for wisdom or judgement – and given her cruel words to Corisande it would be a fitting end. Corisande might weep but Antoine would not: he still had her sister Anne.

And if, against odds, Catherine did not founder in scandal? She would have shown herself fit to be a queen, yet would still need allies, an army and a husband in order to survive on the throne at Kellouique. Antoine could supply them, and she might have learned the good sense to ask.

He decided as well to see to an altogether more pleasant responsibility. When he returned to the capital Antoine would summon Corisande home.

Solange stood on the parapet of the Richebourg citadel, her cloak pulled about her shoulders against the sharp breeze that blew in off the sea. 'Turn and turn about,' she said to Madeleine, who with her had answered the summons from M. de Chirac. 'Was I not right that the good sisters would find Mademoiselle too much for them?' She related the tale, which Armand had summarized in a letter. Some of the novices at Ste-Lucie-en-Avers, it seemed, had exercised small tyrannies over the rest – not much different, thought Solange, from much that went on at Court. Those novices had not reckoned with Catherine de Guienne.

Madeleine laughed softly. 'Honour triumphed over humility,' she said. She worked loose a tiny chip from the parapet and tossed it over, aiming for the young soldier – rather well-favoured – who walked guard below. The chip struck nearly at his feet; startled, he looked up. Both demoiselles leaned over and waved, and Madeleine impishly blew him a kiss. 'There! Surely he has a girl in the town. Let him go to her when his duty is ended, instead of drinking and dicing.' She sighed. 'If only the

Chevalier de Batz-Castelmore were here! Yet we shall be back at Aix-le-Siège soon, and he shall seek me out.'

Madeleine's complacency was infuriating, thought Solange; the more so for being justified. 'Then you must sooner or later do the honourable thing,' she said, 'and yield him your favour. Else you are a cruel demoiselle, unworthy of the sonnets that shall be composed for you.'

'Sonnets?' Madeleine shook her head emphatically. 'Affairs of honour, Mademoiselle de Charleville! Blades crossed for me, and my favour to the victor!'

Solange clucked in mock disapproval. 'You are quite impossible, Mademoiselle du Lac!'

'And you are not? Sonnets indeed! Any poem written for you should be burned in front of the churches. As you are quite without morals,' Madeleine added, 'I feared you might request not to serve Mademoiselle in the Hôtel de Guienne but to stay with the Princess du Pré. I know you find her outrages rather amusing than otherwise.'

'Amusing? I suppose,' said Solange; 'yet not my sins of choice, so I leave poor Allyriane to her fate.' She shrugged. 'Such is the world! You do not escape me; nor Mademoiselle – and none of us escapes exile.' It was not precisely the ends of the earth, but the South Bank of the capital was not Court, and although the Chevalier de Batz-Castelmore might seek out Madeleine there, Solange fretted over how to do battle for Armand de Fossier from so remote a fastness, clear across the city.

'What of the Hôtel de Guienne?' she asked. 'You have been there.'

'Princess Catherine will love it,' said Madeleine, 'because it has the royal arms of the goddams over the gate. You will not. It has all the charm of a prison. A dusty, abandoned one too, full of spiders.' Madeleine made a most expressive face. 'To think that I feared a little scrubbing in a convent! The Hôtel de Guienne needs a great deal, and even the best servants work better for being shown their duties. I shall be on hands and knees for a year, and still only make a start.' Madeleine shrugged. 'Yet on the bright side – my own household! Well, Mademoiselle's, but mine to govern! At Court we had no real use, any more than Mademoiselle did.'

In her simple way, thought Solange, Madeleine had reached the heart of the matter. 'Yes,' she agreed. 'If we perform our duties, they'll leave us be. So!' she continued, 'we must be Mademoiselle's loyal councillors, for until she returns to her own country she shall have no others. So long as we are in her service, *you* shall be Sénéschal, and have charge of her household, and *I* shall be Ministre d'État, and have charge of her policies . . . or as nearly such as makes no difference.'

A trumpet blast rang out below the citadel, and a royal galley set forth from the quayside, oars rising and falling like the wings of a great bird, the hollow boom of her drum carried on the breeze. Galleys constantly patrolled the waters off Richebourg. The Lord High

Admiral of Lyonesse was said to be an old drunkard, but not too old or drunk to sign letters of reprisal: privateers had already taken Aquitanian merchantmen.

Madeleine leaned against the parapet and watched the departing galley intently – as though hoping that raiders would appear and she would get to witness a battle. 'We shall do well, you and I,' she said. 'Yet Mademoiselle shall not be in the Hôtel de Guienne for ever. What then?'

'Then? She goes to her country,' said Solange. 'And we go with her.'

'It will not be the Court of la Trémouille, Solange!' Madeleine hiked one foot onto the base of a crenel in the battlements. 'Not who has preference, or who is having affaires with whom! Mademoiselle shall be Queen of Lyonesse, her husband King – and you and I shall be dancing very close to the fire.'

'I won't set my gown alight!' said Solange. It was a subject to which she'd already given thought. 'I have no intention of becoming maîtresse-en-titre, if that is what you are worried about. "King's Whore" – the goddams might at least have a more graceful term! In any case I will leave it be, even if Mademoiselle's future husband is well-favoured. She might call for the executioner's sword.'

'In Lyonesse they use an axe.'

'Would my neck care?' asked Solange wryly. 'I told you, my head and shoulders go well together. I mean to keep them that way – and advise you to do the same.'

'That is not the half of it, Solange.' Madeleine straightened up and turned – holding a poniard. Gleaming in the afternoon light, the blade looked a foot and a half long.

'Put that away!' Solange ordered. Madeleine was entirely too intrigued by steel.

'You don't like it?' asked Madeleine. 'If you go to Lyonesse, best get used to it! Remember how Mademoiselle came to l'Aquitaine in the first place! Her father shot in a hunting accident – so they called it – and she hauled up onto a saddle to flee. She can kneel to any flag in Christendom, but when her grandfather dies, *that* is what she goes back to.' Madeleine's blue eyes regarded Solange. 'Every robber with a coat of arms will think to take her by force. And if so? We are only minor prizes: given to captains of ruffians if we are lucky, thrown to the soldiers if we're not.' Madeleine turned the blade towards her own neck and flicked it crosswise. 'Or left by the roadside with throats cut, if haste permits no more.'

'Need you be so vivid?' cried Solange. She knew well enough the perils of Lyonesse, and did not need Madeleine to remind her.

'Life is vivid,' said Madeleine, 'and so is death! You can still go back to Monsieur de Chirac, and ask to remain with the Princess du Pré.'

Solange's temper flared. Straightening up, she

looked Madeleine in the eye. 'Do you question my courage?' she asked. 'If so, I demand satisfaction!' In the distance the galley's drum sounded like a great slow heartbeat. Solange gulped. She had said it without thinking – careless folly! It was too late to take it back; she would have to see it through. At the end the final embarrassment, explaining herself to God. '*Hélas!*' she cried, blinking at tears. 'I may be a coward, Mademoiselle du Lac, but I am a daughter of the house of Charleville!'

'No, Mademoiselle de Charleville,' Madeleine said softly. 'I do not doubt your courage. I only wondered if *you* doubted it.' She flipped the poniard and held the hilt out to Solange. 'Take it! Show me how you would strike an enemy!'

Gingerly, Solange took the poniard from Madeleine's outstretched hand, and raised it as though to strike.

'Not at me!' cried Madeleine. 'And not like that! An overhand thrust is easily warded off!' She caught Solange's upraised arm by the wrist. 'See? Worse, your enemy can twist it down, and impale you on your own blade.' She took the poniard, turned it end-up, and put it back in Solange's hand. 'Strike upward, below the ribs. With all your strength, if you must do it, and suddenly! While the assassin still thinks you a harmless woman! Do it!'

Solange jabbed the air, feeling foolish.

Madeleine laughed. 'Well, *that* will stretch out a two-hundred-pound highwayman at your feet! I'll teach you some other time. Yet steel drawn between friends must be cooled.' She held out her hand, palm down. 'Now! Scratch me with it. Deeper than that! Draw blood!' Solange pressed harder, and a tiny stitching of red appeared on Madeleine's hand. 'Now – your turn.'

'I was afraid of this!' cried Solange.

Madeleine reclaimed the poniard, then took Solange by the hand. 'This will sting,' she said. Solange closed her eyes and winced. It did sting. 'There!' said Madeleine cheerfully. 'The steel is cooled, and we are blood sisters. Name your rival and she is my enemy! Name your lover and I admire only from a distance!'

Solange wondered at what distance a man could bask in Madeleine's admiration without being tempted. Surely it would be measured in leagues.

The antechamber of the Superior General's study in the convent of Ste-Lucie-en-Avers faced like Janus in two directions. On one side it opened into the world of the cloister; on the other side onto the secular world beyond. Catherine stood at a window above the outer courtyard. A white coach, emblazoned with the arms of the Aquitaine, waited to bear her to her new quarters in the Hôtel de Guienne. Two score escort riders in the livery of the Gardes de Maison waited in the saddle, and – wonder of wonders – Solange de Charleville stood by the door of the coach. Ten times more than coach or escort, she signified the world beyond. For two months Catherine had seen no woman not clothed in convental black or white, yet there stood Solange, clad in bold crimson as on the day she'd last seen her.

She genuflected to the crucifix on the wall, and passed through the door to the outer stair. The brightness of day made her wince as the captain of the escort brought his lance upright, and the other riders came to attention in their saddles. As she came down the stair, Solange knelt and Catherine raised her up and embraced her.

She wanted desperately to know how Solange had returned to her service – and what had become of Madeleine. There was no way to ask, and Solange herself might not know. In the beginning her ladies had not been friends; perhaps they had not parted friends in the end. She stepped back. 'It is great joy,' she told Solange gravely, 'that you are restored to me! I shall not forget the faith you have shown me in my exile.'

Solange curtseyed. 'We hold it great honour to return to your service, Mademoiselle,' she said, and handed her into the coach. Catherine had only an instant to notice that she had used the plural. Then she climbed in as well, and the waiting guardsman closed the door. 'I ask your indulgence,' said Solange, 'that Mademoiselle du Lac does not attend upon you with me. The King's coachman would only take one of us.' She shrugged. 'So I abused my rank! Madeleine will express her displeasure, I'm sure.'

Catherine was too happy to care. The coachman cracked his whip; with a lurch they were in motion, rolling across the outer courtyard and onto the royal highway, away from Ste Lucie en Avers. Ahead lay the capital, and her new home.

CHAPTER SIX

The Hôtel de Guienne

The great grey mass of the Hôtel de Guienne rose above the rue Frontenac, quite near the river. Once it had fronted on the water, permitting easy communications in the days when the Kings of Lyonesse had ruled half the Aquitaine. Now the river was tamed within a great embankment, the water gate bricked up and forgotten, a row of houses sprung up along the new riverfront; and the hôtel itself was fallen in estate. A grim, fortified pile of stone after the fashion of its day, it offered no attractions to the Kings of Aquitaine, and now served as a storehouse. Its fine furnishings and splendid tapestries had long since vanished: removed, stolen, or simply fallen to pieces. The Great Hall, under whose lofty hammer beam roof Edmund III – *le Conquérant* – had once compelled the greatest lords of the Aquitaine to swear fealty on bended knee, now gave shelter to barrels and sacks, while the barracks were rented out as shops and tenements, the proceeds making a useful contribution to the bailiff's pay. Still, in law it remained Catherine's, as Duchess of Guienne.

The autumn sun was low by the time her coach reached the city and rumbled through the Porte Ste Valerie, turning away from the direction of the palace and heading instead towards the South Bank. The narrow streets were deep shadowed by tall houses, but bright with life. Merchants and workingmen, their wives and their children, pressed hastily up against houses and shops to make way for the splendidly arrayed riders and a coach bearing the royal arms. A few youths waved or blew kisses on spying two courtly demoiselles within. With equal impudence Solange blew kisses back at such as caught her fancy.

The coach rattled across the Pont Ste Monique. It was a modern bridge of stately marble, bare of houses and shops. To either side was only the river, with here and there the dark hulls and bright awnings of barges. They plunged again into the shadows of houses: the South Bank, shabbier and livelier. 'The rue Frontenac!' announced Solange as the coach turned a corner. The crowd thickened; the arrival of a princess – even one out of favour – surely the news of the neighbourhood. Houses gave way to the massive lofty walls of the Hôtel de Guienne, with arrow slit windows. It looked unpleasingly like a prison, yet over the gate were the Royal Arms of Lyonesse: the lion rampant guardant quartered defiantly with the fleur de lis. The coach rolled beneath them into the courtyard.

The coachman pulled to a stop, the door opened,

and Madeleine was waiting to hand her down. Servants were lined up in the courtyard to receive their new mistress; Catherine was surprised and pleased to see familiar faces from her old household within the palace. Her ladies must have retained them, though Solange had said nothing of it. Her sense of homecoming was further sharpened by the liveries of the guards. Shabby and faded though they were, their coats were the red and green of the House of Guienne.

'Mademoiselle—' Madeleine tugged at her sleeve. 'Permit me to—'

Impatiently, Catherine shook her head. 'Wait!' She ought first to address her people. Across the courtyard a stair rose to an open upper gallery. Drawing her ladies after her she went up and turned to look over her assembled household. One of the waiting figures caught her attention: a woman in a blue cloak and – startlingly unexpected here – a gabled headdress in the manner of Lyonesse.

'Listen to me, all of you!' Catherine cried. 'The Aquitanian king, in thinking to shame me by dismissal from his Court, has done me great favour. By his command have I come *here*, to a house of my fore-fathers!' She paused. 'To those of you who have served me before, your loyalty will not be forgotten. To those who are new to my household, I demand only good and faithful service, and shall reward it with good and fair dealing. I am Duchesse de Guienne and this is my house; with God's help I shall govern it well and justly. Yet I hold it in fee from my grandfather and lord, Edmund IV, *Roi de Lyonesse*! I shall most humbly strive to be worthy of him.' Catherine did not suppose the people below cared what she said, so long as she did not go on too long. She had only a little more to say. Changing to the Saxon tongue she cried: 'God save King Edmund!'

The upturned faces stared blankly, not knowing the foreign words. All save one: the woman in the blue cloak and the gabled headdress knelt upon hearing them. Catherine nodded to her assembled people, and started back down the stair, wanting to seek the woman out.

Then the woman was before her, kneeling again, stiff with age. Looking upon her face as she rose, Catherine felt a dizzy shock of recognition. Stunned, tears welling suddenly in her eyes, she stared at the old woman she had not seen in so many years. 'Your . . . your Ladyship?' she whispered.

'Well!' said the woman, speaking in Catherine's native tongue. 'Don't be looking at me as if I were a ghost, Kateryn! I may be old, but not *that* old!' She smiled. 'Your Highness!'

Still hesitant, half-disbelieving, Catherine reached out and raised her up. 'Lud's blood – your Ladyship!'

'My little Kateryn!' her Ladyship answered. 'God preserve me, how tall and fair you've grown!'

Then they were in each other's arms, and kissing one

another's cheeks. Catherine wept till she could not see, and had nearly to support herself against the frail woman's body, for she could scarcely stand.

Lying on his somewhat tatty bed in the best room of the King's Crown inn, William de Havilland tried to imitate the deep slow breaths of a man sleeping in a drunken stupor. As he did he listened to the small sounds of night. The last roisterers had staggered back to their chambers, or collapsed in corners of the common room. The couple whose huffing and moaning sounded earlier from a room close by had evidently slaked their desires, or at any rate worn themselves out. All he heard now were occasional sleepers' grunts, the footsteps of someone rising to use the privy, and now and then a slight rustle or snort from the stables. His servant Pietro snored from the other side of the chamber; William envied the man his useful skill of snoring while wide awake.

The voyage to Lyonesse aboard a merchant galley of Ravenna had been a festival of sleep: a sea-passage with no ship-master's responsibility, nor even watches to stand. Sleeping ashore, here in his homeland, ought to be easier still, on a bed that might be tatty but was perfectly dry, with no heave of the sea nor shift of the wind. On top of that he'd celebrated his return to Lyonesse by eating his fill of roast beef, washing it down with more than passable ale. The food and drink in the common room had been good plain fare. The talk was less good:

too much to do with robbers, not just in the depths of the Wold but striking boldly on the King's highways.

William knew his countrymen. They would complain of the weather at the drop of a hat, and complaining of robberies made a better tale. But the sober merchant-princes of Ravenna had warned him that the law in Lyonesse was poorly kept in these days of an old, slowly failing king. Thus he lay awake, listening.

A sharper creak sounded from another room, then footfalls. William kept his breathing slow and steady as he listened to the steps. They drew closer, but he half dismissed them. It was the unmuffled tread of a man on the innocent business of nature, not the careful steps of one bent on theft, or worse.

The footsteps went past, and on towards the stair. No doubt another drinker seeking the privy. Perhaps, thought William, he was mistaken entirely, and the man drinking with two others in the common room had only been eyeing him out of idle curiosity. He journeyed in the guise of a gentleman of slight means and less consequence, one who had but a single servant, and had to stay in inns for lack of connections beyond his native shire. Yet how many country thanes of the Saxon Pale went on their way in Enotrian garb, and with an Enotrian servant? William had not intended to be secretive, merely unobtrusive. He suspected that he was failing even at that.

A little later the footfalls came back, the man no

doubt having eased himself of his ale – but when he opened a door, it did not seem to be to the same chamber he had come from. William's fingers lightly touched the hilt of his sword, but he kept his breathing even. Sounds came again, softer this time, more careful; the earlier journey must have been to test the floor-boards. A faint scraping came from his own door, the scraping of a dagger blade being used, with slow care, to turn, then slide the bolt. The work went on for what seemed for ever, the bolt being worked back hair's breadth by hair's breadth, until it seemed to William that dawn must surely come before the thief's task was done.

Then, still ever so slowly, the door was eased open. William opened one eye, and sensed a grey space amid the deeper blackness. A shadow passed through, faintly silhouetted by the light of the night candle at the end of the hallway. Shadow and soft footsteps ghosted across the chamber towards the corner where he'd set down his gear . . . William grunted and stirred. The shadow froze. William stirred again, and half lifted his head. 'What?' he cried in feigned surprise.

The intruder whirled and ran for the door as William came to his feet, sword in his right hand, dagger in his left. 'Thief!' he shouted. 'Thief, by Wott!' He jabbed his dagger into his pillow, and with two long strides was at the door. 'Thief!' he cried again, thrusting the pillow through the door. As he had suspected, a blade ripped through it. He dropped, rolled through the door, thrust his rapier up and to the right, to be rewarded with a howl. A heavy body fell on top of him, jerking spasmodically, spattering blood onto him even as Pietro kicked it aside.

Uproar spread through the inn, other figures stumbling out into the half-lit hallway. 'Thief!' cried William again, in his heavy-weather voice. 'Innkeeper! Thief! Raise the hue and cry!' He turned to Pietro behind him. 'Roust out the innkeeper, lad!' Then he swerved back into the chamber, leaving wiry Pietro to make his way through the hallway to the stair. William had left the shutters unlatched against just this chance; throwing them open, he swung himself over, hung on the sill for an instant, then dropped and rolled to his feet in the inn yard.

Three or four other men and youths converged on the stables. The stable door was open, and one figure lay on the ground in front of it. A sudden brilliant light blazed within: a deafening crack, and a bullet whistled past William's ear. A dozen horses bolted from the stable, followed by two more with men astride them.

William sheathed his sword in his sword belt – he had on nothing else but his shirt – and angled towards one of the riderless horses. Casting away his dagger, he made a flying leap, caught it by its shoulder and vaulted onto its back. 'Yaaah!' he cried, and clung tight with his knees as it galloped out of the inn yard. One of the fleeing thieves caught sight of him in pursuit, reined back, and levelled a *pistole* at him. William leaned down behind the horse's neck. The shot went wide and he heard no bullet, but his mount had had its fill, and threw him.

The surviving robbers disappeared into the night, west across the Northengleshire countryside towards Cheltenham Wold. William picked himself off the ground and hobbled back across the inn yard to the stair. Nothing felt broken, but his backside hurt like the very devil. He was a better shipman than horseman.

'There is nothing in this world,' declared her Ladyship, 'half so lovely as a lady with a fine hawk on her fist.' Her governess, thought Catherine, was proof of her point. Erect on her hunter, a fierce peregrine – Rowena, her favourite – on her outstretched arm, she looked like some great lady from the unsullied youth of chivalry. Her Ladyship glanced at Solange. 'You should heed *that*, Mademoiselle de Charleville,' she added, 'if you heed nothing else!'

Madeleine started to laugh; Catherine's sharp glance silenced her. Catherine felt some pity for Solange, for whom these first weeks in the Hôtel de Guienne had been a shock. Madeleine might ask nothing more of life than to hunt and hawk through the royal Forêt de Numières on an autumn day, but Solange thought great ladies should travel by chair if they must travel at all –

certainly not riding astride. Yet astride they were, for the Aquitanian courtly fashion of side-saddle had not come to Lyonesse. Her Ladyship made it clear that Catherine's household must ride as ladies of Lyonesse did. Catherine had obeyed with joy.

Her Ladyship! For seven long years Jane Gower, Countess of Lindley, had bided her time in this foreign land, awaiting the day she could return to Catherine's service. Catherine could scarcely think of it without bursting into tears. They rode along the brow of a ridge, overlooking a grassy valley. 'Falconry is an art,' said her Ladyship, 'and like every art is gained only by dedication and a great deal of hard work! A taste for roast game fowl doesn't hurt.' Removing Rowena's hood, she let her slip. With a burst that blew back the lappets of Lady Lindley's headdress the peregrine was on the wing, spiralling into the grey autumn sky. Her Ladyship urged her steed down the gentle slope, explaining the training of hawks as Catherine and her ladies followed.

'Your Ladyship!' interrupted Catherine. Ahead, among the brush and reeds, the dogs had gone on point.

'Well done, Kateryn!' Lady Lindley said. 'You were listening *and* watching.' She glanced up at Rowena, then signalled the huntsmen. They started into the brush at a jog, beating as they went. A mass of shapes burst up above the stream, a score of grouse, breaking cover to escape the beaters –

– and a dark shape hurtled down on them. Unerringly Rowena found her mark; with a burst of feathers a grouse fell tumbling into a meadow. As Catherine and her ladies followed at a little distance, Lady Lindley dismounted and gently approached peregrine and prey. She urged Rowena onto her glove. With a sharp twist she took the head off the grouse – a fine cock – and gave it to the huntress as reward before hooding her once more.

Two more flights each yielded another grouse; by the time the last was taken the afternoon was well along and Rowena growing tired. 'Enough for today!' said her Ladyship. 'Grouse tonight, and tomorrow it shall be crossbows, and venison; we'll feast better than Charles of Aquitaine in his palace. Poor soul,' she added. 'By the time his dinner is passed from viscount to count to duke, and finally gets to him, it is stone cold.' She glanced over at Catherine's ladies and made a shooing motion. 'Go now, mesdemoiselles – I must speak with your mistress. Away with both of you! If you fall in with young men, I don't wish to hear of it!'

Catherine's ladies-in-waiting inclined their heads, then turned and rode down the valley of Montpassier. For all Solange's complaining, she was a skilled horse-woman – from the country breeding she so wanted to leave behind her – and the ladies made a fine sight together, the falls of their headdresses flying up, hair streaming free, sable and gold. 'Good maids both!' said her Ladyship. 'Even Lady Solange, once she puts foolish notions out of her head.'

'If it please your Ladyship,' said Catherine, 'be not over hard on her. She being from the provinces, and poor, her life's dream was to be at Court. Now she half fears herself back at her father's old castle!'

'Foolish notions, I say!' repeated Lady Lindley. 'Lady Solange is too proud to tell you, so I shall: her forefather defied Edmund III, rendering no homage after the Battle of Châtelhardie. A rebel in Edmund's eyes, so of course his estates were seized, all that King Edmund could lay hands on. But de Charleville was true nobility: a loyal champion of the Aquitaine. Poor thanks that his lands were never restored, but handed over to the Lusianes instead. She could not come from finer stock! Good maids both, Kateryn – no matter what churchmen might say of them! And the better for you showing them their worth!'

'What is *my* worth now, your Ladyship?' Catherine asked. 'Here in the Aquitaine, in the power of King Charles? Richborough was taken, and I did nothing but wear a mourning dress.'

'Do I hear a touch of self-pity?' Her Ladyship rode up beside Catherine and put an arm on her shoulder. 'I dare say you have earned a dram, child,' she said gently. 'But a dram is all you get! You have set the King of Aquitaine by the ear, and made the finest maids in his kingdom your loyal retainers – which says to me that you know perfectly well what your worth is. I wish that the burden meant for your father should not fall upon you. Yet so it shall, my lady Princess Kateryn, so it shall. You can but do your best, and so you have. No man can ask more.'

Catherine had never before heard her Ladyship call her by her title save in reproof. They rode on in silence under the lowering sky. She had one more question she was tempted to ask: what did her Ladyship think of Madame Corisande? Yet what was the point of asking? The answer was obvious. Corisande had been King Charles's whore – and, like her husband, was still his loyal servant.

Madeleine pulled the hood of her cloak over her head and adjusted her feet in the stirrups. Now and then the sharp wind brought the sting of raindrops. She did not mind the bracing air; she did mind Solange's complaining of it, and said so.

'I should be glad of the season,' admitted Solange. 'Even more for winter, and an end to this galloping about the country. I should like to walk properly again, instead of going bandy legged like a Monite from living in a saddle! *Hélas*, come spring it shall all start again. I shall have a slender figure, but shall also be dead!' She sighed theatrically. 'Ah, my fate!'

Remind me to weep, thought Madeleine. Their new life was doing Solange no harm. She did in fact slip easily into her tightest gowns, without having to struggle with lacings. 'Your duties at least take you abroad in the city,' said Madeleine. 'When we cannot go into the country, the Hôtel de Guienne shall be as much my prison as Mademoiselle's! You have found an arrangement, have you not? Do not lie, or I'll have you out of that saddle for a proper thrashing!'

'An arrangement?' cried Solange. 'With Monsieur de Fossier? How? Don't be simple, Madeleine! Thrash me? Run me through and shorten my misery!'

'Do not tempt me!' Madeleine warned her. 'At least you get out! Yet where would I go, save to assure Maman and Papa that their daughter is still intact? With the Chevalier de Batz-Castelmore sent to a garrison, my virtue is not even tried.' And I should like it to be! she added to herself. 'Not only de Batz-Castelmore, but everyone else I might have an eye for, all off in some wretched fortress or other, staring out over the sea! What his Majesty is thinking, or Monsieur de Chirac, I can't imagine! Are the goddams going to set upon us in the dead of winter?'

'If their men are as mad as their women, well they might!' said Solange. 'The Comtesse de Lindley can ride a strong man out of the saddle. By the time she is done, I shall be dead, but Mademoiselle will be ready to lead her own armies, like Yolande d'Asturias or Queen Rowena in that Saxon book of hers. Or Hippolyta, Queen of Amazons, of whom the ancients said—'

Madeleine escaped learning what the ancients said. 'Hush!' she called out, and reined in sharply. The land to their right opened up and sloped down to a lower reach of the stream from which the grouse had been flushed. Something on the far bank caught her eye. Her first thought was those mysterious horsemen she'd caught glimpses of during earlier rides. Solange – no doubt rightly – thought them spies set to keep an eye on Princess Catherine. Yet these were no spies. Riding along on the far bank came another hunting party, one with several ladies, and numerous servants and pack horses in train. Madeleine tried to make out the livery, but could not.

Solange pulled up in turn, and her gaze followed Madeleine's pointing finger. 'Ah!' she said. 'So we are not the only fools out in this weather!'

'Interesting!' said Madeleine. 'They're riding towards Montpassier. If they mean to stay there, we shall all be in close quarters, but at least we shall have company. I wonder if any young men are among them?'

'I thought all the desirable ones were in the garrisons.'

'Hold your tongue, Solange. I don't think they see us. If we circle around to the ford, we'll be able to get up close and see who they are – and warn Mademoiselle, if it is no one with whom we wish to share quarters.'

'*I* shall get up close, dear Madeleine,' said Solange.

'You've no sense of stealth. You'd storm up at the gallop and they'd bolt in panic, fearing a band of robbers was upon them.'

'I would not!' cried Madeleine, though rather pleased by the image.

'I am the senior,' declared Solange, 'and the matter is closed. Wait for me behind the rise.'

Madeleine opened her mouth to protest, but gave it up. Solange rarely asserted her higher rank; when she did she would not be swayed. She rode off towards the rise, and after a little while returned. 'You won't believe it!' she said. 'It is entirely too rich; I shall have to tell Armand, so he can put it in his memoirs.'

'Never mind your de Fossier and his memoirs!' said Madeleine impatiently. 'Who is it?'

'La Fontenelle!' said Solange. 'And all her gaggle with her. At least they are permitted to ride side-saddle.'

'Margot? In this weather?' Solange was an Amazon, thought Madeleine, compared to Margot. 'And riding to Montpassier? Whatever for? The foresters surely told her that ... we'd best go warn Mademoiselle.' She and Solange spurred to the gallop together, towards the lodge of Montpassier.

Catherine had scarcely stepped through the door of the lodge, thinking only to warm herself before the fire that crackled at the side of the hall, when Solange announced her news. 'Margot?' Catherine repeated, needlessly, as she handed her cloak to Madeleine. 'Coming *here?*'

'Yes, Mademoiselle,' said Solange. 'I saw her with my own eyes, not fifty paces away.'

'And the way leads nowhere else,' added Madeleine. 'She'd not get back to the château at Pont St-Gérard before fall of night.'

'Well, then,' declared Catherine, 'she shall get back to Pont St-Gérard *after* fall of night. *Sang de Lud!* I'll not have her here if she comes with two angels to ask her admittance, and ten thousand devils behind her in pursuit.'

'I saw no angels, Mademoiselle,' said Solange. 'Only her usual praise singers. And far more servants than she needs, or befit her rank if you ask me.'

'How long until they get here?' asked Catherine.

'They're not riding hard, I can tell you that!' said Madeleine. 'I should say at least half an hour. I'm glad you got back in time – I do not know what we would have done.' She smiled wickedly. 'I know what I should like to do. Give the command, Mademoiselle, and the huntsmen can put the house in a state of defence, then order them begone.'

'Margot!' muttered Catherine, and shook her head in disgust. 'By the body of Christ,' she said, 'I should like to beat her about the head till her hair is redder than mine!'

'Mademoiselle—?' said Solange suddenly. 'I . . .' She

paused, unwontedly hesitant. Catherine nodded for her to go on. 'If I may be so bold,' continued Solange, 'I think you should receive her.' A peculiar silence fell across the hall, broken only by the crackle of the fire. Madeleine stared at Solange, head cocked in puzzlement. Her Ladyship did not look up from her needlework.

'And why, Mademoiselle de Charleville,' asked Catherine gravely, 'do you think that?'

'Because, Altesse,' answered Solange with equal gravity, 'Margot has come to seek something of you, and in seeking you out, she reveals herself; in receiving her you need reveal nothing.'

What Margot might want of her, Catherine could not begin to imagine. Yet Solange's logic was flawless. 'Very well, then,' she declared. 'I shall receive her with every courtesy. Madeleine, have the huntsmen open the gate to her. Mmm – how many of rank were with her?'

'Three ladies, and I should say half a dozen gentleman attendants and officers of her household. Of servants and others, not less than two score.'

Catherine frowned. The quarters in lodge and outbuildings would be crowded indeed. 'Have her people quartered in the gatehouse,' she ordered. 'My servants must pitch tents for themselves – poor reward for good service, but there's no helping it. Solange, have the cooks dress all the deer, rabbits and fowl that we have taken for tonight's table. We shall see if Margot's women are good enough seamstresses to let out her gown for her! And serve the best wine in the cellar, if the steward has to broach every cask to find it. It is Charles of Aquitaine's wine, and this is his harlot – let him pay for her entertainment!'

Scarcely had the essential preparations been made before the clop of hooves and clink of horse bells declared Margot's arrival. Catherine took her place on the high seat of the hall. Dumont the huntmaster, brought to her household by Lady Lindley, took the part of the doorkeeper. 'Mademoiselle de la Fontenelle begs that she might be received, Altesse,' he declared.

Catherine took a deep breath and nodded. 'Bid her enter, and be welcome.'

Dumont stepped back and in swept Margot, her attendants in train. She glanced about uneasily for a moment, as though expecting to see bowmen taking aim at her. Then she advanced the length of the hall – which was not far – towards Catherine's chair. Her golden curls, for once not elaborately dressed nor hung with bells, spilled across the shoulders of her russet gown. By Margot's standards she was plainly and modestly turned out; Catherine thought she looked rather better that way. Inclining her head, Margot took the folds of her gown and went to one knee. If she had not, Catherine would have tossed her out straight away.

'Rise, Mademoiselle de la Fontenelle,' she said. 'I bid you most welcome. This house and all I have are yours, as long as you shall wish.' She offered her hand for Margot to kiss, and Margot did – she would have to take particular care to wash that hand!

The Princess honours me far beyond my poor desserts,' declared Margot.

'On the contrary,' Catherine lied, 'the honour – and the pleasure – are altogether mine.' She rose and embraced Margot, and they kissed one another's cheeks. She would have to wash her face as well. Introductions were made, her Ladyship rising from her stool to curtsey as though she had never enjoyed higher honour than introduction to the King of Aquitaine's mistress. 'I beg you the kindness of supping with us,' Catherine said when the introductions were done. 'Surely you are weary from such long and hard riding!'

If Margot had a grasp of irony, thought Catherine, she did not show it. 'You are very kind, Princess de Lyonesse,' she said. 'But please – I should like to be your friend, and beg that you may simply call me Margot.' She smiled, though Catherine suspected she was enjoying the occasion no more than she herself was.

'As you must call me Catherine, my dear cousin Margot,' said Catherine, smiling back. 'By rights I should call for music, and we could have proper merriment among us – but I fear I have no musicians.'

Margot, however, had brought musicians among her great train of servants – Catherine wondered if she had brought any huntsmen – and Catherine was thankful for this; without them the wait for supper might have been very long. The servants at the lower end of the hall did well enough, laughing and jesting freely among their own order, but at the High Table, conversation in the musicians' interludes was painfully stilted.

Whatever Margot had come for, thought Catherine, it could scarcely be broached here, amid so many idle ears. She took the matter in hand. 'Dear Margot,' she said, 'I am remiss! It is nearly dark; shall we take the air together while we can?' Margot assented; Catherine offered her arm and they went out together into the little garden of the lodge. Clouds blazed purple red against the deep blue of dusk. Sky and air were glorious, and Catherine wished for better company to enjoy it. She turned to Margot. The maîtresse-en-titre was four years her senior, but Catherine was the taller; for once she was thankful. 'Your company is a pleasure I had not looked for, Margot,' she said.

Margot made a small curtsey, then looked Catherine up and down. 'You are prettier than I once thought,' she said.

'You rode here to Montpassier to tell me that?' asked Catherine, noting that Margot had not actually called her pretty.

'Some might ride a great deal further,' replied Margot. 'After all, the marriage prize of Christendom ought to be pretty, no?'

'The marriage prize of Christendom is as pretty as my

grandfather's kingdom,' said Catherine. 'No one needs to look at me – only at a map.'

Margot laughed. 'A princess without illusions!' she said. 'His Majesty's daughters might learn from you! Yet the man who marries your crown will end up looking at you – and bedding you as well. His duty, yes, but he may as well find it pleasing.'

Catherine flushed. The occasion called for a witty reply, and she had none. 'What is it to you?' she asked. 'I did not know you were so concerned that a king should find happiness in his queen's embrace. Her Majesty would be surprised.'

'Her Majesty does not defend her own cause,' said Margot without a blink. 'The Court may blame me as they wish, but I came late to the affray. My sainted predecessor broke the Queen when I was scarcely out of my crib. That woman must have been quite the archeress in her time, I confess, for her shaft pierced the King to his heart before Queen Isabelle could raise shield against it. Alas, with time she grew plump and lazy, and I bested her.'

Plump? thought Catherine. Madame Corisande had simply been big with the King's child when Margot had overthrown her. 'So what are you saying?' she asked.

'I am telling you the ways of the world, dear Catherine,' said Margot. 'As that woman obviously did not! A princess without illusions should know these things. Tell me – I know you were young, but courts keep few secrets, and even little girls hear the talk if they listen. Did your father keep a mistress?'

For a moment Catherine was too stunned even to be angry. Then she slapped Margot, so hard it stung her hand. The smack resounded wonderfully in the quiet of dusk.

Margot was shocked, then looked murder at Catherine. Finally she laughed. 'Well!' she said. 'I suppose I deserved that!' She put her hand to her cheek. 'Ouch! Now I shall have to apply some powder to disguise it.'

'Insult my father again,' said Catherine, 'and a shipload will not be enough!'

'I meant no insult!' cried Margot. 'I am only speaking of life as it is, my dear, not as romancers would have it. All kings take mistresses. At least, those kings do who are men. Since the other sort cannot hold your kingdom for you, you will need a husband who is a man. He will therefore take a mistress.'

'I shall forbid it!' snapped Catherine. 'I cannot command armies, Margot de la Fontenelle, but I can command the headsman! And so I will, if the likes of you meddle with my husband!'

Margot raised an eyebrow. 'Behead the King's mistress?' she said. 'What executioner would obey that command, save from the King himself? His office might soon pass to his assistant – who would perform it first on him!' She laughed. 'You do have more spirit than her

Majesty: I grant you that. Your husband might come willingly to your bed, even if he strays into others as well. Have no fear that I will cross the sea to haunt you in Lyonesse. I am quite content where I am – and have no wish to challenge queens who even think of the executioner's sword! Others, though, may be bolder. Or labour under greater necessity.' Margot glanced, significantly, towards the shadowed bulk of the hunting lodge.

'What are you talking about?' Catherine decided that Solange's logic in proposing this conference had a flaw – it called for a Solange, skilled in the thrust and parry of intrigue. Margot had laughed off her slap, and was drawing blood at every crossing of blades.

'Your *très charmant* ladies-in-waiting,' said Margot. 'That is not their designed purpose, of course – that woman chose and trained them to do battle with me.' Her voice hardened. 'If either attempts it I shall destroy her, and you'll need no executioner! But otherwise?' Margot shrugged and spread her hands, her tone bantering again. 'When one day you cross the sea, dear Catherine, all their prospects go with you; they'll have no choice but to go as well. Once there, what are they to do? Their reputations will follow; no men of rank would marry them, not even goddams. La Charleville, one need only look at her . . . she is made to ornament a bed, as surely as I am! As for *la Chasseuse* – need I say more? She prattles about chasing stags through the forest, but she is young. In a year or two more she will discover more challenging game, if she has not done so already. Trust me to know sisters in my own profession!'

'You came all this way to warn me against my own ladies?'

Margot shook her head. 'Of course not! I tell you only because you voiced your disapproval of royal mistresses,' she said. 'Natural, given your rank. Amusing though that you spent so many years with that woman – what his Majesty was thinking, I don't know! You were always in her company at Court, and I associated you with her. Until today I had never really met you. Do you know – I rather like you!'

Catherine wondered if she was now expected to wear bells in her hair. She would sooner cut off her locks.

'Yet as you ask,' continued Margot, 'it was my friend the baron who inspired me to call upon you.'

'De Moine?' asked Catherine. Margot nodded, and Catherine puzzled over it. The Baron de Moine was a famous swordsman, but what had that to do with her? Then she remembered: De Moine was in the service of her uncle the Duc de Septimanie. Away from court, how easy it had been to put him and all the Lusiane family out of her mind! Uncle Gérard de Lusiane, thought Catherine, was proud, ambitious – and his interests were not those of the King of Aquitaine. Yet how might Lusiane ambitions possibly serve the interest of Lyonesse?

Margot leaned against a low garden wall and looked

sidelong at Catherine. Plucking a long twig, she twirled it in her fingers so it brushed against her full lips, exactly like a bold maid seducing a shy youth.

'Are you trying to seduce me, Margot?' Catherine asked.

Margot's eyes went wide for an instant. Then she laughed. 'Not that way!' she said. 'You're scarcely to my taste. If you wish that adventure, you would better ask your own Mademoiselle de Charleville – she did after all serve in the Princess du Pré's household for a while.'

'I would rather . . . not.' Catherine stumbled over the words, and felt herself reddening. She'd started to say that she would rather be seduced by the Dauphin, but that was nothing to say to Margot. It was nothing even to think – she could close her eyes and feel his strong arms around her, his lips on hers. If the Dauphin ever tried her, she was not sure she could resist. She stepped back and shook her head to break the spell. 'Is the Duc de Septimanie trying to seduce me, then?' she asked. 'Or my kingdom – my grandfather's kingdom – by seeking to arrange a marriage for me?'

'And if he were?' Margot replied.

'It is not my decision to make,' said Catherine. 'Well, yes, it is.'

The realization gelled abruptly. By all right and propriety her grandfather and his council should determine her marriage, with consent of Parliament. Yet her grandfather was too old and sick to decide anything, and the Privy Council was riven by disputes among the great lords of Lyonesse. That left only Catherine herself – and why *shouldn't* she settle her own marriage? She was to be Queen of Lyonesse by right: her hand alone, by grant of the Crown Matrimonial, would make the next King.

The thought, once formed, was both heady and alarming. 'It is no decision to be made in haste,' she told Margot. 'Yet you may let the baron tell the Duc de Septimanie: if he wishes to convey offers to me, I will listen.' She realized she was stepping onto the marital auction block, an act not unlike mounting the scaffold.

'You are learning, my dear!' said Margot. 'There will be offers, I am sure – offers that Monsieur de Chirac may not wish you to hear.'

Catherine nodded, and suggested that they go back inside to the waiting feast. It was nearly dark. She had indeed learned something from Margot, she thought, that Madame Corisande had not taught her in seven years: she had the power to arrange her own marriage, and give her country a king. Yet it struck her odd that Margot, mistress of the King of Aquitaine, was dangling alliances before her that might not be in the Aquitaine's interest.

The morning sky was lowering, stray raindrops spattering down, when William and Pietro turned south from the high road that led from Rosemouth towards

Kelliwick. They'd risen with the dawn, finally leaving the King's Crown behind.

The robbers had made away with nothing, but robbed them of a day's journey. The constable did not attempt pursuit deep into the Wold, but his men did round up some of the stray horses, including William's and Pietro's, then took down the witnesses' testimony. As for the robber left behind at the inn, William's sword thrust had delivered him to a higher justice than the quarter-session of Northengleshire could dispense. The common room of the King's Crown had ample fresh talk to drink over that night.

Riding in company with a well-armed party of travellers, William and Pietro skirted the Wold and its outlaws as far as Cheltenham Bridge. There they parted ways from the rest to cross the river Rose, so passing from Northengleshire to Southengleshire. The country south of the river was open fields – safer than the Wold, but William had a *pistole* with the wheel locked back and the pan filled, and his sword ready at hand; Pietro likewise. For Lyonesse, as they had learned, was a troubled paradise, even in the Saxon Pale.

Yet paradise it was all the same, and as the road wound southward William's heart rose with it. The poets of the Middle Sea, Christians and Monite infidels alike, went on at length about paradise: gardens it had, so they said, with marbled fountains and sheltering walls from the hellish blowing sands without. Poets knew no more about paradise than they did about women, which was nothing. To William, *here* was paradise: made green by nature rather than art, and peopled by a sturdy lot who might sometimes become bandits, but did not fear them.

Keeping up a steady trot, he and Pietro passed through the ploughlands along the Rose valley, and by late morning were amid the rolling hills of Stockshire. At midday William called a halt, and in the shelter of an oak Pietro served them from a basket of roast fowl. Then they were in the saddle again, the road steepening into the Pelling hills. The sky had lowered further, clouds swirling around the upper slopes, the rain now coming down steadily. Paradise, it turned out, could be soggy. William slightly pitied his servant, who being Enotrian was not accustomed to the weather of Lyonesse.

Yet the clouds broke as they came through the pass above Pellingham. If the breeze was cool, it carried familiar smells, fresh and damp – and below the line of blue sky William caught a glimpse of the sea. Following the horizon he picked out the curve of the Bight, and, just visible in the afternoon sun, the rooftops of Halverstrand town. Home!

It was a joy and a pang, all tumbled together. He could not go there, not yet – not, sad folly that it was, while his father lived. Yet there it was, patiently waiting for him after all these years! William spurred to a gallop – for a couple of furlongs – before reining in.

It had been a long day's ride, and miles yet to go.

The sun was low when he reached his destination, the house of Jamie Strickland, closest friend of his boyhood. The place was as he remembered: the original fortified tower flanked by half-timbered wings. As boys he and Jamie had favoured the old tower, fit for standing off armies of imaginary foes. Now, William suspected, he'd appreciate the roomier accommodations in the wings.

An ostler and stableboy roused themselves on seeing two riders. The old ostler – William remembered his name as Hobbes – looked sidelong at him, and suspiciously at Pietro. 'If you be looking for Sir James, milord,' he said, 'your luck is with you. He was off away at Kelliwick all the last month – only got home Tuesday last. Good to have him back among Christian folk!' Old Hobbes studied William again. 'Begging pardon, milord – you looks familiar, but I can't rightly say where.'

'I know Jamie – Sir James – but I've not been this way for some time. And I best save my name and business for him.' William suspected that his secret would not last much longer, but he would try to keep it for a little time more. Sir James Strickland! The world had changed indeed, and in some ways for the better.

Hobbes took the horses' reins and, with one last suspicious look at Pietro, told the stableboy to see master and man to the door.

The butler was another old family retainer, named Jenkins, even older than Hobbes. William identified himself as a friend of Sir James, lately come from abroad. Jenkins bowed, and peered at him. 'Sir James will greet you anon, good sir,' he said, and withdrew into the hall. The sun had set but the sky was still bright; by comparison the interior was deep in shadows.

Voices came from within – was one Jamie Strickland's? Then came another voice, a woman's, young and lively, also with a familiar ring. 'Best you come, Jamie,' the voice sang out. 'A gentleman to see you. Like as not another foreign devil, but— God's teeth! Jamie! Come here!'

Now William placed her voice exactly: Mistress Margaret Shipley, the first girl he had ever kissed, not long before the final time he set sail for the Middle Sea. She came into the light. The Meg Shipley he remembered had been a scrappy hoyden who had the use of her fists, handy too with a skiff; pleasing to hold all the same. Ten years had transformed her, magnificently so: she was clad in sober black, but God could be well pleased with His handiwork. She was a well-shaped Halverstrand woman, descended like William himself from Halfor Broadaxe's Northmen. William had only a moment to stare before she threw arms around him and drew him into the hall.

'Lud's blood,' said Jamie Strickland's voice behind her. 'It's the earl's prodigal son! What in the Devil's name are you doing here?'

A joyous confusion followed, along with more

questions than could be answered in a week. Presently chaos was brought to order, chiefly by Meg's doing: she ordered meat and wine set out at once, and had even the presence of mind to dispatch Pietro – foreign devil though he might be – to the kitchen, with orders to give him food and drink as well. Mistress Meg Shipley, as William recalled, had always had good sense.

He soon learned that she was Meg Shipley no longer, but Margaret Lady Hollingsworth – and a widow. Jamie told the tale while she was seeing to the refreshments. 'Lord Hollingsworth,' said Jamie, 'good Halverstrand man that he was, made trading voyages to Tearnac. He was in the Karnow Channel, coming back from Eniskillen, when pirates set on him. He gave them a stiff fight, and his men drove them off, but a cutlass thrust did for him.'

Lady Margaret returned with pots of hopped beer. 'Talking about me behind my back!' she said. 'You men wear such guilty expressions, just like dogs. That's why you durst not let women serve on juries: we'd hang the lot of you for your misdeeds.' She set down the pots, and took a goodly draught from her own. 'Sir James here – an honest man, as men go – has offered to make this fine house my own. But I've too much liking for my widow's freedom, high though the price be I paid for it.'

'I fear I'll not be staying,' William said. 'Not as long as I would like, not yet.'

'That oath you swore your father?' asked Meg.

'Aye,' said William. 'A witless boy's oath, but my father will have it kept. In Sicania and Enotria they'll break a score of oaths before they break their morning fast, and a hundred more before supper. But that's not the old devil's way.'

Jamie Strickland nodded. 'I feared as much,' he said, 'but you have the right of it. None dares speak your name in his hearing, Will. Not even your lady mother. We've spoken your name often enough out of his hearing. I know you must go, but I'd be a liar not to say we could use your service in these waters. Are you off again to the Middle Sea?'

'Not so far,' said William. 'To the Free Estates – so I'll be in these waters, even if for now I can but rarely set foot in Lyonesse. Jamie, your man Hobbes said you're only just back from Kelliwick. God save the King – but does the Privy Council show any stirring of life?'

'Little enough,' said Sir James. 'They mumble and turn the other way in their beds. I did get them to issue letters of reprisal. Privateers won't restore Richborough, but we can take some prizes to remind the Aquitainers we are here.'

William looked at Sir James Strickland over his pot of beer. 'Well done!' he said. Nothing, he thought, would win back Richborough – not when Charles of Aquitaine had thirty thousand men under arms – yet something indeed should remind the Aquitaine that while the lion of the sea might slumber, it still had teeth and claws.

Sir James hoisted his pot. 'To King Edmund, and Lyonesse!' William and Meg raised their own pots, and all three drank to their old and feeble king, and their distracted kingdom.

Then Margaret Lady Hollingsworth raised her pot again. 'And to the Lady Katrin, Princess Lyon!' she said.

A woman, a child and half a foreigner! thought William. Yet the heiress to the throne had bearded the King of Aquitaine in his own hall. That was more than he, or any lord, knight, or captain of Lyonesse had done. He raised his pot. 'To the Princess Katrin,' he said, and drained it dry.

CHAPTER SEVEN

An Essay on Jovinian

Armand de Fossier, courtier, diarist, admitted dilettante at *belles-lettres*, looked up from his essay on the *Annales* of Jovinian. From his window he could look over rooftops of this dull (but affordable) quarter to behold, half a mile distant, the centre of the Universe. Magnificent by day, with evening the Palais de la Trémouille came truly into its own: a great glittering lantern, shining through a hundred windows with the light of ten thousand candles. The Court was again in residence, returned from his Majesty's progress through the west – a journey Armand's sinecure in the treasury had allowed him to avoid – and not yet departed for its winter quarters at Montmorency, which he would not be able to avoid.

If anything the palace was more brilliant than usual tonight. Tonight was a feast and ball, and Armand knew he should not waste it scribbling. Too much absence might lose him favour with the delectable Estelle de Grinaud. His tastes, unlike the King's, did not run to young demoiselles; their much-praised freshness was a euphemism for clumsiness. Armand preferred women of experience and sophistication, like Mme de Grinaud. Every rule has exceptions, however, and his had been Solange de Charleville.

She had first come to him for advice in her studies; matters had proceeded from there and Armand found himself smiling. No tutor ever had so delightful a pupil, even if lessons tended to end amid scattered clothing. She was an apt pupil as well – this very essay, on the celebrated rivalry of the empress Servilia and her daughter Constantia, was sparked by Solange's insight: worldly Servilia and virtuous Constantia had quarrelled not because they were so different, but because they were so much alike. Alas, now Solange was in the grim old Hôtel de Guienne, and might as well be half a world away. He would have to settle for Estelle de Grinaud.

Downstairs he heard the housekeeper expostulating, then footfalls on the stair: no courier from M. de Chirac, but a woman's light tread. Had Estelle left the palace to call on him? The thought was too flattering to be plausible, yet who else could it be? A knock on his door, he bade her enter – and stared with amazement. 'Mademoiselle de Charleville!' he exclaimed. Her cloak was thrown back, revealing the same black and crimson gown she'd worn on the day of her mistress's departure. Armand rose and bowed; she curtseyed, and he admired what the gown displayed.

'Monsieur de Fossier! I find you at home, as I hoped.' Solange's great dark eyes regarded him under long lashes, then glanced out towards the great glow of the palace. 'Had I come all this way and found you gone, I would have been vexed!'

'I would have been vexed,' Armand replied, 'had I gone and missed you.'

'Then you considered it!' Solange laughed. 'Like all men you are false! What are you writing?'

'An essay on Servilia and Constantia, in fact, as you brought them to my attention.' Armand gathered up the sheets and handed them to her. Solange was wearing the bracelet he'd sent her during the royal progress. She had sent a reply from Richebourg, thanking him with sentiments so warm he'd been forced to seek out Mme de Grinaud – surely not the girl's intent. She sat on his bedside, reading.

'Perhaps,' said Armand, 'I should be writing instead of the new alliance between Princess Catherine and la Fontenelle. The entire Court is surprised!'

Solange looked up. 'Princess Catherine is surprised!' she said. 'I fear Madame Corisande must be worse than surprised, but it is policy and nothing more. His Majesty might wish for a mistress who looked out for his interests!'

'Do you plan to offer yourself?' asked Armand. 'I should regret that!' He sat on the bed behind her.

'I look out for Princess Catherine's interests,' said Solange. She smiled over her shoulder. 'Sometimes I look out for my own interests – which might be yours as well. But not if you hold me in your arms and wish I were Madame de Grinaud!'

'I shall hold you in my arms and wish you were *you*!' said Armand, undoing a lacing and slipping her bodice from her shoulders . . .

Dawn was already hinting in the east when Solange, riding pillion behind M. de Fossier, reached the corner by the postern door of the Hôtel de Guienne. A sharp chill hung in the night air, and she pulled her cloak tightly around her. She hated leaving the warmth of Armand's bed at this wretched hour, but there was no avoiding it. Under Mademoiselle's rule, the Hôtel de Guienne came to life with the sun. Armand dismounted, helped her down and embraced her. They kissed, then kissed again. 'You must go now,' Solange told him. 'I shall come again when I can!'

'Shall I not see you safely in?' protested Armand.

Solange shook her head. 'It is only a few doors,' she told him, 'and two are more easily noticed than one!'

'As Mademoiselle wishes,' said Armand reluctantly. He bowed, Solange curtseyed, then he mounted up and retreated into the darkness. Solange slipped into darker shadow, and waited until the clop of hooves faded away. Then she stole along the deep shadowed alley that led to the river, descended a stair on the embankment and slipped into an arched tunnel.

It was Madeleine who had discovered the ancient

water gate, buried under the embankment. A sub-terranean stream, rather a sewer, flowed from the tunnel; to one side was a raised walk, just wide enough to be safe. Sadly, however, it gave no protection against odour, and by night the interior of the tunnel was black as the heart of sin.

With slow, careful steps Solange made her way, count-ing but one pace for each two she took. Five . . . six . . . seven . . . surely the most evil denizens of the city made their home in this tunnel. Twelve . . . thirteen . . . four-teen . . . she would be raped, murdered and flung into the water, her fate never to be known . . . twenty-three . . . twenty-four . . . twenty-five . . .

All at once the wall cut away, so that she almost stum-bled against the ancient iron strapped door. And – *grâce de Dieu!* – around the edge was a faint crack of light. Solange sighed with relief, then breathed deeply, heed-less of the stench. She gave the prearranged signal: two knocks, a pause, then three, then four. A bolt scraped, and the door swung open. Behind stood Madeleine, lantern in hand, and at that moment Solange would rather have seen her than a hundred lovers. 'Madeleine!' she exclaimed. 'By all the saints, I am so glad to see—'

Something in Madeleine's expression made her fall silent. Behind her were two other half-shadowed figures: her Ladyship, and Princess Catherine.

'Where have you been, Mademoiselle de Charleville?'

asked Catherine. She tried to keep her voice as judge-like as possible, betraying neither her anger at this betrayal of her trust, nor her anxiety at what it might imply.

'I – I could not sleep, Mademoiselle—'

'You may address me as "Altesse",' snapped Catherine. Not since the day they entered her service had she made her ladies address her as Highness.

With less than her usual grace, Solange curtseyed. 'Yes, Altesse.' The light of the lantern showed tears glistening in the girl's eyes.

'You could not sleep!' repeated Catherine. 'Instead of rising to walk in the courtyard, you went by this hidden way to the river? With Madeleine to wait for you? Close and bolt the door, Madeleine – we've stench enough here within, without enduring that without!' Madeleine hastened to obey. 'I know you for a very good liar, Solange de Charleville,' continued Catherine. 'Is my honour not even worth a convincing tale? Where have you been – and with whom?' She awaited no answer. 'A fine lot, the both of you! What will the world say of me, that I permit such comings and goings at every hour of night? As the servants, so the mistress!' she cried. 'That is what the world will say!' Tears welled in her eyes at the thought. 'What have I done to you, that you should thus expose me to calumny? Have I used you unjustly? Have I treated you as scullery maids, and not as befits your rank?'

Solange went to her knees. 'The fault is altogether mine, Altesse!' she cried. 'I swear before God that Madeleine had no part in it – she but waited by this door, as I bade her, telling her nothing of my errand! Send me back to Charleville, to my father, if you wish, but spare—'

'She is lying!' interrupted Madeleine hotly. 'I found the old water gate, and showed her the way, and arranged everything, that I might in my turn—'

'That is not so!' cried Solange. 'Madeleine tried to dissuade me but I—' She threw her arms around Catherine's legs. 'I beg you—!'

'Silence!' ordered Catherine. She wrenched herself back, and Solange fell weeping on the clammy stone floor. 'To the chapel, both of you! I shall summon you presently to pass judgement on your offences!'

'Your Ladyship!' Catherine said when she and Lady Lindley were alone. 'What am I to do?'

'That I cannot tell you, Kateryn,' said her Ladyship. 'You are mistress of this hall, as by God's grace you shall one day be in Lyonesse. Will you beg your councillors tell you what to do?'

'Shall I not seek good counsel?'

'Yes,' said Lady Lindley. 'A wise prince, or princess, always seeks counsel. Yet the Princess must know her own thoughts first, so she can weigh the counsel she receives.'

'I think I have been ill used by mine own,' said

Catherine, 'whom I thought loyal! You know what is said of me! That I will work my own ruin soon enough, and save my enemies the trouble.'

'And how do you know that, Kateryn?'

'Why, Solange herself told me!'

The Hôtel de Guienne outwardly resembled a prison, but Solange had been first to discover that its keys conveyed nearly total freedom. The great officers appointed to rule her household – the Secretary of State, the Treasurer, the Comptroller – were drawn from M. de Chirac's chief personal servants, who Catherine knew well: all exceedingly busy men. They had no wish to ride across to the South Bank to supervise a demoiselle's household. Thus, as Madeleine governed the Hôtel de Guienne's servants, Solange tended the business of the household, meeting with advocates at law and keepers of accounts, looking like some great married lady whose name drew no smirks at Court. Afterwards she would report to Catherine, relating also every rumour current in the city.

'Does that not make it worse?' she asked. 'Knowing as she does how it stands with me, does Solange have a care, if not for her own repute, then for me?' Tears welled in her eyes. 'She – both of them – have made one more tale against me! God's mercy, your Ladyship, I have done nothing, yet all the world shall think me like Solange, rolling around on some man's bed!' The image of the Dauphin came to Catherine unbidden: their kiss in the garden, his arms about her waist – what would he think of her now? 'By Wott,' she cried, 'were I this day already Queen, Solange should answer with her head, and have no more pleasuring from anyone!'

Her Ladyship raised an eyebrow. 'Ah!' she said. 'Is that not the heart of the matter? That Solange de Charleville, daughter of an impoverished count, may disport herself, while Kateryn de Guienne, heiress to a kingdom, must not? Yet if you would live among saints, you should have remained with the sisters at Ste-Lucie. You'll find none in any royal court! All you can ask is discretion – and I shall say plainly, your Highness, that Lady Solange was discreet for one of her years.' She laughed. 'None should know of her adventure, save that you awoke in the night, called for your ladies and found them not at hand. She and Madeleine had not planned for that!'

Catherine had not expected her Ladyship to speak in defence of her ladies. She remembered a question she could not answer with certainty, but that Lady Lindley undoubtedly could. 'Your Ladyship,' she asked hesitantly. 'Did my lord father keep a mistress?'

'Princess Kateryn!' Lady Lindley frowned. 'What makes you ask such a question?'

'Margot asked me when we were at Montpassier. She warned me that when I am married, my ladies will think to . . . to be swived by my husband.' Catherine flushed. 'Margot knows all about *that*, at least!'

'Well!' exclaimed Lady Lindley. 'So *that* is why you have been sharp with your ladies since we came back from Montpassier! What Margot knows is that both are more charming than she is, and at least as pretty. She has small concern for any husband's fidelity, but much fear that King Charles might recall you and your ladies to Court, and his eye fall upon one of them!' She paused. 'As for your question, Kateryn, your father kept no mistress. Why would he? You remember too well your mother's sorrow at the end, but she was right merry with your father. Few men stray from a wife who makes them laugh!'

Catherine sat silent for some time, then summoned her ladies. They came in wearing sober expressions, unadorned with jewellery, hair modestly covered. Solange was dressed as for her occasions of business, turned out as precisely as an empress, hair neatly covered by a chastely fashionable headdress and veil. Both girls knelt, and Catherine bade them rise. 'Solange de Charleville and Madeleine du Lac de Montpellier,' she declared, 'you have the both of you done great foolishness! Have you any excuses to offer?'

'None,' said Solange.

'No,' said Madeleine.

'Very well. Solange, do you swear before God that this was your doing? That Mademoiselle du Lac had no part in it save to wait for you beside the water-gate door?'

'I alone am at fault, Altesse,' she answered softly.

'Madeleine sought to dissuade me, and only when pressed did she consent to—'

'Enough!' Catherine turned her gaze on Madeleine. 'Madeleine, did you discover this door, and contrive the means of Mademoiselle de Charleville's escapade, thinking to avail yourself of the same in future?'

'I – I was a coward, Madem— Altesse. Knowing that Solange . . . no, no, I – I told Solange of the door only after making her swear that she would – that she would go first.'

In spite of the solemn occasion, Catherine burst out laughing. 'Madeleine, how could you be raised at la Trémouille, and learn so little of the art of lying?' With some effort Catherine forced a sober expression. 'This is a great wonder! Each of you bears the chief guilt, the other being but her unwilling confederate. And this from two demoiselles who, when first you came into my household, could scarcely bear the sight of one another! Very well,' she continued. 'As you each claim the greater guilt, you must bear the same punishment. From now until Advent you shall each sup by evening upon nothing other than bread and water, and each night go for an hour to pray in the chapel. Of what use to your immortal souls, I know not – but with the work that I shall require of you, you'll have less time for mischief. You are dismissed. Attend your duties!'

Solange and Madeleine curtseyed low together, and retreated towards the door.

'Wait!' said Catherine. 'One other matter. If either of you ever uses the water gate again, other than by my leave and command, I shall truly dismiss you from my household! Speak of it to no one! A hidden postern is to be cherished against great need – it must be kept our secret! Madeleine, see that barrels and other stores are so placed as to hide it.'

Madeleine nodded. 'Yes, Altesse.'

'"Mademoiselle" will do,' said Catherine.

'Light, ho! Five points off the starboard bow!' The look-out's cry was a sharp whisper. In the night and mist and silence, otherwise broken only by the soft pad of bare feet on the deck and the slap of water against the *Dawn Thief*'s hull, it was startling as a shout. William de Havilland stared into the darkness in the indicated direction and saw nothing. Somewhere off in the black mist, a league away, lay the coast of the Aquitaine and the old port town of Caramec in the Duchy of Ys. There, before night ended, he would by Heaven's grace exact the first repayment for the fall of Richborough.

A low lying star winked into being, shone dimly for a few heartbeats and vanished again. 'There's our man,' whispered Arthur Ridley, sailing master of the *Dawn Thief*, pinnace.

'Aye,' agreed William. Or our trouble, he thought. 'Show our light, and have the rowers pull us bow on to him. Order all hands to stand ready.' The word was passed, the lantern cover was raised, and for a few moments light poured out. It illuminated the deck and lower rigging of the pinnace: her half-raised forecastle and short poop; the oarsmen on the mid deck, a single file to each side, tugging at the looms of their oars. In their midst gleamed the long bronze barrels of two sakers, taking up between them a third of the deck space. Another, firing over the bow, was hidden among the shadows of the forecastle.

Three great-guns on carriages and a dozen murdering pieces on stocks: the *Dawn Thief* was not a large hunter – seventy-five tons and as many feet stem to stern – but she bore formidable teeth. The guns were reassurance, and William was glad of it. He did not like waiting; he never did. He found it too easy to imagine that the light was not the returning longboat with his own men but an oncoming galley of Aquitaine, ready to discharge her bow gun into his men as her iron-shod spur crashed through the *Dawn Thief*'s bulwarks. Then would come the lash of crossbow bolts, and finally cold steel from a hundred Aquitanian boarders . . .

A minute later the longboat scraped softly alongside and tied up. Two figures swung up over the rail. 'My Lord!' Sir James Strickland jogged aft and up to the poop, and saluted. 'Away and clear, and no trouble.'

William nodded. 'A good piece of work, Jamie. What lies in the port?'

'Two of those small galleys – foysts?'

William laughed. 'I'll have no Gallic, Jamie. *Fuste.* To be a proper galley man, let the Enotrian roll off your tongue.'

'Give me a tall ship with good archers and great-guns, my lord, and I'll answer a dozen galleys in honest Saxon.'

'Till the wind dies or turns. Then you'd have to stand and watch them do what they will. But enough of that – what of the *fuste?*'

'One tied up to the quay by the custom house, armed and fitted out. Her crew is quartered in the town, and the oarsmen kept in the gaol. How fit to row they are, you'll know better than I. The other one is drawn up ashore, with her gear in the harbourmaster's warehouse. They'll be a day at least fitting her out before she can give battle. There's also a merchanter carrack, anchored in the fairway. She's Theudish built and manned, but an Aquitanian merchant owns her, so she's a fit prize. She has a hundred men, but half are ashore drinking and swiving, and the rest sleeping it off. She carries a cargo of wine from Citti, in the Middle Sea.'

'*That* will quench many a thirst in Halverstrand town!'

'There's more, my lord—' Strickland's voice was so serious it was almost sombre. 'Let Master Rhyse tell you himself. He did the speaking to the townfolk.'

'Aye.' William turned to the other man who had climbed aboard from the longboat, a smaller, slighter figure than Jamie Strickland. 'Go on.'

'Now, your Lordship—' Master Rhyse spoke swiftly. He was from the west country, and had the lilting accent of one whose mother speech was not Saxon – it was for precisely that reason that William had sent him into the town. The forebears of the townspeople, and across the Duchy of Ys, had long ago passed across the Narrow Sea from Lyonesse. The native speech of Ys, like the country dialects of Lyonesse beyond the Saxon Pale, was an off-spring of the ancient Tongue Bardic.

Master Rhyse's speech was sometimes hard to follow, but his meaning was clear enough, and when he was done, William let out a whistle. Waiting in Caramec was a prize he had not looked for. 'Lud's luck! A hundred and fifty thousand pieces of gold! Seventy-five thousand pounds. In the cellars of the Farmer-General's house, you say?' Rhyse nodded.

'You'll risk it?' asked Sir James.

'I'd be a fool not to,' replied William. 'We have till midday at the least, and gold speaks a language even our lords Privy Councillors can understand. Not to mention Charles of Aquitaine.' The Farmer-General was the entrepreneur who served as the King of Aquitaine's tax-gatherer for all the Duchy of Ys: the most hated man in the duchy. William had meant to rob his fortified house – but had not expected that its strong-rooms would be overflowing with a year's worth of taxes, collected but not yet forwarded to Aix-le-Siège.

William knew what sort of guards a tax–gatherer

would hire: sufficient against common robbers, perhaps, or angry townspeople, but not such as would stand up to a landing force of determined men who knew the use of arms. He stood silently for a while, picturing the port of Caramec in his mind, working out how to deal with this new situation. He briefly sketched out his plans to Sir James. 'Now back in the boat, Jamie,' he said. 'Row around and bespeak the other captains. If any object, press 'em. We've no time for a Council of War, but must take the tide or lose it.'

The minutes dragged long after the boat pulled away towards the other ships of the flotilla. Presently it returned, lying to under the *Dawn Thief*'s stern. 'All say "aye", my lord,' Sir James called out softly.

'Like true Halverstranders,' answered William. 'I reckoned on no less. We'll tie you up to our taffrail and tow you in.' He turned. 'Master Ridley! Pass the boat a line, and show the light astern! Get the leadsman into the forechains, then make sail, fores'l and mizzen!'

'Aye, milord!'

Sharply whispered orders were followed by sounds cacophonous after the silence of the misty night: feet slapping on the deck, the thump of oars being shipped, the creak of rope and flap of canvas. Then came the soft boom of sails filling and bellying in the breeze. The *Dawn Thief* heeled slightly, and the sea gurgled around her bow and hissed past her rudder as she picked up way. 'By the deep eight!' came the cry of the leadsman forward as he cast his lead and found the sandy bottom. Behind them, invisibly, the rest of the flotilla was getting underway.

William stood at the break of the poop, looking forward across the main deck, hands behind his back, his right leg slightly bent to meet the heel of the ship. The danger ahead was twice what he had anticipated, but the reward vastly greater still. How that devil Antoine de Chirac will howl, he thought, when he learns that he's been robbed!

Advent had come and gone, and Christmastide and Twelfth Night. Revelries were ended, and the streets of Aix-le-Siège were swept with cold rain and bitter winds. Sensible folk stayed inside by their fires, if they could. The students of the University were not sensible, thought Catherine as she stood at the arched entry to her chambers, looking over the throng gathered in the Great Hall. She had hit on Sunday evening scholars' disputations as an entertainment more respectable than stage-plays, and the University was after all on the South Bank. A mere couple of dozen scholars and students had come to the first, but their numbers had grown quickly; tonight two or three hundred filled the hall.

Perhaps they could not afford fires to warm their garrets, and preferred to trudge through the streets for the warmth from the fire that blazed in the Great Hall. Or – since only a lucky few could find places near the fire – they came for the warmth of their own numbers, and the hot mulled wine and fresh loaves that were set out.

The disputants were at the lecterns flanking the High Table, ready to debate whether classes were entities in themselves, or only a form of words that men imposed upon created things. Catherine was about to signal the under steward to ring the bell when she sensed a sharper excitement roiling through the Great Hall. She thought she caught the words *Lyonessans* and *goddams.* Presently Solange appeared, working her way through the crowd, a cloaked and booted figure in tow. He was a late arrival; fresh mud still clung to his boots, not yet tracked off onto the rushes that covered the floor.

'Altesse,' declared Solange, 'this is Laurent de Tremarais. He bears news you may wish to hear.'

The young man studied Catherine frankly. 'You are the Princess Lyonne?' he asked. Catherine nodded. He bowed slightly; she sensed a youth accustomed to bowing before no one. 'I live in the Charenne quarter,' he said. 'As I was crossing the Pont Lagrange, a horseman rode past, crying out news from the West.'

A tingle ran up Catherine's spine, and her heart began to pound. Was her grandfather dead? Was she now . . . ? At once she dismissed the thought. Surely such news would not be brought by a student. In her excitement she missed his first few words.

'. . . at Caramec in Ys,' he was saying, 'defeated the

205

garrison there, and took the place. The Maréchal de Lanier has been commanded to raise an army to march on the town in case les goddams' – Laurent de Tremarais halted, and smiled wryly – 'you will forgive me, les Lyonessans – seek to advance.'

Goddams, indeed! thought Catherine proudly. She made him repeat all he had heard. 'You are certain of this, Monsieur de Tremarais?' she asked.

The young man smiled again. 'I can be certain, Altesse, only of what I heard. To launch a campaign in the dead of winter would be great folly!'

Catherine smiled back at him. 'Monsieur surely knows much more of war than I do, who am but a demoiselle. Yet great folly indeed to take a walled town, no?'

De Tremarais laughed aloud, then bowed again, more deeply. He rose and looked her straight in the eye. 'The Princess, I believe, has it in her power to make men foolish.'

Presumptuous! thought Catherine, blushing. She turned to Solange. 'See that this good gentleman receives a livre for his news. And let him be seated between yourself and Mademoiselle du Lac, where he can meditate upon folly!' She gestured to the under steward to ring the bell, and hastened to take her own place at the centre of the High Table.

The bell rang out and the Great Hall fell into greater silence than usual for this throng. There was no sound but the slight shuffling of feet and the crackling of the fire. Catherine stood behind her chair. At her right hand was her Ladyship – who had not yet heard the news. At her left sat Solange and Madeleine, with the hapless or fortunate Laurent de Tremarais between them. Catherine glanced up at the hammer beam roof of the Great Hall, and the stained-glass windows below it, then, looking across the gathered throng, she took a deep breath.

'I bade you all come here,' she said, 'to hear the disputation of learned men, the common property of all Christendom. We are all brothers and sisters; there should be amity among us. Yet I am a daughter of Lyonesse, and do not love my country less than you who are of l'Aquitaine love your own!' The silence of the hall grew even deeper, so that Catherine heard only the roar of the fire and the pounding of her heart. 'I speak not in boastfulness, but only to say what has come to pass. Mariners of my country have landed in arms and raised the Croix St-Pélage over the city of Caramec in Ys.' She shifted to her native tongue. 'God save King Edmund!' From the corner of her eye, Catherine saw her Ladyship bow her head.

'That is all I have to say,' Catherine concluded. 'Let the disputation begin.' Slowly the murmur of conversation returned to the hall, an uneasy murmur, receding only when the disputants began their Latin arguments. In spite of the heat of fire, wine and the press of bodies, something of the chill without had entered into the Great Hall and Catherine wondered briefly if she had spoken over hastily. No unease betrayed itself in her Ladyship's visage; she listened as intently to the disputants as if she could follow them, though she had scarcely any Latin. Catherine set aside her own doubts and offered instead a silent prayer, in humble thanks that she had been permitted to proclaim in this hall, for the first time in generations, a victory for the arms of Lyonesse.

Three weeks later, word reached Aix-le-Siège that sea rovers had descended again, raiding the town of Louselles. It did not fall such easy prey as Caramec; the defenders fought bravely. Yet fall it did. Great-guns aboard the ships pounded down the harbour wall, and the breach was forced. The following day a royal proclamation was read and posted. For the defence of the realm against the cruel depredations of the pirates, the tax upon wine was increased by one tournois per barrel, and a new tax of three liards was imposed on every hundredweight of fire-wood brought into the city gates.

Lady Jane Gower, Countess of Lindley, looked up from her needlework at Princess Catherine, who sat reading across from her. She'd never known a maid to read so. In her day ladies read only their *Book of Hours*, as Mistress Madeleine had good sense to do. Now the world had a multitude of new follies – Lady Solange was off seeking out the wise-woman she claimed could read the future in cards!

Lady Jane had herself once sought out a wise-woman, who had filled a bronze bowl with water, sprinkled incense over it and wailed hair-raising things in the Tongue Bardic. The dark little woman had said she would have a happy marriage and long life, and so she had. The prophecy had not mentioned her children's deaths, or that Earl Thomas too would die before his time, struck down while pursuing robbers. Jane Gower sighed. Wise-women were not to be relied on. Princess Catherine looked up from her reading. She had heard the sigh. 'Your Ladyship?'

Lady Jane smiled. Regrets were vain; better to number her blessings. ''Tis nothing, Kateryn,' she said. She switched to Gallic for the sake of Mistress Madeleine, who sat at Catherine's feet playing with Asterion and Chara, Catherine's two wolfhound pups. 'I was merely thinking of how foolish wise-women can be.'

'Mère Angelique? That is nothing – if it amuses Solange, I'll hear her out,' said Catherine, 'though I needn't believe her!'

Madeleine glanced up. 'Solange will believe anything, if you say it with long words. Though this Mère Angelique must be persuasive – Solange usually prefers her follies in male form.' Asterion barked agreement.

'Did I not see you,' Catherine said, 'studying Latin with Monsieur de Tremarais on Sunday last?'

'I do what I must!' said Madeleine. 'God knows when I'll see the Chevalier de Batz-Castelmore again. The King will never recall the garrisons now; your grandfather's pirates – mariners – have seen to that! Surely Batz-Castelmore will meet some provincial baron's daughter, and that shall be the end of him. I wish him the best!' She tossed her golden hair, which proved to be a mistake. 'Chara, no!' she cried at the pup. 'My hair is not a toy!'

Lady Jane laughed. Batz-Castelmore's loss was Laurent de Tremarais' gain. But mention of the sea-raids put her in mind of something weighing on her. 'I think it best to consider, Kateryn,' she said, 'whether you should be flying the Cross of St Pelagius over the tower. It does my old heart good to see it, but have a care. The King of Aquitaine is ill-pleased. It affronts his dignity.'

'And what of the affront he gave to my grandfather?' demanded Catherine. 'Let Charles of Aquitaine restore Richborough, and he'll have no trouble from me!'

'It is not only King Charles you must think of, Kateryn,' said Lady Jane. 'The people of Aix-le-Siège will shed false tears for Caramec or Louselles – they despise provincials – but their tears will be true and bitter for those new taxes to fund the defences. Apprentices will be reminded every time they go into a tavern for a cup. When they come reeling back into the street, and look up to see the Cross of St Pelly . . .'

Princess Catherine closed her book. 'I do not fear

drunken apprentices, your Ladyship! If common ship-men can brave winter tempests to take fortresses for Grandfather's honour, shall I meekly hide who I am?'

Her father's daughter! Lady Jane smiled in spite of herself. 'None doubt your courage, Kateryn! Yet there is a place for defiance, and for policy and discretion. Let the shipmen give your defiance to King Charles! None will think less of you.'

Catherine turned to her lady-in-waiting. 'Madeleine – go see to the guards and huntsmen, that they know their places if we have trouble.' Madeleine rose, curtseyed and withdrew, followed by the two young hounds.

'Margot came to me to no purpose, your Ladyship,' said Catherine when they were alone. 'And the Duc de Septimanie's allies also court me to no purpose,' she added. 'I have discovered what an ambassador-resident is: a man who lies abroad for his country!'

Lady Jane laughed once again. The King of Aquitaine's mistress had arranged for a series of emissaries to visit the Hôtel de Guienne. Lady Jane had sat in on the conferences. Her grey hair probably made a useful impression (good for something, after all!), but her advice was scarcely needed. Lady Solange was no fool at all – she had the lawyer who managed the household's business attend and speak, so that emissaries would not think themselves dealing only with a young maid, while she herself made notes of all the evasions and meaningless promises offered for the throne of Lyonesse.

'I know it is the fate of princesses to be courted for the cause of state,' said Catherine, 'not for ourselves. But can the ambassadors not keep up a pretence? They want only my grandfather's realm, or at least his ships. They'll not get a one, not from me! As well as our shipmen have set about the Aquitaine, I'll have use for their ships myself!' She sighed. 'Now, if only someone would have a use for *me*.'

'Don't be bemoaning yourself, Kateryn! You may be courted for a crown,' said Lady Jane, 'yet your husband will count himself lucky for winning you.'

Catherine managed a smile. 'Cannot a princess even grumble, your Ladyship? One day I shall have to marry, of course. Yet if I marry one lord, it will ill-please all the others.'

Which was all too true, thought Lady Jane. A princess might grumble: lords did little else. Jane did note that the girl spoke only of marrying a Lyonessan subject – a wise choice, if she kept to it. 'Marrying within the kingdom will please your people,' she said.

'Good!' said Catherine. 'I do not wish to marry any foreign prince!'

You are a liar, Kateryn! thought Lady Jane. I know exactly which foreign prince you would wish to marry should you be free to do so! Princess Catherine never spoke his name – but she didn't need to; her reaction was obvious when her ladies spoke of him. Jane had not yet come up with any clever solution – had not even dared raise it with her young royal charge – for what young maid would *not* wish to marry the Dauphin?

Catherine looked up. 'I shall weigh your words touching the flag,' she said. 'If it is better policy I'll not hoist it tomorrow – but by Wott, I hope the shipmen will go on flying it if I cannot!'

'Now *that*,' said Jane, 'is the Kateryn I am accustomed to hearing.'

CHAPTER EIGHT

A Riot in the Rue Frontenac

Catherine was still considering all that her Ladyship said when the door flew open. In burst Madeleine and Solange. 'Mademoiselle—' gasped Solange. Her head-dress was awry, and her gown clung to her with perspiration.

Madeleine held her hunting crossbow. 'A crowd is gathering in the street, Mademoiselle,' she said briskly. 'I commanded the bailiff to make fast the gate. Solange got in through the postern.'

Solange had caught her breath. 'I rode as fast as I could, Mademoiselle. Mère Angelique would not come – she begged me stay with her, but I would not.'

'Your wise-woman does well,' muttered Catherine, 'to prophesy what has already come to pass. Her Ladyship said as much, and needed no devilries!'

Solange ignored her. 'Mère Angelique called this the first trial of many. She said that you may one day be instructed by a very good geometer – and that two of the bravest knights in Christendom shall do battle over you.'

'Not without my leave they won't!' retorted

Catherine. She went out to a balcony over the courtyard. Sounds of disorder floated from the street beyond and the townspeople who dwelt in the Hôtel de Guienne stood below in tight clusters. At the sight of her one man stepped forward, a draper named Renaud.

'Altesse!' he cried. 'What are we to do? The people cry out against taxes, and hold your grandfather to blame! We have done nothing, but now the gate is closed and we are trapped here!'

'My daughter is out there!' wailed a woman. 'She went to buy eggs! For the love of God, Altesse, what is to become of her?'

Catherine's stomach muscles tightened. The girl was about her own age. Surely she'd have the sense to stay away from a riot . . . but if she didn't? What could a washerwoman's daughter know of the enmity of kings? Suddenly terrified, she raised her hands. 'Listen to me, all of you!' The people in the courtyard fell silent, which only made the riot outside sound louder. 'You are all under the protection of two kings,' she cried. 'King Edmund and Charles of Aquitaine. I swear before God that anyone who would hurt you must strike me first, and answer with his life! This is only boisterous apprentices and boys,' she added, praying to God and St Pelagius that she was right, 'and will end directly the gens d'armes arrive!'

Some tautness went out of the crowd, and Catherine slipped back into the gallery, then went on, Madeleine leading the way, up a winding stair to the guardroom over the gate, a large chamber of rough stone with a low vaulted ceiling. Racks for arms lined the walls, but filling most of the chamber was a massive contrivance of wheels, pulleys and chains. Though clean and free of cobwebs, all was old and worn, unused for many years. Catherine recognized it as something she had read about but never seen: an engine for raising and lowering a portcullis – she'd never known the Hôtel de Guienne even had such a thing.

'I had the bailiff test it last autumn,' said Madeleine. 'It does not work.'

'Why did you not repair it?' snapped Catherine. At once she regretted her words. How many maidens would have thought to test a portcullis?

Madeleine looked down. 'Forgive me, Mademoiselle.'

Catherine put her hand to Madeleine's chin and raised it. 'You did nobly!' she said. 'I should have seen to our defences! Yet the gate is stout enough – it should hold against a few drunken apprentices.' She stepped to the slit window and peered down into the rue Frontenac. 'God help us all!' she whispered. She'd expected to see a few dozen apprentices and boys. Instead the street was packed with humanity.

A man in labourer's garb climbed onto a cart. 'Listen to me!' he cried, his voice cutting through the sounds of the throng. Heads turned towards him. 'Are we not taxed for firewood in the cold of winter?' Assent rippled through the crowd. 'A tournois for wine! Three liards for firewood! We are poor! Yet the royal brat of Lyonesse lies at ease within this fine palace! Where is justice?' The answer of the crowd was louder and angrier. 'Where is justice, that the child of the raping goddams should have her fire, and her wine, and servants to answer her every whim, while the widows and innocent babes of Louselles starve? While you – every one of you – bears the burden of her keep? Where, I ask you, where is justice?'

Catherine was nearly caught up in the oratory, then realized the man was speaking of her. Flushing with anger, she pressed her head into the slit. 'Send me back to my country,' she cried out, 'and I'll trouble you no more! I never asked to be here!' She thought her voice lost in the uproar, but an instant later the speaker raised his arm in accusation, and a thousand eyes turned on her.

'Kateryn!' snapped her Ladyship. A man let fly, and something clacked sharply against the wall. Catherine backed hastily away and Madeleine pressed in to take her place. 'Mistress Madeleine!' cried her Ladyship, and wrenched the girl bodily aside. Moments later a rock sailed through the opening and ricocheted off the portcullis engine, nearly hitting Solange.

'*Mon Dieu!*' wailed Solange. Wide eyed, she retreated to a back corner.

'Witless girls!' cried her Ladyship. 'Back to your chambers, both of you!' She propelled Madeleine with a firm swat on her backside; Solange needed no encouragement. Then she whirled on Catherine. 'Princess Kateryn! You know better than to bait an unchained bear!'

Tears stung Catherine's eyes. 'Yes, your Ladyship.' Her peril sank in upon her. What if the rioters burst through the gate, stout though it was? Would they tear her limb from limb? She felt dizzy with fear.

Her Ladyship took her hand, and spoke firmly but more gently. 'What is done is done. Come! You must command the bailiff to station the guards with crossbows. This place is strong, but no castle can hold without defenders. They must not shoot unless the rioters try to force entry, but then they must shoot without hesitation. I shall speak to the huntmaster. If a huntsman can get through the postern, we must send word to the Hôtel de Ville for the Provost to send his train band.'

Catherine was still terrified, but her Ladyship's calm words drove her dizziness away. 'Y–yes, your Ladyship. Yet what if the Provost does not? I am his enemy too!'

'Less than rioters in the streets, Kateryn!' Her Ladyship led Catherine by the hand. 'Disorder in a crowded city is like fire – once taken hold it will spread as the wind carries it. No governor dares abide that! What if the mob should turn against King Charles next?

Now go! And remember, the guards must not shoot unless rioters are forcing the gate!'

'Yes, your Ladyship!' Catherine picked up her skirts and ran along the gallery. She went first to her chambers, to have her ladies attend her. She found them amid chaos and adding to it – Madeleine had clothing chests open, pulling out garments, most of which she flung on the bed; a few she tossed into a smaller chest. Solange was rifling through Catherine's jewellery.

'What are you doing?' demanded Catherine.

Solange swept rings and bracelets into a casket. 'Gathering your best things, Mademoiselle, for escape through the water gate.'

The water gate! Since Solange's escapade, the ancient gate had been hidden behind stacked casks and Catherine had wholly forgotten about it. They were not trapped here, after all! She felt as giddy with relief as she had with fear. Yet now that escape beckoned, she could not go that way, not yet. 'Leave off,' she ordered her ladies. 'I shall clear the water gate for the servants and in-dwellers, but I will not flee save in extremity. Now come!' Her ladies glanced at one another, then followed her out.

The bailiff was in the Great Hall, amid servants he was making no effort to command. He fairly threw himself at her feet. 'Altesse!' he cried. 'They are mad in the street! Mad! Why has the Prevôt not sent soldiers?'

'A messenger has been sent to the Hôtel de Ville,'

Catherine told him. She wondered if a huntsman had got out. If not, one could be sent by the water gate. 'For now we must see to ourselves. Where is the guard captain?' The bailiff only stared at her. 'Send for him!' snapped Catherine. 'Now! And where is the steward?'

'He – I think he is in the courtyard, Altesse.'

The bailiff was useless in this crisis. Catherine hastened to the courtyard and found the steward at the well. Two husky servants heaved furiously on the windlass; as the bucket came up, two more seized it and tipped it into a barrel. Seeing her, the steward pointed to the barrel. He did not bow, nor address her as 'Altesse'. 'We must have water at hand,' he said, 'lest fire be attempted against us.'

The plain-spoken competence of the steward was as inspiring as the bailiff's helplessness had been unnerving. 'Very good!' Catherine said. 'But you must— no, carry on!' She had thought to have him clear the water gate, but he was making good use of his men, as the bailiff was not. She hastened back into the Great Hall.

Nothing had changed within. 'What is to be done?' cried a servant.

'Listen, all of you!' ordered Catherine. 'Go to the cellars with Mademoiselle du Lac and do as she commands.' She beckoned Madeleine. 'Clear all but the last row of barrels,' Catherine whispered, 'but say nothing of the water gate save by my command. Or her Ladyship's. If she sends a huntsman, speed him through!'

Madeleine curtseyed, and with a word to the servants set off towards the cellars. All followed her save the bailiff. 'Altesse! You must—'

'I know what I must do!' snapped Catherine. 'Go with Mademoiselle du Lac, and see her directions are carried out!' For an instant he stared at her, then ran huffing after Madeleine. Attended only by Solange, Catherine found herself alone in the Great Hall awaiting the guard captain. She wished her Ladyship would come and tell her what to do next.

'Mademoiselle?' said Solange.

'What is it?'

'The man who was declaiming against you in the street – what did he look like?'

'What? What does it matter?' Catherine looked sharply at Solange. 'Why? Do you think you know who he is?'

Solange shook her head. 'No. But what manner of man? Well clad, or ill?'

'A big man. He wore a working man's cloth cap. A woodcutter, perhaps – he made a great thing of the tax on firewood.'

'Madeleine says that firewood is a great thing in the cold of winter,' replied Solange. 'But – his words were not those of a simple man, Mademoiselle.'

'What do you mean?'

Solange glanced down. 'I am not certain what I mean, Mademoiselle. But if he is a simple man, he is most bold and well spoken, is he not? Perhaps he is no simple man at all.'

Before Catherine could ponder her meaning the guard captain appeared, a large florid man in red and green livery. His bow was scarcely more than a nod. 'Altesse?'

Catherine swallowed. Commanding men at arms was less simple than commanding servants. 'You must place your men at the gates,' she said. 'They must take station with crossbows, but shoot only if an attempt is made to force entry.'

The guard captain's eyes studied Catherine coolly. 'It is not your place to give commands, Princess. You are here by his Majesty's leave and in his custody. My guards serve his Majesty, not the King of Lyonesse – or his granddaughter.'

His words struck Catherine like a blow. She stared at him, fighting tears. Then with a silent oath to Wott she willed herself to anger. 'If the rabble burst through these gates, Monsieur Capitaine, you will be serving the King of Heaven, else the Prince of Hell.'

The guard captain's eyes shifted uneasily. If a thousand rioters burst in, they would not stop to ask who those within served. 'My men will loose against the King's loyal subjects only if their own lives are in peril.'

'I do not ask them to shoot otherwise.'

'The necessary measures will be taken, Altesse – in his Majesty's name.' The guard captain bowed slightly and jogged off in the direction of the courtyard. Catherine cared not in whose name the orders came, so long as they were given.

Her Ladyship and Madeleine appeared at the same instant, her Ladyship from the courtyard, Madeleine from the stairs to the cellars. 'The rioters have found their way to the postern gate,' her Ladyship said. She took Catherine's hand. 'We must hope the town watch bears word to the Provost, Kateryn,' she added quietly, 'before this becomes more than can be dealt with.'

'There is the water gate, Comtesse,' said Madeleine. 'Mademoiselle commanded that it be cleared and made ready.'

Her Ladyship stared at Madeleine. She gave a sudden snorting laugh. 'God's breath! The water gate!'

'My ladies suggested it,' said Catherine. 'I had not thought of it.'

'No more than I had!' admitted her Ladyship rue-fully. 'Well!' She looked at Madeleine and Solange. 'Not such witless girls after all! Kateryn – you and your ladies wait by the water gate. Dumont the huntmaster and his huntsmen will escort you to safety, then carry word to the Hôtel de Ville.'

'Nay, your Ladyship,' declared Catherine in her own tongue. 'This is my grandfather's hall. I'll not slink off in a gutter and leave it!'

'This is no time to be a stubborn fool girl, Kateryn!'

'What better can I be, your Ladyship?' Catherine scarcely knew what came into her, but plunged forward regardless. 'The world reckons me useless, save to convey a crown. If I do not stand for my right, who will? Let the steward ready the servants and others to make escape. As for me? I am but a maid, yet my forefathers built this place to withstand armies, and I can hold it against a riot in the street! If not, let the world call me useless – I'll be dead, and won't have to listen!'

A silent tableau held for long moments. Then her Ladyship made a grave curtsey. 'As your Highness commands.' She changed to the Gallic tongue. 'Shall not your ladies be permitted to go? This is not their quarrel.'

Her ladies glanced at one another. Catherine could not read their expressions, but Madeleine's words were plain enough. 'Mademoiselle,' she said, 'I came here in your service and shall leave in your service.'

Solange nodded, but smiled anxiously.

'Well then,' said her Ladyship. 'Madeleine! Convey Princess Kateryn's command to the steward! Go – quickly, now! Then to the tower, where we can best see what passes.'

'What shall I tell my father?' Louis le Dauphin repeated the question that the Duc de Numières, his closest friend among his gentleman attendants, had asked him as they rode through the streets of Aix-le-Siège. 'For one thing,' he said, 'I shall tell him to come to la Fleur himself, so the soldiers and people can see him, and he them.' His riding party had left the Conciergerie at mid morning for the journey to Montmorency. In a more clement season Louis would have left at dawn to make the journey in a day, but in this weather it was impractical, and Louis would not punish good horseflesh to no purpose. All the same he disliked being so long from his post at la Fleur – even at his father's command.

'So it is to be a war?' asked de Numières.

'It already is a war, Jean. You saw the people of Louselles. They weren't warming themselves by their kitchen fires and bouncing their children on their knees, were they?' Louis spat into the street. Louselles had showed him a face of war he'd not known about. Such a needless war too! The goddams were fighting their own future king, though they didn't know it. It was time for a first lesson. 'Vanguard!' he called. 'Cross by the Pont Ste-Monique.'

'The Pont Ste-Monique?' asked de Numières. 'But that—'

'– takes us half a mile out of our way,' interrupted Louis. 'You will see why.'

Ten minutes later they crossed the bridge. In the open the wind was sharper, and the river below was grey.

'Well!' exclaimed de Numières. He pointed upstream. 'Is that what you came this way to see?'

The Hôtel de Guienne rose solidly above the houses around it. Above its walls rose a tower, and over the tower fluttered a flag, blue on white: the Croix St-Pélage. Louis stared at it. '*Pardieu!*' he muttered under his breath. He felt hot under his collar, half with anger, half with something else.

De Numières chuckled. 'Why do the goddams trouble with sea raids, when their flag already flies over our capital? There is presumption for you!'

'There is courage for you, Jean,' corrected Louis. 'If one of my sisters were at Kellouique, in Lyonesse, would she would hoist the fleur-de-lis over her hall?' Now that he had come this far, Louis felt an utter fool. He'd thought to march into the Hôtel de Guienne and speak to Princess Catherine about the suffering children of Louselles, but mostly he wanted simply to see her. Save for glimpsing a black-clad figure during the Richebourg parade, he hadn't seen her in nearly a year – not since he had kissed her in the garden.

De Numières urged his mount close beside Louis. 'Forgive me, Altesse, but it seems their flag may also fly over our Dauphin!'

Louis flushed, then abruptly laughed. 'No, Jean, you misunderstand completely! She has not conquered me. *I* shall conquer *her*!'

He sensed trouble before he saw or heard it. The day was cheerless, yet the street from the Pont Ste-Monique should have been filled with humanity going about its business. Instead, the shops were nearly empty and some were shuttered, while people looked down from upper windows, or peered furtively round corners. The only sound was the clop of hooves and clink of gear from his own party. His escort – guards, companions and servants – rode in silence, taut now with readiness.

A rider came round the corner, a middle-aged man in the conspicuously rich cloak and doublet of a prosperous bourgeois. He reined in sharply, staring at Louis and his party. 'Capitaine!' he shouted. 'Are you mad? You have not enough men – it is a riot!'

'A riot?' demanded Louis. 'Where?'

Only then did the man recognize the riders' livery and grasp that he was speaking to no ordinary officer. He hastily dismounted, and bowed low. 'Forgive me, Altesse! I did not know—'

'Never mind!' snapped Louis. 'Where is this riot?'

'In front of the Hôtel de Guienne. They are crying out against the goddams! Hundreds of them – thousands! They are mad!'

Louis glanced back and picked out a capable officer. 'You, Montcalm! Quickly, to the Hôtel de Ville, and have the Prevôt turn out the gens d'armes! The rest of you – forward!' He spurred into a canter.

Turning into the rue Frontenac, he found that the bourgeois had exaggerated less than he'd thought – the crowd filled the street, a great heaving mass with a life of its own. Its ragged fringe dissolved into running figures at the approach of armed horsemen, but two hundred paces from the Hôtel de Guienne the way became impassable. The rioters' first hasty retreat only thickened the press of those behind, each rank falling back and jostling the next. Awareness of his arrival swept down the rue Frontenac, and for a moment the crowd's roar was stilled and Louis found hundreds of eyes staring at him. A new murmur began, a murmur of derision as those at the front could see how few men he had. A column of gens d'armes was needed, thought Louis – but none was at hand. Yet for him, the Dauphin, to retreat before a street mob? It was unthinkable.

'De Numières,' he said in a low voice. 'Take charge. Draw swords, but keep them raised. Do not charge save on my command, or if I am beset.'

'Altesse—!' de Numières began to protest. 'You cannot—'

'Do as I say, Jean!' Louis rode forward to the very edge of the crowd, which shrank back a pace or two. Behind him came snapped orders and the sound of drawn steel.

One man – a sturdy fellow in a baker's apron – did not retreat as Louis rode up, but held his ground, feet apart, large hands on hips. Louis dismounted and instantly regretted it since the baker was nearly his height, and considerably greater in girth and reach. Silently cursing his own folly, Louis looked the man straight in the eye. 'You! Why are you not in your shop?

Does no one want bread?' A titter of laughter came from those nearby.

'Who can buy bread,' retorted the baker, 'when their last liard is taken for taxes? For what? For the goddams to steal, while our soldiers sleep and our nobles drink and whore? While their precious princess lives at ease in our street?' He bowed low. 'Altesse! Why are you here, and not at the coast?'

I wonder the same thing, thought Louis. 'I have been summoned to prepare a campaign,' he said. 'But you! All of you! You are brave men? You wish to fight the goddams? Then places await you in the companies! Or are you brave only against a demoiselle – a girl of fourteen years?' He looked over his shoulder. 'De Numières! This courageous baker has volunteered his good loaves for our soldiers at la Fleur! Take him!'

Three riders dismounted and advanced upon the baker. The man's eyes went wide and he tried to retreat into the crowd, but could find no escape in the press behind him. 'Altesse!' He fell to his knees. 'I beg you, Altesse! My wife! My poor babes!' But the soldiers seized him and dragged him forward.

Louis leaped back into his saddle. 'Who else wishes to fight the goddams?' he demanded. No volunteers were forthcoming. 'Then return to your houses! All of you! The gens d'armes are on their way. Every man they find in the street will be enlisted and sent to the coast!' He motioned to de Numières. 'Form in double column, and advance at the walk.' He drew his sword, lowered his reins and urged his mount forward.

Unable to retreat against the mass behind them, the foremost ranks of the crowd fell back instead to either side. Louis leaned over and whipped the flat of his blade down smartly against the backside of one fat shopkeeper. The man squawked and broke into a joggling run, followed by the laughter of Louis' escort. Another man ran, then another – then the street was filled with figures, pushing and scrambling past the riders, or slipping back into alleys. Louis struggled to keep his seat amid the surging, swirling mass of retreating humanity.

Soon all that remained in the rue Frontenac was a litter of rubbish and the groaning or silent figures of those trampled in the rout. Louis rode slowly among them, passing the boarded-up shops. Shattered crockery lay piled before one shop; scattered about another were ghastly objects that might have been decayed heads, but proved to be mere cabbages. A glutinous yellow-white mass oozed into the gutter: dozens of baskets' worth of smashed eggs.

Through the broken shopfront Louis saw one face that did not hide from him – a wide-eyed young girl was staring out at him. 'Come here, child,' he ordered gently. The girl came into the street and shyly curtseyed. She was in her early teens, he judged, her cloak and gown slick from broken eggs, her hair matted with goo. She lowered her tear-streaked face and Louis dismounted and raised her chin. Cleaned up, she would be a pretty girl. As it was, her ragged innocence and fear touched him – there are been so many demoiselles and children huddled outside the ruins of Louselles, and so little he had been able to do for them.

'You've nothing more to fear,' he told her. 'The trouble is ended.' He fished for a coin and handed it to her. 'This will buy you a new gown and cloak.' The girl stared at the coin – a pépin d'or – then mumbled her thanks. 'If it's cabbages and eggs you came for,' Louis told her, 'you'll find plenty, but none fit for your mother's pot and skillet.' He laughed, and the girl smiled. 'Where do you live, child?' he asked her.

'In – in the Hôtel de Guienne, Altesse,' said the girl. She looked down again. 'I . . . I am not of the Princesse's household,' she mumbled apologetically.

'There would be nothing wrong if you were,' said Louis. 'Princess Catherine is my friend, and bears no blame for her grandfather's pirates.' He'd forgotten her in the heat of the riot. Now a smile crept over his face. 'Come, child – I shall see you safely home.' He remounted and rode at an easy walk, the girl by the side of his horse, towards the looming mass of the Hôtel de Guienne. Loose paving stones littered the street outside the gate. Less creditable missiles had been hurled as well; wood and stonework were spattered with dung.

Louis adjusted doublet and cap, rode up to the gate and rapped sharply with the pommel of his sword. It swung open and he rode like a conqueror under the carved arms of Lyonesse. A dozen guardsmen in red and green bent the knee as he passed.

The image of conquest did not outlast the ride through the gate. Behind the guardsmen, partway up a stair, stood a demoiselle with thick golden hair, a milk fresh complexion and a hunting crossbow held at port-arms. She failed to throw herself as a supplicant at his feet, but merely dipped in graceful curtsey. 'As you come in peace, Altesse,' she said, 'I welcome you in the name of Princess Catherine.'

Louis dismounted and inclined his head as she came down the stair. '*La Chasseuse!*' he declared. '*Enchanté!* I bring you safely home a child who dwells in this house. I trust that your mistress too is safe and well?'

'She is quite safe – now!' said Madeleine du Lac. She took by her hand the girl Louis had rescued from the wrecked shop. 'You may go to your mother now, Jeannette, and I shall tell the Princess that you are safe among us once again.' She turned back to Louis and dipped again. 'Princess Catherine shall receive you, if you wish.'

'I am honoured.' He followed her between ranks of kneeling servants to the threshold of the royal chambers. All around were hangings charged with the Cross of St Pelagius and badges of the House of Guienne – most peculiar surroundings, Louis thought wryly, as another demoiselle, dark haired and voluptuous, curtseyed at his approach.

'Your timing is most fortunate, Monseigneur,' she declared as she rose. Large brown eyes studied him without warmth.

Louis hid his frown. Solange de Charleville had her admirers; he was not among them. Intelligence in a demoiselle was admirable, but she thought herself entirely too clever. If only Catherine had two like Mlle du Lac, and none like her. He smiled faintly and dropped his gaze to her bosom. 'Admirable,' he remarked dismissively.

'The Dauphin does me honour I scarcely deserve,' answered Mlle de Charleville, unflustered. The two ladies-in-waiting exchanged sharp glances and Louis surmised a difference of opinion, the subject being himself. Then Mlle de Charleville performed her duty, drawing aside the curtain. '*Son Altesse le Dauphin,*' she declared.

Louis was suddenly more nervous than in the face of a thousand rioters. Princess Catherine sat on a dais, an aged handsome woman in Lyonessan attire standing by her side. Catherine rose as he entered. He'd forgotten how tall she was, not a hand's breadth shorter than he was, and he found himself acutely aware of everything about her: sea-green eyes, high cheekbones and strong chin – how had anyone ever thought her features angular and gaunt? Burnished bronze hair swept back from her brow under her headdress. A year had made her visibly more the woman and less the child and the bodice of her green gown – plainly chosen to match her eyes – revealed the freckled shoulders he remembered, but also a delicate bosom and slim waist, while the swirl of her skirts hinted at long coltish legs.

She was a demoiselle to take the breath away. Louis would have driven off ten thousand rioters, or ten thousand dragons, to reach her door. How could this gravely beautiful creature have anything to do with the ale-swilling goddams who burned Louselles to the ground? Yet above her high seat were the Royal Arms of Lyonesse, with the charge of the heiress-apparent.

He swept off his feathered cap. 'The disorder in the rue Frontenac is ended, Altesse,' he declared. 'His Majesty's peace is restored, and you and all of yours are under his protection.'

Catherine took her skirts in hand and swept a low graceful curtsey. 'I and all of mine are under *your* protection, Monseigneur,' she answered, 'and in your debt.'

It was a foretaste, thought Louis, of what it would feel like to be King.

When Catherine had first spied armed horsemen approaching, she could not make out banner or livery, and took them for gens d'armes sent by the Provost, but they seemed hopelessly inadequate to the task – too few in number by far – and with sick fear she'd thought there was to be no rescue at all, but only a derisory gesture. She was about to pass word to open the water gate for the servants and others – her own fate she consigned to God – when with amazement she watched the mob break in the face of that little band.

Then she saw who had single-handedly driven the rioters from her gates. She determined to receive her deliverer in her Presence Chamber, the delay giving her time to collect herself. She told herself firmly that she was the equal of the Dauphin, or any prince in Christendom; he was doing nothing more than his duty. Then he stood before her, unbearably handsome in his plain riding doublet and hose, russet curls falling loose when he doffed his cap, grey eyes sparkling, a faint smile on his lips – and her firm resolution dissolved. She dipped lower than she ever had before his father, or ever would, and hesitantly extended her hand.

He raised it to his lips and kissed it. Catherine's ears burned, and half in a daze she scarcely was able to draw back her hand when he was done – but she had not wanted it to end.

Floating back to reality, she gestured her Ladyship forward. 'Monseigneur, la Comtesse de Lindley. She has been my faithful governess since I was a babe.' She switched to Saxon. 'Your Ladyship, his Highness the Dauphin.' Her Ladyship curtseyed gravely.

The Dauphin bowed. 'The honour is mine, Madame Comtesse.'

'You are a great credit to the House of Heristal,' answered her Ladyship. She glanced towards Catherine.

'If it please,' she said, 'shall I call for wine? The Dauphin must be thirsty – his company too.'

'Y–yes.' Catherine stammered. The noblest knight in Christendom stood before her, having vanquished enemies at her gate, and she had not so much as offered him refreshment. 'Let a table be set in the Great Hall,' she said, collecting herself, 'and you and yours shall dine with us.'

'I fear we cannot stay to dine,' said the Dauphin. 'Wine and bread, however, would be taken most kindly. And by leave of Madame la Comtesse, you have a garden, Altesse?' He grinned. 'A Presence Chamber is no place for an honest word.'

Catherine remembered, vividly, their last encounter in a garden and she glanced sideways at her Ladyship, who smiled faintly but said nothing. After a moment's anxious hesitation, she took silence for assent. 'Solange, Madeleine. Have the steward set out wine, bread and meat, all of the best. Let the Dauphin's companions be received in the Great Hall.' She dipped again to Louis. 'Monseigneur?'

'Mademoiselle.' He offered his arm, she took it and they set off towards the garden, her Ladyship chaperoning a few paces behind them. Catherine's mind raced. The Dauphin was her enemy! One day she would be Queen of Lyonesse – might be already, for all she knew, if her grandfather had died and word not yet reached Aix-le-Siège. Then I must make war, she thought, for the restoration of Richborough! Yet her grandfather's councillors and captains had raised no hand for her safety, and the Dauphin had.

They came out into the garden. The outside air was chilly, but Catherine scarcely noticed it. She was aware only of the Dauphin's arm under hers, and her own pounding heart. Louis gently turned her to face him. 'You are a very brave demoiselle,' he said. '*Catherine la courageuse – et Catherine la belle!*'

Catherine gulped and felt herself flush. 'You . . . you are too kind, Monseigneur.'

'I am merely truthful, Mademoiselle,' said the Dauphin. He grinned. 'No doubt it will one day cause me no end of trouble.'

'I should never wish to . . .' began Catherine, then let it trail off. She'd begun to say that she would never wish him trouble, yet her duty would someday be to trouble him. She looked at him in silence, and he looked back at her, and the silence stretched out.

The Dauphin broke it at last. 'My father has summoned me to Court. We are to speak of war.' The word fell like a stone into a still pool, with all the weight of what they were, and were to be.

'War,' repeated Catherine. I am your father's prisoner, she thought bitterly, and his hostage. She drew herself up. 'Then we shall be enemies, Monseigneur.'

The Dauphin smiled, not his insouciant grin, but a small, quiet smile. 'No, Catherine. We are not enemies.'

His hand settled on the hilt of his sword. 'You are my father's guest,' he said solemnly, 'and my blade is sworn to your protection.'

Catherine struggled between contradictory truths. She turned away, afraid for him to see tears.

'You do not believe me,' said the Dauphin sadly.

'No,' said Catherine. 'I mean yes. I do believe you – Louis. But . . . if there is war—'

'Not by your choosing!' said the Dauphin, more firmly now. 'I came to Louselles, after your grandfather's mariners burned it.' A tinge of anger came into the Dauphin's voice. 'The children were too cold and hungry to weep. The babes died, because their mothers had no more milk. Was that truly done for your honour, or your grandfather's? No, it was done for pride and profit – your cause does not enter their calculations.'

No, thought Catherine, it does not! Yet if she were not Princess Lyon, what was she? 'Richborough,' she said, her voice barely more than a whisper. She turned back to Louis. 'You took Richborough.'

Their eyes met. He looked down. 'Yes.' He looked back up, his grin creeping into his face. 'God kindly made you a demoiselle, *Catherine la belle*,' he said. 'Were it otherwise, I might fear to cross your blade! You would wield it well! Come – shall we walk? Your table will be ready soon, and then I must be on my way.'

They walked slowly around the garden.

The Dauphin turned to her. 'Churchmen make laws,

Catherine,' he said. 'They call them God's laws, with some verse of Scripture at hand to prove it. I think God's law is peace.' Taking her hand, he knelt, and raised it once more to his lips. Catherine had no idea how long it was before he rose again to his feet. It was not long enough. 'I should like to make peace with you, Catherine,' said the Dauphin gravely. He gave her his arm, and they went together into the Great Hall.

Antoine returned home from the palace long after dark, escorted by a detachment of Gardes de Maison. Corisande was waiting up for him. He often came home late – but she had surely guessed that something was amiss today, since very little escaped her attention. He thanked the lieutenant and dismissed his escort. '*Chérie!*' he said, embracing her once the door was closed. 'You have the honour of addressing the most foolish minister in Christendom!'

'Hush!' she said. 'Trinette is safe, I pray to God?'

Practically nothing, Antoine noted, escaped her attention. 'The Princess Lyonne is quite safe,' he told her. 'Thanks entirely to the Dauphin!'

Corisande ordered Paulet to bring them wine, and dismissed their other servants to their quarters. Her old serving woman Jacquenette, lantern in hand, guided them up the stairs and through their private quarters to the withdrawing chamber off the master bedroom. There Antoine allowed Corisande to get him out of cloak, doublet and hose; then he sank down in a chair in his shirt, and she wrapped a coverlet around him.

Paulet arrived with wine, bread and cheese, and Corisande put the tray on her lap and held a cup to Antoine's lips. 'Tell me as much as you wish,' she said. 'Then you must rest! I am sure you were much less a fool than you believe.'

Antoine sipped the wine. He was dead weary, but his mind was still racing. Sleep would be impossible; it was better to talk. 'On the contrary, Madame!' he said. 'I was a much greater fool than it is possible to believe. What would history have to say of a minister who nearly cost his royal master the throne?'

'The taxes on firewood and wine?' asked Corisande. 'I feared nothing good would come of those!'

'You feared rightly, *chérie*,' said Antoine. 'His Majesty will cancel them – and it will be put about that the Dauphin requested it.' Antoine shrugged. 'He knows nothing of it, but deserves the credit anyway. Alas, his Majesty still must pay for the war, taxes or no taxes.' He drained the last of his cup, and Corisande poured more. 'But the taxes are not a dram in the cask of my folly. I teased a sleeping beast – and it very nearly awoke.'

Antoine was not utterly sure yet that he had not, in fact, awakened the beast of rebellion, for the coming day would be the real test. Would the South Bank, humbled by the Dauphin, stay quiet and go about its business? Or would the embers of riot flare up again amid the litter along the rue Frontenac?

Corisande was looking at him over the top of her own wine cup, and Antoine knew at once that exhaustion and wine had made him say too much.

'Monsieur – *cher Antoine*—' she said. 'What is this folly you speak of?' A long pause. 'Surely, surely you did not . . . have a hand in the trouble in front of the Hôtel de Guienne?'

'I meant only to get that wretched girl's attention!'

'Get her attention?' said Corisande. 'By fomenting a riot in front of her door? Yes, she said words to me she ought not to have! But, Monsieur, she is scarcely more than a child!'

Like the fool he was, Antoine sought to defend himself. 'She is heiress to a throne! She put the Hôtel de Guienne in a state of defence and it would have required an army to take it, not a mob.' Had the rioters turned their anger on the Palais de la Trémouille, thought Antoine, they would have faced not arrow-slits and a stout gate, but spacious windows of glass.

Corisande cocked her head slightly. 'Was the Dauphin also part of this comedy of yours?'

Antoine shook his head, vigorously. 'Not in the least! Only by sheerest good fortune was he crossing by the Pont Ste-Monique, and heard of the trouble.'

Corisande rose from the stool, as gracefully as she had seated herself on it, and set down the silver service tray. 'You say, then, that you charged your men to incite a riot against Trinette, without the least measure to safeguard and protect her? And you call yourself only a fool? Monsieur, you excuse yourself much too easily!'

'I did not intend a riot, *Madame ma chérie!*' cried Antoine. '*Bon Dieu*, that was my folly! I meant only a little shouting, enough to make that girl think twice about flying the flag of the goddams above her tower!'

'*That girl*,' repeated Corisande. 'How easily you dismiss one who has been our guest in this house! This statecraft of yours is a cruel business, Monsieur.'

'Yes, it is a cruel business!' admitted Antoine. 'I confess too that of late I have not much liked your Trinette! Yet I also must confess that as an adversary I respect and admire her. She keeps her household so well that the officers I appointed to it have nothing to do – for which they are duly thankful! She means to be worthy of reckoning when one day she is Queen of Lyonesse. And I am very much afraid that she shall be,' he added. 'I hope it pleases God not to permit the Dauphin to fall in love with her!'

'Above all we must not have that, must we, Monsieur le Ministre!' cried Corisande, raising her voice for the first time. 'No one must dare fall in love, lest it interfere with policy of state!' She lowered her voice again. 'I ought to know that as well as anyone!' She curtseyed to Antoine. 'By Monsieur's gracious permission, I shall retire to the chapel tonight.'

Awaiting no permission, she swept out of the with-drawing chamber, leaving Antoine with only the warm coverlet and tray of refreshments as reminders that he had a wife. Finally, weary and discouraged, he went to his lonely bed. Lying there, still fitful, he had one further thought. Corisande was so often right, but about one thing she was wrong, a matter of the heart at that: even were kingdoms not at stake – and they were – a love affair between the Dauphin and the Princess Lyonne could not possibly end well.

The hôtel of the Lusianes lay in the rue Ste-Valérie, not far at all from the Palais de la Trémouille. Seeing the royal palace – so near yet so far – gave Catherine an unexpected pang. She had come here twice since her meeting with Margot at Montpassier, and now for a third time.

Her reception was proper rather than warm – warmth, Catherine guessed, did not come naturally to the Lusianes. The major-domo showed her in, saw to her ladies and servants, then ushered her into the privy chambers of the Duc de Septimanie, who stood beside an armoire. 'The Grand Duke of Asti received your reply to his proposal, Princess Lyonne,' said the duke. 'He was not pleased.'

Catherine had not expected the grand duke to be pleased. She had enquired about him from the ambassador from Ravenna, who had confirmed what

Solange had found out: the Grand Duke of Asti was greedy for land and money, a petty tyrant to his subjects with a reputation for hatching grand schemes that came to little. Nothing about him was appealing – and more than that, nothing hinted at a fitness to be King of Lyonesse. 'I told him the truth,' said Catherine. 'As gently as I could.'

'Then you should learn to be more gentle!' said another voice behind her. It was her grandmother, the dowager duchess – who must have been behind a tapestry, listening.

Catherine turned, and made the barest hint of a curtsey. 'I see, Grandmère, that I am not the only one who sometimes listens from behind an arras! At Court I learned a great deal that way.'

'You certainly learned to be impertinent!'

'Indeed, Madame.' What more could she say to that?

Grandmère Louise drew a deep breath. 'Come, my child – you must forgive me.' She took Catherine by the hand. 'I too have been impertinent from time to time! And yes, one can indeed learn a great deal by listening from behind a tapestry.'

Catherine allowed herself to be led to a window overlooking a courtyard garden. Fragrances of herbs rose up, but did not make her more comfortable in her grandmother's company. Grandmère Louise was uncomfortable as well, she suspected, and she had to credit her for asking forgiveness of her manner – it could not come easily to her!

'You are young,' her grandmother said. 'And like most young demoiselles, I suppose that you ask only two things of a husband: that he be of fitting rank and estate, and that you be madly in love with him – the second being of much greater concern!'

'Yes, Grandmère,' said Catherine. 'I suppose I am indeed like most demoiselles then!' The Dauphin was of fitting rank and estate, heir of the Aquitaine, and she was most certainly in love with him. But, as always, even thinking of him was a bad idea.

'Alas,' said her grandmother, 'you must learn to live in the world, where fitting rank and station are enough to ask for. They say that peasant girls have no such burden, and are free to marry for love. In my experience it is quite the contrary – no more than nobles do peasant girls marry on mere impulse, for peasants have as keen an eye for a sheepfold as we have for a province.'

'Were I a peasant's daughter,' said Catherine, 'I would certainly hope to have a keen eye for a sheepfold – but even more for a shepherd who knows how to keep the wolves at bay.'

'Ah,' said Grandmother Louise, 'I think I understand! You do not think that the Grand Duke of Asti is a wolf-slayer?'

'No, Grandmère, I do not.'

This time it was the duke who spoke up. 'And you consider yourself knowledgeable about wolves?'

'Of course not!' said Catherine. 'That is why I mean

to take care in choosing a shepherd, since he shall be King of Lyonesse.'

'Yet you should also consider the wolf,' said the duke. 'I believe the wolf you have most to fear is none other than his Majesty, the Most Christian King, Charles of Aquitaine.'

'You are bold to say that, your Grace!'

The duke looked sharply at her, and his mother raised an eyebrow. 'Do you mean to denounce my son to the King?' she asked.

'It is not my place,' said Catherine. The King of Aquitaine was her enemy – but the Duc de Septimanie's liege lord and rightful sovereign.

'My dear,' said Grandmère Louise, 'you must closely consider what your place is. The grand duke is no young man to charm a demoiselle. He is not even a famed captain of troops, which would seem to charm *you*. But he has family connections and other allies, all across Enotria and beyond, along with a treasure room filled with gold. If you think to make war against King Charles, you shall have need of all those things, especially the last. Where there is gold, the *condottieri* offer their services eagerly.'

But will they win their battles? wondered Catherine. The mercenary generals of Enotria had not fared well against the Aquitaine's royal armies. The bowmen and pikemen of Lyonesse had fared no better in the end – Richborough had scarcely held out for a week.

Something else niggled at her mind: one day the present King of Aquitaine would join his ancestors in the vaults beneath the royal chapel of Ste-Valérie, and Louis IX would sit on the throne. Could she so much as imagine being *his* enemy? 'Madame,' she said, 'there is something I must tell you.'

'Yes?'

'You have done me a generous kindness, which I have repaid but poorly,' said Catherine, 'and the grand duke too. I shall have need of allies; I know that! Yet Lyonesse is not a sword to be wielded in another's cause. I hope that I shall love my husband madly, and that he may even love me. But I shall require that he hold Lyonesse before any grand duchy, principality or kingdom whatsoever – even the empire of the world. Even the interests of the Lusianes.'

Grandmère Louise and her son the duke glanced at each other. Silence dragged out. 'Well!' she said at last. 'You do not lack for a sharp tongue to wield in your own cause, for whatever good it will do you. But as you have spoken plainly, so shall I: you are an ungrateful young snip, and his Majesty did well to turn you out of his court!'

'Then I shall not impose further on your hospitality,' said Catherine. *Ungrateful young snip*, indeed! 'Madame; your Grace; I shall take my leave.'

As she rode back with her little company to the Hôtel de Guienne, Catherine pondered allies and enemies.

She had made no friends this day, but she knew that allies did not need to be friends. If reason of state ever drew the Lusianes to seek her alliance, she was sure that they would forget any harsh words. So indeed would she.

Her thoughts about enemies were more troubling, especially when she thought on Corisande. Was Corisande truly her enemy? Yes, she was loyal to Charles of Aquitaine – a subject more loyal than he deserved – yet when had she ever treated Catherine with anything but kindness? How foolish it had been to quarrel with her! She sighed. What was done was done – and now, sadly, could not be undone.

CHAPTER NINE

Crimes of Dispassion

'I do not know why you are so simple, Madeleine,' said Solange as they turned into the rue Armignac. 'You'll risk your neck riding down a ravine after a deer, but you're deathly afraid to visit a perfectly harmless woman.'

'Better my neck than my immortal soul!' Madeleine crossed herself. 'How does this woman see the future, if she's not dealing with the Devil?' She ostentatiously pulled her cloak tighter.

'Oh, the Devil indeed!' said Solange. 'No one is making you do this. If you don't wish to come, you needn't. Everyone has consulted Mère Angelique – if we're going to the Devil, then so are half the ladies at Court.'

'That is quite possible,' said Madeleine darkly, but she did not turn back. They came to a jeweller's shop and Solange and Madeleine dismounted and went in, Solange adjusting her headdress as they did. They were gowned, cloaked and hooded like respectable young ladies of rank – her Ladyship having put her foot down about the two of them going abroad in the city dressed in bold courtly attire. The proprietor's wife motioned them towards the stairs leading to Mère Angelique's chamber.

Solange rapped on the door. 'Mère Angelique?' There was no answer. She rapped again, more firmly. 'Mère? It is I, Mademoiselle de Charleville.'

'Well!' declared Madeleine. 'She's not even in. We've come all this way for nothing. If she can see the future, she should have waited for us, or sent word she wouldn't be here. Some prophetess!'

'She has others who consult her, you know,' answered Solange. 'And she has no servants.'

'She ought to – she charges enough.'

But it was odd and annoying, Solange thought, that Mère Angelique was not here. The seeress might have more important clients than herself, but Solange could imagine no client more important than Princess Catherine. 'She *must* be here.'

'Why is that?' asked Madeleine.

'The jeweller's wife sent us up. Why would she, if Mère Angelique had gone out?'

'Maybe the jeweller's wife didn't see her leave. Maybe your Mère Angelique made herself invisible, or turned into a bird, or something.'

'Don't be simple, Madeleine. No one can do such things.'

'No one can read the future from cards, either.

You're the simple one for believing such foolishness!'

Solange rapped once more, sharply. 'Mère Angelique?'

Madeleine shuffled slightly and glanced back at the stairs. 'She must be asleep.' Her tone did not match her words, only adding to Solange's vague unease.

'She may need our help.'

'What kind of help? What can we do for her? Come, Solange, we really ought not stay here.' Madeleine turned to go.

Solange did not; instead she tried the door. It was locked, so she peered through the keyhole, but could make nothing out. 'Something is not right,' she said. 'I'll see if the proprietress has a key.'

'If she did, would she give it to you? Come – let's be on.'

Solange shook her head. 'No. You go, if you wish.'

Madeleine muttered under her breath. 'I must be simple, or I'd not listen to you.' From a fitchet in her skirt she drew forth her ring of keys and tried a couple. Then, as Solange watched with surprise, Madeleine knelt before the lock and inserted a small length of wire. 'Every châtelaine should know this craft,' she explained. 'It renders servants more honest, and husbands more faithful.' She drew out the wire, bent it, inserted it again. Presently something clicked within and Madeleine motioned for Solange to try the door handle; she did, and it moved freely.

Solange opened the door, and her vague disquiet grew acute. Mère Angelique's chamber was often filled with peculiar fragrances, pungent or pleasing; this one was sharply foul. The chamber was dark, the window shutter closed and the hanging lowered. Incense glowed on the table, but that was not . . . then Solange saw Mère Angelique. She stumbled back, clutching her stomach, fighting sickness.

Madeleine squeezed past her. '*Pitié de Dieu!*' she whispered.

Mère Angelique lay on the floor by the little table used for card readings. Her face was blotched and swollen almost out of recognition; her eyes bulged out, staring at nothing. A cord was twisted tight around her neck.

They stared at the dead woman for some time. 'What are we going to do?' asked Madeleine at last. She answered her own question. 'We must send for the Prévôt's officers – if we leave her here, suspicion might fall upon us!'

Solange turned from the body and tried to think clearly. 'Madeleine. Send a servant to Mademoiselle – not to the Hôtel de Ville, but Mademoiselle – with news of this.' The Prévôt's officers would be less bold towards a Princess of the Blood, whatever her standing at Court, than towards herself and Madeleine. 'Then you and I shall see what we can discover.'

* * *

A crowd was gathered in front of the jeweller's shop when Catherine's chair turned into the rue Armignac. She would have ridden, but her Ladyship had recommended the chair; the two burly chairmen were a useful addition to her bodyguard of huntsmen. They shouldered through the throng and set her down in front of the jeweller's shop and Dumont the huntmaster handed her out. Without a glance at the crowd Catherine went in and up the stairs.

Her ladies-in-waiting, thought Catherine, had never looked quite so glad to see her. They no sooner curtseyed than both started talking, speaking with their hands in that Gallic manner that Catherine had never acquired. She hushed them and had Solange give account, Madeleine filling in details. One detail – how Madeleine opened the door – merited a raised eyebrow. Catherine wondered if she should change locks on her caskets of letters and jewels, then concluded that new locks would be no more secure. Instead she would have Madeleine teach her this useful science.

They entered Mère Angelique's chamber, and Catherine looked steadfastly at the body. 'If she could foresee things to come,' she said, 'why not foresee this, and take measures against it?'

'Why not, indeed?' said Madeleine.

'Perhaps none of us can escape our fate,' answered Solange. 'Can a condemned man escape the executioner?'

'I would certainly try!' retorted Madeleine.

'Silence, both of you!' ordered Catherine. 'If ever I condemn you, Madeleine, I'll command the gaoler to permit you no wires.'

Under Catherine's glare, Solange stifled her smile. Catherine studied the rest of the chamber. The little room was in disorder. Bedclothes had been pulled up and a trunk thrown open, Mère Angelique's clothing left spilled out across the floor. Scattered under the table were her cards, what witches of Enotria called *tarocchi*.

'I believe that someone examined her table for hidden compartments,' said Madeleine. 'See?' The table was simple but finely made, but some of the joinery work was scored. 'A dagger was used to test the seams, Mademoiselle.' Madeleine ran her fingers along the marred seams.

Catherine nodded. 'Then they did not find what they sought. Else it was not here to be found.' She glanced back at Mère Angelique's body as Solange gathered the cards, murmuring as she did, as though to remember how they'd fallen. A futile task, thought Catherine; how could anyone learn how they'd lain on the table beforehand?

The cards disappeared in the folds of Solange's gown. 'I spoke to the jeweller's wife and daughter, Mademoiselle,' she said. 'The last people to call upon Mère Angelique were a lady and a chevalier. They left perhaps two hours before Madeleine and I came. The jeweller's daughter said they had come before, but she did not know who they were. Nor did I recognize them from the descriptions – if they were creatures of your enemies, they were none we have met.'

'My enemies?' asked Catherine, startled.

'We came to ask Mère Angelique's counsel regarding a marriage for you,' answered Solange. 'What if some-one feared the advice she might give you? He might choose to silence her.'

'But—' began Catherine, then bit her lip. She had come only to stand behind her ladies-in-waiting when the Prévôt's officers made enquiries into the woman's murder – that the crime might have had to do with her marriage prospects seemed absurd, grotesque. She looked down at Mère Angelique's body and shuddered.

Outside the milling crowd went quiet and there came the tramp of feet on the stair – the unmistakable tread of men with arms and authority – and a tall, portly man entered, a chain of office round his neck. Behind him were two sergeants in the livery of Aix-le-Siège and a man in physician's garb. The officer glanced at Catherine and her ladies, then bowed perfunctorily. 'Mesdemoiselles. If you will be so good as to wait below, I must ask you some questions presently.' His words had the tone of command.

'*Altesse*,' corrected Solange. 'You are addressing a Princess of the Blood.'

The officer looked sharply at Solange, then back at Catherine and his brow furrowed with uncertainty – no doubt, Catherine thought, he'd taken them all for demoiselles of small consequence. He was not accustomed to dealing with Princesses of the Blood.

She had no wish to make trouble; she had ordered the man summoned, and he was only performing his duty. 'I am Catherine, Princess de Lyonesse,' she declared. 'My ladies and myself are at your disposal. Mère Angelique was a good and honest woman, Capitaine.'

The officer removed his cap and bowed properly. 'Altesse – forgive me. I shall not detain you long.'

Catherine led her ladies down into the street to wait. But the captain's interpretation of 'not long' proved relative. Time dragged on and the tableau in the street – Catherine and her ladies, huntsmen and chairmen, surrounded by the guardsmen, all surrounded in turn by the lingering crowd – was awkward at best.

The captain finally emerged, looking portlier than ever. 'Forgive me, Altesse,' he said. 'You are free to go.' He paused. 'Your women, however, must accompany me to the Hôtel de Ville for questioning.' Catherine heard Solange's small gasp, and saw Madeleine's rosy cheeks turn pale. She herself stood utterly still, at a loss for words.

'That is impossible, Monsieur le Capitaine,' she told him at last. 'My ladies are of my household, under my command and protection. When you wish to speak to them, they will be made available to you at the Hôtel de Guienne.'

The officer frowned. 'I have no choice, Altesse – there has been a murder, and your demoiselles are witnesses.' Two guards advanced towards Madeleine and Solange.

Catherine's heart was pounding. 'I have no choice either, Capitaine.' She stepped between the guardsmen and her ladies. In the corner of her eye she saw Dumont's tiny gesture. Huntsmen and bearers closed in beside her, feet apart, staves held ready and Catherine said a silent prayer of thanksgiving for her Ladyship who had brought these good sturdy men to her household. 'My ladies are in my service, Monsieur, and my word is their bond. You may speak to them when you wish.'

Long moments passed; then the guard captain relented. 'You may hold them under arrest at your hôtel, Altesse, until I am ready to question them.'

'Thanks be to God that Mademoiselle is a madwoman of her people,' said Madeleine when she and Solange retired to their bedchamber that evening. 'Else we should be tonight in a place much worse than this! When that woman didn't answer her door, I told you we should have left well enough alone!' She folded her gown and kirtle into her clothing chest, chasing away the wolfhound pup Asterion, who wished to curl up in it. Clad only in her chemise, she went to the fireplace and tipped a log onto the fire, dancing back as sparks swirled up.

'Who contrived to open her door?' demanded Solange. 'Here – unlace me. You must teach me that art with locks.'

'See what I mean?' retorted Madeleine. 'We could both be in cells, being put to the Question, and all you can think of is new ways to get into mischief!' She bent to unlace Solange's stays. On wicked impulse she instead twisted the ties around a spindle, producing a satisfying cry of protest. Relenting, she undid the lacings and helped Solange out of her stays and kirtle. 'We could be in an even worse place still; did you think of that? What if whoever strangled Mère Angelique had come while we were there?'

Solange had no answer, but her hand strayed to her neck.

'A most unbecoming way to die, don't you think?' asked Madeleine. 'All befouled, your head bloated, tongue and eyes bulging out?' She fiddled with her clothing chest, hoping to dismiss the image.

'There are becoming ways to die?' asked Solange. She sat before the fire, head down. 'Poor Mère Angelique! I should have left her to answer harmless questions about ladies' lovers, not the matters of a princess! *Bon Dieu*, Madeleine – she was always good to me, and see what I brought her to!'

Madeleine sighed and again shut her clothing chest.

She went to Solange and put a hand on her shoulder. For some time they were silent, staring into the fire. 'Do not blame yourself,' she said at last. 'If she could not foresee, how could you? Perhaps the murder had nothing to do with us at all!'

Solange shook her head. 'Perhaps not – but crowns draw ambition, and ambition stops at nothing.' She rose and went to her own clothing chest. On top lay the *tarocchis* she had taken. She knelt by the fire and began spreading them out.

Madeleine shuddered. 'Must you?' she protested. 'I've seen enough of those witches' cards for a lifetime. Cast them into the fire where they belong!' She crossed herself by way of precaution. 'Much good they did Mère Angelique!'

'They might provide some clue as to who murdered her,' said Solange. 'We are under a cloud, you know, till the murderer is tried and hanged. Or beheaded, as the case may be,' she added.

Madeleine frowned. Would a member of the nobility stoop to strangling a fortune-teller? Perhaps!

'There is more,' said Solange. 'Whoever killed Mère Angelique was clearly looking for something. She always had papers about, and all were gone when we got there. But they left the *tarocchis*.'

'Now we have them!' said Madeleine. 'The killers might come for us next! You should have turned them over to the Prévôt's officers.'

'What use would they make of them?' retorted Solange. 'They would learn nothing. I owe it to Mère Angelique to see justice done on her murderer! And we both owe a service to Mademoiselle. That was a very great thing she did for us today!'

'Yes,' said Madeleine softly. A sensible part of her mind said they'd been in no real danger – they were not common serving girls, nor even bourgeoises, but ladies of rank. Another part said that her father, though a courtier, was of modest station, without great connections. Nor was Solange of much greater standing. However innocent, their mere presence in the chambers of a murdered fortune-teller touched them with scandal, and any other Princess of the Blood might have abandoned them to their fate. Certainly the Princess de Marsenne would have done so; probably la Pré as well. She knelt next to Solange. 'What can I do to help?'

'These were Mère Angelique's cards,' explained Solange, 'and her presence must be on them. When they were cast onto the floor – even by her murderers – they might still reveal some sign. Alas, I know little of this science, but if only I'd marked properly where—'

Solange got no further, because the door opened and Princess Catherine swept in. Both demoiselles leaped to their feet, curtseyed and stepped forward to help Mademoiselle out of her clothes. She brushed them aside and crossed to the fireplace, where she looked down at the cards. 'Not only suspected murderesses,' she observed, 'but proven thieves to boot. I dare say the Prévôt's officers would be greatly vexed. Lud's blood! Tell no one you took these!'

Solange repeated her explanation of what she hoped to learn, and Catherine was shortly sitting on the stool in her chemise, watching her lady-in-waiting go through the cards. '*Merde!*' cried Solange. 'I can tell nothing! Why did I not properly mark where they fell? See how ignorant I am?'

'They provided no message to Mère Angelique, either,' said Catherine. 'Certainly not one she was able to read.'

'We know this much,' said Solange, 'or at least we can surmise: I believe that Mère Angelique was murdered by someone who either sought knowledge of who you shall marry – or who wished to keep that same knowledge *from* you.'

'God's teeth!' muttered Catherine in her native tongue. 'One woman already dead on account of my marriage! How many more shall die in order for me to say my vows?'

The July sun blazed high above the trees, though the morning breeze was sharp and fresh from the previous night's tempest. Catherine, accompanied by her little retinue of ladies, huntsmen and servants, was riding south, heading for the château of the Comte d'Arlennes. The count's mother was an old friend of her

Ladyship's, and though Lady Lindley herself – abed with a cold – had not come, she thought it best for Catherine's ladies – and Catherine herself – to breathe country air for a time, away from the capital.

Catherine was fifteen now; so her Ladyship trusted her to ride abroad without a governess, though hinting that a princess of mature wisdom would naturally heed the advice of Dumont the huntmaster in every particular. Thus Dumont rode with two huntsmen as vanguard, while his assistant and another huntsman brought up the rear behind servants and pack-horses.

There were not twenty in her party, but Catherine imagined twenty thousand. She rode not by herself, her ladies behind her, but at the side of her husband, Lewis I of Lyonesse and Louis IX of the Aquitaine. The royal highway would not skirt the Duchy of Septimanie to reach the sea at Freinet, but drive through its heart to the great port of Herclée. Whatever Uncle Gérard might suppose, her husband would surely reduce that province to obedience. At Herclée they'd embark in a great fleet of all Christendom – ships of Lyonesse proudly in the van – and sail in triumph to the Holy Land.

A lingering cloud abruptly snatched away the warmth, and brought Catherine back to reality. This was Catherine's first ride abroad since the murder of Mère Angelique. The royal justice of Aquitaine had made what it regarded as sufficient – though inconclusive –

enquiries into the murder and the case-book was closed, and the house arrest of Catherine's ladies ended.

The sun burst from the cloud, again splashing warmth across highway and countryside. They rode in silence, soon reaching the place her Ladyship had told them to look for. Just past a bridge was an old manor-house; a track ran back from the highway and they turned onto it. Ploughlands gave way to pasture, then forest, the trees closing in till they rode through a tunnel of green gloom. Vines clung to the trees, and mistletoe sprouted from overhanging branches.

Catherine wished the Dauphin were here, and not just so they could kiss again. She urged her mount close in behind the huntsmen, and her ladies drew likewise close behind her.

Something snapped, like a cracking branch but sharper. The huntmaster grunted, checked clumsily and threw aside his reins. 'Dumont!' Catherine cried, irritated, 'What is it?' Then he sagged back and she could see for herself what it was – a crossbow bolt protruded from his chest!

Another crossbow snapped behind her. '*Défense!*' cried the huntmaster's assistant. '*Maître! Avant!*' All at once everything had the vividness of sheer terror – Dumont staring at Heaven, blood foaming from his mouth; then a third snap, louder, and something flashed over Catherine's head with a whistle.

'*Mon Dieu!*' whispered Solange.

'*Maître!*' shouted the huntmaster's assistant again – a young man named Lasceaux, still unaware that his master heard no more. Catherine looked over her shoulder and Solange stared back at her, dark eyes wide with disbelief.

Madeleine was bent over; for a horrified instant Catherine thought she too had been shot – then she straightened up, crossbow in hand, and Catherine found a moment to envy her splendid presence of mind. With Lasceaux at the rear, Catherine suddenly realized, she alone must take charge.

As Dumont rolled to his left, out of his saddle, to fall in a heap, his half-pike still upright, held by strap and socket, figures stepped into the track ahead, armed with staves and swords. '*Se rendre!*' one cried.

On impulse Catherine spurred past the huntsmen and seized Dumont's half-pike. It was far heavier than she'd imagined and she had to struggle to balance herself while she got the half-pike clear of Dumont's saddle. Her foot slipped from the stirrup; for a frightful moment she felt herself tumbling. Leaning forward, she clung desperately to reins and pommel with her left hand, the half-pike in her right. Then her foot was back in the stirrup. 'Charge!' she cried in her father's tongue. '*À l'avant! À l'avant!*' Not looking back to see if any heeded, even heard, she dug in her spurs.

The leader of the ambush party swore loudly. His were

scarcely picked men, but were usually sufficient to way-lay demoiselles and servants escorted only by a handful of huntsmen, and he had been advised that the Princess de Lyonnesse travelled with no more than this. The chief of her escort had been dropped, the party trapped at front and rear. Yet now his men faced this mad spectre charging down through the forest gloom, a spectre in the form of a Princess of the Blood on horse-back, eyes wide and red hair flying. Screaming incomprehensible curses in a foreign tongue, she spurred towards them, bearing a half-pike she lowered like a lance. Behind her came the rest of her party at the gallop.

The track was narrow and the forest thick; a dozen seasoned footmen could hold against a squadron of mounted lancers, but there were no seasoned soldiers among his men – only common ruffians and cutthroats. The pounding of hoofs came up, and all but one man dived from the track. That one, a roughhewn fellow named Brun, had spirit to stand against an armed demoiselle on a horse. He planted himself squarely in the path, his stave held pike-wise. The girl's horse made a flying leap – fine horsemanship – and down he went sprawling, the half-pike driven clean through him. His corpse was tossed aside as the following horses pounded over him.

Then the redhead was nearly opposite the captain. He had a loaded crossbow and an easy shot – but his promised thousand livres would be paid only if the Princess were to be delivered to her buyers alive and he did not care to know his reward if he killed her instead. For an instant their eyes met: hers large and green, full of mad fury – then she flashed past, the rest of her party following. A crossbow snapped, its bolt striking the tree-trunk beside him. An instant later another demoiselle galloped past, a discharged crossbow in hand and a curse on her tongue for having missed him.

Catherine rode on up the track at the gallop, head down, scarcely aware of the pounding of hooves for the pounding of her heart. Her mouth was dry, hands shaking. A man had blocked her way so she'd lowered the half-pike as jousters did in the lists, then had it wrenched from her hand. Only the spirited leap of her horse had saved her. She wanted to believe that this was not happening; that in a moment she would awaken to find herself again riding comfortably behind Dumont and his huntsmen – or, infinitely better, lying under coverlets and furs in her canopied bed. Yet surely she was more likely to end up lying under dead leaves, dead herself – or else wishing she were. With awful vividness she pictured Dumont sagging back in the saddle, then tumbling to the ground like a heap of rags. Although she had seen death before – violent death, when some malefactor of consequence was beheaded, and not two weeks ago the strangled corpse of Mère Angelique –

never had she witnessed death so sudden and close.

After a mile, or perhaps a league for all she knew, she came to a glade, reined in and looked back. Three of her company were close behind: Madeleine and two huntsmen. They pulled up by her side, one huntsman raising a sword in salute, Madeleine and the other waving crossbows. Seconds later Solange came up, followed by two servants, and soon the rest came in view, Lasceaux the huntmaster's assistant bringing up the rear. He held reins and a hunting spear in one hand, a crossbow in the other. All were present save the fallen Dumont.

Madeleine sprang down and dug into her saddlebag. She pulled out the cranquin for her crossbow; a moment later she was bent over, stock propped against her right knee, cranking it back. The prongs engaged the cord and Madeleine stowed the cranquin, fairly leaped back into her saddle and nocked another bolt. Shaken as Catherine was, she felt another flash of admiration – mingled with a touch of envy – for Madeleine. Her lady-in-waiting had acted with sense, whereas Catherine had done nothing but seize a half-pike she knew not how to use, ridden off in panic and thrown it away. Such an unfair world, that an Aquitanian courtier's daughter was blessed with beauty, sense and courage, while the heiress to Arthur's throne had so little of any!

Then came muffled hoof beats down the path and Catherine was jolted back from shame to raw fear again.

'Everyone!' she cried. 'Off the path! If you have a cross-bow, follow me! The rest of you get as far into the trees as you can!' The servants hesitated. '*Now!*'

Guiding her horse into the edge of the woods, she dismounted and pulled out her own hunting crossbow. Lasceaux – now the huntmaster – drew something from a long canvas sheath next to his saddlebag, which Catherine realized was an harquebus. Then she, Madeleine and Solange – who now also had her cross-bow out – took position in the trees to one side of the opening of the glade, just past the huntsmen. For all that Solange detested such things, thought Catherine wryly, she was still a country lord's daughter; she went on one knee, propping her arm on the other, levelling her weapon. As the hoof beats drew closer, Catherine knelt and levelled her own as well, fearful she had chosen foolishly, dooming her people. With prayers to St Mary Magdalene – and the White Lady too, for safe measure – she resolved to yield herself up if all was lost, in hope that their pursuers would be satisfied with her death or capture, and let her company go.

Three riders burst into the glade. Crossbows snapped, followed by a deafening report and cloud of smoke from Lasceaux's harquebus, and the second rider howled, jerked up in his stirrups and fell under the third horse's hoofs. The lead rider pulled up so sharply that his horse reared and whinnied. Catherine shot at him and missed. Turning, he caught sight of her between the trees, and took aim straight at her. She dived for the ground as two crossbows snapped again, and a bolt slashed through the leaves. Shouts and curses bellowed from the clearing, then moments later retreating hoof beats. Catherine looked up in time to see the two surviving riders head back down the track, the leader swearing and clutching his shoulder. Madeleine turned to Solange, who still knelt with her discharged crossbow on her knee. 'Well shot, Mademoiselle de Charleville!' she declared.

Solange made a vague sound and nodded weakly. She got slowly to her feet. 'They're . . . gone?'

'I – I think so,' answered Catherine. 'For now.'

Solange leaned back against a tree and closed her eyes. She was trembling, and a tear splashed from her cheek. 'I want to go home,' she whispered. Catherine shared her sentiment.

Practical as ever, Madeleine went to her horse and pulled a wine skin from her gear. She brought it to Solange. 'So do we all!' she said softly, hugged her and pressed the skin into her hands. 'Here. Drink.'

Without opening her eyes Solange upended it and gulped the red wine till it spilled from her mouth and stained the front of her gown. She gave it back to Madeleine, who handed it to Catherine.

'Mademoiselle?'

Catherine took it with a nod and drank no more delicately than Solange had, then gave it back to

Madeleine to take her own turn. The skin made the round twice more, and was empty.

'Best we be on,' Catherine said. She joined Lasceaux in examining the dead man, but found no clue as to where he came from or who had hired him. 'We ought to go back for Dumont,' she said, 'not leave him out here. But—'

'The highwaymen?' asked Lasceaux. 'They've two dead and their leader wounded. With luck it will fester and he'll die of gangrene.' He spat on the dead man. 'They'll want no more to do with you! I'll ask volunteers to go and retrieve Maître Dumont, and follow them in case of trouble. The rest will stay here to keep guard.'

'I'll go back with you too,' said Catherine.

Lasceaux shook his head firmly. 'No, Altesse. You are—' He paused, and looked at her thoughtfully. 'You are our captain, and must not risk yourself without need.' Before Catherine could protest he turned away.

They returned shortly, Dumont's body trussed over a horse as Catherine's father's corpse had once been. Borrowing Madeleine's little *Book of Hours*, Catherine mumbled a prayer over the huntsman, then they resumed their journey – Dumont would receive a Christian burial at the estate of Arlennes.

'It should not be far,' Catherine declared.

The forest closed in again, then gradually thinned out, becoming an open woodland. Then they passed the lightning blasted trunk of a great tree: a mark, her

Ladyship had said, that they were nearing the château of Arlennes. Catherine was relieved – there had been few landmarks for a long time, and she'd begun to fear they'd lost their way. 'We're almost there!' she cried aloud.

Moments later the report of an harquebus echoed through the forest. 'Hold!' cried a voice out ahead of them. 'Hold, I say!' Another harquebus shot made the meaning clear and Catherine reined in sharply, her company behind her. She tried to swallow, but her mouth was too dry – twice they had escaped; there could be no third time. Nothing was left but to yield and accept her fate . . .

Half a dozen riders appeared, five armed with harquebuses, the sixth with sword drawn. At a gesture his companions reined in, and he rode forward alone. He was a man in his thirties, not un-handsome, and though clad in plain riding gear, from his bearing he was plainly a gentleman of rank. He looked with puzzlement at Catherine and her armed, grim-faced companions.

'My ladies!' he said. 'I am Étienne de Clery, Comte d'Arlennes! If I may beg to know whom I have the honour to address?'

Before Catherine could reply, Solange answered for her. 'My mistress is called Hippolyta,' she declared, 'Princess of Amazons! She has this day slain an enemy by her own hand, and is surprised that you should receive her not as befits her station, but with armed men.'

The Comte d'Arlennes stared for a moment at Solange, then turned a thoughtful gaze on Madeleine. He showed no hint of the appreciation most men showed – understandably so, thought Catherine, since a gentleman looking straight down the stock of Madeleine's crossbow might be forgiven for not noticing her golden hair and lithe figure! Sheathing his sword, he raised both hands in the gesture of peace. 'I beg your forbearance, my ladies!' he said. 'One of my foresters heard a shot, and found a dead man in a glade. I was riding out to investigate.'

Catherine nodded. 'Madeleine,' she said. Madeleine lowered her crossbow.

The Comte d'Arlennes doffed his cap. 'You are most kind, noble Hippolyta,' he said. 'If it please you, I shall conduct you to my house – and introduce you to my noble mother, Jeanne de Cléry. I suspect that she will be delighted to make your acquaintance!' He turned his mount and set off at a trot.

Catherine and her party followed. As they rode towards the château, Catherine motioned Solange up beside her. 'Hippolyta, indeed!' she whispered. After the terror and tension of the last hour, she felt light headed and giddy. 'Would that I *were* an Amazon, and had killed an enemy, instead of just riding off in panic!'

Solange looked at her oddly, through half-lowered eyelashes. 'You *did* kill an enemy, Mademoiselle,' she whispered in reply. 'The man in the path!'

'What!' Catherine's startled reply made the Comte de Clery look back over his shoulder.

'You ran him clean through, Mademoiselle!' Solange said softly. 'Not a chevalier of the Gardes de Maison could have struck more true!'

'God's mercy!' cried Catherine. She felt for the rosary that hung from her belt, and nervously counted its beads. As she did she made a decision. Life was precarious and friends were precious. If she made it back to Aix-le-Siège alive, it was time to end her foolish rift with Madame Corisande. She counted her rosary again, this time in prayer that Corisande would deign to receive her.

Gerard de Lusiane, Duc de Septimanie, received his distant cousin the Baron de Moine in the private study of his hôtel in the rue Ste-Valérie, where he resided when his presence was required in the royal capital.

Gerard acknowledged the baron with a nod, then got directly to his point. 'You have gravely disappointed me, de Moine!' he said. 'I expected better of you! I did not hold you at fault about the fortune-teller, though we learned nothing from either her cards or her papers. It was a chance we took. But this latest business! How in the name of the Devil could a party of women and servants drive off your men? Not even women. Mere girls!'

'I too am disappointed, Monseigneur,' said the

baron. 'And I take full responsibility for this misadventure.'

He was buttering his words carefully, thought Gérard de Lusiane. 'As you should!' he said.

'Yet the outcome, if I may say, is as I feared,' de Moine added, 'given the insufficient means provided.'

The butter, it seemed, had run short. 'You accepted the task!' said Gérard. 'Along with my gold.'

'I made the best of what I had to work with,' said de Moine. 'I regret that they proved insufficient. Unfortunately, mercenaries of a better class are exceedingly costly to hire.'

Gérard de Lusiane knew exactly what the better class of mercenary troops cost, but he also knew that none of the better class of mercenaries would have taken on the commission to abduct a royal princess. 'Whereas common ruffians come cheap,' he retaliated, 'leaving you more of my gold for you to pour down your gullet.'

De Moine reddened. Gérard glanced down at the fat man's sword. He had failed in executing a campaign, even a small one – but his personal skill with the blade was not in doubt. It would not do to drive him too far. Gérard laughed. 'I don't begrudge you a good meal, my good Henri!' he said. 'But I require your diligence! What should we do now about Princess Catherine?'

'A second attempt to take her by force is out of the question,' said de Moine. 'She will be on her guard now. Along with de Chirac, and all of King Charles's officers.'

Gérard nodded. 'Alas, you are no doubt correct. Take no further direct action against Princess Catherine or her household.' He paused. 'However, you must see to it that the men you hired receive their just reward.'

De Moine nodded. His hand strayed to the hilt of his dagger. 'It will be seen to.' He bowed and withdrew, leaving Gérard alone with his thoughts.

Catherine, he decided, seemed scarcely a Lusiane at all – no wonder that she so proudly and defiantly called herself Catherine de Guienne. Gérard wondered if there might be a better way forward. Marie's other daughter, Anne, was still at la Trémouille: a pretty and demure child – still a child, yet at eleven years old now almost on the verge of young womanhood. She stood only one precarious royal life further from a throne, and might be a much more fitting marriage prize of Christendom than her reckless sister.

It was something to think about.

CHAPTER TEN

Alliances

Catherine and her company set off from Arlennes after a two weeks' stay, returning to Aix-le-Siège by a different and longer way, their escort reinforced by a party of the Comte d'Arlennes' men.

As they neared Aix-le-Siège the countryside changed. Open fields gave way to market gardens. Modest old houses of country gentlemen gave way to the larger, elegant châteaux of nobles who had preference at Court, or sought by expenditure to imply that they did. Catherine and her party were still some two leagues from the city when a column of horsemen appeared, not less than a hundred strong, white cloaked in the livery of the Gardes de Maison.

Catherine reined in, surrounded by her company, and awaited them. Then she saw who rode at their head, and her heart leaped. At an unheard command his company halted and the Dauphin alone rode up to her, dismounted, and swept off his cap.

'Altesse!' He helped her down from the saddle, and she found herself in his arms. His lips touched one cheek, then the other, then he stepped back and bowed.

Catherine barely found presence of mind to curtsey. 'Monseigneur!'

'I heard of your encounter in the forest, Princess Catherine,' the Dauphin said. His voice was almost gruff. 'You were a very great fool to undertake such a journey.'

For all that he was the Dauphin, Catherine's back stiffened. 'Many have travelled that way before, including ladies. If the King of Aquitaine cannot keep the peace,' she added pointedly, 'a traveller must look to her own means!'

At that the Dauphin laughed. 'Ah, my Catherine, you are altogether impossible! As you grow more beautiful, so you grow more courageous, and I do not know what to do about you.' His expression turned grave again. 'Were you seated in your grandfather's place, I should much fear to hear such news as I have received today.'

'Louis?' blurted Catherine. 'Monseigneur?'

The Dauphin frowned. 'I bear news of great import, Altesse, which should be given to you alone, and not in the highway.' He looked back at Catherine's ladies, his gaze lighting on Madeleine. 'Mademoiselle du Lac,' he said. 'would you do me the honour of accompanying your mistress and me, that there may be no question of impropriety?'

Madeleine and Solange glanced at one another, and the latter's eyes flashed darkly – as the senior of Catherine's ladies she should have been chosen.

Catherine was sure that the Dauphin's small breach of protocol was deliberate: he had no more fondness for Solange than she for him.

They rode up a side path to a meadow at the edge of a grove. The Dauphin dismounted, helped Catherine down and tied their horses to a tree. Madeleine rode another hundred paces, where she could watch without being in earshot. 'Louis?' asked Catherine when they were alone.

'My news is sorrowful to me, *ma belle*,' he said. 'Your grandfather – or rather, your grandfather's ministers – have declared war upon l'Aquitaine. War there already was; now it is proclaimed.'

Catherine stood utterly still. 'I am in your power, Monseigneur,' she said. 'I am alone, and have no means to resist.'

'*Pardieu!*' cried the Dauphin. 'I am not your prison warder, Catherine! I told you my blade is sworn to your defence! If for an instant I thought my father meant ill towards you, I would ride with you to the frontier of the Estates and cry my defiance to him.' He smiled slightly. 'Yet my father does not fall short of his honour as King. You remain his guest, and he commands only that you not ride abroad in the country unescorted – unless you give your parole of honour that you will not seek escape. Is that unjust? There is danger on the roads in any case, as you have learned!'

Catherine nodded. 'Then escorted I must be! I am a

princess of Lyonesse, and swear no bond to the enemies of my house and country.'

The Dauphin grinned. 'I never supposed you would, Catherine *la belle*! In your place I would do no less.' For a few moments he stood silent, and his grin gave way to an almost shy smile. 'Over the present we have no power,' he said, 'yet the future is ours if we make it so. Listen to what I say, for I have given it great thought.' He drew his sword. Holding it hilt up in his gloved left hand he went to one knee and took her hand with his other. 'Catherine, daughter of Henri! If it be your will and pleasure, I, Louis d'Héristal, pledge you my troth, *per verba de futurus*, to marry when soonest we may. I beg you consider my most humble suit. In token I offer that which of earthly possessions I hold most precious, this blade.'

Catherine gulped, and stumbled, and only with uttermost effort kept from fainting dead away. 'Monseigneur? . . . Louis?' she whispered.

'I ask a great thing of you, Catherine – my love,' said the Dauphin, his own voice shaking. 'Do not accept in haste; but I beg you, do not reject in haste.'

All of Catherine's heart bade her accept, and half her mind, but the other half held back, hesitant, uncertain. 'But . . . your father – the Church – Parliament—'

'I have considered all those things, *chère* Catherine. My father will bellow for a time, but in the end he must accept my decision. As for the Church, I have studied the matter, and your Pelagian church is less stubborn than ours . . . As to your *Parlement*? You shall be Queen! For now it must be secret; a great shame – but a greater shame to let our declarations pass by us.'

Catherine knelt on the grass facing the Dauphin. 'Louis, you know my heart is yours! It has been yours since I was an awkward child, laughed at by all others at la Trémouille, and you alone did not laugh at me.'

'They were great fools to laugh, *la plus belle* Catherine! Never has l'Aquitaine had so radiant a Queen as I shall give her!' Louis thrust the point of his sword into the ground beside them, put his strong arms around her and drew her close till their lips met. Catherine hesitated, then did not, and her blood roared as they kissed. They slid down onto the grass, his arms still around her, and she kissed his ears and his neck, intensely aware of the warmth of his body against hers. His hands eased into the back of her riding gown, and it began to slip from her shoulders . . .

Catherine knew where this journey was headed, yet wanted desperately to ride onward. Instead, abruptly, she half raised herself. 'By God's grace, Lewis . . .' she began, then realized she was speaking in Saxon. 'Monseigneur – *mon cher Louis* – is this how we keep our secret?'

He sighed, then leaned his head back and laughed. 'Alas, you are right! It is no way to keep a secret. *Pardieu!*' He sat up, got to his feet, shaking off bits of grass and dirt, then helped her up and bowed. 'I forgot myself . . . Mademoiselle will forgive me?'

Catherine curtseyed, and smiled. 'I shall try very hard, Monseigneur!' She took several deep breaths. 'I think, Louis le Dauphin, that when you seek to conquer, very few shall long resist you!' She adjusted her gown, blushing as she did, and looked down at her skirts. 'Fortunate that this gown is green! Else I should have much to explain to Mademoiselle de Charleville.'

'Mademoiselle de Charleville can go to perdition!' said the Dauphin. He pulled his sword from the ground, cleaned the blade and sheathed it, then glanced at Madeleine in the offing. 'Mademoiselle du Lac shall be a useful ornament of our Court, a lesser jewel to call attention to the greater. But when I am King, I shall . . . ah, I shall consign that Charleville piece to a convent. She will make a most formidable abbesse, no? The novices will go in great dread of her!'

'I do not care to see women sent to convents against their will!' retorted Catherine.

The Dauphin looked sharply at her, then smiled wryly. 'Ah, *ma belle* Catherine – that was foolish of me. You are right: not a convent.'

'Not anywhere, Louis,' answered Catherine gravely. 'Mademoiselle de Charleville is of my household. She serves me well; it is not for another to dispose her fate.'

For a moment the Dauphin looked as though he were searching for a retort. Then he smiled again. 'You are right, *ma chère;* you speak as should the Queen who shall reign by my side. Let us say no more of her! You have not answered my suit though, Altesse. You will consider it?'

Catherine dipped. 'I shall consider it, Monseigneur – with all my heart!' With sudden anxiety, she recalled that there was to be war, so surely the Dauphin would be at the head of his troops. What if he were to fall in battle, struck down by her future subjects?

He noticed her expression. 'Catherine?'

'Have a care for yourself, Louis,' she said, and felt like a traitor for saying it.

He frowned. 'You are thinking of the war. Monsieur de Chirac,' he said, 'hopes that it may pass without a full meeting in arms. I pray it will be so.'

'I shall pray so as well,' answered Catherine. 'But now we must go back to my people. We have been too long already. No – we have not been long enough, yet I should go back.'

'So you should, and it shall be my honour to escort you to the Hôtel de Guienne.'

They rode back together to her waiting company, and the Dauphin rode at Catherine's side the rest of the way back to the city and the Hôtel de Guienne.

'You shall have to let out all your gowns, Madame,' said old Jacquenette. She held up one against Corisande. Her swelling was scarcely visible yet, but Corisande could feel it when she dressed. Afterwards, she'd need a great deal of walking in the garden to restore her figure. 'You've no one to blame but yourself,' continued Jacquenette. 'And Monsieur, to be sure. Indeed, since he is the cause, it should be charged to his wardrobe, not yours; I'll speak to Paulet. And at his age too!'

'Monsieur is not so old as all that!' observed Corisande. *And I am not so young!* she added to herself.

Jacquenette glanced down at Corisande's waistline. 'No, Madame, he obviously is not!' She laughed. 'You could have gowns made in the Enotrian manner – they'd conceal your condition for a little longer – but Monsieur might not approve. He'd rather show you off to his friends, no? For them to admire his handiwork? Not that it was done with his *hands.*'

'Jacquenette! I should have taught you to keep your tongue long ago.' Corisande aimed a mock slap at her, then shrugged. 'I suppose it is too late now.'

Jacquenette had been her chamber woman almost from the day King Charles's eye had fallen on her, an obscure singing girl, and she had suddenly found herself maîtresse-en-titre. 'There were others before you, girl,' Jacquenette had advised her at the time, 'and there'll be others after. You'll have nothing to fall back on but the kindness of those to whom you show kindness now.' Corisande had learned: to give favour to those who had no favours to give in return; to humble herself before ladies of less beauty but greater rank; above all, to honour the Queen by being invisible in her presence.

A little serving girl burst into the bedchamber. 'Madame!' she announced, without so much as a curtsey. 'Monsieur Paulet says to tell you—' Jacquenette gave a short harrumph. The girl remembered, dipped to Corisande, and turned to Jacquenette. 'Monsieur Paulet says to tell Madame that a lady has come in a chair, with others in attendance, and servants.'

'Very much better, Fleur!' said Jacquenette. 'Have Paulet admit her, and ask whom Madame has the honour to receive.' The child nodded, then fairly skipped off.

Corisande was puzzled. She expected no friends. She snatched up a shawl and joined Jacquenette at the window. The party below was not large: a chair with its bearers; three ladies riding astride; a handful of servants. '*Pardieu!*' she whispered. Two of the mounted ladies were young, and familiar, but even before she recognized them, the trapping and livery identified the party – the red and green of the House of Guienne.

Corisande sighed. Whatever her feelings, whatever the purpose of this visit, her duty was plain: she must receive Princess Catherine, and entertain her appropriately until Monsieur arrived. 'Jacquenette! Leave off gawking and help me dress. Then you can stare to your heart's content.'

Jacquenette took a gown from a chest trunk, and helped Corisande into it. She was lacing the false sleeves when little Fleur returned to say that Paulet was waiting to announce the visitor. Paulet entered and bowed. 'Madame,' he said impassively, 'Mademoiselle Trinette begs that you might receive her. The lady gives no other name.'

So! thought Corisande. The princess had come not to call on her husband, but on her. For an instant she flashed with anger that this proud demoiselle should think to turn up in a chair and erase with a word all the tears that she, Corisande, had wept. She cast the unworthy thought aside. Proud demoiselle, indeed! She was heiress to a throne! 'Admit Mademoiselle Trinette,' she ordered Paulet, 'and see that she and her party are refreshed and at ease. I shall be down directly.'

A few minutes later Corisande went down the stairs, Jacquenette in train. Waiting was an unmistakable figure in a dark green gown, her ladies drawn up behind her. What a difference time makes in a young demoiselle! thought Corisande. The Catherine who stood before her was even taller, by a little, than the one she remembered, but the thin and lanky girl was nearly gone. Gown and headdress accentuated her colouring and red hair without overwhelming; her décolletage made elegant display of her bosom, the freckling of her shoulders adding to her charm. Corisande had worried at times that she had overplayed her hand in selecting Mlles de Charleville and du Lac to attend the Princess, but now, standing behind her, the two ladies-in-waiting only accentuated Catherine's splendour. She looked already the Queen she would one day be.

Corisande took her skirts in hand and knelt. 'You do me profound honour, Altesse.'

Catherine's hand was under her chin, gently bidding her rise. For long silent heartbeats her green eyes held Corisande's. 'I should have come long ago, Madame,' she said.

Corisande showed no sign of what she felt; otherwise she could have sunk to the floor. Catherine had come to her, as the King – who did her infinitely greater slight – had never done. 'You are always welcome in my house, Altesse,' she said.

'"Altesse", Madame?' Catherine smiled almost shyly.

'Trinette!' said Corisande, and they embraced, wetness on the demoiselle's cheek mingling with that on her own.

Catherine let herself bathe in relief – Corisande could have received her with the frosty courtesies due her rank; instead she showed her only kindness. Slowly they drew apart. With a gesture she summoned forward the aged woman who stood behind her. 'Madame,' she said, 'do you remember la Comtesse de Lindley, my governess? You met her, long ago, when . . . when I first came to l'Aquitaine.'

The lady dipped, stiff with age, infinitely dignified, and smiled warmly at Corisande. 'I esteemed you always, Madame. Never have I thanked you for the love you showed my child.'

Corisande curtseyed in response. Seven years – an eternity to a young demoiselle, but scarcely yesterday to the Comtesse. 'Madame de Lindley,' she said, 'your child has a heart well worthy of love.'

It was summer's end, a day made for riding in the country, and Catherine wished she were doing so, though it was no longer permitted without an escort of Gardes de Maison. The excuse was the war, though it had produced only more sea-raiding. The true reason, she suspected, was King Charles's embarrassment over the assault on her on the road to Arlennes – it had been followed by a great uproar, with ladies fearing to visit their estates lest they be set upon by highwaymen.

Outside Catherine's window birds sang, free to fly without asking for an escort. Only Madeleine was using the day as God intended, demonstrating the art of the chase to Laurent de Tremarais – who had become a regular visitor to the Hôtel de Guienne following his arrival with the news of the first of the sea-raids. Catherine thought him gallant to consent to a maid's instruction, though Solange was surely right that his quarry was Madeleine herself. Catherine, as a dutiful princess, was instead answering love letters, for falling out again with the Lusianes had not made an end to her suitors: they continued to swarm.

Solange sat at her feet, experimenting with a new open style of needlework called lacework, said to be all the fashion at Ravenna – ready too to assist Catherine in composing replies, for she had compiled a marriage book, listing every suitable prospect and what was known of him.

Five of the six swains who had written to Catherine had never seen her. Nevertheless the Imperial Elector of Angeln was so overcome with ardour as to offer her the city of Theissenburg – she wondered what the Theissenburgers thought of that. A letter from Pedro, Prince of Valencia, she put aside to answer last – he had evidently composed it himself, and Catherine smiled. For a boy of eight he had done his best to express how moved he was by her incomparable beauty, so he deserved a kindly answer. King Hernando's ministers would get a more tart missive, pointing out that the twenty-four galleys whose loan they sought were two dozen more than the Kingdom of Lyonesse possessed; her people were formidable at sea, but did not employ galleys, and if Catherine knew that, they certainly should.

The longest letter was from Marcello di Rinalfi, ruling Prince of Santanni. It proved fit to move the most stone-hearted maid, and Catherine said as much.

'It ought to, Mademoiselle,' replied Solange. 'His secretary is the poet Pietro Castelnuovo, who has conquered some of the noblest bedchambers in Enotria. The Contessa di Lanzeri left her husband for him.'

'No wonder!' said Catherine. The Prince's

sentiments, or Castelnuovo's, went well beyond the call of diplomacy. 'I'm half ready to yield, and I've never seen him, any more than— Hah!' She burst out laughing.

'What is it?' demanded Solange.

Catherine struggled to contain herself. 'My golden tresses! Lud's teeth – I suppose it sounds prettier than brazen tresses, but if he writes ten pages of sweet lies on his master's behalf, he might at least find that much out. "The Tall Redhead" – my hair colour is not a secret!'

'He doubtless means the golden tresses of your soul,' explained Solange.

'He means the golden crown of Lyonesse!' She handed the Prince of Santanni's epistle to Solange, and picked up the sixth letter.

She had written him once, trying as best she could to express her feelings, but saying it was better they have naught to do with each other while their countries were at war. He had continued to write all the same. With a sigh she kissed the Dauphin's seal and placed his letter in her casket unopened.

Catherine had one more letter to write, one that had nothing whatsoever to do with protestations of love. Her Ladyship had suggested that Catherine write to William de Havilland – the Earl of Avalon's son, who was said to be leading the sea-raids – and gently remind him how the war imperilled the heiress to the throne. She dipped her pen, blotted it and set to work:

Jhesu

My lord Willaume de Hauillande. I, Kateryn, dawter of
Harrye, Prince of late memorie, graund daughter of his
Maiestie Edmund, ivth of that Name, Kyng of
Lyonnesse &c, do wryte unto thee to shew my great and
goode approuement of those deeds in armes which thow
hast wroght upon the Aquitaine, in sundrie Places, viz.
Caramec which was taken, and Louselles despoiled, and
brennt, & also shyppes taken upon the sea. Wherein
hath been greyte grief & troubble unto Charles de
Héristal, who ex pretentio calleth himself Kyng in
Aquitaine.

Catherine wondered ruefully what the Dauphin, who
had spoken bitterly of the burning of Louselles, would
think of these words of commendation. Then she
reminded herself firmly that Louis had, after all, led the
assault upon Richborough, so it was no place of his to
question what was done in her grandfather's service!

I do gretely rejoyce, as surely doth euery loyal Subiect,
that thou hast in such manner made defiaunce &
admonyshment unto the same Charles, which sheweth
to the good honour of his Maiestie and the whole
kyngdom of Lyonesse. In this citye of Aix, wherein the
King of Aquitaine most oft sittith, is no thing spoken of
in late daies but thy boldness in address, the which far
surpasseth what hath been dared by any other.

*Yet so also is heard at euery hand infinite wayling
and gnashing, for that the Kyng of Aquitaine hath made
levy of new taxes upon euery order of folk (saueing
only the nobilitie), for that he might have the means to
contryve warre, and so be avenged for such greyte
affront as he deemeth thou hast delyvered unto him,
which was never before seene in the time of this king, or
of his father who rewled before him, for many one year.*

*And in that same wyse do I give trew
advertizment unto thee, that this same Kyng and his
councillors are said to be most resolved upon warre,
and for the same do have many prest to that servyce,
commons and nobilitie alike, and do also seek the hire
of soldiours and shippes, from the Free States and
otherwhere. Have a goode care, then, my lord, that the
Narrow Sea be well kept, and all placed in state of
defence. For if this busynesse proceed as the Kyng of
Aquitaine would have it, then standeth Lyonesse much
in his peril if needful measures be not taken.*

Now she came to the most delicate part of the letter:

*It behooveth no man, nor womman, nor chylde, that
anie privat care sholde be admitted in such case, when
the honour and good keepyng of the common wealth be
at hazard. Nor, in especiall, am I unmindful of my
estate and my dutie, which God forbid sholde euer be
forgot. Yet do I think it not remiss that I bid thee have*

remembraunce of me, that by no wish of mine own I am kept in this place, and so am in the hand and danger of the kyng of Aquitaine, and my sister Anne also. It did of late come to pass, upon the occasion of the spoylyng of Louselles, that a certayn part of the populace of this citie did riot in vent of their fury before my house. The number of them being not less than a thousand, so that I did thynk me that my last hour was nigh upon me, and did commend my soul unto Jhesu, and only by the veriest chaunce was delivered.

Catherine thought it more fitting not to say that veriest chance had come in the form of the Dauphin.

Being as that I am but a mayde, and of small yeares, I have not powre to resist, and have very few of mine own with me. So do I pray thee that thou mayst be mindful that I be not cast away without need. Yet do I humbly protest that I fear not to meet whatever shall be apporciouned unto me, trusting in thine own good loyaltie to his Maiesties Grace, and most especiallie in God, to which euerie heart is seen plaine, and which is our onlie salvation.

    Done by my hand this daie, being the xix of September, in the yeare of the Crown of Lyonesse MXXXIII, at the Hôtel de Guienne.
        Kateryn, Princess Lyon

Catherine read the letter over, aloud, and decided that it was at least more honest than diplomatic love letters. She read it over again, then took it to her Ladyship.

Solange picked a rose, one of the last of the autumn damasks, and watched Armand de Fossier watching her. Her gown was of black velvet trimmed with red ribbons, low necked and high waisted, and she entwined the rose in the ribbons of the bodice, taking care not to jab herself in places she would rather be caressed. 'There!' she said. 'Does it become me?'

'Charmingly,' admitted Armand. He reached to pluck it out, and Solange danced out of reach.

'*Noli me tangere!*' she said, and wagged an accusing finger at him. 'Not until you confess you have been seeing la Grinaud again, and resolve to sin no more!' Armand assumed a gratifying expression of guilt, though Solange would have been more gratified were he innocent. She had no intention of making a scene – weeping and cries of betrayal might embarrass men in the short run, but in the end made them flee.

Margot de la Fontenelle was making that mistake, Solange thought, and it would lead to the predictable end. She regarded Armand through lowered eyelashes. 'What does Madame de Grinaud have, Monsieur,' she demanded, 'that I have not? Oh yes – an exceedingly stupid husband! Is that not it? The conquest is greater if you put horns on another man? Very well, then,' she declared, 'I shall marry! A husband with a very good sword arm and a very hot temper, so that you embrace me at your peril. You would quite forget la Grinaud, no?'

Armand grinned. 'And what, my Solange, if your husband locks you away in a chamber? Or vindicates his honour as the Baron du Chapelle did? The loss would be tragic.'

'Oh!' Solange felt disarmed at a stroke. The baronesse had been quite notorious until her husband – placing honour above his head – stabbed her as the whole Court looked on. Solange's hand went un-consciously to her bosom, so she made the best of it. 'Ah – fate!' she cried. She clutched herself, head thrown back, with a dancing little half-turn as if in her death-throes. 'Shall you not write a poem of me then, Monsieur?' She began sinking to her knees. 'Shall you not at least catch me?' she added with a touch of asperity.

Armand de Fossier did, and his lips claimed a reward she willingly gave.

'Very much better, Monsieur!' Solange declared. Her concentration was broken again, by a little burst of applause – she and Armand had acquired an audience: three students and a handsome young robed scholar watched from the garden gate. 'Bravely done!' cried one. Solange sighed. Students and scholars crowded into the Hôtel de Guienne for the Sunday disputations, unfazed by the war, or what was called a war. 'Away with you!' she cried to the intruders. 'We are rehearsing a play to be presented before the Court. Away, I say, or I shall set my hounds on you!' The intruders retreated, the young lecturer only after a gallant bow, which Solange found satisfying – it would do Armand no harm to see that other learned men were also handsome of face and well knit of form. She turned back to him. 'Now, Monsieur, where were we? Oh, yes. You are to have no more to do with la Grinaud, that empty creature.'

Armand bowed and looked contrite. 'What was I to do, Mademoiselle? The Court removed to Montmorency for the whole of last winter. I had no choice but to go, and fifty miles of bitter winds and snow drifts lay between us. Alone, was I to pine away for you?'

'I pined quite well, Monsieur,' said Solange haughtily. 'In any case, you are back, and have been since spring – so it is long overdue that you show her your door for the last time.' The bells of Ste-Eulalie rang the hour of six and Solange stepped back. 'Monsieur – we have but an hour before the disputation. I must tend to my accounts, or Mademoiselle will be vexed.'

Armand frowned. 'Accounts?'

Solange permitted herself a faint smile. 'Yes, Monsieur. Come – I will show you.' Armand shrugged. He surely had no interest in the accounts of the Hôtel de Guienne, but followed her towards the counting-rooms.

The accounts were already checked – Solange had finished them by candlelight, while brewing leaves of maiden's prayer to ensure that this afternoon left no encumbrance – but she led him through offices to a store room and through a hidden door to a stair, and thence to the household chambers. She ushered Armand into the one that she and Madeleine shared – and Armand's eyes widened as he beheld the scene. 'Mademoiselle,' he said, 'I misjudged you again. You keep excellent accounts.'

'I am most careful with them, Monsieur,' Solange said. She poured a cup of wine and handed it to Armand, then set to work on the fastenings of his doublet. 'I regret that we must be hasty, Monsieur,' she told him. 'Yet what is life, but moments stolen from Eternity?'

Not the least virtue of her gown was that it came off with a minimum of fuss. A flick of her fingers and the ties were released; a shrug of her shoulders and the fabric slithered down about her waist so that only her translucent chemise remained between her bosom and Armand's eyes, then it too fell away . . .

An eternity later – an eternity scarcely long enough – it was over. Armand slid onto his side next to her and lay there, eyes closed, one arm lazily caressing her. She kissed him. 'You are most kind,' she said, 'to the daughter of an impoverished count.'

'No, *ma chère* Solange,' answered Armand, 'it is you

who are most kind, and forgiving of my sins. I swear I shall not stray again!'

When all was in order they went back down again into the garden, the world no wiser of their escapade. They strolled once around the garden, then went in the direction of the Great Hall.

'Mademoiselle—' said Armand suddenly. 'There is something I forgot to tell you.'

'Monsieur?'

'As you asked, I enquired into the affairs of wise women, astrologers and other such mountebanks. A notary in the quartier St-Léger deals also in matters frowned upon by the Church, and one day in early summer he was called upon by a gentleman who sought the meaning of certain fortune-tellers' cards.'

A tingle ran down Solange's spine. 'Yes, Monsieur?'

'He could not answer the gentleman's question himself, but knew others, more skilled, who could. Three days ago, the gentleman came back to learn what the notary had discovered. One of my men was in the neighbourhood and recognized him – he is one Monsieur Vernay.'

'Vernay?' repeated Solange. She made herself show no visible sign, but she knew exactly who M. Vernay was: he was a man in the employ of the Baron de Moine – and therefore, ultimately, in the service of Gérard, the Duc de Septimanie, and the house of Lusiane.

CHAPTER ELEVEN

A Time for Peace?

The first rays of the morning sun spilled over the hills that ran down to the sea east of Halverstrand town. On beyond the Westgate the sun threw a long shadow ahead of the horseman who rode at the gallop westward along the highroad. It cast a golden light on the half-timbered Hollingsworth country house, and through a kitchen window onto William de Havilland, who sat breaking his fast early beside the lady of the house.

It was his second visit home – or nearly home – since he'd come back from the Middle Sea. From Hollingsworth House the town and its castle lay only a morning's walk away, though the time had not yet come to make that brief journey, and while his father lived it might never come. But yesterday his lady mother had ridden out to Hollingsworth House to meet with him. After the tears of joy, and reproofs for his absence that were far more gentle than he merited, she told William what he already had heard. Trade was sick abed, dying of slow starvation on account of the war, yet the Privy Council had – in King Edmund's name – witlessly declared formal war on l'Aquitaine.

'Milady,' cried Meg's maid Bronwyn. 'Sir James is at the gate, and says that he must speak to his Lordship directly.'

'Lud's blood,' muttered William. In this too-brief visit he'd had nothing more from Meg than good solid food – and a couple of nourishing, wholehearted kisses. A splendid prize was Margaret Lady Hollingsworth! Whether she was for the taking he was yet unsure, but he had a fresh and following breeze and no wish to be becalmed by Sir James and matters of business.

'Admit Sir James and show him in, Brownie,' Lady Meg said. 'And lay a place at table for him.'

'His horse was fair lathered, Milady,' answered Bronwyn. 'He says as it's urgent he speak to his lordship straight away, beg pardon. He bears a sealed warrant from the King.'

'Pass the word that I'll hear him out anon,' William told Meg. A warrant from the King – that would mean from the Duke of Norrey as head of the Privy Council. He was in no hurry to read it.

Bronwyn showed in Sir James, who bowed to Lady Meg. 'Beg pardon the intrusion, my lady!'

'You are always welcome here, Jamie!' said Meg.

'More welcome at a better hour, I fear.' Sir James turned to William and fished a packet out of his doublet. 'Will! Sorry I am to burst in on your peace, but this came from Kelliwick under the King's privy seal. Addressed to your father, but yours to deal with given his condition.'

William tore open the packet and read the document within. It was a copy of an Order in Council, commanding his age-stricken father to raise an expedition to retake Richborough. For this his father was granted the King's press of men and ships – but not a farthing to arm and provision them, or keep them on the sea. 'God's teeth,' he muttered. 'The Privy Council commands that Richborough be retaken. With what means, they say not, but it is nothing to be attempted in any case.'

'I thought you desired no less,' said Lady Meg.

William looked Meg up and down. 'I desire any number of things!' Then he shook his head. 'In this war I have sought only to show the Aquitaine that Lyonesse still has teeth and claws. But we'll not get Richborough back, not now that the Aquitainers have it. It is not Caramec or Louselles! Charles of Aquitaine has put his best men and his best captains into the place, with plenty of artillery. And opened up his treasure rooms to pour a flood of gold into his galleys too.'

'I have always thought his galleys rather for show than for service,' admitted Sir James. 'But you know more of them than I do.'

'You'll learn!' said William. 'Once their crews have been seasoned at sea they are the devil to deal with. Galley service makes men quick, or leaves them dead. The heart of the matter is this,' he added thoughtfully. 'War is easier got into than got out of – and the time has come for us to get ourselves out of this one. To go in deeper instead, with no preparations and no supply, is foolish!' He held out his mug. 'Another pot, darling Meg, and I'll thank you kindly!'

'Give him another pot, Lady Meg,' advised Sir James. 'Ale is but water in the cup of this news. And I'll trouble you for one myself, by your kindness.'

'By my kindness the two of ye are drinking away a poor widow's substance.' But Lady Meg refilled William's pot, and poured two more for Sir James and herself.

Sir James spoke up. 'Will – there's another letter sent, this one for you alone.'

'Another letter? From whom?'

'The Princess Lyon,' said Sir James. 'At least it has her name and seal.' He drew it from his doublet and passed it to William, who broke the seal and opened it. It was written in an elegant Enotrian secretary hand, but the language was the honest Saxon tongue.

William read it aloud. ' "I, Kateryn, daughter of Harry, prince of late memory, granddaughter of His Majesty Edmund, fourth of that name, King of Lyonesse . . ." ' He read it through to the end.

'Well!' said Lady Meg when he was done. ' "Cast away without need." The maid might have wished a word or two with the Privy Council.'

'She might wish a word or two with *me*,' said William. 'She tells how a riot broke out in front of our old royal castle where she now lives, after we burned Louselles. And there's more. The word in the Free Estates is that she was waylaid in the country, accompanied only by ladies, servants and some huntsmen. Her party fought off the attackers. Princess Lyon indeed!'

Lady Meg studied William with a thoughtful expression, then raised her pot and drained the lot of it, as heroic a draught as William ever saw any woman take. 'So what is to be done?' she asked at last.

'I wish I knew,' said William. 'I'll try to compose some empty words to the Privy Council, and hope that they will sober up and go no further. You heard my lady mother last night: the merchants are grumbling. They grumble in the Free Estates as well – I have got an earful of it. Ravenna too wishes an end to this war. Their merchant galleys sail in convoy and fear no one – but where trade is strangled they find no buyers for their cargo, nor outbound merchandise to load. Senator Falier has spoken of it to me.'

'But what of King Charles of Aquitaine?' Sir James asked.

'If he chooses to spend a million in gold he can have all the war he wishes for,' said William. 'But he is not a fool. He might prefer to spend his gold on wenches, as has been his custom aforetime. I shall have to speak more with Senator Falier, before he goes to take up his post at the court of Aquitaine.'

* * *

For the first time in a year and a half Catherine found herself at the Palais de la Trémouille, Charles of Aquitaine having relented of her exile. She did not know why; perhaps the Court wished to see and gawk at Hippolyta, Princess of Amazons. She declined the offer to return to her old quarters – the Hôtel de Guienne was hers now – but, to her ladies' unconcealed delight, had accepted the royal invitation to be received at Court again.

In spite of herself, Catherine felt rather overawed by the vast splendour of the palace: its marble walls and great wide rows of windows, brilliant in the autumn light. The Hôtel de Guienne had been built in its time to convey the power and majesty of the Kings of Lyonesse, yet by comparison it was shabby and poor. Most intimidating of all was the palace's utter lack of defences. Nothing proclaimed more loudly the might of the King of Aquitaine – he had no need to dwell in a fortress: all the Aquitaine was his fortress, garrisoned by thirty thousand men.

She steeled herself to meet again with her uncle Gérard. Had the Duc de Septimanie truly contrived the murder of the fortune-teller – and then attempted to abduct Catherine herself? She had not raised the question with M. de Chirac yet, for she had not a scintilla of real evidence – only the slenderest of third-hand rumours.

She put speculation aside to concentrate on

practicalities. For her ladies the return to la Trémouille might be uncomplicated pleasure, but Catherine's first order of business was to see her sister, for the first time in a year and a half. Although she had written to Anne regularly – in both Saxon and Gallic, simple letters about everyday things – Anne's replies had been far less regular, and never more than perfunctory. With her Ladyship in train, along with Solange and Madeleine, Catherine made her way to Anne's Presence Chamber.

Moments later Anne's governess, Mme de Dampierre, emerged with Anne: her sister richly attired in a wine-coloured brocaded gown, her curly golden hair spilling out under her headdress. Anne was nearly twelve now, and looked it – Catherine realized that one day not so far off she would have to deal not only with her own marriage but also with Anne's.

'Catherine!' cried Anne. She glanced back at Mme de Dampierre, then came tentatively forward and made a grave curtsey, as though Catherine were a dignitary from abroad. Anne had always been attentive to proper form, if not to her studies.

Catherine gave not a farthing for the forms of the Court of la Trémouille. With perhaps more display of enthusiasm than she entirely felt, she swept up her sister in her arms and whirled her around. 'Nan! My little Nan!' she cried in the Saxon tongue. 'What a great girl you've grown into!' Only when she had twirled herself half dizzy did she set Anne down. 'Look at her, your

Ladyship!' she said. 'Do not lie, but confess that Nan was always the pretty one, so fair and rosy cheeked as she is! Do you remember her Ladyship, Nan? Of course you do! Curtsey to her now, to show her you can!'

Anne merely looked back at her, and it was plain that she remembered not a word of the honest Saxon tongue! Catherine felt she had failed in her own duty: Anne stood next in the line of succession, yet could not so much as speak the common tongue of her people.

Her Ladyship saved the hour. She knelt and addressed Anne gently in the Gallic tongue. 'Anne, *ma petite*,' she said, 'you do not remember me; you were so very young. I am the Comtesse de Lindley, and when you were little I was your governess too. Now we can get to know one another again! And surely you will come to see Kateryn in the Hôtel de Guienne, as she has come to see you.'

Anne bade her Ladyship rise, then turned back. 'But, sister!' she said. 'Are you not restored to favour? Madame de Dampierre told me you are, and shall be again at Court.'

'I shall come to Court, yes,' Catherine replied, 'but I have my own household now in the Hôtel de Guienne. A house of our forefathers!' she added. 'When you visit we'll go riding in the country, and you can resume your lessons.'

Anne looked doubtful. 'More lessons, Catherine? I

am made to spend so much time at them, and they are so dull!'

Her sister had small taste for learning, Catherine reflected. 'We'll speak of lessons another time!' she said. 'Now, by permission of Madame de Dampierre, we shall go to the garden. I have much to tell you – and you must have much to tell me!'

Mme de Dampierre gave her assent, with a stern warning to Anne to mind her deportment. She ushered forward two maids of twelve or thirteen, Anne's ladies-in-waiting.

They withdrew to the Montfaucon garden, turning bare now with the coming of autumn, and she, Anne and her Ladyship retreated to one side, away from their ladies and the other groups of courtiers in the garden. 'Do not go hard on Nan,' said her Ladyship softly. 'She is too young to remember Lyonesse. Rather give thanks to God that you do.'

Catherine made herself smile. 'Yes, your Ladyship; you are right, and I am indeed thankful.' She turned to her sister and addressed her in Gallic. 'You must listen to me, Anne. You do not remember Lyonesse, but you must know that we are at war with l'Aquitaine. We must hold ourselves as befits our rank and station, and I shall be at your side.'

Anne looked soberly back up at her. 'Please, Catherine – you are not going to make a scene as you did last year, are you? I shall be humiliated before everyone!'

'Anne!' cried Catherine. 'Our kingdom is at war, and you think only of the Court of Aquitaine?'

'Kateryn—' interjected her Ladyship. 'Bear easy—'

Catherine took a great breath, and closed her eyes in wordless prayer. 'Anne, I am sorry . . . this is all you know.' She took Anne by the hand. 'You must never forget that you and I are of Lyonesse, and of the House of Guienne, and our grandfather is as great a king in this world as Charles of Aquitaine. Do you understand that?'

'*You* do not understand!' cried Anne. 'Grandmère Louise explained everything to me. Lyonesse is ruled by the King's councillors, who send pirates to burn the towns on the coast, and turn mothers and babies out naked in the rain to starve.'

Catherine stared at her, momentarily speechless. Grandmère Louise! Their grandmother – and matriarch of the Lusianes. Was Anne slipping into her orbit? And how was Catherine to answer a lie that came so near to the truth?

'Our grandmother de Lusiane says that, Anne?' Catherine sought for words. 'What does she know of Lyonesse?' she demanded.

'I know quite enough!' said another voice behind her – Grandmère Louise.

Catherine turned slowly to face her. 'Indeed, Madame?' she said.

'I know that it made you a wild reckless demoiselle,' said her grandmother, 'more fit to live in a forest than among civilized Christian people. You may take pride in that; I am sure that you do! But consider this: were you not a royal heiress, where would you find a great enough fool to marry you?'

Burning with fury, Catherine raised her hand. Her Ladyship caught her arm and restrained it. 'Nay, Kateryn!' she said softly in Saxon. 'This is my quarrel as much as yours – and it is high time for me to do something I ought to have done years ago.' With that, her Ladyship took one step forward and firmly slapped the dowager duchess of Septimanie across her face.

It was so quick that Catherine could scarce believe it and Grandmère Louise stared in utter shock. The frozen tableau held for a few heartbeats; it seemed a near eternity. Then Grandmère Louise turned abruptly and strode away without another word spoken.

Her Ladyship turned to Anne, who shrank back, eyes wide with alarm and disbelief. Kneeling, her Ladyship addressed her: 'Anne, daughter of Henri!' she said in Gallic, her soft voice as firm as any king's command. 'I much grieve that you had to witness this, but you must heed what your sister has said! You too are a princess of Lyonesse, and the Lusianes have no authority over you. Not even your grandmother.'

Anne only shook her head. 'Madame la Comtesse must forgive me,' she said, 'but I am not like my sister! I would dread to be set upon by ruffians in a forest!' Before Catherine could say that she too had been terrified, Anne curtseyed – then fairly fled across the Montfaucon garden, towards the safety of her ladies-in-waiting.

Her Ladyship sighed. 'I am the one who must ask forgiveness, Kateryn!' she said. 'I fear I did you no good service this day.'

'You did me a great service!' said Catherine. 'And so you always have, and your service today was noble! But I have done poor service towards Nan, I fear. When I was dismissed from Court I thought only of myself! Now I see that I left Nan alone there, with none to watch out for her.' Catherine felt somewhat of a hypocrite in saying it, for it came to her that she did not truly like her sister very much. All the same she had failed in a duty.

'You have done what you can, Kateryn,' said her Ladyship. 'Some things are not in our power to change.'

Catherine felt now as if she had no power to change anything. For all of her Ladyship's magnificent gesture, everything about this day was dragging Catherine back, turning her again into an awkward gangly girl adrift in a vast and alien court. Yes, she had ridden down and slain a man in the forest, and yes, that befitted a prince of Lyonesse – but who indeed would marry her, were she not heiress to a throne?

Young men's voices carried across the garden. One hushed the rest with a sharp word – the last voice Catherine wanted to hear at that moment. But here was her answer to Grandmère Louise, if she wanted one –

the noblest chevalier in Christendom sought to marry her, and he was no fool, even if marriage between them was surely impossible. Booted feet approached along the gravel path, and it took all Catherine's will to turn and face him.

He doffed his cap and inclined his head. 'Altesse.'

Catherine curtseyed in reply. 'Monseigneur.'

He glanced at her Ladyship. 'Comtesse. If you will excuse us.' He gestured towards a corner of the garden. Catherine followed him, her Ladyship delicately withdrawing a few paces. The Dauphin faced her. 'You have not answered my letters, Catherine.'

'Yes I did, Louis.'

'Only the first.'

'I could answer a hundred,' said Catherine, 'and it would be the same. We are at war. What else is there to say?'

'Louis and Catherine are not at war.'

'Louis and Catherine do not decide.'

'You are the most stubborn demoiselle in the world!'

Catherine smiled in spite of herself. 'I try to be.'

For an instant the Dauphin glared at her, his face darkening. When he was Louis IX, the world might fear that expression – she feared it now. Then, explosively, he laughed. 'Certainly you succeed!' he cried. 'Catherine, Catherine, what am I to do with you?'

Don't lay siege to me! It was at the tip of her tongue; she held it back, wished she hadn't even thought it, because her next thought was how very much she'd like to fall to him. 'Remember who we both are,' she said at last. 'If I were Louis and you were Catherine, would you say any less?'

He smiled, that insouciant smile so hard to resist. 'I hope I would say more! But you will have to decide that for yourself. In time, I think you will.' He stepped back and bowed, and Catherine managed to dip in reply. Then he turned, and was gone.

Attended only by a minimal escort, Margot de la Fontenelle made her way through the bustle of the South Bank to the rue Frontenac. The hour was well past dark, the crowds in the streets vaguely menacing. The torchbearer's light showed a looming blackness filling out half the sky, then a massive gate flanked by stone towers: the Hôtel de Guienne. A light shone faintly through a tiny window at one side.

Margot hesitated. There was still time to draw back – but time was something that she could no longer waste. His Majesty was growing restless, too attentive in his flirtation with other women, and for the first time, she sensed that her hold on him was beginning to slip. Perhaps it was nothing! But if it were not, she needed . . . something . . . to fall back on.

And so Margot had come here, to the gate of the Hôtel de Guienne. Princess Catherine might be her enemy – was certainly her enemy – but Margot had found her curiously refreshing to deal with. The girl was forthright! Even the slap at Montpassier, though unforgiveable, had at least been honest. If only she could win her over to the cause of the Lusianes, thought Margot, she might gain favour with her family. And the family interest would be something to hold onto, even if she lost favour with the King.

She motioned her servant to knock on the great door.

'Saliarde, that most perfect of knights, drew from his pouch the golden tooth of the dragon Oriandel, and laid it at the feet of King Dolado. 'I bring this in token, Sire, that Oriandel troubles your land no more, and that ladies and humble pilgrims may journey without fear.'

No sooner had Saliarde spoken these words than the golden dragon's tooth burst into flame, and a great smoke billowed forth from it. And when the smoke cleared, where the dragon's tooth had been now stood King Dolado's lost daughter Therasiane. And she knelt before him, saying, "O Father, by this brave knight's deeds am I restored unto thee. I beg of you that you may give him that boon he has sought from you . . ."'

As Catherine closed the book of *Saliarde of Cockaigne*, Solange sighed ostentatiously. She picked up her needlework from her lap, where it had lain quite neglected while Catherine read aloud. 'Ah, Mademoiselle,' she said, 'where shall we find such knights in our time?' Their conversation was interrupted by a knock on the door; the under-steward bade entry and Catherine told him to come in. 'As please,' he said, 'Mademoiselle de la Fontenelle is at the gate, and begs that she may be received.'

This was a genuine surprise. Catherine had met with Margot half a dozen times, sometimes in the country, sometimes in city gardens. She had never expected, however, that the maîtresse-en-titre would show herself at the Hôtel de Guienne – especially now, when Catherine's breach with the Lusianes was complete. Yet here she was. 'Show her in, Leclerc,' she told the under-steward. 'And let her servants be taken to the kitchen and offered food and drink.'

Presently Margot was ushered into the Privy Chamber. 'The Princess Lyonne is most kind to receive me!' she said. She curtseyed and unfastened her cloak, revealing another minor surprise, for her gown was in the Ravennate style that Solange and Madeleine had made popular. Catherine herself was wearing a similar one, made for her by Solange – though the style made so little pretence to modesty that she could wear it only in her own chambers. Margot looked fetching in it: daring, certainly, but not the least like a whore. Madeleine took her cloak, and set a stool for her by the fireplace, and tray of bread, apples, forcemeats and wine. Margot thanked her and sat down.

'Welcome to my house, Mademoiselle de la

Fontenelle!' said Catherine. It was all a bit odd, she thought. Seated by the fire, Margot might have been taken as another lady of her household. 'You missed a romance of chivalry,' Catherine added. 'The adventures of Saliarde, knight of Cockaigne.'

'I am sorry to have missed them,' said Margot. 'But I have come to beg you to see reason, and not be at war with your family.'

Catherine bit her lip on the impulse to say that her family was the royal House of Guienne. 'My country is at war with l'Aquitaine,' she said, 'but I am not at war with anyone.'

'The Duc de Septimanie and his mother – your grandmother – believe that you make war against them,' said Margot. 'They did not send me here! Nor the Baron de Moine, nor the duke, nor even his Majesty – I have come to you of my own accord.'

'I believe you!' said Catherine, and decided that in fact she did. 'Yet I am not at war with the Lusianes, whatever they think. Even the Countess of Lindley is not at war with them, whatever my grandmother might think. And I am not at war with you – you are not my enemy, Margot.' Certainly not my friend, added Catherine to herself – but who could say what might come to pass?

'That woman – Madame de Chirac – is my enemy!' said Margot. 'And you are her friend. Does that not make us enemies?'

'You are mistaken about Corisande,' Catherine told

her. 'Do you truly believe that she wishes to resume her old place with King Charles? She does not love you, Margot – but she does not hate you! She is Monsieur de Chirac's happily married wife – they even have a child on the way. She has left the past behind.'

'Yet this involves her!' said Margot. 'Was it not she who turned you against your uncle de Septimanie, and your own grandmother?'

'No—' began Catherine, then cut herself off. What did she really know?

'You hesitate,' said Margot.

'I was a child,' Catherine replied. 'And I was here in a strange land, scarcely speaking the Gallic tongue. I understood little, but I have learned much since then. When my mother the Princess Marie brought me here to l'Aquitaine – after my father was killed – her family demanded that she remarry, to make another alliance for the Lusianes. They had no regard for her, or for me, or my sister, or for the realm of Lyonesse! And they so hounded my mother until she retreated into the convent where she died.'

Catherine had pieced the whole story together by degrees, from things said by Corisande, by her husband, and by her Ladyship. She had never really spoken of it to anyone – how was she speaking of it now, and to Margot de la Fontenelle?

'I was a child then too,' said Margot, 'and not at Court. But I have also learned much! Did Madame de

Chirac befriend you for your own sake? Or to further the policy of the man who is now her husband?'

It was, Catherine acknowledged to herself, a very good question. Margot de la Fontenelle might be a harlot, but she was no fool. 'How can I say?' she admitted. 'Perhaps it was both! Madame Corisande has always shown me kindness, strange though that may seem to you. But yes, she is a woman of policy. She is loyal to King Charles, and loyal to her husband.'

'Madame de Chirac and her husband have always poisoned his Majesty against our family,' said Margot. 'The duke fears that the crown might move against him. And because he is afraid, I am in disfavour with him!' Abruptly she looked away from Catherine. She might have said more than she intended.

'I suppose you owe much to the duke and the Lusianes,' said Catherine. 'They brought you to Court, and saw that you were placed before King Charles's eye.' In plain and simple truth, she thought, Septimanie and the Lusianes had been Margot's procurers – offering an unimportant but pretty relative for the royal bed. And Margot surely knew it better than anyone. Margot's misfortune was the same as hers: they were both tied to the Lusianes. 'Yet you need not be their servant!' she said. 'You are not without friends.'

Margot shook her head. 'You do not understand! His Majesty has become impossible to please!' she cried. 'Without him . . . and if the Lusianes have turned against me – I shall have nowhere to go!' She looked genuinely distraught.

Catherine said nothing for some time. She and her ladies had speculated more than twice about Margot's uncertain standing with King Charles, but what Catherine had never thought of was how it must feel to be falling from favour, and to know it. Corisande had fallen from favour, and into the bed of a loving husband. Could Margot de la Fontenelle expect such good fortune? She had as yet no husband, even in name, but having a husband had turned out badly for Corisande's predecessor, Diane de Trièxe ... Were those tears in Margot's eyes, or was it just a trick of the fire?

Catherine made a decision. 'You have a place to go if you wish, cousin Margot,' she said. 'The gates of the Hôtel de Guienne are always open to you! You may stay here as my guest, as long as you wish. At least while my grandfather lives!' she added. 'Then I must return home to Lyonesse.'

For long, long moments Margot looked back at her. Then, slowly, she shook her head. 'That is impossible, Princess Lyonne. I am as I am, and cannot transform into another creature. There is no place for me here.' She rose to her feet. 'You have been most generous to receive me, but I must go. I ask you one more time to reconsider your enmity with the House of Lusiane!'

'I too am what I am,' said Catherine. 'A daughter of the House of Guienne – and of Lyonesse.'

This time it was Solange who rose to her feet, fetched Margot's cloak and saw her out. Not a word more was spoken.

'Name this child,' ordered the priest.

Catherine stepped forward with the swaddled infant. 'She is to be called Catherine, *Père*,' she declared. Beside her stood Madame Corisande, clasping by one hand her son by the King, M. de Chirac at her other side, along with the Duc de Numières and Catherine's ladies-in-waiting, all in the baptistery of St Marc, parish church of Clermont-sur-Brassy, on this day after Twelfth Night.

'*Catharina, ego te baptizo in nomine Patris et Filii et Spiritus Sancti,*' intoned the priest, and sprinkled holy water over the infant's brow. Little Catherine de Chirac let out a squall, then subsided into happy burbling and drooled spittle.

The service ended, the priest charging de Numières and Catherine with their duties as godfather and godmother, and all retired to the modest château on the rise of the hill. The feast was not modest at all, and Catherine teased Madame Corisande that this was no way to restore her figure, though in truth her friend was as resplendent as ever.

When the last course was done, Corisande's husband drew Catherine aside, and his expression turned more serious. 'We believe, Altesse,' he said, 'that we have found the leader of the men who beset you on the road to Arlennes.'

Catherine looked at him sharply. She had not expected such news. 'You believe, Monsieur?' she said. 'He has not confessed?'

'If so,' said de Chirac, 'it was only to God. He will not confess to us even under the severest questioning. You see, he was found dead.'

Catherine bit her lip. After some moments' hesitation, she did confess to him what she'd learned about the murder of Mère Angelique.

De Chirac looked sharply at her. 'You said nothing of this, Altesse!'

'I had no proof,' said Catherine. 'And the assault was upon me – a matter of Lyonesse, not l'Aquitaine. Does King Charles come to me for aid?'

De Chirac allowed a slight smile. 'No, Altesse, he does not. Happily, Armand de Fossier is in my service, and told me as well as his mistress about what he had learned! In any case, we know some things and suspect a good many more.'

'And do these things involve my loving uncle the Duc de Septimanie? Is he to be arrested?'

'*Hélas*, Altesse, that is impossible, at least for now.' De Chirac spread his hands. 'It would reach too high, and touch too many. Yet a conspiracy discovered is a conspiracy broken.'

'But my uncle of Septimanie—'

'– Regards you, just as he regarded your mother before you, as a rightful legacy of the Lusianes. By his lights, by her refusal to marry again your mother defied the family to which she owed everything. Many – among the nobility, perhaps most – would say that his view is only reasonable and just.'

'Do *you* think it reasonable and just, Monsieur?' asked Catherine. 'Does King Charles?'

'I did everything in my power to keep you out of the hands of the Lusianes,' said de Chirac. 'Of much greater consequence, Madame did all that was in *her* power – which at that time was much greater than mine.' De Chirac smiled again, wryly. 'You owe a great deal to her!'

Catherine nodded gravely. 'I owe Corisande more than I can ever repay in life,' she said. 'I realized that on the road to Arlennes. God kindly gave me the chance to ask her forgiveness.'

'Even more kindly,' said de Chirac, 'God gave you the will to do so! The gratitude of princes is measured, and necessarily so. But I do not think it will be the worse, for yourself or for Lyonesse, that you had the courage to embrace one who cherishes you.' For a moment he hesitated. 'You are not a stranger to policy, Altesse, any more than his Majesty is. You have no love for your uncle of Septimanie, or for the house of Lusiane. Yet you did not hesitate to deal with them! Even with Margot de la Fontenelle. Which I confess surprised both myself and Madame!'

'That was only a matter of policy!'

De Chirac nodded. 'Indeed it was, Altesse – as I was saying.'

Catherine had blundered right into it. As grave as the subject was, she nearly laughed. 'Ah, Monsieur! You have caught me out!'

'The truths of statecraft have caught you out,' said de Chirac. 'As they catch all of us who deal with crowns. You play a higher game than your uncle: he thinks of estates; you think of kingdoms. He may come to rue that he used you so poorly. All the same, you are right. His Majesty would not be sorry to put the bridle to Septimanie. But this matter reaches higher.'

'Higher, Monsieur?' Who could be higher than a duke? Oh, of course!' she exclaimed. 'Margot!'

De Chirac shook his head. 'No, Altesse. I shall speak in confidence, trusting to your judgement.' He lowered his voice. 'This matter touches Pépin.'

'*Pépin?*' Catherine blurted it out loud enough that those at the table looked up. She certainly could not imagine Pépin at the heart of a conspiracy. 'But—'

'But why?' de Chirac finished her question. 'Your friend the Dauphin is heir to the throne, Altesse, and Pépin is not. Yet he too would very much like to wear a crown. And the Duc de Septimanie has placed the dish of temptation before him.'

Catherine did not know whether to shudder or laugh. 'They meant to seize me and force me into a marriage with Pépin?' I would sooner die, she thought, but not before cutting Pépin's throat! If she would not give herself and her crown to Louis, who had every princely quality, she would certainly not give them to Pépin, who had none. 'But the Church,' she said. 'The Patriarch would not give a dispensation.'

'The matter was not pressed as it could have been, Altesse,' said de Chirac. 'His Majesty thought better of it.'

For once Catherine was thankful to the King of Aquitaine. 'But then,' she asked, 'how could Pépin overcome not only the Church but his father the King?'

'You are not yet a mother, Altesse,' de Chirac said, 'as I hope you one day shall be. I have only this last fortnight become a father, and am still amazed. Yet already I am learning how one can dote on one's child! You may not love Pépin, but his father does.' He paused. 'The world may sometimes think his Majesty a foolish king, but in fact he is a wise one. He set aside his heart's desire for the good of his realm. Pépin as King of Lyonesse would only make trouble for his brother – which is surely what the conspirators have in mind. Moreover, a cadet branch of the royal house on the throne of Kellouique might one day pose a deadly danger.'

That, thought Catherine, was plain enough. A branch of the House of Héristal would have a stronger claim on the throne of Aquitaine than the House of Guienne alone ever had. 'I shall be content with the throne of

Lyonesse,' she told him. And would not marry Pépin for the throne of the *world*, she said to herself.

Then she thought of someone else whom Pépin might sooner wish to marry – and who had already showed herself all too compliant towards the House of Lusiane. '*Bon Dieu!*' she cried. 'Anne!'

Her sister was not heiress to the throne of Lyonesse. But if some mishap should befall Catherine herself . . .

'You see,' said de Chirac, 'how . . . delicate . . . this matter is.' He sighed, and again spread his hands. 'You are discovering, at a young age, the perils that can go with a crown. Or even the prospect of a crown. Yet the less said of it, the better! I beg you keep it in uttermost confidence, Altesse.'

'I shall do so,' she said quietly.

CHAPTER TWELVE

Disputations

The disputants made their closing arguments and bows, and applause filled the Great Hall, the under-steward ringing his bell for some time to no avail. This disputation had been particularly spirited: the battle of Ancients and Moderns fought out in rhetorical cut and thrust, though the disputants' flourishes came down to two things Solange already knew: the Ancients were dead, while the Moderns were fools. The Moderns, she decided, had the better of that argument. They might be fools, as she was, but they were actually *alive*.

Gradually the applause subsided, and the second part of the evening's business began. Robed scholars, workmanlike painters, young gentlemen wearing their whole wealth, gathered around the High Table to press their works, proposals and petitions on the royal heiress of Lyonesse. Statesmen might ponder what prospect, if any, Princess Catherine had of one day sitting on her grandfather's throne, let alone keeping herself there. Those crowding around the High Table made a simple calculation: Mademoiselle's favour *might* one day bring great fortune. Some made even a simpler calculation, to flirt with ladies of rank.

Solange's concern of the moment was neither place-seekers nor flirters. A young man had come late into the hall. His bold, red, slashed apparel set him off from the students around him; more to the point it marked him as a Theudish gentleman. Envoys from the Imperial Elector of Angeln had recently come to Court, and the Elector was in the marriage book Solange had drawn up: indeed, he had once written to Mademoiselle, offering her the Free and Imperial City of Theissenburg – which, as it turned out, was not his to give, though princely suitors rarely let such details trouble them.

More to the point, the Elector had ties by marriage to the Duc de Septimanie and the house of Lusiane, so his retainers and servants would need to be watched like hawks. Solange had suspected that one of them might seek to enter the Hôtel de Guienne – and that beefy young man in garish red looked the part. His presence here, thought Solange, would doubtless be reported to M. de Chirac before the night was done. For now it was her duty to investigate him further herself, on Mademoiselle's behalf.

At a nod from Mademoiselle, she stepped down from the High Table and made her way through the crowd. At first they gave way, albeit with appraising glances; regulars knew her for a lady of the household. Then she was in the thick of the press, threading against the tide.

The Moderns, as their disputant champion had noted, were exploring seas and finding lands unknown to the Ancients. One Modern's hand was overly eager to explore her waistline; Solange firmly slapped it away. Presently her quarry came into view, unmistakably one of the gentleman-attendants who had come with the Elector's ambassador.

His slashed doublet was in spectacularly bad taste. The man himself was well-favoured, in a large, florid way – not Solange's usual preference, but as God had made men pleasing in variety, she accepted the divine bounty. The Theudishman's bushy eyebrows went up on seeing her. He made a fine bow, and Solange curtseyed in reply.

'Monsieur?'

'*Fräulein!*' he said in his own tongue, then changed to good if accented Gallic. 'At your service, Mademoiselle!'

As Solange soon discovered, he was a gentleman-attendant to the Elector, by name of the Ritter von Holtmann. He was in good spirits, and hence talkative – Solange guessed that he had visited a tavern or three while making his way to the rue Frontenac. Intending to keep him talking, she refilled his cup in the kitchen, passing near enough the High Table to catch Madeleine's eye. Madeleine looked annoyed – she plainly thought the task of prying knowledge out of a handsome Theudish soldier should be hers, whether she had any talent for it or not.

The evening was mild even for May, and students

drifted out of the Great Hall into the courtyard, in no hurry to disperse to their garrets. Solange and von Holtmann drifted out with them. She kept him talking, plying him with wine, tasty bits of gossip from la Trémouille, and questions about court affairs of Angeln. Frivolous women's questions; men at least would take them for frivolous, and Solange found his answers instructive. He explained in detail how the Elector's chief envoy kept two mistresses, blissfully unaware that his young and pretty wife warmed the Elector's own bed. Von Holtmann, Solange decided, was a touch naïve – the envoy doubtless knew exactly how his wife diverted herself, consoling himself with his office, stipend and mistresses.

Someone in the Great Hall struck up a drinking song. Students in the courtyard joined in, till the Hôtel de Guienne echoed with three hundred voices:

Vivant omnes virgines,
Graciles, formosae!
Vivant et mulieres,
Tenerae, amabiles
Bonae, laboriosae!

How admirable of students, thought Solange, to praise good, hard-working women as well as pretty demoiselles. They ought to, given how many lived off their mistresses. Their singing made conversation impossible, and she guided von Holtmann through the garden gate, beginning to wonder as she did so if he was the minor retainer he claimed to be. He drained his cup again, and she refilled it from her own. *In vino veritas!* He'd had a great deal already; she would ply him with as much more as it took to get the truth out of him.

She guided his tale of conquests back towards the Elector's mistress, a lady whose most intimate secrets von Holtmann seemed to know remarkably well, and a suspicion took form in Solange's mind: this was surely no gentleman-servant, but the Imperial Elector of Angeln himself! She decided to flush him out. 'So,' she asked, 'do you still wish to marry Princess Catherine? Or have King Charles's daughters so batted eyes at you that you will leave my lady mistress disconsolate?'

'Indeed I would rather marry her!' he declared – his careless words an admission that he was indeed the Elector. He laughed. 'Your princess is prettier than Charles of Aquitaine's daughters! Yet I confess, Mademoiselle, that I like you even more! Yours are larger,' he added by way of explanation. It was factual, if scarcely diplomatic; for some time he'd been looking covetously at what her Ravennate gown displayed in the flaring torchlight. 'Round as melons!' he exclaimed.

Solange began edging towards the garden gate. The Elector edged along with her, staying between her and the gate. Abruptly he tested her 'melons' for ripeness, less gently than he might have, splashing wine over her bodice, and Solange gasped, then managed to turn it into a sort of laugh and spanked his hand away. 'Monsieur!'

The Elector roared with laughter – then grabbed her about the waist and kissed her roughly. The wine on his breath was overpowering, and Solange wondered if she could be suffocated by fumes as his other hand started pulling up her skirts.

'Monsieur!' she cried, and struggled again, without effect. Over the roistering singers in the courtyard, no one would hear her cries. The time for diplomacy was past. Hiking up her own skirts, she tried to knee him in the codpiece. He grunted, but kept his grip – then ripped her gown off her shoulder and shoved her down, landing on top of her and nearly knocking the wind out of her. 'Monsieur – I beg you—!' she gasped. He laughed again and said something in Theudish.

She had only one measure left to protect her honour, an extreme one. As he pawed at her and began pulling up her skirts in earnest, Solange hesitated for a moment, then decided: the Elector of Angeln had forfeited the rights of a chevalier, of a prince of the Empire, even of a drunkard, and the Comte de Charleville's daughter would do what she had to do. Her right hand worked its way through a fitchet in her overskirt till she found the ivory hilt. She would have one chance only, and would have to strike true . . .

* * *

'Me as Diana?' said Madeleine, and laughed. 'You waste good flattery, Maître van Guilder!'

'I never flatter, Mademoiselle du Lac,' said the young man, 'save when very well paid.'

Princess Catherine heard it and gave him a sharp look across the High Table. Van Guilder, a painter from the Free Estates, had been retained during the winter to paint a miniature of her for use in marriage negotiations, though no suitor had yet been so favoured as to receive it. He had also offered to paint her as Helen of Troy, an offer declined but not ignored. He was an excellent flatterer.

Van Guilder turned, produced a heavy sheet of paper from his packet and passed it to Madeleine. 'You may judge for yourself!' The drawing was the merest sketch, but a clear likeness of the demoiselle: turning, raising her bow to defend herself against a pursuing Actaeon. Madeleine blushed – Diana's tunic made only the very slightest concession to modesty.

Mademoiselle snatched it out of her hand, studied it and looked over it at van Guilder. 'Not very practical for hunting, good master,' she said. 'Her arms and legs would be scratched by the underbrush! I suppose goddesses aren't troubled by such things?'

'Of course not, Altesse,' said van Guilder.

'Yet you would make *me* a mere mortal. Don't tell me what Helen would wear – I can guess. But what of

Mademoiselle de Charleville? Does she win no honours from you?'

The painter bowed again. 'The Empress Servilia, Altesse.'

'In her bath, I presume,' said Madeleine, 'witnessing the arrest of the conspirators?' It was one of Solange's favourite stories.

'Where *is* Solange, anyway?' asked Mademoiselle. 'Still conversing with the gentleman from Angeln?'

'In some form, no doubt,' replied Madeleine. 'I wonder what Armand de Fossier would think of it?'

'He would protest her infidelity all the way to Madame de Grinaud's door,' said Mademoiselle. 'He and Solange deserve each other. Servilia in the bath, indeed! Madeleine, go see what she is up to. Master van Guilder will try and abduct me to Troy, but I shall resist him. A thousand ships might not be launched for me, but I would settle for a dozen ships of Lyonesse.'

Madeleine stepped down, and made her way through the Great Hall to the courtyard, her cloak draped over her left arm. She had no need of a cloak on this pleasant evening – but under its folds she carried her scabbarded sword. A brawl had erupted following a disputation the previous autumn – the guards had broken it up with only a handful of wounded – and as her father said, honour was dead in the world. The crowd in the courtyard was thinning, but Solange and the Theudish chevalier were nowhere to be seen there. She called through the garden gate. 'Solange?'

'Call the guards!' cried Solange from somewhere in the shadows. '*Now!*'

'Hold your tongue, girl!' shouted a man. Then a blow and a yelp.

Madeleine pushed through the gate. A man sprang to his feet; amid the shadows cast by the flaring torchlight Madeleine could just make out a figure on the ground. With fury and sick fear, she threw back the cloak over her left hand and drew her sword. 'You – hold!' she shouted. 'In the name of Princess Catherine, you are under arrest!'

'You know who I am, girl?' demanded the man. 'I am the Elector of Angeln!'

'Do I care?' retorted Madeleine.

The man laughed, and drew sword and dagger. Amid the crowd in the Great Hall, Madeleine had not seen he carried a sword – but she should have known he'd wear one, whether he was a gentleman-retainer or a prince of the Empire. This was not good at all.

Shouting something in Theudish, the man charged her. Madeleine had just time to think, *Bon Dieu,* he's going to kill me! – then she brought up her sword to parry, as her dancing-master had taught her, and Papa before him. Blades clanged, her hilt twisting so sharply in her hand she thought she would lose it, but her wrist turned with it and she held on. Springing to her right, she swept her blade at the torchlit figure before her, but he parried with his dagger, then lunged. Twirling her cloak she caught his sword-tip on her blade, twisted it aside and danced back out of reach – dancing was something Madeleine knew how to do.

It gave her a moment to catch her breath as her assailant glowered at her, sidelit by the torch near the gate. He lunged. She skipped left; their blades rang, and they were apart again. His moves were swaggering, incautious; a skilled swordsman would have the advantage of him. She could only dance, and hope for a mistake. Solange had got to her feet, holding up her torn bodice with one hand, her poniard in the other. Madeleine stayed at guard, on the balls of her feet, the tip of her blade describing small circles, steel glinting in the torchlight. She wanted to cry out to Solange not to be a fool, but dared not – and Solange was no fool; if she could slip up behind the Theudishman it might be their only chance.

Her approach was ghost-silent, but of his own the Theudishman began to circle left, spied her – and whirled on her, blade flashing. 'Run!' screamed Madeleine, heart in her throat, springing after him even as Solange cried out, stumbled and fell across a low hedge. The Theudishman turned back and charged Madeleine, but carelessly – she snapped out her cloak to catch his blade, then lunged. His dagger came up to ward off her thrust, but too late. Her point found his shoulder, and she drove it in with all her strength.

His bellow shook the air. He staggered, but stayed on his feet, then ripped his sword free of her cloak and lunged at her. Madeleine jumped back, but had to let go of her sword, leaving it pinned through his left shoulder. Cursing in Theudish, he ran after her, and with a little cry of sheer terror she dodged and scrambled away. She had run him through, but now was disarmed – what an absurd way to die! She tripped on something and nearly fell, then heard behind her a crash.

The Theudishman – the Elector of Angeln, as he had proclaimed himself – lay on his side, groaning, his sword still in his right hand, his left tugging at the blade through his shoulder. Solange appeared out of the shadows, still holding her gown in place.

'Stand back!' ordered Madeleine. 'Find my cloak and throw it over him!'

The man glared up at her. 'I'll see you in Hell, girl!' he gasped.

Solange answered him. 'You may see *me* there, Monsieur, but do not look for Mademoiselle du Lac!'

'This has caused no end of difficulties, Altesse!' said Antoine de Chirac. Unless infection took hold the Elector would live; but Antoine was not sure whether that made matters better or worse.

His chief difficulty sat facing him. Just turned sixteen, Catherine de Guienne looked and carried herself like a young woman. More to the point, she conducted herself like a prince. 'The Elector of Angeln caused both of us difficulties, no, Monsieur?' she said.

Antoine shook his head. 'The Elector caused his own difficulties,' he replied. 'You cause mine! You persist in embarrassing his Majesty – fighting off brigands, who are not supposed to exist in this kingdom, and having ladies who defend their honour entirely too well.'

'Should ladies not defend their friends' honour?' asked Princess Catherine. 'Or indeed their own?'

'They should perish in the attempt, Altesse. Poets gain subject matter; the Church sometimes gains a saint.' Antoine shrugged. 'Everyone is happy, except the unfortunate lady. As it is, Mademoiselle du Lac has caused something of a scandal. The world will be told that it was a drunken accident – in a sense, perhaps, it was – but some will guess the truth.'

'And if they do?'

'They will blame *you*, Altesse!' said Antoine. 'Whether Madeleine du Lac ever finds a husband with the courage to enter her bedchamber is her concern. Whether *you* find one concerns the world, including his Majesty, and therefore me. You are gaining a reputation, Altesse, as the most beautiful princess in Christendom – and the most dangerous.'

'I am content to be the most dangerous!'

Antoine permitted himself a smile. 'Why am I not surprised?' Placed in her own household, with none to supervise her save an aged dowager who could not compel obedience, Catherine de Guienne should have foundered in a sea of scandal. Instead she had annoyed half the princes of Christendom with her tart replies to their suits. Still they were drawn by her prospect of a crown – a few, perhaps, even by her bold spirit.

She posed one further difficulty that he could admit only to himself: her reconciliation with Corisande. It had been far easier to deal with her when he had no reason to like her.

'Madeleine du Lac de Montpellier,' said Catherine, 'the Elector of Angeln, through his ambassador the Markgraf, demands that your life stand forfeit for the injury done him.' She drew Madeleine's sword. 'With this sword I give him answer. Kneel.'

Madeleine knelt before her, as ever with perfect grace.

'I have no power to dub any man knight,' declared Catherine, 'and none has the power to knight a demoiselle. Yet I have the power God grants us all, to give honour to courage and loyalty.' She tapped Madeleine with the blade, on one shoulder and the other. 'Rise, Madeleine the Valiant.' Madeleine rose, blue eyes glistening. Catherine sheathed the sword and handed it back to her. 'Wield this blade as you have, for right and justice!'

The ambassador exploded. 'You do greater insult, Princess Lyonne, and I tolerate no more! The world shall know of this outrage!'

Catherine whirled on him. 'The world shall know what? That your master laid forcible hands on my lady-in-waiting? That when my other lady made protest, he drew steel against her and she vanquished him in single combat? By all means let the world know! The world has always need of mirth, and the Elector of Angeln has given it something to laugh about when we are all in our graves!'

Armand de Fossier sat in a wine shop in the quartier St-Léger, nursing his cup. It cost a liard and was worth less. The cheapness of wine sold in St-Léger was one of the two virtues of this quarter. The other was that his creditors were unlikely to seek him here. In his purse he had precisely one douzaine and six more liards. Along with his sword and clothing, and some personal effects not yet pawned, they constituted his worldly possessions. Enough for two more cups of this wretched stuff, and a loaf of bread. That would be his supper, and he'd buy another loaf in the morning. Beyond that . . . ? Armand had not yet determined among the rather few choices open to him.

'*Pardieu!*' he muttered. His empty reflections were drawing him away from the immediate situation. Bourgeois! Ah, for the days when that rabble of shop-keepers and pawnbrokers would fall to their knees, wailing at seeing an inch of a nobleman's bared blade! Now they came, gens d'armes in tow, to demand repayment to the uttermost sou. Armand had of course read M. de Chirac's treatise on the finances of the crown. He understood that the prosperity of the bourgeoisie was doubly beneficial: it not only brought in taxes, it increased the wealth of the realm, his Majesty's estate. As reason of state the argument was faultless, small comfort to a poor nobleman in debt.

The simplest recourse would be to ask M. de Chirac for an advance on his subsidy. But how would his patron regard a man who came begging vulgar coin to relieve a debt? It was not to be thought of. A second option was to borrow from a mistress. Estelle de Grinaud's purse was as ample as her bosom – but Armand had at last cut her loose. That left Mlle de Charleville. Having won the battle for his favour, she could scarcely begrudge him a few coins. Moreover, thought Armand wryly, in a manner of speaking she – or the household in which she served – owed him.

He had joined in a syndicate to purchase a shipload of wine, a sound, sensible investment. Alas, while the goddams could evidently neither read history nor look at a map to see that Richebourg obviously belonged to l'Aquitaine, their talent for robbery at sea was not to be doubted. The carrack now sailed under the Croix St-Pélage. Her cargo – and with it Armand's fortunes – had long since vanished. Ah, my sweet Solange, thought Armand, shall you not restore me, when your royal lady mistress has left me poor?

Louder voices cut through the murmur of the crowd. Drinkers and whores fell back in retreat, and Armand at once cursed himself for not positioning himself near a window. Gens d'armes? Surely his creditors would not be coming for him here! Then the source of disturbance emerged out of the swirl: the vast, well-adorned figure of the Baron de Moine. He planted himself directly in front of Armand. 'Ah, de Fossier,' he proclaimed.

Armand rose and bowed. 'At your service, Monsieur. I seem to have the finest of company, no?'

'Better company, my good de Fossier, than you are likely to find in debtors' prison.' The baron laughed, his great belly heaving. 'No doubt you will go squeaking to de Chirac to rescue you – if you haven't already. But perhaps he finds you a broken sword, to be discarded for a better?' Customers and whores, reassured that there was no trouble for them, now formed a circle around Armand and de Moine. Great names were being spoken. Entertainments of this order seldom found their way to St-Léger.

Armand knew he was being baited; he had to reply without giving offence. 'It is the Duc de Septimanie,' he answered, 'who should give thought to his weapon. It grows, perhaps, too large and heavy to wield.' A ripple of laughter.

The proprietor pushed his way to the front of the circle and threw up his hands, pleading, 'Monsieurs – I beg of you – take your quarrel elsewhere!' Slowly de

Moine's head turned, and he fixed the man with an icy stare. The proprietor subsided. Armand thought the man a fool in any case; this episode could assure him more custom for weeks to come.

'No,' said de Moine, again addressing Armand. 'I do not think you will go to de Chirac. Ah – perhaps it is to Mademoiselle de Charleville you will go! Yes . . .' He smiled broadly. 'She has charms most definite. Young, but ripe and full.' He held his hands up in an unmistakable cupping gesture and made squealing sounds. 'Perhaps you noticed the improvement in her skills? She has given me some slight entertainment.'

'Indeed, Monsieur?' said Armand. Neither poverty nor drink could rob a nobleman of his honour, but both could rob him of good sense. Even as he spoke, Armand knew in a detached corner of his mind that he was being a very great fool. Yet speak he did. 'I confess I am surprised,' he said. 'I did not think her to your tastes. I was given to understand, on the contrary, that you were a frequent guest at a certain house in the rue Ste-Valérie.'

More gasps from around the circle. Everyone knew what house was meant. From somewhere in the back of the throng came an interjection, imprudently loud, '*Un pédéraste? Non!*'

The accusation was indeed false; Armand knew that quite well – De Moine's pleasures were the table and the blade, and to enticements of the flesh he was indifferent, by whichever sex they were offered. But he could guess what de Moine was thinking: true or false, this accusation would cling, and not even an answer in blood would truly wash it away.

Finally, with grave formality, de Moine spoke. 'Monsieur understands, I am sure, that I must require satisfaction.'

With equal formality, Armand bowed. Now that it was too late, he felt entirely sober. 'Of course, Monsieur.' With sudden good sense he added, 'There is some business of his Majesty that must take precedence, but if your representative will call, an occasion can most assuredly be agreed upon.'

'His Majesty?' said de Moine, smiling now. 'Indeed – complete your service. Regrettably he will have to dispense with it in future.' He bowed, turned and was gone.

CHAPTER THIRTEEN

A Most Dubious Gentleman

'His Excellency the Senator Enrico Falier, ambassador of the Most Serene Republic of Ravenna.' The newly arrived ambassador was announced by Solange, who then hastened forward to kneel at Catherine's side. A fire in the kitchen had called Madeleine away, leaving Catherine with only one lady-in-waiting in her Presence Chamber.

A man in his sixties or seventies came forward, his posture erect, his robes richly and stylishly old-fashioned. He bowed gravely. He could pass for a first cousin to Senator Morosini, Catherine thought, and possibly was. She addressed him in Enotrian, praising the wise government that made Ravenna shine along-side the great republics of antiquity. The words were expected formalities, but she was sincere. Senator Falier praised her beauty and princely virtues, and she hoped *he* was sincere.

The senator then ushered forward his attending gentlemen. Among them was none other than Lord William de Havilland, the Earl of Avalon's son and heir,

who had led the sea-raids against the Aquitaine. The
raids had ended and the war now only smouldered,
though prizes were still being taken at sea. Had her
letter to him been of some effect?

Lord William was easy to pick out from his Ravennate
fellows – a tall, sturdy young man, very well turned out
in a doublet and short cloak of Enotrian style, but hardly
to be mistaken for any Enotrian. With sword at hip, hair
golden as Madeleine's spilling from under his cap, his
northern complexion burned by the wind and sun of
the Middle Sea, he was not handsome, precisely, but
certainly well-favoured. For all his modern finery he put
Catherine in mind of his Northman forebears.

He came forward and knelt. 'Your Highness,' he said
in Saxon.

'Rise, Lord William,' Catherine replied. 'Your
services are much approved,' she said, 'and well worthy
of the mariners of Lyonesse!'

'My lady princess flatters me beyond my merits.'

'Indeed?' she asked. Perhaps I do, Lord William! M.
de Chirac had expostulated about the privateers, who
fought chiefly for plunder: he called them little better
than freebooters. But even though Lord William was
now under the diplomatic protection of Ravenna, this
journey, she thought, must be more perilous for him
than any sea-raid. Forgetting herself, she smiled at
him.

'Perhaps,' he said, 'the Princess Lyon flatters in

innocence, as one unaccustomed to it – flattery of herself being neither necessary nor possible.'

Catherine laughed in spite of herself. 'Flatterer!'

As they rode away from the Hôtel de Guienne, escorted by a guard in the royal livery of the Aquitaine, Senator Antonio Falier motioned William to ride up alongside him. 'At least,' he said, 'you now know that the gentlemen of Morosini's household are truthful.'

'Truthful?' William replied. The praise from Senator Morosini's servitors had seemed extravagant. 'Envoys set out gristle on silver service and call it a roast, Signor Senatore, but that maid should be offered up on a platter of gold.' Sitting on her canopied chair of state, she'd looked as self-possessed as though already Queen – slim and elegant as a galley, perhaps as dangerous, with skin like cream against her black velvet gown; sea-green eyes; and hair like a burnished bronze culverin. By reputation she was a fierce virago, but he liked what he saw. So would her future subjects.

'You may as well know,' said Senator Falier, 'that the minister of Aquitaine has refused you any private conference with her. In his place, I confess, I would do the same. Principessa Caterina is not to be trusted, and neither are you. You might get a chance to speak to her this evening at the ball, but expect to be closely watched!'

* * *

The sun was low when the party from Ravenna arrived at the Palace of la Trémouille. A court should express its lord's magnificence, and this one did. Certainly its women were magnificent – William had never seen so splendid an array; even the plain ones made the most of such charms as they had, and the fair ones . . . he had seen their equal nowhere, even among the celebrated courtesans of Ravenna.

A man in his fifties was studying him, from his manner and lawyer's robes doubtless a royal secretary. Far more interesting to William was the woman at his side, perhaps in her late thirties, a streak of premature grey in the dark hair peeking under her headdress. She made no effort to disguise it, nor needed to. Even at the Court of la Trémouille she stood out. She glanced towards William, raised an eyebrow, and for a moment smiled. She and her companion exchanged a few animated words; she laughed, curtseyed and withdrew. His wife? Mistress? William was disappointed.

Her companion in lawyer's robes walked over to William and bowed slightly. 'Signor de Havilland?' he said in Enotrian. He was a little man with a large Gallic nose, not handsome; but seen close up he had presence.

William nodded. 'Signor?'

'Permit me to introduce myself,' the man said. 'I am Antoine de Chirac, minister to his Most Christian Majesty. Your journey here to l'Aquitaine is surprising,' he went on.

'I am surprised myself!' said William. De Chirac! The lady, then, must be the King of Aquitaine's former mistress, Corisande d'Abregon. She fully merited her renown.

De Chirac smiled. 'In most circumstances you would find yourself lodged in a royal fortress, for a very considerable ransom.'

'It would not be paid.'

'A gallant reply, which happily I don't mean to test. I have no reason to trust you, Monsieur de Havilland, but I trust the Republic of Ravenna to look after its own interests. Trade suffers from the war in the Narrow Sea.'

'Let your king indemnify Lyonesse for the taking of Richborough, and the war will end,' William said. 'Trade will flourish again.'

'Is that the position of Ravenna?'

'Senator Falier will express the position of Ravenna,' replied William. 'It is not my place. For here and now I am in the Republic's service, and express no position of my own. Still, I know my countrymen. The war grows burdensome, but they will ask some recompense for the loss of Richborough. A subsidy would cost your master less than troops and galleys do.'

Chance movements of dancers opened a momentary line of sight across the hall, and William spied the Princess Lyon conversing with a young gentleman and maid – she was a tall, unmistakable figure. For an instant her eyes met his across the open space and William

346

raised his cap and genuflected. She made the barest hint
of a curtsey, then a dancer interposed himself with a leap
and William could see only the bronzy coronet of her
hair. He turned back to the King of Aquitaine's minister.

De Chirac had been watching. 'The Princess de
Lyonesse is under his Majesty's protection,' he said, and
smiled. 'Also that of my wife, whom you might find an
equally formidable guardian.'

'Madame de Chirac bears no outward resemblance to
a dragon, Monsieur.'

'She can be one, when it comes to her Trinette!' he
said. 'Yet her Trinette will presently succeed to the
throne of Lyonesse. Which has not felt the hand of a
strong king, Monsieur de Havilland, in very many years.
She is a young demoiselle – no ordinary one, I confess,
but still a demoiselle. She will need protection.'

'By prison guards, otherwise known as Aquitanian
troops?'

'You have a good deal in common with Princess
Catherine, Monsieur!' he said. 'Yet you must know that
there has been talk of usurpation.'

'I have no claim on the throne of Lyonesse, Monsieur
de Chirac – not even a usurper's claim. If I seek a throne
I'll win it by honest conquest. There must be a thousand
islands in the Ocean Sea. Some are surely in want of a
king.'

'You are a young man,' said de Chirac. 'You know
how to sail and you know how to fight. In the absence of

a strong royal hand at Kelliwick, you might be tempted.'

'You hold out the apple of temptation to me?' William laughed. A shrewd devil was de Chirac. He'd said no word but what was true and reasonable, but his purpose was the King of Aquitaine's. Lyonesse had no army but the guards of Kelliwick Castle; its strength in arms lay in its lords' retainers, the train-bands of its cities, the militia of its shires – and its ships, one day his to command.

Over the heads of dancing gallants and ladies of the Court of la Trémouille, he could just see the Princess's braided red coronet. She had laughed and called him a flatterer. Did she know how formidable a temptress she might be in her own cause?

It was late when Catherine and her party returned to the Hôtel de Guienne. She half listened to her ladies, talking and laughing in low voices as they followed her up to her chambers. While she had spent the greater part of the evening closeted with the envoys from Ravenna, they had spent it spying on the Earl of Avalon's son.

'Perhaps we can throw dice for him,' said Solange.

'Not your dice!' retorted Madeleine. 'They are dishonest.'

Her ladies were not improving Catherine's humour. 'If he slips into a disputation,' she told them, 'I'll have the huntsmen thrash him and toss him into the street before Madeleine can take steel to him.'

'Take steel to him, Mademoiselle?' said Solange. 'Madeleine would cheerfully yield herself, I'm sure.'

'Something no one could imagine of Solange de Charleville!' Madeleine retorted.

'Hold your tongues, both of you!' Catherine cried. 'Can I not have peace in my own chambers? A word more and I'll pike your heads to either side of the gate, and de Havilland can choose which is the prettier!' Her ladies fell silent. Both were vain of their necks. 'And there will be no more suitors,' she added. 'Not sons of earls, nor sons of emperors. So I told Senators Morosini and Falier, and now I am telling you.'

Solange forgot her vanity. 'But, Mademoiselle! What of marriage?'

'What of it?' snapped Catherine. 'I cannot marry before my accession anyway, save by writ of Parliament. So this is all angels dancing on pins. Why then should I be asked for a promise I cannot make, and hear promises never meant to be kept?'

'Indeed, Mademoiselle?' said Solange, unlacing Catherine's kirtle. 'Of what use to tell that to a Ravennate? His republic cannot marry you, and you could not bear its child if it did. "La Serenissima" – Ravenna is plainly a woman anyway, or in the nature of one. Such a marriage could amuse only the Princess du Pré.'

'Do not try me, Solange!' suggested Catherine. She raised her arms and her ladies got her out of her kirtle.

'I tell their Senate because it will tell the world,' she explained. The Republic had licensed a printer to publish every month a broadsheet called the *Gazetta*, with the acts of the Senate and accounts of all that came to pass that month. 'Let every prince, grand duke, condottiere and highwayman in Christendom – even every pirate – find out at once that I am done with them,' she said, 'so I do not have to tell them all one by one!'

'Will they listen, Mademoiselle?' asked Solange, still impudent. 'You are still heiress of Lyonesse, whatever the Senate says, or even what you say.'

'The suitors will not listen,' Catherine admitted. 'But I need not listen to them, either! Let all the princes in Christendom stand in a line outside my gate if they wish. I'll have nothing more of them.' She sighed. 'Now! I am going to go see that her Ladyship sleeps easy, and then to sleep myself. You two can scheme as you wish.'

She checked on Lady Lindley, who had lately taken another chill, then came back to her bedchamber. She could hear her ladies in the other chamber, but not what they were saying – much to the better. She picked up her hairbrush and wrestled with her problem as she brushed. Once on the throne she knew it would be her duty to marry, and provide her kingdom with a king and an heir. At least, Catherine thought, she would then have soldiers, if her suitors became too importunate. Ships of war too.

At last she was done. She blew out the candles and climbed into bed, crawling far under the bedclothes where none of them could find her.

Three days later, Madeleine and Solange sat in their bedchamber while their mistress tended to her Ladyship. Solange was describing her plan to arrange a meeting between Mademoiselle and the Earl of Avalon's son.

'You are quite mad, Solange!' said Madeleine. 'If Mademoiselle consents, she is mad as well!'

'That has taken you so long to discover?' asked Solange. 'Yet if we do not take this chance now, it may not come again. And it is essential that they meet! When the time comes for her to return to Lyonesse, it is he who shall hold the sea – for her or against her.'

'If it goes awry,' said Madeleine, 'I could end up bending my head to the executioner's sword! Right after you!' She could think of any number of ways that Solange's scheme could go awry. For all that, it was a plan of wondrous audacity. Solange had outdone herself. 'But this gentleman of yours, the Chevalier d'Hardouin?' she asked. 'Will he be able to play his part?'

Solange smiled. 'When has he ever failed us?'

When, indeed? thought Madeleine, and shook her head.

* * *

On the following day the Court headed for the royal château of Tertrianne for a few days' hunting. Solange was in a gallery there, surveying the crowd of courtiers and servants, when Madeleine turned up beside her and tugged eagerly at her false sleeve. 'He came!' she whispered sharply. 'I just saw him!' She pointed. A little group of Enotrians had entered the courtyard below, along with the unmistakable figure of the Earl of Avalon's son.

Solange smiled. 'Well! I shall see what truth I can get out of him!'

'A pleasing duty, I'm sure,' said Madeleine. 'Should we not both—'

'No, you are wholly unfit by nature to be a spy,' said Solange. *Because you are detestably pretty, and he would favour you!* she thought. 'Besides, you must go to the Chevalier d'Hardouin, and bid him be ready to do his part.'

Madeleine shook her head, but turned and headed for the chambers set aside for Princess Catherine's household. Solange went down to the courtyard and threaded her way through the crowd. Wine flowed freely, and she foresaw a day lively and indiscreet – some in the crowd were already weaving, and one or two tried to grab at her as she went by. She shook them off. Counts and valets would be sleeping in doorways, she suspected, before the horns sounded, but a noble of Lyonesse, she judged, would drink his share if not more.

She hoped he would prove a truer chevalier than the Elector of Angeln had, but if not? It was a risk she would take to get truth, and this time she knew better what to beware of.

William had come to the hunt along with several younger Ravennate nobles. He had much to think about. King Edmund was declining, as was his own father. When they were gone he would be Lord High Admiral, in the service of a young queen who did not lack for either courage or good sense (or for that matter beauty) – but was nearly a stranger to her homeland. Yet in the meantime, here he was at the Court of Aquitaine, a place not lacking in fair maids or lively ladies.

Perusing the crowd just after arriving, his gaze lighted on one courtly lady of the Aquitaine: a shapely young maid, olive-complexioned, who might pass for Enotrian. Their eyes met for a moment and she smiled, then was lost again behind a group of gentlemen. William set course towards her, working his way against the head-wind of the throng. Shortly he had her in sight again. Wavy dark brown hair showed beneath her curved head-dress and spilled down her back, loosely bound by a net. She was uncommonly pleasing to look at – but more than that, she was the lady-in-waiting who had knelt at the side of the Princess Lyon's chair of state in the Hôtel de Guienne. He closed in on her, more deliberately now. To flirt with any maid of the Court of Aquitaine would be pleasing; to flirt with this lady of Princess Katrin's household might rank as service. He bowed, sweeping off his cap. 'Mademoiselle,' he said, 'will forgive the intrusion of a plain mariner, and of a foreign country?'

She curtseyed, displaying finely the warm curves of her shoulders and bosom. 'I forgive readily, Monsieur!' she replied, and smiled. 'Yet you are of Lyonesse, son of the Comte d'Avalon – and your country is one day to be mine as well! I have the great honour to serve in the household of Catherine, Princess Lyonne.'

William bowed again. 'Lord William de Havilland, at your service,' he said. 'Is it true, the sorrowful news I hear? That the Princess took a chill and has kept to her chambers?' William found it suspiciously convenient that on this – the last occasion when he might have spoken freely to the Princess Lyon – she was reported to be indisposed.

The maid nodded. 'It is a small thing, Monsieur. Mademoiselle has rarely a day of ill health, but she awoke yesterday stuffy in her head. We begged her to stay at home, and she assented.'

'I shall give report, Mademoiselle,' said William, 'as to how well Princess Katrin is served!' Was this charming maid truly her faithful attendant, or her keeper? She was not more than eighteen or twenty years of age, he reckoned; surprisingly young to be entrusted with such a task – unless she had artfully concealed a few years. Whatever she was, he intended good service with her. 'Would it please Mademoiselle,' he asked her, 'to have a draught to warm you against this cold breeze?'

She curtseyed again. 'You are most kind, Monsieur de Havilland.' She smiled. 'Ah, but you have given me your name, and I have not given you mine. I am called Comtesse Solange de Charleville.'

Wine by the cask was at hand, but William had with him a flask of brent wine, a distillate essence of wine he had discovered in his student days at Torcello. He took a cup, poured a small quantity of brent wine, and handed it to Mlle de Charleville. 'Drink carefully, Mademoiselle,' he warned her; 'this burns in the mouth, but you will find its warmth pleasing within.'

She sipped, and her eyes went wide. 'Monsieur!' she gasped. They drifted towards the edge of the throng. 'Do you think to conquer me, Monsieur?' She laughed. 'Perhaps I shall conquer you!'

Either fate sounded pleasing, though William had every intention of winning the day. The maid spoke of life in the Hôtel de Guienne; of the Princess Lyon's good treatment of her and of all in her household; and of how fine a horsewoman and huntress her mistress was. William spoke in turn of adventures by sea, and others ashore.

Mlle de Charleville found no fault in his service. 'The courage of your mariners is much approved,' she said. She studied him under her long lashes. 'Princess Catherine shall be fortunate to have such brave men in her service, Monsieur – may I call you Guillaume? And you must call me Solange!'

William found possibilities here; the maid was nearly asking him to enter the Princess Lyon's personal service. 'You must tell me more, Mademoiselle – my good Solange,' he said, 'of how Princess Katrin is maintained, and what manner of life you lead.'

'So I shall, Monsieur Guillaume,' she said. 'Now, there are in Mademoiselle's household, besides myself, Mademoiselle du Lac de Montpellier – Ah! But here she is. You shall see for yourself.' William caught a hint of displeasure.

He followed her gaze. A young gentleman came through the crowd, a maid by his side – and such a maid that William was hard put not to catch his breath, even in the company of his own very pleasing companion. Blue of eyes and gold of hair, it was no wonderthat even the delightful Solange de Charleville was ill pleased at seeing this rival. What woman would not be?

The golden-haired maid curtseyed, and her companion bowed – with an odd brief hesitation, and awkwardly. William bowed in return. 'Monsieur,' said Solange, 'this is my companion in the service of the Princess, Madeleine du Lac; and with her the Chevalier d'Hardouin. Monsieur, Mademoiselle, this is Guillaume, son of the Comte d'Avalon in Lyonesse, a captain at sea, now in the service of Ravenna.'

'Monsieur!' said the youth, and studied William with undisguised fascination. 'I heard that a noble of

Lyonesse had come with Senator Falier! A captain at sea, you say?'

William nodded.

'Surely good service to Christendom, then, Monsieur Capitaine de Havilland,' said the Chevalier. 'The mariners of your country are of goodly repute! Yet should you not rather serve—' Abruptly the youth turned bright red, and swallowed visibly in embarrassment. 'That is,' he stammered, 'is not that service most perilous?'

'Life is perilous, Monsieur,' said William. The Chevalier d'Hardouin, though tall for an Aquitanian, was a slight, beardless youth, who surely had never tasted battle.

'Indeed life is perilous,' said the youth. 'I shall not fear battles!'

'You will if ever you are in one,' William replied. 'I can tell you that first hand. The man who says other is a liar or a fool.' In truth the wait for battle was hardest. The sooner joined the sooner done with – one way or the other.

The Chevalier d'Hardouin bowed, again awkwardly, no credit to the Court of Aquitaine. 'I am sure that you speak the truth, Monsieur le Capitaine,' he said. 'I shall not forget what you have told me.'

That, thought William, was much better. He produced more brent wine and offered it all around. He turned his attention back to Mlle Solange – a pleasing duty, and a fine prize herself. She spoke wittily of the King of Aquitaine's hunts, though William guessed other pastimes more to her own liking. All at once horns sounded, to make ready for the chase. Grooms led saddled horses from the stables, and he shortly was mounted beside his new companions, amid two hundred others, and hundreds more servants afoot. He presented d'Hardouin – why did that name seem vaguely familiar? – with his compliments and the flask of brent wine. He had another for himself and Mlle Solange.

The horns sounded again and the King of Aquitaine and his immediate following rode out through the gate, followed by his Court, rank upon rank. William and his companions, gentlemen retainers and ladies of slight consequence, were among the last. Once across the moat, riders fanned out into the fields and William bade his leave of d'Hardouin and Mlle du Lac and angled off, Solange riding at his side. Their game was not yet past opening gambits, and he wanted no others watching the board.

As the two pairs parted, William stole a glance back at fair Madeleine du Lac, and caught the Chevalier d'Hardouin staring at him. The youth blushed, and looked suddenly away and William chuckled under his breath. He'd already noticed that the lad seemed more interested in him than in his own splendid companion, and he decided that his suspicion was right – the

Chevalier d'Hardouin was a catamite. He was in truth most handsome, or would be so judged by those who prized such: well shaped of calf and fine of features, with pure fair skin, and red hair tucked up under his cap. Such youths were greatly prized in some princely courts.

Catherine, with Madeleine at her side, rode across the meadows north of the château of Tertrianne. Her chance to ride and converse with the Earl of Avalon's heir had vanished almost as soon as it came. Madeleine put her finger on the reason.

'Mademoiselle de Charleville,' she said with some asperity, 'seems to have snatched away Monsieur de Havilland for herself! How did that happen?'

Catherine shrugged. 'She will of course have a very good explanation, being more skilled in those things than you or I, or anyone else for that matter. We shall suppose that his being well-favoured has no part in it, of course. Monsieur de Fossier should look to his woman!'

Madeleine laughed. 'Indeed he should, Mademoiselle. Solange is not a fool, and she would like to marry an earl! Yet we shall see how she fares if I enter the lists against her!'

'Ah!' said Catherine, and grasped the obvious: she might want a lord of Lyonesse to serve her – but her ladies saw a prospective husband. Now here was one well-favoured young man, and two maids. Three, in fact, she thought with annoyance. Could you not see, Lord William, that I too am a maid?

'Monsieur de Havilland,' said Madeleine presently, 'might wonder that you showed greater attention to him than to me!'

'Was I supposed to take your hand and kiss it?'

'It is the custom among chevaliers, Mademoiselle.'

'Well, then,' asked Catherine, 'should I take a mistress as well? And should it be you or Solange? I could make you bitter rivals for my favour, as well as his! *Pardieu*, I feel a great fool! My legs bare to the thigh, nothing but hose, for all the world to see! How I ever let Solange talk me into this, I don't know. If the Dauphin were to find me out—'

Madeleine laughed. 'He would think you the handsomest chevalier he ever saw!' she said merrily.

'It would do neither of us any good,' retorted Catherine. Sadly, she thought, nothing was going to do her and the Dauphin any good. She would succeed to her throne, and the Dauphin to his, and they would be enemies. The next Earl of Avalon would not be an enemy, but the Queen must marry a husband of royal rank, a duke at the least – even an earl would scarcely be fitting. Such was the order of the world.

She rode on in silence. Lofty, billowing white clouds had risen from the north and they drew overhead, with flashes of lightning and rolling peals of thunder. Rain spattered down, let up for a time, then began again.

'Best we make for our cottage,' said Madeleine. 'We're too far to get back to the château.'

Without a word Catherine wheeled and spurred to the gallop, Madeleine riding after her. Scattered through the country about Tertrianne were shelters and cottages, intended for use in the royal hunts – most often as places of assignation. The one provided for Catherine's household could not be far, she thought; perhaps a mile or so.

They had gone scarcely a furlong when the skies opened up. Catherine's male plumage was quickly sodden, hose wet and frigid against her legs. Her hair, soaked and heavy, pulled from under her cap to slap in a wet mass across shoulders and back. At last they rode down to the stream below the cottage – now a raging torrent. They made it across, and with blessed relief arrived at the cottage. It was a simple building: one side had a tiny stables with a handful of stalls, the other a single chamber without even a loft. Catherine and Madeleine led their horses in, pulled off their trappings and wiped them down, then retreated into the other chamber where Madeleine stacked logs in the fireplace, and in short order had a fire roaring.

'Now help me out of this foolishness!' said Catherine, fumbling at the points of her doublet. Madeleine assisted her – showing good working knowledge of male attire – and with great relief Catherine unwound the cloth she had bound about her chest for the sake of imposture. Servants of the château had left ample coverings on the rude platform bed, so Catherine dried herself off, wrapped a coverlet around herself and huddled before the fire.

Madeleine peeled out of her own sodden clothing, swathed herself in another dry blanket and settled at Catherine's side. 'It shall serve Solange justly,' she declared, 'if she gets twice as soaked as we were!'

'Then she will be drowned,' said Catherine. 'Do not wish for that; you'll have to perform her duties as well as your own.'

'Hmph!' said Madeleine. 'No doubt Monsieur de Havilland will keep her warm and dry!'

Catherine remembered something, and scrabbled through her wet pack. 'Here!' she declared, and drew forth the flask. 'His brent wine! We have at least this to warm us within, and the fire without, and so could be worse off than we are!' As before, it burned cruelly at lips, tongue and throat, but was pleasing warmth within.

She passed the flask to Madeleine.

CHAPTER FOURTEEN

Brent Wine

William and Lady Solange followed the body of hunts-men north from Tertrianne, then drew away till the horns faded in the distance. They rode alone across a wooded valley, spotting deer that were perfectly safe from them. As he'd suspected, the brilliant sun gave way to clouds, bearing down under full press of sail. He had noted a possible shelter, a simple open lean-to at the head of a glade. As the storm's vanguard passed over and the blackness of the main body loomed, he urged his mount round and rode back up the glade at a canter, Solange at his side.

They reached the shelter just as the first raindrops fell, and were safe under cover when the storm broke in full force. Lady Solange spread a cloth; they supped on bread and cheese, washing it down with brent wine. William let the maid talk, which she did freely and at length. If she was Princess Catherine's guard she was an indiscreet one – else a very clever one indeed, painting herself her mistress's loyal retainer, and saying much to the credit of the Princess Lyon. The talk wandered, and

William found himself propounding Salviani's doctrine of the heavens turning on the Sun. He'd rarely done so, certainly not in such good company.

The celestial orbs of her dark eyes regarded him. 'Are sea-lords of Lyonesse so learned, Monsieur?' She laughed. 'I had not known this!'

'I attended university once, my fair Solange,' William explained. 'At Torcello. I thought to learn more of geometry and astronomy, needful for navigating to the Spice Islands and other far places.' He leaned back. 'Alas, I never took a degree. The rectors misliked it that I hanged a professor.'

The maid's eyes went wide.

'Oh, I cut the wretch down alive,' William hastened to add. 'He gave his lectures drunk, mumbling nonsense. I care not if a professor is drunk, but will not pay good coin for mumbling! The rectors took offence all the same.' He had decamped across rooftops, five minutes ahead of the guard. 'I found safer learning on the poop of a Ravennate galley.'

The storm blew over, and at Solange's suggestion they rode not back towards Tertrianne, but to a cottage a mile or so distant. It was set aside for the use of the Princess Lyon's household, the maid explained. 'I ought to see,' she said, 'whether Madem– Madeleine and the Chevalier d'Hardouin were able to reach shelter there before the storm burst upon them.'

D'Hardouin . . . the name teased at William; he knew

it from somewhere, or thought he should. *D'Hardouin . . . Hardwin!* The forebear of the House of Guienne had been a Saxon thane, Harold Hardwin. Four hundred years ago he had crossed the sea to the Aquitaine, offering his sword to Pippin the Great for the deliverance of Sion. For his service he had been made Duke of Guienne. His descendant, John of Guienne, had married an heiress to the throne of Lyonesse, then returned across the sea to rule. The example, thought William, was all too apt. Like its predecessors, the House of Guienne – and the crown of Lyonesse – had come down to a maid.

He pondered this as they rode up along a storm-swollen brook to a cottage. Was d'Hardouin, wondered William, the descendant of some royal bastard, forgotten in Lyonesse? The youth had the colouring and nearly the height of a Guienne prince, though that slight and effeminate boy did poor justice to the blood royal. What was he about, and why? William swung down from the saddle, helped Solange down and strode towards the door of the cottage. Suddenly the maid was at his arm, pulling him back.

'Wait, Monsieur Guillaume!' she said. 'You must not – it is not proper—'

'I scarcely think I'll find Mademoiselle du Lac compromised,' said William. 'Not by the Chevalier d'Hardouin! Yet I should like to know precisely who he is, and why he is privy to Princess Katrin's household!'

* * *

Time had passed in the cottage, and so had the flask, back and forth between princess and lady-in-waiting. The rain let up, and light brightened through the windows and Catherine and Madeleine fell to talking of those things that concerned every maid, whatever her station. 'Monsieur de Tremarais is gallant to me,' said Madeleine, 'wretched scholar that I am. But ah, Mademoiselle! Truly, truly I had once set my heart upon the Chevalier de Batz-Castelmore – and he forsook me utterly!' She sighed. '*Hélas!*'

'The g-greater fool he, then!' said Catherine. 'If he cast away a pearl, then he is a swine!' She laughed at her wit. 'You see how Mademoiselle de Charleville, how she is wiser than you! She made de Fossier dismiss la Grinaud. *Pouf!* She is gone! But Solange, you know, is all given to worldly things. A bishop could preach whole texts upon her!' No bishop, thought Catherine sadly, could preach an interesting text upon *me*! Kateryn de Guienne, Princess Lyon, who alone has no true love! She held up the flask. Only a little golden fluid was left. 'Here, Madeleine, you shall have a little more, and I the rest!'

'No, no, Mademoiselle,' said Madeleine. 'And I think you too should not—' She reached for the flask.

'I shall as I will!' cried Catherine, fending her off. 'Do you think I cannot hold drink better than you, being as I am of Lyonesse? Nay!' She upended the flask and finished it off. What a wonderful potion, she thought, is this brent wine! She held up the empty flask. 'The great good gift of an earl's son of Lyonesse!' she exclaimed. 'Yet think you not, good Mistress Madeleine, that Lord William should serve me, who shall be his dread sovereign lady?'

Madeleine looked at her, confused. 'Mademoiselle – Miledi? I can non so well spek ze—' She stumbled over the words, then gave up.

Catherine realized she had spoken in Saxon. She laughed. 'Now there's a pretty jest, girl; you scarce know what I say. Brent wine cannot rob me of my native tongue! And I shall have a prettier jest for his Highness, Lewis the Dolphin of Aquitaine! Ah, Louis,' she sighed.

Suddenly there came a rapping on the door. Catherine got to her feet, stumbled, and her coverlet slipped off. She laughed, pulled it back around herself and had a profound revelation: she was quite drunk. 'Madeleine!' she cried. 'See who is at the door! Tell them the Princess is indisposed, and will see no one!' From outside came voices – Solange's, and another she realized was Lord William's. The door flew open.

The interior of the cottage smelled of damp, of the fire, and – unmistakably – of brent wine. As William's eyes adjusted to the relative darkness, he picked out two figures within. It took only an instant to see that one was Mistress du Lac, wrapped in a coverlet, wet golden hair spilling across her shoulders. It took even less time to see, with the uttermost surety, that her companion was *not* the Chevalier d'Hardouin – and never had been.

'Lud's blood!' he cried aloud. Then he went to one knee and doffed his cap. 'Your Royal Highness!' William had not felt such a fool since, at age eleven, he'd been ordered to splice the mainbrace. He'd gathered a work party before the boatswain told him it meant to pipe up the ale ration. All made perfect sense now! 'D'Hardouin's' height and colouring, slender build, high cheekbones, red hair and green eyes: the marks not of a royal bastard but of the royal heiress. No wonder she'd had more an eye for him than for Madeleine du Lac! Like that maid, Princess Catherine was wrapped in a coverlet, their clothing spread before the fire to dry.

The Princess Lyon advanced, with careful unsteady dignity, her blanket revealing glimpses of her long legs. 'You may – you may rise, Lord William,' she said in deliberate Saxon. 'It does much pleasure – please – does much please me to receive the heir of Avalon in my p-presence.'

William rose. 'My Lady Princess must forgive—'

'Forgive, my lord?' The princess laughed merrily. 'Shall I – shall forgive you the brent wine? How it is burned I know not, yet by Lud it has burned *me* to a cinder!'

That, thought William, was truth beyond doubting.

He spied the flask near the hearth. Every drop had been drained. That much, between two maids who must each weigh but eight or nine stone – it was a wonder both were not insensible to the world!

'I am the one who must ask forgiveness, Mademoiselle!' said Lady Solange. 'I should not have brought Monsieur de Havilland here; I did not consider that you might have been caught in the storm, and that—'

Princess Catherine turned to regard her. 'Truly, Madem . . . Mademoiselle de Charle . . . Solange. Truly I must forgive you much! For I see that while I have been sh– soaked utterly to the skin, you have kept most warm and dry! I doubt not in Lord William's arms!' She turned back to William. 'Is that not so? She is a most bold maid, and did s-snatch you away, to have you for herself! For I see that you are most goodly and brave!' she declared. A tear glistened on her cheek. 'For I have been alone, alone in this country, and thought me cast away and lost, yet you have overset the Aquitainers more than twice! And now, now you have come to me, and that is great joy in my heart!'

She studied William up and down, blinking with the effort of concentration, her cheeks flushing. 'You are goodly and brave, Lord William! Should I not be well served by sh-shipmen, shipmen goodly and brave? For though I am but a maid, yet shall I yield to no p-prince of Christendom. Not Charles of Aquitaine, nor even the

Dauphin, how so he think the contrary.' She drew herself up proudly. 'He shall not rule Kateryn daughter of Harry! For I shall be a queen of shipmen, goodly and brave! And you shall be my admiral, and captain-general upon the sea, and thrash them as – as aforetime. Is that not so, Lord William?' She changed over to Gallic. 'Ah, Solange, you think yourself so high, and M-Madeleine too, but I am – I am not plain awkward Trinette! Non! I shall be well served—'

Solange took her mistress by the hand. 'Mademoiselle – I beg you, you are not well—'

'I am well enough!' cried Princess Catherine. She shook her hand free and spanked Solange across the nose like a disobedient puppy. The maid jumped back with a little cry. 'See you, Lord William?' said the Princess. 'I shall cuff me my servants whenso'er I will!' Her abrupt movement loosened the coverlet and it slipped off one freckled shoulder. 'Oh!' She yanked the coverlet back into place and laughed, blushing all the brighter. 'You did not know me for a maid, but now you know better!' Green eyes regarded William, unfocused but glittering bright, and her breath came short and sharp. 'Shall – shall you not serve me well, Lord William, William de Havilland?'

'With all my heart, your Highness,' said William before he could catch himself.

'And so you shall!' answered Princess Catherine, and brought herself up to him. He put his arms around her

– had to, to keep the royal heiress from falling at his feet. He was intensely aware of her body under the coverlet, the eager body of a maid just discovering her own powers, too befuddled by potent drink to guard herself from their effects. Her arms went around his shoulders; she clung to him as for life in a shipwreck, and her lips found his.

How long they remained thus William could not say. It seemed an eternity, and he could not pretend to be a statue, not with the warmth of this maid against him, though she was his future sovereign. He received her kiss and answered it gently, as best he could. Gradually her breathing slowed, her arms slipped away and her head sank down to rest upon his shoulder.

He eased the Princess Lyon round, picked her up and carried her to the bed.

'Goodly and brave . . .' she murmured.

Silently Lady Solange followed him. Once William had laid Princess Catherine down, she adjusted a pillow under her head and drew more coverlets over her. Her other lady-in-waiting, golden Madeleine du Lac, was beyond rendering service; she had sunk down by the hearth, half undraped, singing and laughing to herself.

When Solange was done tending to her mistress, she turned to William. Her dark eyes regarded him steadily. 'Monsieur must not think ill of my mistress,' she said. 'She is by her proper nature a grave and noble princess, who knows well her place and her duty. What has happened here is altogether the effect of the brent wine – and of my own great folly! For I thought that in the guise of a youth, she could meet with a noble of her own land, as otherwise would not be permitted. I did not consider that – oh, *pardieu*!'

William smiled and bowed. 'I think no less of Princess Katrin than that she is a fair and noble demoiselle,' he said, 'overcome by drink stronger than she knew. As you too, Mademoiselle, are fair and noble, well worthy to be in her service.' But the improper nature of Princess Catherine had been all too well revealed: a true daughter of the House of Guienne, as gallant and passionate as any of her royal forebears.

William bade Solange tend to Mistress Madeleine, and went to see to the horses. He laughed aloud, and cursed Lud for a trickster and devil. Here he was, in the company of three of the fairest and liveliest maids in Christendom – certainly the fairest and liveliest princess – and he could do not a thing about it. He returned to the cabin and settled himself by the door, sword at hand lest any intruder come in the night.

Catherine woke up to sunlight through a horn-covered window. The light was far too bright, and she ordered it to go away. It disobeyed. She rolled over, but could not fall back to sleep. The bed was plain and hard, covered by no canopy; it was certainly not her own. Where was she?

She came all at once awake, bolted upright – and her head burst asunder. She moaned and fell back, reduced to throbbing half unconsciousness. When the pounding subsided her contentment was gone. Her mouth tasted like a stables. Every inch of her body ached, and in a hazy tangle she remembered the cottage, the brent wine, and herself, clad only in a wrapped blanket, enfolded in a man's arms and carried to the bed.

'God help me!' she whispered. Tears formed on her closed eyelids, and she prayed to the Magdalene and her name saint. Oh! Sweet holy Mary Maudeleyn, lady of mercy, and good, wise St Kateryn – please, let it be but an ill dream, that I am not where I think, nor in such state as I fear I have come into! Her earnest prayer availed her nothing. At the memory of Lord William's arms about her, holding her tight, his lips on hers, her traitorous body responded. By an act of sheer will she sat up again and tried to rise, only to tumble over the side of the bed, crashing half naked onto the floor. The jolt sent more pain tolling through her head. She climbed back onto the bed, and the hammering subsided to where she could think.

By too bright day she examined the cottage. On a pallet in one corner was a mass of blankets, blonde hair spilling from one end: Madeleine. Solange was nowhere to be seen – but a man lay stretched out by the door. She needed to be out of here, to get back to Tertrianne – or better, the Hôtel de Guienne and her own bed. Ah,

Princess Kateryn, she thought, what was doubtless done to you last night – and most by your own folly – can by no means be undone. All the wishing and praying in the world shall not make it otherwise!

She wanted to dress, but none of the clothing spread by the hearth was hers; only Madeleine's, and the man's gear of her imposture. Between frustration at having nothing to wear, and anger at Solange for leading her into this folly, her head was pounding again. 'Solange de Charleville,' she said aloud, 'by Wott shall I give you such a thrashing as never you'll forget – and when I am too tired to go on, shall command Madeleine to beat you more!' Her pack lay by the bed. She found a wine skin and drank, hoping to dull the pain. It had the desired effect, so she drank some more.

Gradually a philosophical mood asserted itself. *Sic transit gloria virginitatis!* As well I never thought to be a virgin queen, since I have ill-succeeded in being a virgin princess! God's teeth, she wondered, what would the Dauphin think of me now? She had shown neither modesty, nor wisdom, nor discretion, nor common sense, but had disgraced herself utterly. She had not prayed for guidance from St Mary Magdalene, nor brewed maiden's prayer, precautions that were the duty of every maid of sense. Merciful God, what if . . . ?

She heard a stirring, and looked up to see that her ravisher had arisen and was looking at her. Stumbling to her feet, she whirled to face him. '*You!*' she cried. 'How dare you presume! Have you not done enough, you false traitor, you—' She snatched up the empty flask whose contents had led her to her ruin and hurled it at him. He let out a sharp yelp as it hit his elbow, then crashed against the wall and shattered into a hundred pieces.

'Peace, good lady!' he cried. 'Peace—'

'Peace?' answered Catherine. 'Know you, Lord William de Havilland, what says the law of Lyonesse about the seduction of a firstborn daughter of the King? High treason, my lord!' she said. 'That says the law!' She was not at all sure that the law applied to her, yet the sound was pleasing . . . and she would in any case be Queen. 'For the which,' she continued, 'the penalty be thus: that you be hanged, and cut down alive, and opened up, and your entrails drawn forth and burned before your living eyes. And your privy member hewn off – the which shall be most especially tended to! Then your head cut off and your body quartered' – her voice rose to a shout – 'that all other traitors may know the fate of such of any rank so ever as ravish a princess of the realm!' She paused, and panted for breath. 'Now, Lord William, heir of a race of pirates! What say you to *that*!'

He laughed merrily, then bowed with all elegance. 'I say, my lady Princess Katrin, that a most splendid Cat you are – pleasing to stroke when you purr by the fireside, but a terror to disobedient mice! So are you well fit to succeed to your grandfather's realm, much in need of mousing, and with some over-mighty rats as well. A Cat for Lyonesse to make the kingdom well kept!'

Catherine listened amazed, not sure whether to be furious or pleased. Lud take me! she thought. I threaten this man with a death most fearsome – no threat to take lightly, being as who I am – and he laughs! What manner of man . . .? He looked frankly at her, and she flushed, realizing that her coverlet had slipped half open. Glaring at him, she pulled it tight, then made a resolution and swore a mighty oath:

'By my immortal soul, Lord William,' she declared, 'I, Kateryn, daughter of Harry, born of a race of kings, shall not be governed, nor afeared of you, but truly shall I govern you, and all my kingdom's lords! Nor shall I await meekly my husband, but give him as dowry a kingdom in good order!' How to put that noble resolve into effect was a question, however, she could not begin to answer. She was saved from answering it by a knock at the door, and Solange's voice.

'Mademoiselle?'

'You may enter,' said Catherine sharply.

Solange came in, fully dressed; a ribbon loose here, a curl astray there, ever artful in disarray. She curtseyed, spied Lord William and curtseyed again. It was as much as Catherine could take, and more. The problems of this over-bold lord and her disorderly future kingdom she could not now resolve, yet by Wott she could set Solange in her place. So she did, without a word, her whole strength behind her fist, snatching her coverlet before it could fall.

Solange – soft, shapely Solange, who so disdained riding and hunting (or indeed any exercise not to be had in bed) – was not one to stand up to such a blow as Catherine could deliver. Over she went: her legs flew up in the air and her skirts cascaded like rose-petals, leaving no secrets to Solange de Charleville.

'For making me lose my virginity!' cried Catherine, and burst out laughing.

Lord William stared at her a moment – then knelt, and with faultless gallantry flipped Solange's skirts back over her legs. He helped her up, then looked coolly at Catherine. 'The better the service the sharper the blows?' he asked. 'A poor way to govern a ship, nor better a kingdom! You lack not spirit, my lady Princess Katrin, but have somewhat to learn of policy. Now! If you would strike blows, strike me, who can well bear them!'

Catherine did, and yelped at the hurt to her knuckles. She might better have struck an oak. 'Away with you, then!' she cried.

'As your Highness wishes,' said Lord William. He made a fine leg and withdrew to the door, then turned again and said firmly, 'In whatever state you came here, my lady, you leave in the same. I've never taken maid too drunk to have pleasing from it.'

Then he was gone.

* * *

Madeleine met Solange as arranged, secluded atop one of the towers of Tertrianne. 'I've dealt with Lasceaux and the rest,' she told her. 'Three extra days' pay calmed them down.' The servants had been nearly frantic by the time the 'Chevalier d'Hardouin' and Mademoiselle's ladies returned to the château. 'The reward must come from our purses, I fear,' she said. 'Mademoiselle is of no temper to approve the disbursement.'

Solange shrugged. 'I'll contrive to get it out of the household account. Not all at once, of course. But we'll get it back, one way or another.'

'Well, that's fine! A little silver is the least of it. *Bon Dieu!*' cried Madeleine. 'Do you realize what could have happened? Monsieur Guillaume could have had his way with Mademoiselle – or with all three of us, for that matter! I for one was in no condition to resist!'

'Dearest Madeleine,' replied Solange, 'you were in no condition even to know. Fortunately he is the more honourable sort of pirate, taking only prizes who can give him a lively engagement. What were you thinking, getting Mademoiselle drunk? Is that how you serve her?'

'I did not get her drunk!' Madeleine protested. 'How was I to know? That potion of his! Half a cup and you don't know who you are kissing, nor much care! Besides,' she demanded, 'what service were *you* performing for Mademoiselle? Playing Comtesse d'Avalon?'

'Hold your tongue,' snapped Solange. 'We only kissed. I should have ventured more when I had the

chance! He can never go back to Lyonesse to serve
Mademoiselle. She said she would have him hanged,
drawn and quartered. In her ill humour, she might just
do it.'

She got no further, because booted feet were climbing the tower stairs. Moments later Lord William
appeared. He bowed and doffed his cap. 'Women
plotting,' he said, 'are never up to any good. Will the
Chevalier d'Hardouin be joining my ladies?'

'Regrettably no, Monsieur,' said Solange, dipping.
'He was so overcome last night that he renounced the
world for ever, and will be seen no more. Our mistress
the Princess Lyonne, however, has renounced the world
only till she recovers from her chill, so in
the morning we must return to the Hôtel de Guienne.'

Madeleine curtseyed in turn. 'Pay no attention to
Mademoiselle de Charleville,' she said. 'One day she will
deliver a brilliant oration from the scaffold. In the mean-
while, both of us have been clumsy fools, for which
Monsieur may forgive us.'

Solange sighed. 'Mademoiselle du Lac is right,' she
admitted. 'We thought that in disguise, Princess
Catherine could meet with you, a noble of her country,
without anyone being the wiser. Yes, it was great folly on
our part, for which I especially am at fault! So think
nothing of that blow the Princess dealt me – I have merited a hundred. Indeed, a thousand!'

Madeleine found herself annoyed. Solange was

monopolizing his attention once again. Direct action was called for, and she took it. She smiled at Lord William and flourished a deep curtsey. 'The Princess expresses her gratitude, Monsieur,' she said, 'for your noble preservation of her chastity – now that she knows the truth! Yet she thinks it unseemly to do so directly. It therefore falls to us to render thanks in a becoming manner.' Only when she had said it did she realize just what rendering becoming thanks would entail – a debt of honour could only be repaid in the coin of honour!

'The Princess Lyon expects a great deal of her retainers!'

'Some services are their own reward,' Madeleine said. 'As Mademoiselle de Charleville can doubtless attest.'

'Indeed, Mademoiselle du Lac.' Solange turned to Lord William. 'We are at your command, Monsieur.'

'Both of you?'

'Monsieur!' cried Solange. Madeleine gulped.

Lord William laughed. 'Alas, the laws of hospitality require me to content myself with just one. Now, how am I to choose?'

Solange of course knew. 'The custom, I believe, is to present an apple – it would necessarily be an apple – on which is inscribed *Calliste*! "To the fairest!"' She curt-seyed again, produced an imaginary apple and handed it to Lord William, who bowed and accepted it.

Lord William held out the invisible apple – then snatched it back. 'The apple of discord!' he declared.

'Paris, Prince of Troy, was a fool to bestow it. By doing so he made enemies of two goddesses.'

Solange laughed. 'Here you need make an enemy only of one!'

'But suppose, Mesdemoiselles,' said Lord William, 'I would confer it upon the goddess who is not present? You spoke of folly? What kind of fool stands not five feet from the fairest maid in Christendom and doesn't see her for what she is?' He bit into the apple of discord, then tossed it over his shoulder. 'Think it not less honour to yourselves, but greater to your mistress.'

With that he bowed, and left. Madeleine and Solange were left looking at one another. Madeleine found herself rather disappointed. 'Well!' she said at last. '"The fairest maid in Christendom!" We have been passed over!'

Solange laughed. 'The Dauphin would have cause to be jealous, if he knew! Had Mademoiselle not passed out, it might have been not Lord William having his way with her, but Mademoiselle having *her* way with *him*. Whoever becomes King of Lyonesse will dare not keep a mistress – but also may have no need of one!'

William went down the tower stairs shaking his head. How had he just turned down two fair maids who offered themselves freely? Because the goddess not present was the fairest of all: kiss not the maid, went the saying, when you'd rather kiss the mistress. Folly!

Heiress to the throne, she was as out of reach as if set among the fixed stars.

All the same, William liked her. If her words this morning were less than kind – she had thought herself violated – in her place he'd have said no kinder ones. It was time to break an oath. He had sworn he would never go home – truly home – while his father lived, but King Edmund might not cling to life as stubbornly as his father did. When the King died, Princess Catherine would be Queen, and in need of men who could fight for her cause.

And that was something he knew how to do.

CHAPTER FIFTEEN

An Affair of Honour

Catherine sat in her study, reading. Senator Morosini was gone back to Ravenna, his place taken by Senator Falier. The Earl of Avalon's son was gone as well, back to the war at sea. Thus Catherine found herself once again alone in the Aquitaine, with none of her own realm beside her save her Ladyship. Senator Morosini had, as she'd asked, left her books of history and policy. Lord William had left her with her virginity, though she had done nothing to ask for it. She'd greatly chided Solange for the whole mad scheme, then given her a ruby ring.

She decided to walk in the garden. On impulse she went first to her bedchamber, and the chest in which Solange had placed the 'Chevalier d'Hardouin's' clothing. Catherine was quite done with him, but one item struck her fancy. She untied her couvre-chef, brushed out her hair with a few strokes, then took from the chest the feathered man's beret. She set it on her head and examined herself in the glass. Not quite right. She adjusted it a few times, finally setting it at a rakish angle. Now, she thought, this does very well! Bold indeed, but no more than the be-ribboned Enotrian fashion originally introduced at Court by Madame Corisande. Certainly better than Margot's bells. The Kateryn in the glass looked no mere princess, but rather a prince in form of a maid, one day to be sovereign of a mighty realm.

'Mademoiselle?' It was Solange. Catherine turned, awaiting pronouncement on her new fashion, but Solange made no comment; indeed didn't seem to notice. 'Mademoiselle . . . forgive me . . .' she began awkwardly. She looked down, in a manner most unlike her. 'It is Monsieur de Fossier—'

'What of him?' asked Catherine, irritated. Armand de Fossier was vastly less important than her daring innovation in fashion – though Solange might rate matters otherwise. 'Has he gone back to la Grinaud again? If so, he deserves no better. Put him from your mind!'

Solange shook her head, still looking down. 'No, no, Mademoiselle! It is not Madame de Grinaud. It is . . . the Baron de Moine spoke insultingly of me, in Armand's hearing. In the heat of the moment he answered in kind – and the baron has demanded satisfaction!' With that Solange burst into tears, something Catherine had never seen. She guided her to a bench and let her cry for a time on her shoulder. As the tears subsided, Catherine got the story out of her: the tavern encounter, the exchange of insults, the demand for satisfaction in steel. 'Armand thought it could be put off longer,' Solange told her. 'Oh, Mademoiselle! *Bon Dieu*, it is all my fault!'

'Something can be done,' Catherine told her. 'I am sure of it.'

But what? Go on her knees to de Moine? To Margot? to her grandmother? – and beg that the matter not be carried through, or at least de Moine be content with first blood? That was impossible. All at once she grasped the heart of the matter. The encounter could be no accident – the baron had deliberately sought out Armand de Fossier at an obscure wine shop in St-Léger. It was a double thrust, thought Catherine: striking at her ally M. de Chirac, whom Armand served, and delivering the cruellest of insults to her own loyal-lady-in waiting. Such could only be an act of revenge, for Catherine's defiance of the Lusianes.

She rose and faced her lady-in-waiting. 'Mademoiselle de Charleville,' she declared. 'No man affronts my household or its friends with impunity!' Solange's great dark eyes looked up at her, with an expression Catherine had not seen before. Hope and faith shone in Solange's eyes. This slyest and cleverest of maids believed that Catherine, daughter of Henry, could somehow deliver a miracle. The realization exhilarated and terrified her. She put out her hand to Solange, and raised her to her feet. 'I shall speak to the Dauphin,' she said, 'and seek his counsel.'

Solange looked doubtful for a moment – Catherine knew well her suspicions of the Dauphin – but then she nodded in understanding, and curtseyed. 'You are most kind to me, Mademoiselle,' she said. Then she smiled, if somewhat wanly. 'The beret, Mademoiselle – it becomes you very well.'

With a flick of his hand, Louis d'Héristal wrapped his cloak around his left forearm. He swept his blade to the side, inviting the Duc de Numières to attack. De Numières grinned and shook his head. 'Too eager, Monseigneur; I regretfully decline.' He circled to the left. 'I suppose we shall spend another winter in garrisons, awaiting the pirates of the goddams?'

The Dauphin nodded. 'They'll find us ready this winter! Yet I doubt they will come.' He turned as de Numières circled, but stepping sidewise as he did, to draw his partner towards a corner of the salle d'armes. De Numières would then be able to circle no more; would have to address himself directly to Louis' blade. 'Edmond de Lyonesse is dying by degrees,' Louis said, 'and all must change.'

'Perhaps the Princess will change?' de Numières asked.

Louis shook his head. 'I fear not, Jean,' he said with regret. 'She is the fairest princess in the world, but she thinks herself a prince.' Bitter irony, thought Louis. Setting aside beauty and wit (as if those could be set aside!), her very pride made her a fitting consort. Yet in the most important decision she would ever make – her marriage – she would consult that pride instead of her heart. '*Diable!*' he cried. He'd let himself be distracted. De Numières' blade flashed around and in, Louis' wrapped cloak flying up barely in time to catch the capped point. He feinted low and thrust up, but de Numières' cloak caught his blade.

Recovering, the duke stepped forward, his sword a silver arc whistling towards Louis' chest. Louis caught the blade under his cloak, and his own tip found the padding directly over the duke's heart.

'*Touché!*' gasped de Numières, and dropped to his knees. Louis swung to his feet and helped his groaning friend back up. The Duc de Numières would have a good bruise to mark this encounter. 'That was for the Princess!' Louis declared as he returned de Numières' bow. 'And when next I see your Madame de Jordanes, I shall tell her your downfall came as you spoke of another woman.'

'That thrust would truly find my heart, Monsieur,' said de Numières, still gasping from the blow. 'Then may I tell Princess Catherine that you were speaking of *her*?'

Louis grinned. 'Not as you value your life, Jean.'

A liveried servant appeared and bowed. 'Altesse. A letter has come from the Princess Lyonne. She asks that she might be received at your earliest convenience.' De Numières looked sharply at Louis, who frowned.

'Reply at once, Clouet,' Louis told his man, 'asking the honour of her company. I shall receive her in the hall – set out a suitable refreshment, all of the best.

Then tell my valet to draw a bath.' He turned to de Numières. 'Well . . . you spoke of her, and suddenly she is coming here – do you know something I do not?'

De Numières shrugged. 'Only that you are still in love with her – but you seem quite aware of that yourself.' Louis grunted. De Numières knew him too well.

He was scarcely bathed and dressed before Clouet returned to announce the Princess. When Louis entered the hall, his eyes were drawn first to the feathered chevalier's beret set boldly on her head. His gaze slid down, following the red hair that spilled from her cap, across her freckled shoulders. What it would be like to undo her lacings one by one . . . His mouth went dry at the thought. Her green eyes regarded him steadily; did she ever indulge a like fantasy?

'Princess Lyonne,' he said. 'You do me an honour I had not looked for this day.'

'It is Monseigneur who does me great honour,' she replied, 'to receive me on such brief notice. The more so, since at our last meeting I spoke words you did not wish to hear.'

'You spoke as befitted the day and your place, *ma chère*,' said Louis. He ushered forward de Numières, and Catherine her ladies; courtesies were exchanged all around, then servants ushered host and guests to a table.

Louis drank to peace, and the Princess to friendship, and they conversed lightly over veal and game birds. When the plates had been cleared away, Louis refilled Princess Catherine's cup and his own, ready to hear her reason for coming. She spoke plainly – as always.

'In a moment of foolishness, Monsieur de Fossier spoke words to the Baron de Moine. The latter took them as affront, and demands satisfaction.'

Ah! thought Louis. So that is it! Everyone knew about the affair; he and his friends had spoken much of it. The consensus was amazement that someone of de Fossier's intelligence had talked himself afoul of de Moine's blade. None would be sorry to see the baron meet his match, but it was most unlikely to be at the hands of Armand de Fossier. Louis had failed entirely, however, to draw any connection to Princess Catherine's household – and was annoyed that she should have come to see him for this, of all things. His gaze slid over to Mlle de Charleville. She looked down.

'Monseigneur must know,' said Catherine, 'that this was no happenstance in a tavern! De Moine went seeking Monsieur de Fossier, and insulted a lady of my household. In so doing he insulted me. If you wish, you may also consider it an attack on Monsieur de Chirac, who as you know has shown signal favour to de Fossier.'

Louis sighed. She was correct. He leaned back in his chair. 'The problem of de Moine has been frequently discussed,' he said. 'And I had thought on a matter of this nature before.' He related an idea to the demoiselles. 'It is a ... possibility,' he said. 'Nothing more. I can make no promise.'

'In matters of arms,' added de Numières, 'there can be no certainty, for the Baron de Moine is a most skilled and dangerous man.'

'Yet it is a very good plan,' said Princess Catherine. She nodded gravely to Louis. 'Monseigneur, if it please you, I should like a moment's speech. In the garden, perhaps?'

Louis nodded. The party arose and retired into the garden, and Louis and Catherine walked between the rows of flowering plants, now turning bare, and on among the apple trees of the orchard. At last, Princess Catherine turned to face him. '*Cher* Louis,' she said, her voice halting. 'Whatever ... whatever may come to pass, I shall not forget this day.

'I shall not forget many days, *ma plus belle* Catherine,' answered Louis.

She held out her hand. He took it, and drew her to him. They kissed, and embraced long and close, her body trembling against his. At last they stepped apart, and she said words in her own tongue. Louis did not understand them, but bowed, and again took her hand. Silently, hand in hand, they returned to where the others awaited.

Servants were summoned, horses led out, and moments later Catherine, her ladies and their escort rode out through the gate. Louis and de Numières said nothing as they walked together back into the hall. It had begun in a garden, thought Louis; must it end in a garden as well? Clouet had with his usual efficiency had the table cleared of all but two wine cups. When he and the Duc de Numières had sat, Louis raised his cup.

'Long life to the King of Lyonesse,' he said.

Time was his ally.

The combat between Armand de Fossier and the Baron de Moine took place at dawn on All Souls' Eve, a day cold but brilliant with sunshine. The designated place was the old cloister of the Cordelières, deconsecrated when that house moved to its new establishment across the river from the palace. On this occasion, wide knowledge of the dispute, and the reputation of the Baron de Moine, rendered the pretence of secrecy purely nominal. A great part of the Court was there, and many others – vendors selling oranges, and filles de joie selling themselves.

Catherine solemnly escorted Solange to her place of honour on the west side of the gallery above the courtyard. She took her place at Solange's right hand, and Madeleine on the other. Beside Catherine was the Dauphin, and with him his household – save the Duc de Numières; his place was in the courtyard below. M. de Chirac had not come – attendance at so flagrant a violation of the law ill befitted the minister of state – but Corisande came, as did a great number of ladies. Mme de Grinaud was not among them. Lady Lindley came, though Catherine sought to dissuade her, for her Ladyship's constitution had never truly recovered from her recent bout of fever. Her colouring was pale, and she moved more slowly than before. At times Catherine had to give her hand to steady her. How would she fare, Catherine wondered, when she no longer had her Ladyship to guide her?

Along the opposite gallery, more numerous and boisterous, were the adherents of the Baron de Moine. Fewer ladies were among them, but an excited stir announced the arrival of Margot de la Fontenelle, and then Prince Pépin. Never before, thought Catherine, had the parties of the Court been quite so overtly displayed. She whispered as much to the Dauphin. He nodded. 'Pépin and la Fontenelle should never have come here,' he whispered back. 'But then, nor should I, yet here I am!' His lips formed the ghost of a smile. 'If I were my father, I would enforce the edict, call out the gens d'armes and send the whole lot of us to the Tour St Martin!'

If the Dauphin were King of Aquitaine, thought Catherine, he would never allow it to go this far. Further meditations were cut off when the doors to the old refectory swung wide and a lone figure strode into the courtyard. He wore a tabard, white without charge. The buzz of conversation in the galleries died away. 'Henri, Baron de Moine,' the herald cried, 'having been given mortal affront by Armand de Fossier, demands that the latter answer upon his life. Monsieur de Fossier, having the choice of arms, has chosen the manner of old – the encounter will be with broadswords, the combatants armoured cap-à-pie.'

A collective murmur rose from the crowd. Such arms were familiar from tournaments, but none could remember when they had been called for in an encounter to the death. Only a few – Catherine guessed from their expressions – understood why the Dauphin had advised this form of combat. From the far side of the courtyard strode in a great vast figure, clad in glittering steel: the Baron de Moine. Three friends followed bearing arms and helm. From a door below her Armand de Fossier likewise entered, accompanied by two friends and the Duc de Numières.

The herald spoke a few whispered words to each principal's second, then shook his head and stepped back. The crowd was not to be disappointed. 'The dispute cannot be mended,' he announced. 'The combat is *à l'outrance.*' Each man turned back to his friends, to be fitted with his helm and receive his weapon. Before the helm was placed over de Fossier's head, he bowed to Solange in the gallery above him. She in turn undid a hair-ribbon and cast it over the balustrade. When she resumed her seat Catherine put an arm around her shoulder and hugged her.

The two men advanced on each other, circling, their

plate clinking in the still morning air. De Moine swung back his broadsword, then – with surprising speed for so big a man, moreover encased in steel – advanced on de Fossier. The latter swung up his sword, too late to fully ward off the blow that slammed against his shoulder. He staggered and went onto one knee. De Moine stepped forward and raised high his great blade; Solange gave a muffled cry, and Catherine's breath caught in her throat. But Armand de Fossier recovered enough to swing at de Moine's legs, forcing him back, and his great stroke crashed down through empty air. De Fossier got to his feet and backed away, circling, as de Moine came after him.

So it went, de Fossier retreating, de Moine advancing, broadsword always swinging, now kept back by de Fossier's defensive arcs, now delivering a clanging blow. If de Moine's great bulk was beginning to tell on him, Catherine saw no sign of it. His weight seemed only to give more power to his swings. At one point de Moine stumbled and went to one knee; Armand stepped in and got in a glancing blow to the arm; then the baron was back on his feet, advancing again, more furiously now. His broadsword rang against Armand's helm, sending him staggering back. On came de Moine, de Fossier dodging sideways past him, to jeers from the baron's partisans in the opposite gallery.

De Moine turned and fairly ran at him. Blade met blade with a sharp clang, and again Armand was retreating as his opponent advanced. Once more Armand dodged past. This time in turning de Moine lost his footing; he fell clattering to his knees, the great sword dropping from his hands. Once, twice, thrice, Armand landed solid blows – then the huge man was on his feet once more, broadsword in hand and swinging, Armand able only to back desperately away.

De Moine went again to his knees. He began to stumble back to his feet – then his sword crashed to the pavement, his gauntleted hands clutching his breast-plate. He sank once more to his knees and with a great clatter fell forward and was still. With a sob, Solange went to her own knees, crossed herself and whispered the Paternoster.

De Fossier stepped back, lowering his broadsword, as the baron's seconds came forward to examine him. They shouted for a physician and began to unstrap his armour. The physician appeared, briefly examined him, then rose and spoke a few whispered words to the herald. The herald raised his hand, and the crowd in the galleries fell silent. 'The Baron de Moine's heart appears to have failed him,' he declared. 'This matter is closed.'

As the crowd began to disperse, Madeleine ushered Solange towards the stair that led to the courtyard. Armand de Fossier walked slowly towards the side and sat on a bench, his seconds drawing around him to take off his helm and begin freeing him of his armour. The

Dauphin took Catherine by the arm and led her down to the courtyard.

Now at last, with the combat ended and the crowd dispersed, a squad of gens d'armes appeared. One knelt and examined the corpse of Henri, Baron de Moine. His body was bruised, but showed no mark of a fatal stroke. The officer got to his feet, muttering – then he and all his fellows knelt as the Dauphin stepped forward. 'It appears,' said the Dauphin, 'that the Baron de Moine has at last paid the price of his excessive table.'

'The murder of the baron was an insult to me, Sire,' said Margot de la Fontenelle. 'All the Court knows that he was my relation, and' – she hesitated a moment – 'my friend. All know as well that he was of the party of your son Pépin. Therefore it was an insult to Pépin . . . and to you.'

Charles VI, King of Aquitaine, was indifferent to the fate of the Baron de Moine. With a smile he contemplated the demoiselle who perched fetchingly on the foot of his bed, clad only in a transparent chemise. 'Murder? My lovely Margot, it was a fair fight, and one he chose – in violation of my edicts, I might add. And how can murder be claimed when there was no fatal wound?' He shrugged. 'De Moine should have indulged himself in fewer quarrels, or at least fewer sauces. In any case he lies in God's hands now. As you shall lie in mine.' He crooked a finger at her. 'Come, and I shall help you forget de Moine.'

'I tell you, Sire, it was an insult!'

'Do not vex me, Margot—'

'If you could have seen the Dauphin there, hanging on Catherine de Guienne!'

'Enough!' King Charles's voice rose to a shout. He took a deep breath, trying to calm his irritation. What right had this creature to make him lose his temper? 'Either come, Margot – or go!'

For once she knew when to subside. She came to him, her hips swaying, her chemise slipping off her shoulders. With a sudden motion Charles pulled her on top of him. 'Sire!' she gasped, then laughed and kissed him hungrily.

Charles's moment of ill temper left him, but afterwards – even as Margot lay beside him – he felt a lingering irritation. What right had she to speak of his sons, especially the Dauphin? He, Charles d'Héristal, was King of Aquitaine and master of the Court of la Trémouille – and it did not lack for women. It was amusing, he found, to lie next to Margot, weighing possible successors.

Fleetingly he thought of taking Corisande back. She was still magnificent, but it would be undignified, and she and de Chirac seemed happy. That time was over. Perhaps he'd acknowledge their son, belated thanks for those happy years. It was good sense in any case: acknowledged bastards were the stuff from which loyal generals were made.

No, he wanted a young demoiselle; they were so fresh. He considered Marie, daughter of the Comte d'Annabault, she with hair the colour of honey. She was a possibility – a shy, gentle girl, her figure just taking form, pretty as a flower waiting to be plucked. Or her cousin Allyriane de Marac, equally pretty, and with a hint of wildness. There were stories, outrageous and amusing, of what went on in the household of the Princess du Pré. Or for a different flavour, that smoky de Charleville girl, mistress of Armand de Fossier who'd brought low the mighty Baron de Moine. There was one with a lively eye! Pleasing to the eye too, with a good shape to her. Or Princess Catherine's other lady-in-waiting, golden Madeleine du Lac. An excellent equestrienne too ... and in Charles's experience, a woman who rode well was also lively in the bedchamber.

Charles smiled. 'Margot, my sweet – you say the Dauphin attended the duel with Princess Catherine?'

'Of course, Sire,' answered his mistress. 'The Dauphin and the Princess have been quite often in one another's company,' she said, as if he didn't already know. 'Indeed, I believe she persuaded him to assist in de Fossier's preparation for that duel.' She lowered her lashes. 'What persuasion she used, I do not know.'

Charles laughed aloud. Margot, Margot, foolish creature, you understand nothing! My son leads a very jewel of Christendom towards his bed – or has already – and you ask what persuasion *she* used! An audacious youth! For perhaps the first time, Charles found himself actually liking his elder son. 'I see,' he told Margot, 'that I have been remiss in duty to my royal brother, to see that his granddaughter's virtue is kept safe. I shall have to keep closer watch on her.' And on her lovely ladies-in-waiting, he thought. He did not say *that* part to Margot.

Advent came, and after a spate of storms brought with it a week of fine autumnal weather. The King of Aquitaine led his Court once more into the country, riding to the hunt amid the fallen leaves. Madeleine rejoiced in the weather, less in the circumstances. Their household had been invited to ride with the King's own party, but Mademoiselle herself stayed to tend her Ladyship, who again was ill. Hence the honour fell entirely on her ladies.

For a full day Madeleine found herself riding at the King's side. In his presence she was permitted – which was to say commanded – to bring down a stag with her crossbow. Through all she was uncomfortably aware of how many eyes were on her. Not till the sun was below the trees did the royal party return to the meadow where the Court was to make camp. Pavilions had been raised, and servants were hanging lanterns from branches while others turned spits over cooking fires. Excused to prepare herself for supper, Madeleine had at last a chance to retreat to the edge of the meadow for a few precious minutes with Solange.

'So – all goes very well, no?' Solange grinned slyly at Madeleine. 'His Majesty shows you high honour, permitting you to take a stag he could have taken himself.'

'A blind man could have taken it,' retorted Madeleine. 'It was no test of my shooting!'

'How you shoot a stag is no concern of the King's, I assure you,' answered Solange. 'He has given you Cupid's bow, with an easy shot to his heart. Draw the shaft and let fly, and he is yours.'

'You may find it endlessly amusing,' snapped Madeleine, 'but the jest is quite lost on me – even though I'm at the centre of it. Do you know how many great ladies swept me deep curtseys today, looking as though they'd cheerfully strangle me? Or how many men have been tearing my clothes off with their eyes?'

'Madeleine my dearest, they've been doing that since you were thirteen. You've just not noticed it before.'

'Well, I notice it now! And tonight – a feast, and dancing, and the King has bidden my presence at his table. What am I to do?'

'Feast and dance, of course,' answered Solange. 'None does either better than you do. You looked splendid riding beside the King! I wish Madame Corisande had come to see it. She would kiss your hand in sheer admiration.' Solange laughed. 'Margot certainly looked as if she'd like to throttle you! Did I not say her star is fading? The King is looking for one to replace her, and today he is looking at you. Tomorrow it may be me, or some other, till he finds what he is looking for. But today he looks at you. A hundred ladies at Court would give anything to be where you are now.'

Madeleine sat on a rock, staring at red and gold leaves. 'A hundred ladies at Court are welcome to it!' she said. 'I wish Mademoiselle were here! She could command me not to dine beside the King, and I would be safe. I do not wish to wake up in the King's bed, or anyone's but my own – not yet. All I wish is to stay in Mademoiselle's service and go to Lyonesse when her time comes. There I shall be content to wake up one fine morning in my husband's bed, with a household of my own.'

'I only want you to think about it,' Solange told her softly. 'Because if you close this particular door behind you, it won't be opened again.'

'That is fine with me!'

'So be it,' declared Solange. 'I expected nothing otherwise – in truth, I should terribly miss you if you did not come to Lyonesse with Mademoiselle and me. But close it gently: one does not slam doors on a King.' She bit her lip, then smiled. 'Indeed, perhaps we should open another for him? You must ask the King if Allyriane de Marac may accompany you at table.'

'Allyriane? But—' Madeleine felt herself colouring slightly. Madeleine had never quite put from her mind the stories Solange told about the household of the Princess du Pré.

Solange raised an eyebrow. 'Allyriane's tastes are varied,' she said. 'But for all her love of variety, Allyriane's adventures are chiefly with men – and what greater adventure than to be maîtresse-en-titre? She might return some grace to the office, sadly lacking since Corisande.'

'Well, that would be well and good,' said Madeleine. 'But what has it to do with me, now? Within the hour I must sit at table beside his Majesty, in my best gown, with the entire Court wondering if he will take it off me tonight! Is that not bad enough, without being made Allyriane's procuress as well?'

'Think it a service,' answered Solange. 'Let us guide him towards Allyriane, who is well disposed towards us. We will have served Mademoiselle well, and ourselves too.'

'I came back aforetime, Father,' said William, addressing the figure who lay face to the wall.

'Then you've come to the wrong house, boy!' said his father. 'I have no sons! One lost to Selsey Rock, the other an oathbreaker. The de Havillands are at an end! I thought Petronilla an honest woman – yet she surely bore some other man's get and called it mine, damn her.'

'You call my lady mother false?' William had vowed patience: a second oath broken. 'By Wott, if you were still a man I'd have your answer in steel!'

Now his father lay no more facing the wall, but reared himself up in the bed. He turned to face William. 'I'm man enough for the likes of you, oathbreaker!' he roared. 'Now, out, afore I call the guards and have you cast out.'

'They'll not come,' answered William. 'If I go, it will be my own choosing.' The look of the old man's face, thought William, could break a strong man's heart. Here was Black Jack de Havilland – the man who sailed into Finngard haven and sailed out with Sven Torvaldsen's head on his bowsprit, a pirate the King of Gottland never dared touch. Now he lay as much a ruin as the legionary fortress of Stanbury. 'Now!' said William. 'Will you hear me out, or die a greater fool than I have lived? Yes, by God I broke my oath – and a bloody witless one it was. I'd have kept it all the same, but for a woman!'

For long moments his father looked at him in silence. One eye was broken with cataracts, but the other could yet see. 'Eh?'

William had hoped for that. Women were the de Havilland weakness. When his father had sailed to claim a second bride – his own lady mother – the van den Kempens had been the wealthiest merchant house in the Free Estates. He'd arrived to find them ruined, dragged down in the great fall of the banking house of Orsini, but he'd asked for the daughter of the house all the same, and took her to wife, saying he'd come for a woman, not a counting-house.

His father sank back on the bed, his broken strength spent but his good eye still on William. 'What maid is this you broke your oath for, boy?'

'A maid,' said William. 'Fair and goodly. What more needed to break a fool's oath? Her name is Katrin.'

'Katrin,' murmured his father. 'Good name. Never knew a Katrin to lack spirit. What sort of Cat is she?'

'A ginger one,' answered William. 'Pleasing enough by the fireside. Not yet tried for mousing; she doesn't lack claws.' He paused. 'God willing, she might clear rats from a barn in Kelliwick.'

'Kelliwick?' His father eyed William suspiciously. 'They told me you sailed from Flyssingen. I've sailed that course more than twice – it makes no landfall at Kelliwick.' No course did. Kelliwick lay in the heart of the kingdom, on the western marches of the Saxon Pale.

'The course hasn't changed,' said William, 'and I've not seen Kelliwick since Prince Harry's wedding. I met the maid in the Aquitaine.'

'The Aquitaine?' His father frowned. 'Beware Gallic maids, my boy. They're clever.'

William thought of two Gallic maids. 'So I have found out,' he said. 'Yet this maid I speak of is as much of Lyonesse as you or I. Half Gallic by birth and bearing a Gallic name, she swears by Lud all the same.'

The old earl made a grumbling sound.

'I'll not riddle you more, Father,' said William. 'Her name is Katrin de Guienne. The Princess Lyon.'

The silence this time was the longest yet. Below in Halverstrand town the bells of St Mary Magdalene rang the hour. 'Little Ned died,' said his father at last. 'Then Prince Harry himself, and I thought this kingdom cast away. Yet I heard tell the little wench knelt to the flags taken at Richborough. Bloody more than I or many others did.'

If it weren't contrary to natural law, William would have sworn his father's good eye was moist. 'She's no little wench,' he said. 'Rather a lofty one. Taller than my lady mother.'

'Taller, eh? Well! Yet there was never lady nobler – I spoke in haste, my boy.'

'And I did not?' said William. He poured a cup of water, eased his father up and held it to his lips. 'The palest pale, Father – Mother says it's best for you.'

The old man sipped, then settled back, closing his eyes. 'The Princess Lyon!' he said. 'You're firing on the uproll, son.'

'So I am,' William agreed. 'And a stern chase is a long chase. Yet with a fair wind and good laying aboard, the de Havillands are not done, Father. They might even wear a crown.'

'Mind it's not a paper one, your head on a pike over Farrington Bridge! Yet if the maid be worthy . . . serve her well.' His father raised his arm and pointed across the chamber. 'There. On the table, in a leather pouch. You'll find something of use in her service. And draw the bedcurtain, if you will. Best I sleep a while, afore Petronilla comes to force soup down my gullet.'

William rose and closed the bedcurtain, then went to the table. He opened the little pouch. Within was a gold bosun's call on a silk cord – the Lord High Admiral's badge of office. He stared long at it. He kept his eyes dry. Then he turned, drew his sword and knelt in salute to his father. Rising, he slipped the silk cord around his neck and departed the chamber.

CHAPTER SIXTEEN

Monk's Hood

Margot sat before her great glass and carefully examined herself. Nothing was wrong with her, even to the discerning eye. Her eyes were not reddened from weeping, for she had not wept. If her cheeks were slightly pale, a touch of rouge would restore her colour. Yet which bottle held the elixir to restore her favour with the King? The entire Court talked of nothing but how he was testing young demoiselles one by one, looking for her replacement. The hunting trip had been the worst, having to ride behind him while impudent Madeleine du Lac rode at his side. Then the feast, with his eye falling on Allyriane de Marac – Margot knew la Marac would not hesitate to take her place.

As her hold on the King slipped, the family was turning away from her as well. De Moine had been positively frosty before he was so foolish as to get himself killed in a duel – and all over Princess Catherine's other lady-in-waiting. Margot had no illusions as to what the Lusianes saw in her, and there was a service she might yet perform for them, one having nothing to do with the King.

Before his death the baron had let slip that the family interest was turning from Catherine to her sister Anne. Margot thought of a way she could aid their cause.

Briefly she hesitated, thinking of that strange comedy that had played out in the Hôtel de Guienne. The way she'd been received there had thrown her off stride: she had not gone there to ask for sanctuary! Margot could not help but admire such arrogance – the girl was so comfortable in it that it rested lightly on her. Her offer had seemed almost genuine, and perhaps in a way it was. Then, with a deep breath, Margot steeled herself to resolve. Catherine de Guienne must be dealt with firmly, as originally intended, and her conniving ladies too. She had not forgotten the slap at Montpassier. No woman, not even a princess, slapped Margot de la Fontenelle with impunity.

Soon the Duc de Septimanie would appoint another to take de Moine's place – but for now, however, she had command of de Moine's household. It was time to do what should have been done long ago. Margot rang her bell fiercely, and when her chambermaid appeared, she ordered the girl to fetch her steward. 'Send to the late baron's hôtel,' she told the steward. 'Have his man Vernay sent to me.'

The hour was late and the Hôtel de Guienne slumbering when Catherine yawned and set down her copy of Quintilius Postumus's *De Re Imperio*. She had one important matter to tend to before she could go to sleep. Her Ladyship's coughing had persisted, and Catherine brought her a hot posset of milk mixed with mead each night to ease her rest. For greater efficacy she prepared it with her own hands, going each night to the kitchen to mix and heat it on a brazier left ready for her. She set out, with candle and another book in hand.

Not without difficulty had Catherine asserted her right to enter her own kitchen. Madeleine pointed out the jealous pride with which good servants guarded their domains: the better the servant the more fiercely guarded. Only by insisting on royal prerogative had Catherine won Madeleine over, and so on down the ranks: steward, butler, chief cook and his mates. Even so, she prevailed only by lying. She asserted that old custom in Lyonesse held a hot posset to have greater curative powers when made by a princess of royal blood. It was the newest of old customs. Would some princess in centuries to come wonder how it originated?

Catherine was at least able to reach the kitchen easily; a private passageway led from the royal chambers to the kitchen. Perhaps one of her forebears had wanted to claim a cut of roast or leg of fowl without rousing half the household. As she made her way down by the light of her candle, she wondered if he'd had so much trouble getting his servants' permission.

All was in readiness; that much Catherine accepted without protest. A brazier was set up at the far end from the great hearth around which kitchen servants slept, and beside it a kettle of milk, pot of mead, and a little cinnamon. Once the kettle was heating, Catherine sat on an upturned pail and opened her book. She wanted no Latin at this time of night. It was the book of Stiyand Tydder, *The Seven Pilgrimes ifaren biyonde See* – an old and famed book, said to be a tale of morality, though the pilgrims committed many and colourful sins in their journey to Sion and salvation. She turned to 'Lady Alison's Tale', pausing now and then to stir the milk and take a sip of mead. Resourceful Lady Alison was seducing the emir who'd taken her captive when Catherine sensed a rustle, then soft padding of bare feet on the flagstones. A small dark shape approached, like the ghost of a child, silhouetted against the glow of the hearth. When Catherine looked up, the figure froze in its tracks.

'Come here, child,' she said, beckoning the little spectre forward. It was revealed as a kitchen girl, two or three years younger than Catherine. She curtseyed, then stood with head down as though to make herself even smaller. As it was she was a slight little figure, clad only in a worn shift; one of the humblest servants of the Hôtel de Guienne.

Catherine gave the milk another stir, then gently raised the girl's chin. 'You are called Rosine, child, are you not?'

The girl nodded. 'Y-yes, Altesse,' she managed.

Catherine smiled at her. 'Do not be afraid, Rosine. If you wish audience, here I am!'

Rosine shuffled her feet uneasily. 'I . . . I have done wrong, Altesse.'

'Then you must tell me, child, and you shall have a fair hearing. What have you done?' Catherine could hardly imagine what offence this girl might commit.

'I . . . I stole some salt.'

Catherine swallowed her impulse to laugh. Salt! Yet a thief was a thief, even if this one's crime was as small as she was. 'Why did you steal, Rosine?'

'To buy a necklace,' mumbled the girl.

That was honest, thought Catherine – no pretence of a starving little brother or the like. A little necklace of coloured beads would be to her as one of pearls to Catherine. 'You must give it to the chief cook,' said Catherine sternly, 'for it is the fruit of wrongdoing. You must repay the salt, as well, and twofold!' More gently she added, 'Yet because you confessed your crime freely, tell him I shall not dismiss you from my service.'

The girl's mouth was working. 'You are very kind, Altesse. I won't steal, not ever again! But – but I . . .' She began weeping, and Catherine put a hand on her shoulder. The child was quivering; her conscience a far sterner judge than Catherine. In the face of such contrition, Catherine tempered justice with mercy. 'I shall not even tell the chief cook,' she said. 'Tomorrow you must go to the chaplain, confess, and give *him* the necklace. Do the penance he assigns, and none shall speak of it again. God will forgive you, and so do I. Now, go back and sleep, child.'

The girl did not go. Instead she wept even more, till she was heaving sobs. With a sigh Catherine set the milk off to the side where it wouldn't boil over. Taking the girl by the arm, she guided her back to a storeroom. 'Is there more you want to tell me, Rosine?'

The girl wiped her eyes on the sleeve of her shift. 'I – I . . . Maître Bonpierre caught me when I sold the salt,' she said. 'He told me . . . he told me he would have me arrested by the gens d'armes, and I would be hanged, if I didn't – didn't—'

'Bonpierre?' interrupted Catherine. He was one of the steward's officers, one she knew Solange did not trust. 'What did he make you do?' she demanded.

'T-tonight, Master Bonpierre is to send a man,' said Rosine, her voice small and trembling. 'I am. . . to show him where the silver jars of spices are k-kept.'

Catherine frowned. 'To steal them?' Why would Bonpierre use this girl to steal spice jars, even silver ones? Then she abruptly grasped the meaning of the silver jars – they were for her own table: none but her immediate household tasted the spices they held! She gulped.

'Rosine! There is a stair that leads up to my chambers – I will show you.' Catherine gave her the candle. 'Take this to guide you. Go up and rouse my ladies,

Mesdemoiselles de Charleville and du Lac, and tell them to come down at once!'

'M-Mademoiselle du Lac?' Rosine blanched and shrank back, more afraid of Madeleine than of Catherine herself. It was of a piece, Catherine realized, with all she'd learned of her household. To a kitchen girl she was a remote figure, clothed in the aura of royalty. Madeleine was the visible fount of authority – well might this child fear to rouse her in the night! Catherine laughed softly. 'You need not fear Mademoiselle du Lac, Rosine. Tell her you summon her by my command. Now go! At once!'

It seemed an eternity that Catherine was alone in the storeroom. But at last a glow appeared from the stairs and became her ladies, cloaks thrown over their chemises, followed by Rosine. Each had a candle; Solange also held a crossbow and Madeleine her sword. Catherine related what Rosine had said, and Madeleine commanded the kitchen girl to await the man, and do precisely as he ordered.

Many eternities passed, each hour of night yielding only with utmost reluctance to the next. Once or twice there were stirrings, merely kitcheners rising to use the privy and Catherine began to wonder if the poisoner would come tonight, or indeed at all. Perhaps he was just the fanciful invention of a frightened kitchen girl, conscience stricken over her theft of salt?

Solange nudged her. Catherine roused with a start,

having nearly fallen asleep. Another stirring came from the depths of the kitchen, barely perceptible, more furtive than any servant going to the privy. Presently two shadows appeared, ghosting past the glow of the great hearth: a small shadow that was Rosine, followed by a larger. Catherine stepped from the storeroom. 'You – stand, or we shoot!' she ordered.

For an instant the larger figure froze. 'Run, Rosine!' cried Madeleine, but an instant too late; before the girl could run the man caught and held her, and Catherine saw the glint of a knife.

'I'll cut her throat!'

'Touch a hair of her,' answered Catherine, 'and you'll die by roasting!'

The man backed up. He did not let go of Rosine – but the uproar had roused the kitcheners. Within moments half a dozen were advancing on him, one armed with a cleaver, another hefting an immense skillet, suitable to fell an ox. 'Take him alive!' ordered Solange.

The man backed towards the wall, still holding Rosine – but a servant got behind him. What ensued was too fast for Catherine to follow, but it ended with Rosine sobbing in the arms of the chief cook, while the poisoner was spread-eagled on the floor, held fast by a dozen strong hands. A brief, un-gentle search discovered a small flask of oil. The chief cook handed it to Madeleine, who handed it to Catherine – even here and now, rank was observed. Catherine gave it to Solange. She if anyone would know what it was.

Solange did not disappoint her. She opened the flask, sniffed it and dabbed some on the tip of her finger. 'Extract of aconite,' she declared. 'Known in Lyonesse as wolfsbane or monk's hood. Applied as an unguent it is medicinal. Taken with food . . . this would be quite sufficient for all of us.' She paused. 'If it please Mademoiselle, we ought to question him – and Bonpierre too. Have the servants truss him up, and the huntsmen arrest Bonpierre. Then you may wish to dismiss the servants. Such questioning is best done in privacy,' she added grimly.

Catherine gave the necessary orders. Rosine was delivered to the chaplain for comfort and rest, and huntsmen were summoned to arrest Bonpierre and bring him to the kitchen.

With the great hearth stoked to a blaze, thought Solange, the kitchen soon resembled all too well a chamber of horrors. None were now present but Mademoiselle and her ladies, two grim-faced huntsmen standing guard, and the bound prisoners. In the light of the flames, the innocent tools of the cooks' trade – great cleavers, spits and mallets – looked like implements of torture. A side of beef, hanging in wait for tomorrow's dinner, suggested a victim who had suffered the uttermost agonies.

Mademoiselle stepped forward and looked down at

the bound prisoners. 'As Duchesse de Guienne,' she declared, 'I have the right of high, middle and low justice over this house and all within it. Confess!'

She got no answer but silence. Solange tugged at her cloak and motioned towards the storeroom. Catherine followed her back. 'What is it?' she asked.

'By your leave, Mademoiselle,' whispered Solange. She hesitated and swallowed. She had failed once in her duty – what a reckless fool she had been, not to guard against poison! – and could not fail again. The truth had to be drawn from the criminals. Solange had read how it was done, in books never meant for ladies. It was one thing to read about, another to do it. Yet she had read also how the Empress Servilia, beautiful and courageous, broke the conspirators against her without laying a violent hand on them. Solange could attempt the same methods . . . and not think of what might be necessary if they failed. Quickly she outlined the plan, and Mademoiselle gave her assent. Madeleine was dispatched again to give orders to Lasceaux the huntmaster, and to seek out a suitable kitchen servant.

Lasceaux's arrival was heralded from afar by Asterion and Chara, their baying and barking echoing off the walls. As they entered the kitchen they strained and snapped at their leashes, tails wagging furiously, their howls an eager crescendo. The prisoners cringed back. Well might dogs go mad with joy in this place, thought Solange, it being filled with the accumulated smells of every roast ever turned and every pie baked. Lasceaux came well equipped for his task, clad in a wolfskin, a great knife in his belt. He bowed to Mademoiselle, then turned to Solange. Drawing him aside, she whispered to him the part he must play, and they returned together to the kitchen.

Solange went to the hearth and drew out the poker. Then she turned to the captives, waving it before first one man, then the other. The tip blazed yellow white, its baleful glow illuminating their faces. 'Who sent you?' she demanded. 'Which of you will spare himself by telling the truth?' The glowing iron hovered before Bonpierre's face. He was sweating profusely. 'You, Bonpierre?' Solange turned and held the poker towards the other man. 'You, Monsieur? I do not know your name – but I shall!' She stepped back. 'The iron grows dull. I must renew it!' She thrust the end of the poker back into the hearth. 'The Princess is patient,' she said. 'I too am patient – but Lasceaux and his dogs have been dragged from their rest, and are not patient at all. None, I fear, shall rest till we learn the truth.' She drew the poker from the fire, and walked slowly towards Bonpierre. Once more she held the glowing tip before his eyes. He winced and turned his head; the iron followed. 'Bonpierre! What have you to say for yourself? Has the Princess treated you unjustly, that you conspire to poison her?'

No answer.

Abruptly Solange whirled on her heels and plunged the tip of the poker into a pail of water. She had supposed it would hiss and steam, but was taken aback by the spitting fury: hot droplets flew in all directions, stinging her hands and face, and she nearly dropped the poker. Turning towards Lasceaux, she gestured towards the bound men. 'Separate the prisoners,' she said, 'and we shall consider which to question first.'

Huntsmen roughly picked up each man and carried them to separate storerooms. Solange then nodded to Madeleine, who had with her the same huge assistant cook who had earlier wielded the great skillet. Taking him aside, Solange explained in a whisper the part he must play. Once more she heated the poker till its tip was blazing white. This time she thrust it against the hanging side of beef.

The assistant cook, a good and faithful servant, did as commanded: the instant the meat hissed from the glowing iron he screamed as in death agony, his wailing cry reverberating from the stone walls. 'Enough, Lasceaux!' cried Solange. 'No more!' At her gesture, the cook's false cries of agony subsided into a whimpering moan. After a little time, the whole grim comedy was repeated.

After a further pause, Solange went into the storeroom where the bound figure of Bonpierre awaited her. She guessed him the weaker of the two men. 'Your confederate has told me some of the truth,' she said, 'but I do not believe he told me all of it. He claims he was working for Leblanc,' she said, inventing a name. 'Yet I do not think Monsieur Leblanc had any part in it.' She paused. 'Please, Bonpierre,' she continued, 'do not make me go on! Tell me the truth, that we may have an end to this. At whose bidding did you let this man into Mademoiselle's house?' Long moments passed. Bonpierre's mouth trembled, but he said nothing.

The dogs snarled furiously: a huntsman was teasing them with a beef bone. Then they were at the storeroom entry, held by Lasceaux. 'The night grows long, Mademoiselle de Charleville,' he said. 'You waste your time with Bonpierre. He is a fool, and surely knows nothing. Let me give him to Asterion and Chara, that the other may be encouraged to truth.' The huntmaster let slip a loop of the leashes; his beasts sprang forward, growling and snapping – for behind Bonpierre stood the huntsman with the bone.

'No!' gasped Bonpierre, staring up at the slavering dogs. 'I beg of you!'

'Then speak!' ordered Solange. 'Tell me the whole truth, Bonpierre, and there will be no more. What is your confederate's true name?'

'He – he calls himself Maurras.'

'And who commanded this? It was not Leblanc at all, was it?'

He shook his head, sweat glistening on his brow. 'It was a certain Monsieur Vernay—'

Vernay! thought Solange: the man Armand had told

her of, who had made enquiries about *tarocchi* cards after Mère Angelique had been murdered. Vernay had been de Moine's man – but de Moine was dead. She ordered Lasceaux to withdraw; when he was gone she asked further questions of the broken Bonpierre, but discovered little. Of Vernay's affairs, Bonpierre knew nothing. Solange learned only how he had been ensnared, a tale as pitiful as Rosine's beads, for Bonpierre had consorted with prostitutes and Vernay had threatened to expose him to his wife.

Nothing more was to be gained from Bonpierre. Again Lasceaux teased his dogs with the beef bone. Again their snarls echoed through the kitchen and storerooms, accompanied by screams from the assistant cook. Surely, thought Solange, the man had earned an extra day's pay. She went into the storeroom where Maurras was held, followed by Mademoiselle and Madeleine.

'Bonpierre confessed, Maurras,' Solange told him, watching him start as she used his real name. 'However, I do not believe he was speaking the whole truth, for he claimed that *you* were the author of the plan, that you proposed it to Vernay for the sake of gain. I on the other hand suspect that *Vernay* was behind it. It can profit you nothing to conceal what you know. Are you in Vernay's service?' The man nodded. 'And in whose service is Vernay? Speak – or Lasceaux shall resume his ministrations, this time with you.'

At that the man spoke, his voice a dry whisper. 'The baron's household is – is now – at the command of Mademoiselle de la Fontenelle.'

'Margot!' exploded Mademoiselle, from her place in the shadowed corner. 'But why?'

'That,' said Solange, 'I suspect I can answer better than Maurras can.' She turned to Mademoiselle. 'Altesse,' she said gravely, 'we have done here all that is needful.' She was heartily glad. Just now she did not particularly like herself.

The kitchen was soon restored to its honest purpose. The prisoners were taken to separate places of confinement and a guard set over each. Huntsmen and dogs were dismissed, Asterion and Chara each with a bone for loyal service, and the servants allowed to return. Only one other duty did Catherine have here: as her ladies stood silently by, she prepared her Ladyship's long delayed posset. Dawn was breaking as the three of them went back up to their chambers. Her Ladyship had slept through the disturbance below, but she at once sensed something amiss, and insisted that all be told her.

Solange sat on the side of her Ladyship's bed. 'I thought the sooner Margot fell from favour the better,' she explained. 'I did not think it would lead to this!' She related how King Charles's eye had fallen on Madeleine, and how the two of them had sought to draw his attentions towards Allyriane de Marac.

'But—' protested Catherine. '*Poison?*'

'Margot's place is her life, Kateryn,' said her Ladyship. 'If she loses it she loses all, unless she can act in a way to ensure the protection of the Lusianes.'

'It is my great folly,' said Solange, 'not to have foreseen that she would go so far!'

'How could you foresee this?' asked Catherine. 'I must convey word to the King of Aquitaine. I fear he will not believe me – yet he would not care to have a poisoner share his bed!'

'He will believe the prisoners, Mademoiselle,' said Solange bluntly.

'Impossible!' roared the King of Aquitaine.

Antoine de Chirac kept his head bowed. It was most delicate, as the King might fairly doubt his impartiality. 'Unfortunately, Sire,' he said, 'there can be no doubt. De Moine's man Vernay has regrettably been found dead – we do not know by whose hand – but both men taken at the Hôtel de Guienne have been put to the Question and their confessions are in full accord with what was reported by Princess Catherine.'

'Princesse Catherine!' exclaimed the King. 'By what right does she take such matters upon herself?'

'It is a delicate point of law,' admitted Antoine. 'Nevertheless, as they were caught in her hôtel, with poison in hand, so it was only natural that she should question them.' With some skill too, he thought.

The King looked sharply at him. 'Have you ordered Margot arrested?'

'No, Sire. I judged that beyond my discretion. I gave orders only that she be watched. Alas, she is nowhere to be found; whether she fled or is in hiding, I cannot say.' Antoine had himself sent Corisande into hiding, for fear of her safety – these were clearly dangerous times for any who had displeased la Fontenelle.

The King sighed. He looked weary, and much too old. 'Margot has often strained my patience, de Chirac, but I – I did not expect this. I give you authority to have her held when she is found – but see that she is treated with every dignity. Whatever may come.'

Margot entered the palace grounds through a yard gate, near the larger gate frequented by produce wagons and kitchen servitors. It was humiliating to slip in like this, but she feared now only the greater humiliation: being drawn through the city in a cart, then mounting the scaffold in front of Ste Marie Madeleine, watched by a thousand eyes, to have her head struck off by the executioner's sword.

Everything had gone so dreadfully wrong. The bungler Vernay had relied on agents, and they on some ragged serving girl, who had confessed all to Princess Catherine.

She found herself in the east wing, among work rooms and offices where she had rarely been. She passed through a door, down a gallery reeking of kitchen smells, and into the Montfaucon garden – more familiar surroundings. His Majesty's apartments were not a hundred paces from here. She could be there in a minute . . . but the guards would stop her, attempt to arrest her. They would not succeed. Margot had brought a *pistole*, a new and costly weapon that had belonged to de Moine, to ensure that she would not be seized, held, dragged away a prisoner.

If only she could reach the King! She would throw herself at his feet and confess her faults. He would listen, he would understand, and surely he would take her back! Yet in her heart Margot knew that he would not. For a moment her courage almost failed her, and she thought to slink back out as she had come – but where, and to what? She resolved to go onward. She knew private ways to the King's apartments, but those too were guarded – and what was to come should not be witnessed only by guards and servants. Thus on she went from the Montfaucon garden into the gallery beyond, more crowded than the garden: the gallery that led to the royal Presence Chamber.

A minor countess saw Margot, stared at her and pointed her out to her companion. A buzz of conversation spread along the gallery. As nothing was to be gained by further concealment, Margot threw back the hood of her cloak. All around her the courtiers gasped. Then they drew back, waiting. In front of her appeared a half-circle of Gardes de Maison, resplendent in silver and sable, and an officer with sword drawn. He bowed. 'Mademoiselle de la Fontenelle,' he declared. 'I must ask you to come with me.' She looked back. Three more Gardes de Maison appeared, barring her retreat – not that she would retreat in any case.

'No, Monsieur,' she replied, 'I must not.' She might have done so much differently, thought Margot – yet had she not reached the very pinnacle? For the little time left she was still maîtresse-en-titre. Even now the officer bowed to her! Beyond that, what was there? No, she had reached the pinnacle – and from it she would cast herself down.

More guards appeared. Deliberately, unhurriedly, Margot walked towards the King's apartments, though her heart pounded and her breath was tight. Reaching to her bosom with her left hand, she unfastened the golden brooch of her cloak; with a peremptory gesture she threw it from her shoulders, revealing her crimson gown – and the *pistole* in her right hand.

'Mademoiselle—!' cried the astonished officer. A collective gasp ran through the gallery, then the whir of a dozen swords drawn. The flash of their blades dazzled in the morning light.

'None but his Majesty,' declared Margot, 'may bar me from his chambers!' Even as guards converged upon her, she raised and levelled her *pistole* –

– and gasped as terrible cold fire blazed through her

breast. The *pistole* flew from her hand, she sank to her knees, and the world went spinning about her as she plummeted through infinite space, down from the pinnacle . . .

CHAPTER SEVENTEEN

La Reine Volante

Catherine kept Twelfth Night with the household of M. de Chirac and Corisande, a year less a day since she had stood godmother to their daughter. How great was the variety of Fortune! Here sat Corisande beside her husband, her son at her knee – now acknowledged by King Charles, made Duc de Conté – and her daughter in her arms, while Margot de la Fontenelle lay nearly a month in the grave. Her final scandal had been the talk of the Court, till Christmastide festivities swept it into the past. Catherine thought only that Margot had found a dignity in death that had eluded her in life. Even so a faint sombre pall remained. Her ladies' too clever attempt to promote Allyriane in the royal favour availed nothing. The King took no new mistress, and kept Christmas quietly with Queen Isabelle at his side.

The new order at Court was not altogether an improvement. Catherine was no longer invited, which was of no consequence save that her occasions to see Anne, always few, were now none. Her ladies took on the new tone of sobriety – especially Solange, who subtly transformed herself into a model of chaste elegance. Without her quite saying it, Catherine gathered that she and Armand de Fossier had bid their adieux.

A stronger guard was kept on the Hôtel de Guienne, and a royal escort provided whenever Catherine left it, whether as bodyguard or gaolers she was unsure. Ambassadors came. As the sun set over Kelliwick it rose over the Hôtel de Guienne; those who had business with Lyonesse came now to her. She could give no answers, not yet, but she could listen, and convey her thoughts.

Before departing the next day, Catherine spoke alone to M. de Chirac. 'Is there any new word of my grandfather?' she asked him.

'King Edmond declines, Altesse,' said de Chirac. 'The end cannot be long, but none can say when. The counsels of Lyonesse are gravely distracted. I must tell you – as your friend, not as his Majesty's minister – that you must consider what awaits you. Most hold that your age and sex render you incapable to rule. I, who know you, am persuaded otherwise. Yet the accession of a young prince, in a kingdom long without a firm hand, is always uncertain.'

Catherine nodded. She knew she might be going from cooking-pot to fire; all the same she was eager for it. The sooner faced the sooner met. She wished only for a minister like de Chirac to guide her; there were none such she knew of.

'You should know also,' he said, 'that the old Earl

d'Avalon has preceded King Edmund in death. His son takes his place, also as admiral: I believe you met him? The young man who came with Senator Falier's embassage.' De Chirac smiled almost imperceptibly. 'I understand that another young man was seen with them at Tertrianne – one never heard of before or since.'

'Indeed, Monsieur?' said Catherine, knowing that her colouring was giving her away.

'Not long afterwards, so Madame tells me, you adopted a new fashion in headgear, and quite a bold one. I leave fashions to her, and will not ask what inspired you to it! I will only remind you that even Hippolyta is still a demoiselle! You will find yourself surrounded by ambitious young men, of whom d'Avalon is only one. By report he is fitting out great ships of war – perhaps for your service, perhaps his own.' He shrugged.

At least, thought Catherine, neither de Chirac nor rumour had said anything about brent wine and princesses wrapped in coverlets. 'The ships are for my service,' she said, and hoped fervently it was true. Then she made a firmer resolve: she would see to it that they *were* for her service.

'I must tell you also,' said de Chirac, 'that many still point to the troubles your mariners have already made, and the threat of more – and press the King to demand reparations.'

'But—' began Catherine, then bit off her protest.

Reparations, as the price of her release and return? No sovereign of Lyonesse would assent to such terms. Catherine was not yet sovereign, yet a royal answer was called for and there was none other to make it. 'That is impossible, Monsieur,' she said quietly. 'Yet if l'Aquitaine will provide a suitable indemnity for the seizure of Richborough, then we in turn shall indemnify the people of Louselles for the despoiling of their town.'

De Chirac studied her for some long moments. Gravely he bowed. 'I shall convey your answer to his Majesty,' he said. 'That too is impossible – yet it lies within my office to tell him that no lesser reply could be expected.'

Late the next afternoon, Catherine followed Madeleine in inspection of the cellars. 'All those barrels are empty, Mademoiselle,' explained Madeleine in a low voice, gesturing towards the north wall. 'I thought it best, in case . . .'

Catherine nodded. 'In case,' she repeated. Behind the empty barrels was the old water gate, and the tunnel to the river. She was not sure how well three maids would do at moving even empty casks, but it was something. 'You have done very well, Madeleine – as always. Now,' she said, 'I must go back up to her Ladyship. She is coughing again, and requires hot honeyed wine to soothe her.'

*   *   *

Late February, and in Kelliwick Castle men spoke in low voices if they spoke at all. William de Havilland sat at table in his chambers, opposite Sir James Strickland and Margaret Lady Hollingsworth, his alepot in hand and a sheaf of papers before him. They bore orders to place the Queen's ships – as they must soon be – in readiness: arms and powder, stores and provisions; even paint and arming-cloths to replace the ER royal monogram with CR. The galley *Antelope*, new built at Flyssingen in the Free Estates, lay now at King's Dock in Rosemouth, her taffrail canvas-draped, Royal Arms with the new Queen's device already in place. He would put out a call to all good shipmasters of the realm to serve the Queen. But he could not compel; only the people's hope in a new reign could do that.

Three days past a great thunderstorm had swept over Kelliwick. Rain pounded down in sheets, lightning lashed from the black sky, peal after peal of thunder rolled across the landscape. King Edmund had cried out for Elizabeth, his first queen, dead a generation, and for Henry his son. He had not cried out for his grand-daughter Catherine. Since then he had spoken no word, but lay insensible in his chamber.

From somewhere outside came raised voices and the tramp of booted feet. A fist pounded on the door, and without awaiting answer it was pushed open. An officer of the royal Housecarls stepped in and bowed. 'My Lord of Avalon,' he said. 'Sir James; Lady Hollingsworth. It is over.'

William bowed his head, and his companions like-wise. Then he raised his alepot. 'God save Queen Katrin,' he said softly.

'Long may she reign,' answered Jamie and Meg, and raised their cups to their lips. For a few minutes they drank in silence.

William made a decision. As Lord High Admiral, he was himself the new Queen's lieutenant upon the sea, and as such he would act, though it stretched his authority to the limit and perhaps beyond. One by one he began to sign the papers before him. As he did he found himself smiling. Signing the orders might be some compensation for having got his sovereign drunk.

Twelve thousand years before Edmund IV breathed his last, ice sheets covered the place where Kelliwick Castle would one day stand. Immeasurably far from that place, a mighty star had seethed in its death throes. At a fated hour, far beneath its roiling surface, its innermost furnace ran amok. Naked hearts of atoms danced in mad bacchanalia, combining and promiscuously re-combining. In a heartbeat they were transmuted to massy iron, and could dance no more.

As suddenly as a snuffed candle flame died the immeasurable force of radiance that had borne up the great doomed star. Its upper regions hung sus-pended for the blink of an eye – then cascaded downward, layer upon layer, under the inexorable power of their own ever growing weight. The heart of the star was crushed into a single great atom, then further yet, till fleeting Light herself was trapped in the claws of gravity and dragged back down. In the last instant before entombing itself from creation the star gave a dying gasp – the merest froth of its substance, yet with such power as to catch up the plummeting outer layers and hurl them back outward. A vast burst of radiance flooded across space, brighter than seven hundred million suns: a supernova explosion.

Twelve thousand years later, the first light from the dying star's pyre swept past the earth, and eyes raised to the heavens beheld a new star that night, shining where no star had been the night before.

Catherine saw the star as she stood at her chamber window before retiring. She had learned something of the heavens during all those evenings spent out of doors, but did not know them well enough to recognize the newcomer. She turned from the window and went into the chamber where her Ladyship lay in fitful sleep, knelt and prayed by her bed. Soon, Catherine feared, her Ladyship must leave her for God, and her husband and children.

William de Havilland saw the star from the battlements of Kelliwick Castle. The clouds had blown away to the east, and the starry heavens above shone bright. He glanced up idly – and sensed something awry. After a few moments' puzzlement he picked out the anomalous star in the figure of Auriga the Charioteer. It could not be a wandering star – a planet – since they did not wander through that part of the sky.

Nova stella, novus rex: a new star was said to signify a new king. Might it also signify a new queen? If so, a fortunate sign! For some time William gazed and wondered. Yet he had more pressing matters than the heavens. Holding together a fleet made up largely of conscripted merchantmen would be difficult. But a plan was forming in his mind, in case the King of Aquitaine proved stubborn.

On the second night Catherine beheld the star again. It could not be mistaken now, even by one little versed in the heavens. In the day since it burst forth it had grown in brilliance. Capella, with Castor and Pollux the Twins, dwindled before it; Aldebaran and Procyon, Betelgeuse and Rigel, all were humbled. Only Sirius could yet rival it, and even that fierce mastiff was compelled to yield place as hour by hour the new star burned more brightly. Catherine sensed cloaked figures as her ladies joined her. In silence they looked up with her. At last Madeleine broke the silence.

'Is it a comet, Mademoiselle?' she asked softly. 'Will there be a pestilence?'

'A comet is a star with streaming hair,' said Solange. 'The name is from the Achaean, *cometes*. Like a madwoman running, hair flying behind her.'

Solange knew no more of comets than Catherine did, which was nothing. Yet she was right: this star had no streaming hair. It was a pure and true star, its fierce whiteness darting now red now green in the crisp night. 'I think it a sign,' Catherine said softly, 'though of what I know not. As there are wonders in Heaven, perhaps there are wonders on earth.'

The next morning, Madeleine reported that a larger guard had been placed outside the Hôtel de Guienne. Catherine thought then to flee through the hidden water gate ... yet there was her Ladyship, whom she must care for now, as her Ladyship had cared for her as a child.

On the seventh morning after beholding the star, Catherine awoke to a great tramping in the rue Frontenac. She was out of her bed, Solange helping her dress, when Madeleine burst in. A large armed party was in the street, and the steward wanted to know her command. Catherine ordered the gates held, if held they could be, and hastened to the gatehouse, her ladies running after her. Through the slitted window they watched pikemen march in column of fours down the rue Frontenac, followed by a body of mounted lancers, noble chevaliers all, wearing the livery of the Gardes de Maison.

Catherine gulped. If they had come to arrest her, the Hôtel de Guienne must fall before the bells of

Ste-Eulalie rang the hour. Solange tugged at her sleeve. 'Mademoiselle!' she whispered. 'You must—'

'Wait!' cried Madeleine. 'Look!' Among the coats and trappings of white and sable were three riders in red and green. They rode up to the gate. A voice rang out, in the Saxon tongue – seeking admission in the name of the Lords and Commons of Lyonesse.

Catherine's heart began pounding. 'Bid the steward let them in!' she ordered Madeleine. 'I shall receive them in the Presence Chamber.'

There was no time to change from her plain day gown. Catherine hastened to the Presence Chamber, throwing off her couvre chef as she went, ordering Solange to fetch her feathered cap. She went first to the casket that held the best of her jewels, and took out her mother's pendant necklace with the Royal Arms. Catherine had not worn it since the day of the Richborough parade – the day she was turned out of Charles of Aquitaine's Court. She adjusted it around her neck as she went to take her place on the canopied chair.

Presently Madeleine ushered in three gentlemen, then hastened to take her place opposite Solange beside Catherine's chair of state. Two gentlemen halted just within the chamber. The third strode almost to the dais, a few feet from Catherine, not so much as bowing. 'My Lady,' he said without preamble, 'I bring you word that your grandfather the King is no more.' Whereupon he knelt, and his fellows knelt behind him. 'Your Majesty,' he declared. 'Kateryn of Lyonesse, Aquitaine and the Islands of the Sea, by Heaven's Grace Queen.'

In perfect unison, Solange and Madeleine knelt also.

Catherine's head swam. Somewhere a crow cawed, and from the street a market wife cried the virtues of her fresh loaves. The vast silence within her Presence Chamber awaited her first royal command, and she did not know what to say.

'Arise, gentlemen all, and ladies,' she finally managed. She got unsteadily to her own feet and bowed her head. 'Peace be upon our grandfather, King Edmund,' she said. 'For God's great good mercy and favour vouchsafed unto us we give thanks, and pray that we shall be a good and dutiful prince.'

The side door was pushed open, and there stood the Countess of Lindley, a cloak wrapped over her night-dress. She held the door jamb for support.

'Your Ladyship!' cried Catherine. 'You – you must go back to your bed!'

Lady Lindley shook her head. 'Even my old ears heard such ado, and I could not rest without knowing what it was about. Oft you disobeyed me, Kateryn,' she said, her frail voice scarcely more than a whisper. 'This once I must disobey you. I have lingered long for this day, and shall have my part in it!' Still holding to the door post for support, she knelt. Her old voice found strength to fill the chamber. 'God save Queen Kateryn!'

* * *

Lady Jane Gower, Countess of Lindley, died peacefully in her sleep on the third day after Catherine learned of her accession. The next morning the chaplain said his final benediction, and she was laid to rest in the crypt beneath the chapel. Catherine lingered for some time in the cool silence of the crypt, after all the others left. Silently she wept, for her own loss, and for regret that her Ladyship should lie here, and not in her own soil.

Then she decided that it was not unfitting. Here beside her lay captains and knights who served her fore-bears in the days when they ruled half the Aquitaine. All that was ended now, Catherine surely the last of her house ever to reside here – yet these stones were for ever sacred to Lyonesse. She kissed them, bidding her final farewell to her Ladyship, then turned and climbed the stair to the world of the living. She spoke a few words to Lasceaux her huntmaster and retired to her chambers to rest. That night she would have much to do.

After supper she summoned her ladies into her bed-chamber. 'Mesdemoiselles de Charleville and du Lac,' she said gravely, 'my time here has ended. My royal brother of Aquitaine shows no inclination to restore me to my own people. While the Comtesse de Lindley lived I could not leave her – but she has been called to serve a greater sovereign. I have no cause more to stay. Therefore I shall go, tonight, and entrust myself to the road and to God.' And to Lud, she thought, for this is surely a most foolish scheme! 'I must say something too, before you choose to come with me. You are my dearest friends in the world, you and Madame Corisande. Yet coming into my country a stranger, I must show favour to ladies of my own land. If you come with me, you cannot have places equal to your merits.'

Solange and Madeleine glanced at one another, and Solange shrugged like the lady of l'Aquitaine she was. 'You have shown, *Majesté*, how even a demoiselle can take Fortune in hand.'

Jacques Delors, thief, sat at a culvert in the embankment, drinking from his wineskin. Twilight had long faded; the only light came from houses over on the North Bank, and from the starry sky above. Enough time had passed since the bells of Ste-Eulalie rang curfew for his working day to begin. The owner of a house nearby had gone on a journey, and the servants would be safely drunk. He gnawed the last of a leg of chicken and tossed it into black gurgling water.

He was suddenly aware of shuffling behind him, from the depths of the tunnel. He came more sharply awake. Far down the tunnel was a door; Jacques could not open it and did not know where it led. He turned, pressed against dank stone, straining to pick out whoever moved in the blackness. This culvert was his, Jacques Delors's; no other had right to be here. He slipped his dagger into his hand.

'Drop the knife and put up your hands!' The voice from the blackness was soft – indeed a woman's voice – but had the force of command.

Jacques hesitated, then chose boldness. A woman here could only mean that someone had chosen his tunnel for an assignation. 'I can give you a better time than your lover, girlie,' he said.

'I doubt that,' answered the voice from the darkness. 'I have a crossbow, and will shoot. In the name of the Queen, drop the knife!'

Jacques dropped it. Three figures emerged, women swathed in cloaks. Moments later Jacques Delors found himself bound and gagged, unable to voice his curses at the bold doxies of the South Bank, who not only surprised honest thieves in the dark, but dared do so in the name of Queen Isabelle. Then he recalled that the demoiselle in the Hôtel de Guienne was herself also now a queen. He cursed bold queens.

Catherine chose a skiff to steal, the best of several pulled up on the shingle below the embankment just upstream from the culvert. With some effort she and her ladies pushed it into the water and slid over the gunwale. None of them was any riverwoman, but they managed not to tip the boat and themselves into the river. With her own hands, Catherine took an oar and poled them into deeper water. She was no mere thief, she decided as they drifted out into the stream. Like her shipmen, she had taken a prize.

They were alone on the water. River traffic, so heavy by day, had long since tied up for the night. Down they went, under the Pont Ste-Monique – a terrifying rushing passage – and on around the curve of the river, till ahead on the right bank rose a faerie city of light: the Palais de la Trémouille. Its reflected glory glinted and shimmered on the dark water. Catherine could not resist softly laughing.

'Madame?' asked Solange. Since her accession her ladies had elevated her from Mademoiselle to Madame. Rightly so, Catherine supposed; was she not in a sense married to her kingdom?

'Behold the Court of l'Aquitaine,' said Catherine. 'Behold too the Court of Lyonesse, here in this boat. Now, both of you, bear a hand! We must get to the shore or we'll be too far from de Pelletier's stables.'

Somehow they got the boat to the bank, a mile down from the palace. It slid into a mass of reeds and thumped to a stop. They clambered out – Solange soaking herself, and taking a dozen saints' names in vain. At Madeleine's suggestion, she and Catherine pushed the skiff back out, free of the reeds and mud, so that its presence here would not guide pursuers. The current caught it, swung it around, and away it drifted into the darkness, ending its brief service as a queen's vessel of Lyonesse.

An hour later they emerged from woods by the stables of the Baron de Pelletier, an old friend of M. de

Chirac. He allowed some of her household's horses to be stabled there, taking advantage of pasturage. The stable dog knew them, and barked in greeting as dogs will, defying all efforts to quiet him. The stable boy appeared, armed with a pitchfork, to find three demoiselles leading saddled horses from the stables. 'Who—?' he cried.

'Ssssh!' hissed Madeleine, pointing her crossbow for emphasis.

'I'm sorry, Jean,' Catherine said. 'We have to tie you up, lest blame fall on you or your master. Do you have a wineskin? Good – I'll put it by your mouth, so you can drink.' Moments later she and her ladies rode from the stables towards the royal highway. Shining down was the new star, by far the brightest in all the sky.

Louis did not await the audience the Ministre d'État had requested. He at once ordered horses saddled, and with the Duc de Numières in company rode at the gallop to de Chirac's hôtel. Madame de Chirac met them in the hall and ushered them up to her husband's study. The minister rose and bowed as Louis came in. There was a curious, almost impish expression on his face.

'Has my father decided?' asked Louis, fearing that his father had . . . and foolishly.

'The matter has been taken from his hands, Monsieur,' said de Chirac. He handed Louis a letter. It was in Latin – and in a familiar hand.

Iesu Salvator Noster
Catherine of Lyonesse, to our dear royal brother
Charles. We regret that we must no longer accept your
hospitality, which it seems consists in detaining us
against our will, though all know that we have never
offered offence, nor entered your lands in arms, but
were rather brought to them a helpless child.

Touching such designs as you may practise against
our realm, we rest easy, in good assurance that our
mariners shall commit to the sea any such as would
adventure against our shores. Yet it being our duty to
place ourselves among our own subjects, we shall not
burden you further with the care of us, but have taken
our departure; and though it ill befits the guest to steal
away by night, it does not more befit the host not to
have granted her departure freely.

Your royal sister, Catherine

Louis stared at de Chirac, who nodded. 'Your father's prize bird, it appears, has taken wing. The bailiff of the Hôtel de Guienne just sent word.'

'This is impossible!' protested Louis. 'How? How could she . . . ?'

'There was a secret passage out of the Hôtel de Guienne,' de Chirac explained, 'leading to the river. No one knew about it – except, obviously, Queen Catherine. The fault is entirely mine, for not having made sufficient enquiry.'

Louis felt a moment's dizzy fury at his father's minister, who thought of so many contingencies but had failed to consider this one. Then the implication sank in, and he laughed. '*Ma plus belle* Catherine!' he cried. 'Is she not the most courageous demoiselle in the world? I should dearly love to see my father's face when he learns of this! She went *alone?*'

'No, with her ladies-in-waiting.'

'*Dieu!* Three demoiselles – even those three – alone on the highways? Are they all mad?'

'It is a characteristic of her nation,' said de Chirac.

'But—'

'She is in great peril, Altesse. Whatever she thinks – whatever *you* think – you must find her, before someone worse does.'

Louis nodded. Time had not been his ally after all. He stood silent for a long moment, and considered a score of possibilities. He knew what policy would dictate: Anne was the pliable one, not haughty Catherine. Absolute policy could draw but one conclusion. Yet to that extreme he refused to go – and why should he? She was proud, yes, the proudest demoiselle in the world, but still a demoiselle. 'I shall find her, Monsieur,' he said at last. 'Indeed, I shall find her! And she has delivered herself into my hands . . .'

Rouners, Neville, Alounne-en-Touraigne; the towns fell away, marking Catherine's path to freedom. On the first day, straight north towards la Fleur. When she ostensibly retired on the night of her escape, she'd given the strictest command that neither she nor her ladies were to be disturbed, and they stuffed clothes under the coverlets to feign sleeping forms. Catherine hoped it would give her till midday before her absence was discovered. In her bed were letters to her servants, commanding them to take no risks by concealing her departure any longer, but at once to inform M. de Chirac. Nevertheless, it should be late in the day before word got to the palace. No effective pursuit then, she reckoned, until the second day.

That night they made camp in a glade not far from the royal highway. In the morning they struck out across country – towards the northeast. Surely, thought Catherine, she would be expected to flee straight north to the coast, or even west, directly towards Lyonesse. Yet even if she reached the coast, could she steal a seagoing vessel, or sail one if she got it? A queen of shipmen she might be, but she'd scarcely been able to manage a skiff in a river. Her goal instead was Dorstat in the Estates, free city of a free land. There she could plan her next move. She would land in her country in naught but her shift if she had to, but had no wish to fall into any overmighty lord's hands before she could rally her own.

The winter was mild, and Catherine and her ladies made good time. They rode on lesser local tracks, or through field and forest, avoiding all settlements. This was her Ladyship's gift, she thought: all those days hunting and hawking, sleeping in rough lodges, cooking over a fire. She could not have made this journey as a pampered demoiselle of the Court of la Trémouille. Her sister Anne would never be able to – and, Catherine reflected, would never try. She had lost Anne long ago, neither her own fault nor Anne's.

On the fifth night her little company made camp in the forest above the Trévaine valley. The lowlands west of the Trevaine belonged by law to the Aquitaine, by nature to the Estates. The land ahead stretched low and flat; blue threads marked canals, windmills along their banks. Catherine and her ladies took turns washing in a stream. Putting on their outer clothing they soaked their chemises and hung them on branches to dry. At sunset Madeleine went to hunt rabbits, while Catherine and Solange set up camp. Catherine was tossing wood on the fire when something made her stop. 'Solange,' she called softly. 'Listen!' Catherine moved towards her pack and reached down for her crossbow.

'Stand up there, girl!' ordered a voice from the trees. 'Stand or I shoot!' Catherine stood. Three men emerged from the woods, one holding an harquebus, the others armed with sword and axe. 'Well,' said the man with the harquebus, 'what have we here? Tall, redheaded, good to· look at – all the marks of a queen out of her country.'

'Who are you?' demanded Catherine, fighting to keep trembling from her voice.

He leered at her. 'Does it matter? Ah, but I forget myself.' He bowed. '*Majesté*, you have the great honour of meeting Luc de Ferry, free gentleman.'

He was plainly no gentleman of any sort, and Catherine did not think he had been sent after her by Charles of Aquitaine, or even the Lusianes.

'The King,' said Ferry, 'has men all over the country-side looking for you.' He laughed. 'There is a reward for your safe return. But I, Luc de Ferry, have found you – so I can name my reward, no? How much are you worth, girl? A lot, I think!' As Ferry talked, he gradually let the barrel of his harquebus drop. Catherine dived for her crossbow. 'Don't!' he shouted. 'You'll fetch less if I kill you, but move an inch and I will! Get hold of her, Pierre!' he ordered. One of his companions tossed down his sword and strode up to Catherine. He grabbed her, pulling her up and pinioning her arms behind her back. Ferry walked up to her. 'Now, girl. I don't keep company with royalty, so I don't know the going rate in queens. I'm sure you'll fetch a price, pretty as you are.'

Catherine took a deep breath. 'Do you think any – purchaser – would leave you alive after such a trans-action?'

'Clever girl too,' he said. 'I could just have some fun then, before I get rid of you. Never had a queen before.' He laughed again.

Solange spoke up. 'If you harm her, you'll be paid

447

nothing,' she said. 'But certainly an arrangement can be reached – I know something of such matters.'

'Do you now?' said Luc de Ferry. He turned and looked Solange up and down. 'You're not part of any bargain, girl. I can do as I wish with you.'

'Of course,' said Solange. 'Whomever you might sell her to will surely pay more if she is still a virgin. Is that not so? An inconvenience, Monsieur, but you would in any case find her shy and clumsy. I, on the other hand, am neither.' Solange began unlacing the ties of her bodice. She slipped her gown off her shoulders, and firelight danced off her bare breasts. 'Come; you will not be disappointed.'

Smiling broadly, de Ferry snatched Solange by her open bodice and savagely jerked her up against him. Suddenly his eyes went wide.

'Release my mistress and drop your weapons!' snapped Solange, dagger at his groin. '*Now!* Or I will make you a capon!'

'Let her go,' grunted Ferry to the man who held Catherine. The man's grip loosened; Catherine wrenched herself free and snatched up the sword that lay on the ground. It was an old-fashioned broad blade, amazingly heavy. The third man, with the axe, began to lower it – then stepped back and tightened his grip. 'Drop it!' ordered Ferry. Sweat glistened on his face.

'Well, now,' laughed the man with the axe. 'She's a lively one there, Monsieur Luc.' He hefted his axe and turned towards Catherine. 'The King may want you in one piece, but me, I don't care. Drop that sword, or I'll have to spoil his merchandise.'

Ferry suddenly screamed and fell, clutching his guts, and Solange whirled, her poniard dripping blood. '*Putain!*' yelled the man with the axe, and advanced on Solange. Catherine ran at him, wielding the sword as best she could. He turned, laughing – then stopped short, puzzlement on his face and a crossbow bolt in his chest. '*Quoi?*' he gasped. Dropping the axe, he staggered back and crashed into the fire, a swirl of sparks erupting around him.

'Madame!' cried Solange, her eyes great with fear. Catherine spun round; the man Pierre had drawn a dagger. But finding himself outnumbered – if only by maids – and his two companions dead or dying, he ran.

Out of the darkness from another direction walked Madeleine, holding her discharged crossbow. She glanced down at the writhing Ferry. '*Mon Dieu!*' She picked up his harquebus and handed it to Catherine, then drew her dagger and bent down beside Ferry. After a moment's hesitancy she simply cut his throat. Then she knelt beside the sobbing, retching Solange, holding her heaving shoulders and speaking soft low words to her.

They dragged the dead men as far from the camp as they could, and made the necessary preparations for the night. Catherine's ladies would not permit her to take her turn at watch, but she slept fitfully, and the next morning had no taste for her breakfast. 'If common brigands could find me,' she said, 'so can Charles of Aquitaine's men. There is more trouble here than I thought.' She sighed, leaned back against the tree and closed her eyes. She was weary, more weary than she'd thought possible, and more frightened. 'I am on a fool's errand, and had no right to bring you down in my folly!'

'It was our duty,' said Madeleine sharply, 'and our honour. We slew the brigands, Madame, and drove the other away. So we will any others who would stop us!'

'And the frontier is not so far, now,' added Solange. 'Come, Madame – we should be on our way while the day is young.'

Catherine smiled, if wanly, and got to her feet, ashamed of herself for losing faith when her ladies had not. Soon they broke camp and rode down into the lowlands. The horses of Luc de Ferry and his companions had been found tethered in the woods, and with spare mounts they made better time. Catherine led her little party north along a canal, till fields gave way to windswept dunes. By midmorning they were riding at a canter along the broad sea strand, alone but for gulls that rose screeching and wheeling as they rode past. Out to sea a couple of fishing craft were just visible, almost lost in haze. Ten or twelve leagues ahead lay the mouth of the Trévaine. How they would cross it she was not sure; perhaps they could steal another boat. Cross it they would, one way or another. On the far bank lay the Free

Estates. There she would be a fugitive no longer, but sovereign Queen of an ancient ally.

'You were right the first time, Jean,' the Dauphin told the Duc de Numières, when he caught up to him just short of Auselles-sur-Trévaine. 'Of course she would make for the frontier of the Estates. I'll remember your generalship when the time comes.'

'Don't forget the generalship of Queen Catherine either,' said the duke with a wry smile. 'Thanks to God she is a woman, and unlikely to lead armies against us.'

Over-proud demoiselle! thought Louis. 'You can thank God for it, if you wish,' he said. 'I count it no favour. Your report.' De Numières gave it, and they briefly discussed the lay of the land and possible routes. Agreement was reached. 'Drop down south,' the Dauphin ordered, 'and try to pick up her track. The frontier posts have already been notified, for what it's worth, but I'll push on along the coast.'

De Numières nodded, and the two companies parted again. Louis and his party rode on into Auselles-sur-Trévaine. Brief questioning of citizens in the streets provided no word; Louis had not expected it – Catherine and her ladies had carefully avoided every town.

From Auselles it was a league, along a road raised on a dike, to the sea strand. The Dauphin and his men rode east at a steady canter, till – just as he was about to call a midday halt – moving figures were spotted, far down the strand, almost lost in the haze. At his signal a handful of riders angled across the dunes, lest the pursued try to break inland. Then with a wave of his hand Louis spurred to the gallop, the rest of his company behind him.

Louis had ridden to the hunt since he was a boy of eight, but never a longer, harder ride than this one along the broad northern sea strand. His quarry were well mounted, with skilled hands at the reins, holding their steeds back just enough to avoid blowing them, yielding almost nothing to their pursuers. For a league, two leagues, Louis and his company pounded along the hard sand, and the specks in the distance seemed scarcely closer.

On they rode, pursued and pursuers, Louis wondering exactly how far it was to the Trévaine, and what he would do if against all reason Catherine reached the river, then somehow managed to cross to the far bank – and the Free Estates. At last, though, the quarry was close enough to be made out clearly: five horses, only three with riders. Now and then one rose to look back, without breaking pace.

Onward, mile after mile, the sun lowering behind them to the west. The pursuers gained ever so slowly: five hundred yards, two hundred, one hundred; those in flight now clearly women in riding gowns. They spurred on desperately, and Louis spurred after them, driving his horse till foam blew back from its mouth.

Then at last the chase was up. The demoiselles reined in and swung down from their saddles, and crossbows appeared in sign that they would sell themselves dearly. He signalled a halt to his men and rode up alone, at a walk, hands raised to show he was unarmed. Dismounting before Catherine, he knelt.

'*Majesté.*'

'You needn't stand on ceremony, Monseigneur,' said Catherine. 'I am of course your prisoner.' She lowered her crossbow, and her ladies lowered theirs. Dirty, soaked, bedraggled, hair hanging limp across cheeks and shoulders – magnificent all, thought Louis.

He stood before her amid the great emptiness of the strand. Surf pounded in and rolled back. There was an infinity of things he wished to say, to make this moment other than what it was; none of them was useful or possible. He could only hope that time – time, and the nature of women – would bring her to understand and accept what must be. If not? Louis would not think of it. 'If you were Louis and I Catherine,' he told her at last, 'I would surely say the same.'

She lowered her head, then looked up – and smiled. 'Yes, Louis. As you have done, I would surely have done the same. If I must be a prisoner, I am glad to be yours.' She brought her crossbow to port-arms, then handed it to him.

Catherine was conducted to the ducal château of

Auselles. She and her ladies were lodged in the duke's family quarters, attended by his servants. Within the hour a bath was drawn for them – blessed kindness! – and fresh clothes set out, their own taken to be pounded clean by laundresses.

The next morning, as Solange arranged her hair, Catherine contemplated her situation. Reason informed her that she could expect no deliverance. It would be mad folly for the new Earl of Avalon, or any other, to land on this coast to attempt her rescue. Yet in all ages men had done mad folly for the sake of what they cherished, men of Lyonesse not less than others. Would any attempt it for her? What would it avail her or her kingdom if they did?

Someone rapped on the door, and Madeleine answered it. 'Madame?' she said. 'Monseigneur le Dauphin seeks audience.' Catherine's heart skipped a beat, yet she kept her composure and bade Madeleine show him in.

In place of soaked riding clothes Louis was clad in the silver and black of the Gardes de Maison, resplendent in simplicity. He swept his own cap from his head – freeing the curls of his hair – and knelt low. '*Majesté*,' he declared.

Heart pounding, Catherine bade him rise. She was a regnant queen, he a prince – the noblest prince in Christendom, heir to a mighty realm. She stood before him in a borrowed gown and what seemed a borrowed life: a queen beyond reach of the people she affected to rule, for all she knew disregarded by them. For a mad instant she wanted to throw herself as a supplicant at his feet. She did not. She was Queen of Lyonesse. 'Monseigneur,' she said quietly, fighting to keep trembling from her voice.

'By your gracious leave, *Majesté*,' he said, 'I beg audience of you.' He glanced briefly at her ladies. 'Alone – for I would speak to you not as Prince to Queen, but as Louis to Catherine.'

With a turn of her head Catherine dismissed her ladies, and with a glance at one another they withdrew.

'Catherine *ma belle*,' said Louis. 'Once before I knelt before you, and sought of you the greatest boon ever asked by any prince of any lady. You were then still your grandfather's subject, and could not give the assent I know was in your heart. Now you are Queen, no subject but God's, and so I kneel before you again.' He went to one knee. 'I ask your hand in marriage, though it be in defiance of my father and the Patriarch. Reign beside me, Catherine, as my wife, my lady, and my queen. I, Louis, shall swear myself your defender, your champion and your faithful husband all my life. Through us the fruitless quarrel of our houses shall be at an end.'

Catherine swallowed dry. She knew what she must say, not how to say it. At last she spoke. 'It cannot be, Louis. I shall not, I will not marry without consent of my Parliament. And such consent they will never give.'

Louis stared at her in puzzlement as he rose. '*Parlement?*' he asked, rendering the word in its Gallic form. 'Mere gentlemen of the Long Robe? What voice have they in the marriage of their queen?'

'Not councillors of the law, Louis, such as the *parlements* in your country.' Amid all her feelings, Catherine thought he might have learned more of the realm he was asking to rule beside her. 'I speak of the Estates General in Lyonesse,' she explained. 'The assembled Lords and Commons of my realm. Without their consent I must not marry – and they will endure no marriage to l'Aquitaine.'

Louis shook his head in dismay. 'Catherine! *Pardieu!* You are Queen! You do not seek consent of your subjects. You command! I am disappointed in you, Catherine – Catherine *ma belle* – that you would say such a thing! You have much to learn about kingship. But I shall instruct you!'

Even though it was Louis who spoke those words, the hairs on the back of Catherine's neck stood up. 'I need no instruction in my duties, Monseigneur,' she answered sharply. 'Not from any prince in Christendom! Not even from you.' She paused, swallowed and went on more quietly. 'It is the custom of my realm, Louis: the sovereign rules by consent of his – her – people. Once I asked you how it would be were I Louis and you Catherine – but you are not Catherine! I am! When you marry, you give your people a queen and consort; when

I marry, I give mine a king. Never shall I do that, save with their assent and their blessing.

'Happily would I marry Louis d'Héristal,' she continued, 'before any prince in Christendom. You know that! Yet I will not make my realm a province of another. Will you renounce the inheritance of l'Aquitaine? Will you swear before me now, and before my Lords and Commons at Kelliwick, to hold no other kingdom before Lyonesse?'

Louis stared at her, nostrils flaring. 'Do not toy with me, Catherine!'

'Do not toy with *me*, Louis!' she retorted. 'If you cannot assent, no more can I.'

Louis could not have looked at her with more amazement, thought Catherine, were she a horse that refused the saddle. For a moment she almost laughed. Then he replied, and drowned her mirth. 'Will you marry no one, Catherine de Guienne?' he asked. 'Will you live and die a virgin queen? Is the castle of Kellouïque to be your convent cell?'

What right had he to ask her such a thing? 'I hope to marry,' she said, 'as any demoiselle might. Yet I am not the footstool of a throne. When I marry, I shall give my husband as dowry a kingdom in good order, and nothing less.'

Louis was long in answering. 'You are a proud and stubborn demoiselle,' he said at last.

'I am of a proud and stubborn nation.'

Louis half smiled. 'So de Chirac has often told me. Yet I pray that you do not cast all away for pride and stubbornness.' With that he stepped back, swept a fine bow, and withdrew, leaving Catherine alone with her thoughts.

It was market day in the town of Auselles, and the odour of baked bread filled the air. Caged chickens squawked, protesting their confinement though unaware of their fate. A boy stole an apple and dodged away, pursued by the apple seller's futile cries. Then a sharper commotion ran swift as quick-match along the street: pounding hoofs, jangling bells, shouts to clear way for the Royal Post.

The rider's passage spurred further speculation and gossip. The Duc d'Alemain was not in residence, but in his place the banner of the Dauphin flew from his towers. A splendid youth, agreed those who had seen him the afternoon before, riding to the château amid a company of chevaliers and demoiselles. Rumours spread that the demoiselle riding at the Dauphin's side was Queen of the goddams.

The royal courier burst in through the gate of the château and threw his packet to the sergeant of the watch, who passed it to his captain, who read the superscription and sent a runner to deliver it to the Duc de Numières. Moments later the duke was ushered into the Dauphin's chamber; he bowed, and handed the letter to the Dauphin. Louis glanced at the address and seal. 'Wait, Jean,' he said, as de Numières started to withdraw. 'From the Comte de Plassey, at la Fleur.' He chuckled without mirth. He broke the seal, read the letter – and his chest went tight. '*Diable!*' he cried. He read it again; the contents did not change. 'You may as well see for yourself,' he said, and handed it to de Numières.

De Numières' eyes widened as read. 'But – how can they . . . we have . . . could de Plassey be mistaken?'

Louis shook his head. 'De Plassey does not jump at shadows, Jean.' Louis stared out the window. 'Never enough time,' he added quietly to himself. He turned back to de Numières. 'Make speed to la Fleur, Jean, and put yourself at de Plassey's disposal. I – I will follow as soon as I can.'

'La Fleur?' De Numières looked sharply at Louis. 'What of Queen Catherine? Your father?'

'She shall accompany me,' he said. 'To la Fleur. Now go! There's no time to waste!' Even as de Numières withdrew, Louis calculated times and distances. He had three or four days, perhaps, before Catherine's future was taken from his hands.

Four days, to somehow make her see reason.

CHAPTER EIGHTEEN

The Galley Royal

The sun was high when the cavalcade rode forth from the ducal château. To the townsfolk, thought Catherine, they must look a fine and royal company. She rode at the Dauphin's side as though she were his lady, not his prisoner. He set a firm, brisk pace. At mid afternoon they reached a fork in the road – taking not the left-hand way towards the capital but the right, continuing along the coast. A league further along, the road climbed from the lowlands through woods and meadows, with now and then a glimpse of blue sea.

The sea! This could only be the way to la Fleur, Catherine realized – and her heart rose in silent song. Louis, dashed in his impossible high dream, had resolved as her true knight to do what his father would not: set her free. No wonder he rode now so tight lipped and silent, for the risk he took was grave. Yet she would remember this. In the time of Louis IX there would be peace and friendship across the Narrow Sea.

Late on the third day they reached la Fleur. They did not pass into the town. Instead, Catherine and her ladies found themselves installed in tower chambers of the Porte St-Michel, a massively overgrown gatehouse in the wall of the town. Familiarity teased at her mind until she remembered: here she had been lodged with her mother and Anne, till Corisande had arrived and led them to the Court of la Trémouille. Full circle! She would have liked to look out over the sea, and imagine Lyonesse beyond it, but the tower faced the other direction. She could see only the countryside of the Aquitaine, from which she must soon depart. In all of this the Dauphin spoke no word.

That night she slept fitfully. Shouted commands, grounded pikes and the tramping of boot-shod feet went on all through the night. At dawn Catherine rose and stood at the arrow-slit window. The countryside was awakening, ploughmen going to their fields, their wives to feed chickens and milk cows. Country smells were borne upon the breeze; now freshly ploughed earth, now pungent manure. Closer at hand, nothing was bucolic. A company of horsemen came over a rise and rode in at a canter below her. Then there was dust above the rise, and tiny figures that drew closer and became columns of footmen, harquebusiers and pikemen. Catherine's ladies joined her, the three of them watching as the companies marched in to the tattoo of their drums.

The last pikemen passed through the gate, and for a while quiet returned to the countryside. More squadrons of horse arrived, then three great bronze guns on their limbers, each drawn by scores of horses. Behind them were wagons piled high with bales of hay. What those were for she could not begin to imagine – and why such mustering of arms? Servants brought a morning repast of pastries and cheese. A little while later came booted footsteps at the outer door of the chambers. Without word of announcement the door was opened – and there stood the Dauphin. Quietly her ladies withdrew. He bowed, and Catherine dipped slightly, as befitted a reigning queen before a great and noble prince. 'Monseigneur!' she said.

'*Majesté*,' he replied. How drawn and weary he looked, thought Catherine, as though all the burdens of a kingdom lay upon him. For a time he studied her in silence; then, almost hesitantly, he spoke. 'Catherine *ma belle*,' he said. 'I have come to ask, one last time, if you will hear my honourable suit.'

He had that right, now at the end. Gravely Catherine inclined her head. 'I know what is in your heart, Louis,' she replied, 'as you know what is in mine. Yet we have each of us our duty: mine to the people I rule and yours to the people you shall one day rule.' Her eyes grew moist, and she was not ashamed. 'Let it be sufficient to one day be said that for their love Louis of Aquitaine and Catherine of Lyonesse made peace. That in their time their armies fought not one against the other, but side by side, in the defence of Christendom against the M—'

'Enough!' cried Louis. 'I did not come to hear empty words, Catherine, even words as pretty as yours!'

Catherine was taken aback, but rallied at once. 'I can say no others, Louis,' she answered quietly. 'You know that.'

'I know that you are a proud demoiselle, and a foolish one!' The Dauphin's voice rose to a shout. 'You speak of rule! What do *you* rule? Two demoiselles who hold themselves far too high, near as high as you do! Nothing more!' He paused, and with visible effort lowered his voice. 'You are a fine rider, Catherine – no demoiselle finer – but can you put spurs to a kingdom? I think not! By your own words, you confessed that you cannot; did you not say that when you marry, your husband will be King? Yes – and a king is what Lyonesse needs most! Women are not born to rule; it is a man's place.'

That was the truth Catherine most feared – but she would not yield, not now, not to anyone. She struggled for words. 'Yolande d'Asturias ruled in her time,' she cried, 'and made the Monites fear her name!'

'Do any fear yours?' asked Louis sardonically. 'Surely not your own subjects! The Duc de Norrey rules at Kelliwick, and the Comte d'Avalon lies with his fleet before the ports, ready with sword and fire to bar you from your own shores.'

'He stands guard as my loyal lieutenant!' retorted Catherine, and hoped she was right. With sudden, dreadful insight she grasped the meaning of the gathering soldiers: Charles of Aquitaine was preparing to invade her kingdom – in *her* name. She pressed on in fury. 'It is not I who am barred, Monsieur d'Héristal. My Lord High Admiral bars your father, and your father's soldiers! So he shall bar you too, if you should dare seek to enter my land in arms! Never by God shall any set foot in Lyonesse but by my will and pleasure – and I will it not, for I am ill pleased!'

The Dauphin stepped back and looked at Catherine through narrowed eyes, with a coldness she had never seen before. 'Your will and pleasure?' he said, and laughed without mirth. 'Your will is the caprice of a proud and foolish girl, and you know nothing of pleasure. I would have taught you' – he looked her up and down – 'I could teach you now, in this very chamber! But I see you have no wish to learn. So be it, then! I asked you – I went on my knees, and begged of you – that you reign beside me as my wife and queen, and so make peace. But I see that you will have war! War it is, then . . . and by the law of war, you are my prisoner!'

'Yes, Monsieur le Dauphin,' said Catherine, her voice very low and soft, scarcely more than a whisper. 'Indeed I am your prisoner. But not a prisoner of war. I am a prisoner of foul deceit and treachery!'

'No, Madame!' cried another voice – Madeleine's. She burst from the inner door, sword in hand. In four quick steps she was at Catherine's side. Solange followed, poniard drawn. 'Monseigneur!' commanded Madeleine. 'Yield yourself prisoner, in the name of la Reine Catherine!'

The Dauphin stared wide eyed at her . . . and at the sword-tip hovering a foot from his chest. 'Don't be a fool, Mademoiselle!' he snapped. 'I have two thousand men outside—'

'I have you, Monseigneur, here inside!' retorted Madeleine.

The Dauphin's lips curved in a faint smile. 'So I see.' He began to lower himself, as though to kneel in surrender at Catherine's feet – then pitched backward. He went down, rolling over one shoulder, even as Madeleine flew after him. The next moments were a ringing blur – then the Dauphin and Madeleine were standing apart, swords raised as if in salute. Had Mère Angelique truly said that two of the bravest knights in Christendom would do battle over her? Was *this* what she had foreseen?

The Dauphin bowed. 'Do not attempt this dance, Madeleine du Lac!' he said. 'I am not the Elector of Angeln, and a missed measure could be your last!'

Madeleine curtseyed. 'A true chevalier would not compel me to dance it!'

'*En garde!*' cried the Dauphin, and sprang at her. With a flash and clatter of steel their dance was joined. As fast as he came at her Madeleine leaped aside, skirts swirling – then, incredibly, the Dauphin was retreating, a red streak on his white doublet and astonishment in his eyes. Madeleine pressed him at once. Steel flashed and rang half a dozen times, high and low, the empress of dancers driving him inch by inch towards a corner. The Dauphin rallied, casting strength and experience on the scales against matchless courage. Catherine dared not command them to put up their blades, lest she distract Madeleine. The Dauphin advanced, Madeleine dancing back – a piercing cry and her blade flew from her hand. The Dauphin recoiled like a spring, sword at guard, as Madeleine staggered back to the wall.

She looked at Catherine, eyes wide with surprise and alarm. A spot of crimson marred the deep blue fabric of her gown. '*Majesté!*' she gasped. 'I am . . . so clumsy!' She looked down at the spreading stain on her bodice. '*Pardieu!*' she exclaimed, as though it were spilled wine rather than blood. She pressed a hand to herself, and gracefully as a curtsey she sank to the floor.

'*Diable!*' cried Solange, and ran to Madeleine – to stop short, the Dauphin's rapier-point at her throat. For a moment, Dauphin and lady-in-waiting faced one another; then Solange dropped her poniard and knelt at Madeleine's side.

Catherine's blood roared in her ears. By her side was a stool, then it was in her hands. '*Burn in Hell!*' she cried in her father's tongue and charged her enemy, wielding it like a battle axe; heedless in her fury of a rapier or a thousand levelled pikes.

The Dauphin leaped high and kicked; the stool flew from Catherine's hands – and his rapier point was at her breast. 'Hold!' he commanded. Catherine held. 'No more such folly!' he snapped. 'Or Anne becomes Queen!'

The tip of his blade pressed Catherine's flesh, hard enough to sting, and she felt something warm and wet: Madeleine's blood, or her own. Louis' eyes upon Catherine wavered no more than his blade. I am about to die, she thought. Yet she was daughter of a great race of kings, and would meet her death like one. That much she could do.

Trembling though she was, she lifted her gaze from the sword at her breast to meet the Dauphin's eyes, unblinking. 'Have a care, Monseigneur,' she said. 'What touches one monarch touches all.'

Long heartbeats passed as the Dauphin glared back at her. Then he stepped back. Slowly, sword still at guard, he backed towards the door. He opened his mouth as though to speak, but no word came forth. Then he turned to the door and was gone.

Catherine stared at the door for a few moments after it slammed shut. Then, as though a spell were broken, she hastened to Solange's side and knelt over Madeleine. 'Is she—?'

'She breathes, Madame,' replied Solange, 'but she is insensible . . . I do not know.'

'Help me undo her bodice,' Catherine said, 'so we

can examine her.' Her hands were still shaking, too clumsy to do anything, but Solange quickly and deftly unfastened the lacings, unpeeling layers of velvet and buckram. Catherine helped her push the fabric down around Madeleine's waist. Only a trickle of blood seeped from the wound, but Catherine had heard that even some mortal wounds scarcely bled.

Solange recovered her poniard, cut and ripped away a piece of linen from Madeleine's chemise. As she pressed it to the wound, Madeleine groaned and half opened her eyes. 'Fetch her wine!' said Solange. 'If you would, Madame,' she added, realizing that it ill befitted a lady-in-waiting to give commands to a monarch.

Catherine did not care. She rose, filled a wine cup and brought it to Madeleine. Madeleine raised herself up, wincing, before Solange could help her, and shook her head at Solange's remonstrance.

'It is – *oww!* – the merest nick!' she gasped. 'Forgive me, Madame! I am disgraced! Fainting like a silly girl!'

'Enough!' cried Catherine. 'You did nobly, Mademoiselle du Lac! It is I who have been the foolish girl! I loved him! I thought he . . .' Her heart was breaking, but it was Madeleine who lay wounded in Solange's arms. Catherine looked up through tears at the door. 'To the Devil with you, Lewis of Herstal!'

Louis snapped out orders for a strict and strong guard to be kept around the guest quarters of the Porte St-

Michel. No servants were to pass without close inspection – it would be entirely in keeping, Louis thought, for those girls to attempt escape in servants' guise. Perhaps not Mlle du Lac; he ordered a physician fetched for her. He'd always liked her, and so merely jabbed the fool girl instead of running her clean through, but one never knew what a sword-thrust might do. La Charleville he would have run through without a moment's regret. Louis ordered his attendants to leave him and he walked the battlements, alone with his fury.

The ladies-in-waiting were nothing, their offences the merest echo of their mistress's. Haughty demoiselle! Had he not knelt before Catherine, ready – in defiance of father and Church – to give her a place by his side, Queen of two mighty realms? What was her answer? First evasion: that nonsense at Auselles about the Estates of Lyonesse. Then, invective and insult! Even with his sword's point at her breast she had been defiant, daring him to thrust, cocksure that he would not. *She* was the one he wished to run through, for all the impossibility of doing so. It would be a thrust for justice and honour . . . and in the moment of death she would know that she had at last pushed him too far.

'*Connasse!*' he shouted aloud. She had made him lose his temper, was making him lose it even now. The fault was his own, Louis told himself sternly, for letting himself to be ruled by heart rather than head. From the moment de Chirac had told him of Catherine's escape, he'd been aware of what absolute policy dictated: a sword thrust or harquebus shot in the wilderness, and her ladies likewise. Her body would have been found and decently mourned over . . . and her sister would be Queen of Lyonesse: Anne, who could be governed as Catherine never would be.

God, Louis decided, had made a mistake. Why had He made Catherine heiress to a throne? Of any other rank – daughter of a duke, or a peasant – she would have made a splendid maîtresse-en-titre. Her very hauteur would have been delightful, and found its natural channel, instead of leading her to think herself a king. Louis looked out from the battlements, over the town, and then towards the sea. He made himself look out to sea. Nothing was left but to take this lesson to heart, lest any such case arise in future.

A physician arrived – accompanied by half a dozen guards – and pronounced Madeleine's hurt a small one, the thrust stopped by a rib. He did not ask how she got it, or from whom. At Solange's insistence he also examined the tiny scratch dealt Catherine, and confirmed that she probably would not die of it. He rubbed some evil-smelling potion on it, but offered no balm for betrayal. She had wept more tears than Louis d'Héristal deserved, and would shed no more. Love, she decided, was the most dangerous illusion of princes. No wonder the Aquitaine had the institution of maîtresse-en-titre! Then she went to the window and looked out. Another company of footmen was marching down towards the gate.

'My ladies!' Catherine declared, turning to face them. 'You must know, as I do, why I am brought here, and why Charles of Aquitaine gathers his armies. He means to invade Lyonesse in my name, and so make me traitor to myself. I cannot put stay to them – but my shipmen can! I pray and trust that they will not let foreign soldiers land on my shores on mere word they come in my name. They will ask my command, and command them I shall – to give battle.' Catherine took a deep breath. 'I commend my fate to God, and pray that mine own shall have the advantage of the day. As for the Dauphin, the fish shall learn how to lie in Gallic when they dine upon his heart.'

There was a long silence, broken only by the martial sounds below. At last Solange spoke. 'What will the fish learn from me, Madame?' she asked.

'How to seduce fishermen, of course,' answered Madeleine.

All three laughed. Catherine embraced Solange, and knelt by the bed to embrace Madeleine. They were the best of the Aquitaine, everything the Dauphin was not. These maids might at a hundred turns have deserted her, and been rewarded with the finest marriages the magnificent Court of la Trémouille could bestow. Instead, their reward for good faith was to be swallowed up with her in the sea.

Rising from Madeleine's bedside, Catherine went again to the arrow-slit window. Another company of pikemen approached along the road. On some unheard command they fell out to either side. Between their ranks came a coach bearing the arms of the Aquitaine, with a mounted escort. Not King Charles, surely, for the escort was not of kingly scale, but some great officer come to attend upon the invasion fleet. It passed through the gate below. Presently came the sound of booted feet, climbing the stairs of the tower.

Catherine's heart pounded and her mind raced. This surely was the word being brought that Lyonesse was to be invaded in her name. Should she answer now with defiance? Or seem to yield, biding her time till she could reveal her will to her own? She whirled from the window. 'Solange!' she ordered. 'No, Madeleine, you must stay abed!' She was not obeyed; Solange helped Madeleine to her feet, and they followed Catherine into the outer chamber. Catherine seated herself on the stool, determined to receive her captors as befitted a queen.

Arms were grounded; a key worked in the door, and it swung open. In came an old soldier Catherine recognized: the Comte de Plassey. He bowed gravely. '*Majesté.* Monsieur le Duc de Conté begs audience, for himself and his mother.'

Conté? Catherine knew the name, but could not place him. And why – for such business as this – should he be accompanied by some dowager duchess? Solange, standing at Catherine's side, echoed her puzzlement. 'Conté, Madame?' she said in a low voice. 'But that is—' Before she could finish, Catherine remembered exactly who the Duc de Conté was: he was King Charles's now-acknowledged natural son, the Dauphin's half brother – Corisande's son.

For all her terrible plight, Catherine nearly laughed at the absurdity. A child of six, sent to proclaim Charles of Aquitaine's intent to invade her kingdom? For a giddy moment she thought that it could not be that at all, that she had misunderstood everything. Then, more darkly, she considered that he was Corisande's son, and Corisande was de Chirac's wife. Did de Chirac suppose the entreaties of his wife and her child would persuade her to betray herself, where the Dauphin had failed? For a moment she considered turning them away. Then she resolved to face even this. 'I shall receive them,' she said.

Waiting at the top of the winding stair, Corisande de Chirac heard Catherine's reply, and sensed the coldness in her voice. She dreaded the audience, yet had offered to perform this service. She had suggested too that little Charlot accompany them. Queen Catherine had little reason to believe the word of any Aquitanian – not even hers – but perhaps would accept the word of a child. It was a hard journey to ask of one so young, though in truth he had been its one pleasure, spending the whole trip with his face eagerly pressed to the coach's window. A difficult task too awaited him now, yet he was the

King's acknowledged son. It was not too soon for him to learn the duties of his station.

The two Gardes de Maison at the door turned on their heels, and the old Comte de Plassey stepped aside. Drawing a deep breath, her son's hand in hers, Corisande entered. Nine years ago she had entered these same chambers to be received by the widowed Princess Marie and her children. Little Anne had shrunk back behind her mother's skirts. Seven-year-old Catherine had stood boldly, almost defiantly at her mother's side. Now at sixteen she was a queen; the unwilling ward – in her own mind surely the prisoner – of the man whose kept woman Corisande had been for nearly half her life. Catherine sat on a stool, her ladies beside her, as though it were a throne, and her worn riding-dress her robes of state.

Corisande knelt gravely, and gently urged little Charlot forward. As she had instructed him, he took another two steps, then knelt in turn.

'Rise, Monsieur le Duc; rise, Madame,' said Catherine.

The boy rose to address her. Corisande remained kneeling behind him, though she raised her head to see. '*Majesté!*' declared Charlot. 'I bear glad tidings from my father, your royal brother of l'Aquitaine,' he said, his high child's voice carefully reciting the speech Corisande had taught him. 'He commands me relate to you that his guardianship over you is ended. Tomorrow the royal galley of Lyonesse shall await upon you, for you to be received by your subjects.'

For long moments Catherine showed no expression, and Corisande's heart tightened with fear that she would denounce her son's words as a lie. Then Catherine exhaled like a woman reprieved at the foot of the scaffold. Smiling, she beckoned Charlot forward. 'Charles, Duc de Conté,' she said, 'you are a true and noble chevalier.' Taking his hand, she brought it to her lips. Then, rising, she led him back to Corisande. 'Rise, Madame,' she said softly. Corisande rose and Catherine's green eyes met hers in silence. Then she embraced her, kissing one cheek and then the other, and Corisande felt a wetness on Catherine's cheeks that mingled with the wetness on her own. At last, slowly, they drew apart.

'You have journeyed a long way,' said Catherine. 'I must not detain you from rest, nor your child. Yet I would receive you with such hospitality as I can. Solange!' she commanded. 'Wine for Madame Corisande, and a little wine mixed with water for the Duc de Conté. Madeleine, go rest! She overexerted herself in dancing, Madame.'

Mlle du Lac curtseyed and withdrew; Corisande had noticed her stiff movements. Had she injured herself in Catherine's attempted escape? It could hardly be from dancing – not Madeleine du Lac. Mlle de Charleville filled the cups, then offered to conduct Charlot to his own chamber where he could rest. Assent was quickly given; with a curtsey she departed, Charlot in tow.

Corisande watched them go. 'They serve you well, *Majesté*,' she said. 'They shall be worthy ornaments to your Court.'

To Corisande's pleased surprise, Catherine laughed. 'More than ornaments, Madame!' she exclaimed. 'You chose them well – better, perhaps, than your husband intended! Had they been born men, Madeleine would one day command armies and Solange be Minister of State. But then I would never have had them in my service, no?'

'You are right, *Majesté*.' Corisande smiled. 'Had they been youths, I would have been at pains to keep them away from you.'

At once she knew she had spoken unwisely, for Catherine's bright expression faded. 'Ah, Madame,' she said quietly. 'Had they been youths, however bold and forward . . . they could not have served me more ill than another has!'

Corisande hesitated. 'The Dauphin?' she asked.

'Yes, Madame.' Catherine turned abruptly away. 'The fault is mine! I took the Dauphin for what I wanted him to be, a chevalier out of a tale – not for what he is, a prince ambitious of a crown. Why await his father's? For the price of a few words in the ear of a foolish girl, he thought to have that of Lyonesse. We are warned against flatterers, Madame, but I did not heed the warning. I shall not make that mistake again!'

Corisande studied her young friend, sombre and lovely, standing in profile before the window. What prince in Christendom would not be enflamed by her, whatever her estate? 'It is not my place,' she said finally, 'to ask the Queen of Lyonesse to forgive one who has done her insult. Yet perhaps you will one day understand, my Trinette, that the Dauphin is very much younger than you are.'

The sun was low when Catherine at last insisted that she detain Corisande no longer. They had spoken long, mostly of small things, to wrap up, tie in a bow and lock in a casket the years they had known one another. For half her life, Corisande had been the nearest she had to a mother. After tomorrow they might never see one another again.

Corisande returned early next morning, and with her came servants carrying chests. 'Now!' she declared, as the servants set the chests down. 'We must make you ready!'

The chests proved to contain gowns. Catherine had never made the slightest preparation for this day's occasion, having been much more concerned to see that it came to pass at all. Corisande and her own ladies, she now discovered, had tended to it without her knowledge – and had taken their measures very well indeed. For her ladies, gowns of red and green, the colours of the House of Guienne. For her own, purple velvet trimmed with the red and gold of Lyonesse, with a long train and a pale gold kirtle. Solange laced her in, Madeleine trying to help till Catherine told her to rest or face the scaffold.

As this went forward, her hair brushed, purple ribbons tied into it, a splendid plumed cap placed on her head, and her mother's pendant with the Royal Arms around her neck, martial sounds continued outside: tramping of feet, grounding of arms, shouting of orders, blast of trumpets and roll of drums. 'What is that all about?' asked Madeleine suddenly, putting the question Catherine had not wished to ask of Corisande, and had scarcely dared put to herself.

Perhaps Corisande read her expression, for it was to Catherine that she replied. 'In the way of the world, *Majesté*,' she said, 'what passes is much to your honour – as you and your ladies shall see! You are no longer my little Trinette,' she added wistfully, 'nor anyone's Trinette, and shall never be again.' Then – for she was still Corisande – she turned back to Catherine's ladies-in-waiting. 'Now!' she said. 'We've no more time to waste. Make yourselves ready! Quickly! Quickly!'

Presently the door flew open, and the Comte de Plassey stood there. He looked, thought Catherine, as though he had had far less sleep than she had. 'You are ready, *Majesté*?'

'Yes, Monsieur,' she replied, and stood up. 'I am quite ready!'

De Plassey bowed, and stepped aside, gesturing towards the door. 'If you please!'

Catherine's little company marshalled itself and set forth. The corridors and stairs were lined with soldiers. The courtyard of the Porte St-Michel was filled with pikemen, and harquebusiers lined the battlements above. A dozen drummers rapped out their tattoo. As she entered the courtyard, trumpeters raised their horns, and blast upon blast resounded from the walls. The display of force was so massive that Catherine smiled in spite of herself. *Do you think me so fearsome a maid?* A coach awaited her. De Plassey himself opened the door, and Catherine climbed in. Solange and Madeleine gathered up her train and climbed in after her, then Corisande and the Duc de Conté.

The coachman cracked his whip, and the coach rolled through the inner gate onto the cobbled streets of la Fleur, lined with soldiers, empty of citizens, houses shuttered. The ride through the streets took only a short while; to Catherine it seemed as long as three days' ride from Auselles at the Dauphin's side, when she still thought him her knight and not her betrayer. This, surely, would be her last few moments with Corisande, but neither could find anything to say. It was, indeed, as though her real life was ending, its place to be taken by some mad, incomprehensible dream.

What was Lyonesse, beyond tangled and disjointed memories of her early childhood?

It was her kingdom, and her home.

The coach burst from the narrow street into the great open square facing the waterfront of the city. Catherine stared with amazement – and for an instant with horror – at the array of soldiery marshalled there, with their banners and pennons. Had Corisande betrayed her after all? Her study of the art of war taught otherwise. Here was a mighty army – yet no embarking invasion force, rather one in defensive array. Pikemen and harquebusiers were drawn up in squares as though to repel an assault. Great guns lined the foreshore, muzzles pointing out to sea, the hay-wagons that had so mystified her forming a barrier between them.

Catherine raised her eyes – and the little hairs stood up on the back of her neck. Beyond the harbour lay not open sea to the horizon, but a great forest upon the waters, a forest of masts. Ships! Ships in their score upon score, great ships and small. Now at last she understood why so many troops had converged on la Fleur – understood too, perhaps, the conduct of the Dauphin, so unexpected and cruel. Most of all she understood why Charles of Aquitaine had relented of holding her.

Banners and streamers floated from the lofty masts and yardarms of the fleet: the blue on white of the Cross of St Pelagius; the gold, red, and green of the Royal Arms and the House of Guienne. Before her lay the navy of Lyonesse, in its full array and grandeur upon the sea. Then she could see nothing clearly, for the tears of joy and amazement that welled up in her eyes.

Her people had come for her!

Catherine accepted with mumbled thanks the kerchief that Corisande gave her to dry them. When she had done so she looked out again upon her fleet, too large to take in all at once, and she did not even know what kinds of ships she beheld. Her books, ancient or modern, had said little of war at sea, yet she was Queen of a sea-girt realm – she would have so much to learn! Some details she could pick out even in her ignorance. The great four-masted ships in the centre must be carracks. Men spoke of them as large: these were enormous. Grapnels hung from their bowsprits, great scythes were fixed to their yardarms, and boarding nets stretched over their waists between lofty castles. From ports low in their hulls gleamed muzzles the colour of her hair: great-guns of bronze. Plainly they were ready to give battle, fearing no foe.

Among the great ships were two immense galleys, the banners of Lyonesse and Ravenna flying side by side from their poops – she had already an ally! Most else was incomprehensible: a mystery of the sea. All Catherine saw clearly was that here before her was the might of her realm, as mighty in its element as Charles of Aquitaine's. Overproud lords might command a few ships, her Lord High Admiral perhaps a score. Only the will of her people could have sent forth so many, great and small. Catherine found herself smiling.

The coach rolled to a stop in the midst of the square. At a shouted order, a double line of Gardes de Maison drew swords all together and snapped to attention. The double line stretched away, forming between them a path from the coach to the edge of the quay. Three galleys waited there, spurred prows pointing out to sea. Above the poops at each side flew the flag of the Aquitaine, and their rails were lined with mantlets bearing fleurs-de-lis, sable on silver. The galley in the centre bore no flag, and the awning over her poop and the arming cloths along her sides were all of sombre black.

The door of the coach opened . . . and Catherine found herself looking upon the face of Louis the Dauphin. For an instant she shrank back, away from Louis, away too from that grim, black-draped galley. At that moment she could have retreated into Corisande's arms as she had years ago, to be comforted after some little slight or petty cruelty in the vast, alien Court of la Trémouille. She would do no such a thing.

I am Catherine, daughter of Henry, she thought. I may fear; I do not flee. She rose and stepped down from the coach. Solange and Madeleine climbed out behind her, bearing her train, and the little Duc de Conté helped his mother out. Catherine embraced Corisande wordlessly, one last time, and they kissed one another's wet cheeks. Then Corisande and her son climbed back into the coach and Catherine stood, her ladies-in-waiting behind her, facing the Dauphin.

He bowed, then straightened and looked at her, handsome as ever. '*Majesté*,' he said. 'It seems that we are at an end, you and I.' He gave a wry little smile. 'I find much to regret in that. I once hoped to lose many a night's sleep on your account – but not in this manner, I think.' He paused. 'I shall not kiss your lips as I would like: that honour I must leave to some more fortunate prince.'

You have nothing more to say than that? Catherine would have flown at him in fury if she could. Her station forbade it. Instead she looked evenly back at him. 'No, Monseigneur,' she said. 'In the Porte St-Michel we came to an end. There are no illusions between us now. We are not demoiselle and chevalier – we are Lyonesse and l'Aquitaine.'

Louis' faint smile faded. Catherine turned from him and with measured stride set forth between the white-clad chevaliers of the Gardes de Maison, every pace taking her towards the black-draped galley – and, surely, her Lord High Admiral.

By the quayside stood a little group of men, halberdiers in red and green, alien and incongruous amid the silver and black of the Aquitaine. Behind the halberdiers was a man in a tabard: the chief herald of Lyonesse. As she came up, the halberdiers' arms barred her passage and a tall man stood forth on the poop of the black-draped galley, unmistakably Lord William, now Earl of Avalon. 'Who would enter in state,' his voice rang out, 'into this galley that was King Edmund's?'

The herald turned and called out in reply, 'Kateryn, daughter of Edmund's son Henry, of Lyonesse, Aquitaine, and the Islands of the Sea by Heaven's grace Queen!'

The Lord High Admiral turned on the galley's poop and addressed her crew. 'What say you to that,' he cried, 'loyal shipmen goodly and brave?'

Then arose a great shout from the galley: 'God save the Queen!'

A whistle shrilled, and in an instant the black cloths were taken up all along the galley's length, transforming her into a brilliant dazzle of colour. Along her overhanging rails were mantlets of gold, red and green, some with the Royal Arms, some bearing Catherine's own badges, the White Hart and the Linnet. The royal standard rose and broke from a tall staff above the poop. Below the stern rail were the Royal Arms, flanked by the letters C and R.

The halberds were brought upright, clearing her way, but for long moments Catherine stood in place: dazed, alarmed, furious, above all exhilarated. She stepped past the halberdiers, went down the water-stair – and, carefully, from the stone quay of Charles of Aquitaine's realm to planking that was of her own. 'Lyonesse, arriving!' declared the Lord High Admiral. As Catherine ascended the short ladder by the galley's poop a row of men raised whistles and let out a long, ear-splitting trill.

The Lord High Admiral raised his sword in salute and knelt before her at the gangway. She bade him rise, then added – so softly that none others could hear – 'The Chevalier d'Hardouin sends his regards, my Lord of Avalon. He would have a word with you concerning brent-wine!'

'Yes, your Majesty's Grace,' he answered aloud – then added, softly, 'Tell him that Cat's kingdom awaits mousing, being much in need thereof.'

Catherine felt herself blushing, and cursed as never before this traitorous body of hers, that so often proclaimed to the world what she would most keep secret. She went numbly through the motions as the Lord High Admiral introduced his officers, and representatives of the lords of Lyonesse. All knelt before her. She was ushered to a seat on the poop, made up as a makeshift throne draped in ermine. She took her place, her ladies disposing themselves gracefully on the deck to either side of her.

To settle her disarrayed thoughts Catherine examined this galley – her galley! – aboard which she found herself. She had embarked on galleys when the Court had visited port towns during its summer progresses. She had not liked them. Never had she been able to ignore the convicts, heads shaved but for a forelock, in rows on their benches. Their weary hopeless faces had always deadened her joy.

Looking along this Galley Royal of Lyonesse, she saw

how her own realm differed from that of the Aquitaine. The men on these benches had no empty look of convicts. They were alert, and looked back at her with more than soldierly frankness. They had arms close by them: cutlasses, axes, boarding pikes. Lining the rails were not the familiar crossbowmen, but men clad in forest green, bearing bows taller than they were.

To each side crisp commands rang out in the Gallic tongue: the flanking galleys of Aquitaine, making ready for departure. There were no such preparations aboard her galley. Instead her Lord High Admiral spoke. 'If it would amuse your Majesty,' he said, 'I shall call for a hornpipe while we await.'

Catherine had no idea what a hornpipe was, nor why her galley made no preparations to depart. 'Amuse me?' she asked sharply. 'What you find amusing, my Lord High Admiral, is much a wonder to me! Yet call for it as you wish.'

So he did, and as a pipe played, two burly shipmen rose and danced with surprising grace before her. As they did, a dance of sorts went forward aboard the galleys alongside: orders and replies, smart twirlings and snapped salutes, hauling of lines and man-handling of oars. Shall we not make ready? Catherine wanted to demand. Then a whistle shrilled and a drum rolled aboard the galley to her right, answered by whistle and drum aboard the other. From the first came a shouted report, in the Gallic tongue, that both galleys were in readiness.

An officer approached the Lord High Admiral and bowed. 'Monseer le Frog says as he's ready, my lord!' he said.

'Not a moment too soon!' answered the Lord High Admiral. He gestured for the dance to end. 'If they made such a to-do with the Monites standing in,' he said, 'by day's end they'd be praying to the One God of the Monites, never again to taste bacon!' He turned to Catherine and bowed. 'By your Majesty's gracious pleasure, I'll have us under way.'

'By our pleasure!' answered Catherine. She looked out at her waiting fleet. Insolent he might be; he seemed to know his trade. There was much to be said for that.

He nodded, and turned to a slight young figure – a boy of twelve or thirteen – in officer's garb. 'Master Compton! If you would be so good as to take us out.'

'Me, your Lordship?' answered the boy.

'I see no other I'm speaking to.'

The boy swallowed, eyes wide with anxiety. Catherine wondered at this cruel game – then saw the Lord High Admiral nod and smile at him.

'Aye, aye, your Lordship!' answered the boy. He saluted and turned to face down the length of the galley. In that instant it seemed the boy vanished for ever; it was a young man's high, clear voice that sang out. 'Station the sea and anchor detail!'

'Sea and anchor detail, aye, sir!' cried a petty officer below the break of the poop. He trilled his whistle, and the galley erupted in sudden tumult. In moments order came from chaos, and the Galley Royal quivered like a cloth yard shaft drawn to the ear. Deck hands lined the gangway, bearing a heavy rope; to each side sat oarsmen, three by three from poop to prow, poised with oar looms in hand. 'All in readiness, sir!' called the petty officer.

'Slack all lines,' ordered the youth.

'Slack lines, aye, sir!'

The young officer turned to Catherine and bowed. 'By your Majesty's leave?' he asked.

She smiled warmly at the lad. 'By my leave, good sir!'

He turned again, smartly on his heels. 'Let go all lines!'

'All lines let go, sir!'

'Coxswain! Give way!'

'Give way, aye, sir!' A whistle shrilled and a gong sounded. The oarsmen rose in unison, stepped up on the benches before them and with a great shout threw themselves back. Their oar blades dipped and rose, water streaming from them like fountains of jewels – and Catherine, Queen of Lyonesse, set forth towards home.